Rebel Star

An Apocalyptic LitRPG
Book 8 of the System Apocalypse

By

Tao Wong

Copyright

This is a work of fiction. Names, characters, businesses, places, events and incidents are either the products of the author's imagination or used in a fictitious manner. Any resemblance to actual persons, living or dead, or actual events is purely coincidental.

This book is licensed for your personal enjoyment only. This book may not be re-sold or given away to other people. If you would like to share this book with another person, please purchase an additional copy for each recipient. If you're reading this book and did not purchase it, or it was not purchased for your use only, then please return to your favorite book retailer and purchase your own copy. Thank you for respecting the hard work of this author.

Books in The System Apocalypse series

Main Storyline

Life in the North

Redeemer of the Dead

The Cost of Survival

Cities in Chains

Coast on Fire

World Unbound

Stars Awoken

Rebel Star

Stars Asunder

Broken Council

Anthologies

System Apocalypse Short Story Anthology Volume 1

Comic Series

The System Apocalypse (On-going)

Contents

What Happened Before

Having left Earth, John Lee and his companions journey to Irvina, capital of the Galactic Council, in search of answers about the new Galactic Society that Earth had been forcibly recruited into. Galactic Society is both more peaceful and more dangerous than John could have ever imagined. Dungeons' entrances are carefully regulated, and those without the Credits or prestige to join the higher levels of society are forced to sell themselves to serfdom for a chance at a decent life.

Angered by the inequality and seeing an opportunity for Earth, John arranges to transport the dispossessed to Earth, where humans have more monsters and monster loot than they know what to do with. However, his actions challenge the social order of the Galactic Council and invoke a rapid and violent response.

John and his friends survive the attacks and assassination attempts, but his actions have consequences. Humanity's leaders are targeted on Earth, and in turn, John vows to take the battle directly to those who hired the assassins. Leaving Irvina and the diplomatic corp behind, John, Mikito, and Harry journey to the dark side of Galactic Society.

Chapter 1

I can already taste the chocolate—the bitterness, the velvet smoothness—on my tongue as I stare at the golden foil. The luxurious taste as it melts in your mouth and slides down your throat, that hit of sugar and cocoa that perks you up. Carefully, I unwrap the piece of heaven, slide the piece into my mouth, and let my eyes half-close. I revel in the taste, finding peace. Happiness. Decadence.

"Are you listening, John?" Harry's voice cuts in, forcing me to open my eyes to look at the British journalist.

Harry's dressed in the latest Galactic fashion, which reminds me of the worse of seventies fashion crossed with a gothic ensemble—garish colors on too-tight clothes held down by big belt buckles that crisscross the body. It's a bad clash with his umber skin, but then again, I'm dressed in Adventurer chic. Black armored bodysuit with multi-pocketed vest, pistol and knife strapped to me.

"No." The words come slow, my attention returning to my friends. First, though, I let my gaze sweep over the spartan furnishing of the spaceship we're in. The mess hall is spartan, all in bronze, brown, and used, the smell of hours old cooking mixing with the taste of the chocolate in my mouth. Memories of a better time, an easier time, threatening to return. "Not really."

Harry harrumphs while Ali holds up a hand, the two-foot-tall Spirit floating upside down as he speaks. "What boy-o means is that you're blathering. Just the conclusion."

"I'd like details," Mikito speaks up.

"See? Some people understand the trouble I go through to get this information," Harry says.

"No. I just want the details."

Harry huffs at the congenial ribbing. "Obviously we have System confirmation that the target's still paying into the quest pool for Adventurers targeting Earth leaders. Of course, as we know, that's not enough confirmation these days, since they've started messing with the System data pools. But Slimwese isn't the kind to keep quiet about what he's doing. I have four different independent confirmations of him ranting and boasting of his involvement. On top of that, I checked financing on the fund and backtracked it to two of his companies."

"Good enough." Mikito's black eyes harden, and for a moment, the naked blade that my little friend has become shows itself. Then Mikito leans back and that sense of danger disappears.

"What is it?" I say, interrupting Harry before he can get into the next part. The part where we plan how to kill a man. Alien. Sentient. Everyone else looks at me, but I can't help but ask. "What number? Seven, eight? Since we started this?"

"Nine or eleven," Harry says. "Depending on how you count the Filt incident."

"Ah. Right. Filt…" I say. That had not been our proudest moment. Filt was the reason we'd started double-checking everything we got from the System. Our enemies had used the System to lie to us, to send us against an enemy of theirs. The only good thing was that the son of a bitch was not much better than the ones we meant to kill. He and his friend. And so many uncounted individuals who just were doing their jobs, who got in the way.

"And the six orgs," Ali adds. "However you want to count that."

I grunted. Taking out a corporation was both easier and harder than dealing with an individual. Sometimes it was just a person or two you had to dissuade. Often, it was a board and shareholders who needed convincing—and that convincing was a matter of stealing, destroying, and otherwise taking away their resources and operations. Best part is when you throw the Credits you steal right back into a fund for others to keep doing the same.

"Two years and a bit, a whole bunch of dead sentients, and what have we really accomplished?" I can't help but let the weariness, the emotional exhaustion creep into my voice. Two years of violence against others. Running, hiding, killing. Bringing hell back to those who attacked us first. And for what?

"The bounty fund targeting Earth personnel is down to thirty percent of its original size," Harry says. "There were only three assassination attempts last month."

"One of which succeeded," I say.

The Grandmaster in Hong Kong had fallen in that attack. There might be fewer attacks, but the fellows taking the jobs are more skilled. Even with all the defenses, the training and Levels, being on the defensive is killing us. Slowly but surely.

"Historically, that's pretty good," Ali says. "You should see the numbers in Truinnar and Movana empires. Never mind the Piskies and the Gruthlaks."

"John?" When she knows she has my attention, Mikito continues. "Are we calling this off?"

"No." I shake my head. Whatever I might think, wherever my conscience might fall… Slimwese is a bad man. And we've come this far. Might as well finish it. Somehow though, I can't help but remember an old friend. One who died just before we entered the Galactic arena. Someone who, in her own way, was a much better killer than I could ever be. "Just… no. Go on, Harry."

And he does. He goes into the details of Slimwese's Status, of his security and his routines. Of what we can expect. And then, in the midst of the planning, I forget my reticence for a while. I forget the exhaustion and doubts while I plan how to kill a man.

***

The view from the cockpit of the ship—*Nothing's Heartbreak*—is eye-wateringly beautiful. Without an atmosphere to block the starshine, the Milky Way sprays its glory across our viewport. For a moment, I bask in the wonder of it all, a dream come true a thousand times over. Then the rumbly voice from the pilot's seat catches my attention, dragging me back to the present.

"We doing this?" Dornalor says.

The man is huge, about nine feet tall, with the entire ship shaped to suit his size. The ghatotkaca is entirely hairless, with a head shaped like a pot and a weird, dandelion-yellow skin. Lounging in his chair, the man acts like the lord of his ship—which he is. As I regard him, Ali pops up his information again for me.

Dornalor Xyrralei, Journeyman Trader (Merchant Journeyman Captain Level 41) (A)

HP: 290/290

MP: 4890/4890

Conditions: Shipboard Awareness, Hyperspace Fold, In His Place, Mana Drip

Nearly everything on Dornalor's Status is correct, except for the fact that he's not a Merchant Captain but a Pirate Captain. Well, that and the various other Titles he's hiding. Dornalor's got a few Skills that help keep the ship and us hidden. It's why we hired the man—after saving him from an unfortunate situation involving cockatrices, loan sharks, and a rotating saw.

It only takes a moment to call up the information on his Skill.

False Impressions (Level 4)

An Advanced Skill of the Pirate Captain, False Impression creates a false recording or article of knowledge in the System that will obfuscate events around the Captain. This new recording or impression will now be the default answer. This is a rare Skill that has both passive and active effects.

Passive Effect: A false recording of events as designated by the user will be created. This passive effect will obscure (4) locations and/or pieces of information at all times, with false information provided in their place. Currently selected locations include: cockpit, dining room, storage, and Captain's status.

Active Effect: When False Impressions is in effect, a false recording will be created. User may designate higher levels of realism for the recording or higher cost to breach the recording.

Passive Cost: Permanently reduce Mana Regeneration by twenty

Active Cost: 250 Mana + 200 Mana per minute

"Yes," I say and gesture. The information we've got gets sent over, filling in dashboards.

Dornalor's eyes go blank for a few seconds as he and his AI process the information. The navigation map flickers then updates, a new course plotted.

"Restricted zone, planet-side raid. Additional twenty-five thousand Credits." Dornalor's voice is low and husky, business-like. There's a reason why we never have him on the actual strategy missions. Dornalor's a pure mercenary, but one who has a code. Which was part of the reason he was in trouble before.

"Ali?" I say.

"Transferred."

"Good. We'll be coming in hot and we'll need you all in the dining room," Dornalor says. "You have twenty minutes. I'll stay longer by five for another 125,000 Credits. No more."

"Got it," I say.

Twenty minutes should be enough. More than enough.

***

We drop through the atmosphere undetected. The Pirate Captain's Skills combined with the numerous stealth abilities of the ship allow us to cut through the sensor net around the pleasure planet Rexha like a ghost. It helps that we time our entry with the arrival of another dozen VVIPs, all of whom have their usual entourage of security ships and assistants that have to be cleared. In the brief period when the security team for Rexha are overwhelmed, we slide into the atmosphere and land.

Pleasure planets are a weird Galactic creation. The easiest way to describe Rexha is like taking Vegas, spreading it across the entire damn planet, and adding guided safaris. Due to the System, one of the major points of interest—beyond the usual plethora of kinky pleasures—are guided hunting scenarios. Like big game hunters in Africa, the pleasure-seekers get brought across multiple acres of dungeon land, all with the goal of killing weird, unique, and high-Leveled monsters. In some cases, the goal is more specific—a Title, a Quest, a Level or Class unlock. Pleasure planets cater to all wants and tastes.

Of course, the numerous guides and bodyguards present means that the amount of actual danger the tourist faces is low. But injuries still happen—mostly due to the overwhelming pride and stubbornness of the tourists.

Our current target is on one of those safaris. In a society where violence is often the last and most powerful resource, where Levels are most easily gained from death and mayhem, it's not a big surprise that those who can take what

14

they want stand at the top. Non-Combatants might become powerful via indirect means, but that power can be bypassed by someone dedicated and violent enough. It was true on Earth too, pre-System, though the fact that we were all equally squishy meant that there was only so much damage a single person could do. Not like in the System.

All of which leads to this need for those at the highest strata of society to be able to prove themselves as fighters. Even those who aren't combatants feel the need to flex, to show that they can handle themselves in a combat situation. I'd call it testosterone-laden, except a large portion of these aliens don't use that chemical. In either case, what it means is that Slimwese's out here, having a holiday while keeping the number of his guards to a minimum to keep his experience gain high.

"What's he hunting anyway?" I ask, a cup of coffee in my hand. Not that there aren't better—or different—drinks, but the taste of coffee, like the chocolate spread before me, is a reminder of home. There's a certain point when you've been traveling for ages and you just want something familiar. I admit, I've been past that point for ages.

"A pugot," Harry says. "Headless creature, mouth where its neck would be. Extra-long limbs… yeah, like that." Harry glares at Ali who, rather than speak, has projected an image of the pugot. Arms that end with curved, diamond-tipped claws, sworls around its grey-green skin that look like tribal tattoos, and a frightening lack of eyes float before me. "Pack animals."

"Levels?" Mikito asks.

"Fifty to sixty individually, pack leaders around seventy, and alphas can hit eighty," Harry says. "They move in groups of five to seven."

Not horrible at all. In fact, it'd be easy enough for any one of us to deal with individually. Well, except Harry. The man's Skills lean in another direction. Which, I guess, makes sense since Slimwese is a non-combatant too.

"So…"

"Landing in five. I'll deploy the Dimension Locks when we do. You have twenty minutes from the moment we touch down," Dornalor's voice cuts in via the intercom.

I find myself straightening, banishing idle thoughts. Time to work.

***

I've lost count of the number of alien worlds I've stepped foot on. All too often, it's for instances like this—a drop and dash, a spill and kill. Rexha's gorgeous—towering trees, undergrowth resplendent in a riotous amount of color, foliage literally glowing in all the colors of the rainbow and beyond. My helmet takes a second before it filters out the additional illumination, but it doesn't slow me or Mikito down. The tiny Samurai is on a horse, a ghostly addition to her arsenal, the beast facing me. Her open-faced helm shows Mikito's impatient visage, and I can't help but smile.

"All right, I'm coming," I say.

I take a step, then another, and the armor catches up, wrapping itself around me, cloaking me and boosting my attributes, my Skills. The hidden jets kick in as I take my fifth step, then we're off, ducking deep into the forest.

It's an indulgence and a man's dream, but who doesn't want power armor? Unlike Sabre, which I gave away years ago, my new suit of battle armor is no mass-produced personal assault vehicle but a Master Class-created masterwork. With a warranty and an in-built teleportation function that allows me to send it off once a week to get reserviced. The cost of all that was ruinous, but one of the advantages of going out and playing hired killer against bad people is that often, they have multiple bounties on them. And unlike many others, we're willing to collect those bounties rather than have the bounties disappear.

16

I admit, the System's method of allowing anyone and everyone to contribute to bounties is a minor leveling factor. There are even organizations whose sole job is to set up and manage such bounties, verifying claims and kills and ensuring the secrecy of the contributors. Since the System will take Credits right out of your account, it makes contributing really easy. Not to say there aren't counter-bounties placed on contributors—when they're located—but it's an interesting addition.

In either case, my new suit of armor provides significantly more power, boosting my Strength by nearly a hundred and my other attributes anything from forty to eighty points. There are also three new in-built Active Skills, over and above its teleportation option.

As I fly behind Mikito, letting the Samurai lead the way, I can't help but feel the stirrings of anticipation. Pointless or not, battle is something I've come to crave.

Two minutes from when we are meant to meet our target, I fade out of existence, triggering the Quantum State Manipulator on my arm. It puts me partially in a parallel dimension, making me invisible in the visible and audible spectrum. To someone without a proper Skill, I'm as good as not there.

Mikito has purchased a couple of hiding Skills too, but none of them are that powerful. In fact, the QSM by itself would not be enough to hide from Slimwese's bodyguards. Not without bait. And that's why she keeps riding, as fast as she possibly can, directly at our target.

The bodyguards hit her thirty seconds out, their cordon contracted tightly with the majority of their people focused on the Upper Samurai. One of the benefits of Galactic infamy is that they know better than to hold back. Not if they want to have any chance of beating her.

Magic missiles, beams of power, and hard-shelled projectiles fly toward Mikito. A good portion miss, Another number get cut apart by Hitoshi, her polearm weapon with the extra-long curved blade at the end. Mikito triggers a Charge Skill just before the rest of the attacks land, making a few more miss. The rest glance off her armor, causing a rainbow of sparks and the cacophony of clashing metal to resound through the forest. The triggered Skill allows her to force her way through the attacks, closing in on the trio of melee fighters.

That's the reason why melee weapons are still relevant. When Skills, armor, and health allow people to rush through long-range fire, there's no way to stop those who are intent on closing in from doing so. A good team makes sure to patch all the holes in the defense, including melee fighters and support personnel. I manage to catch sight of Mikito dropping her naginata down like a lance moments before she and her horse slam into the melee group. Then I'm gone, flitting past the group like a ghost.

I catch sight of our target seconds later, the Galactic Mogul standing behind the two Hakarta guards that make up his close-range protection. They have spread out, one in front and the other behind, guiding him to their extraction point where emergency transportation is already on its way. Single-use communication devices are nearly impossible to block, so we didn't bother. Blocking them from teleporting away was more than good enough for our purposes, which is another reason why we're using a pirate ship. After all, Dornalor's needed to lock down entire ships, so a little Galactic Mogul is nothing.

Beside me, Ali floats, his hands darting and twitching, tearing through magic obfuscation and secondary distractions, keeping me on track. The moment they noticed us, the bodyguards deployed magical and technological countermeasures, but all of it is for naught as the tiny Spirit cracks their attempts with practiced ease. It's not really fair, considering Harry helped us learn all their countermeasures well before we arrived.

I make my way nearly directly behind Slimwese, just a little to the side due to his bodyguard's positioning. The Galactic Mogul's five-foot-wide bulk, most of it blubbering flesh and rolling muscle, provides him a measure of innate protection, but it won't be enough. As I ready myself to drop back into reality and attack, my entire body shudders, flesh and muscle tearing as I accelerate without moving.

You have been forced into the primary dimension

You are Dimension Locked

The notifications flicker up and disappear in fractions of a second, every molecule in my body screaming. Reflexively, I block the glowing hook that comes from the bodyguard, the blow caught on my forearms and throwing me backward. The damage is minimal, but I still fly through the air and tear a furrow in the ground.

"Did you think we did not expect you?" Slimwese says. "Did you think we were that stupid?"

Unlike the Mogul, the bodyguards, including the four that have hidden themselves, aren't hesitating. They launch their attacks even as I come out of my roll. The protective shield around me flickers, covering me as I focus for the few seconds I need.

When Sanctum slams down, covering me, the pair of close-in bodyguards, one other of the guards, and the Mogul, I can't help but grin.

"I didn't," I say.

And then all hell breaks loose.

Chapter 2

Slimwese's eyes widen, the corpulent sentient's jaw dropping open even as his bodyguards yank him backward and to the edge of the Sanctum. They don't stop firing, laying down fire to shatter my defenses. I trigger a Soul Shield and watch as my armor bubbles and creeps, reforming damaged portions by drawing in the ambient Mana. Even without my thinking about it, the Aura of Chivalry has turned on, making the group hesitate then focus on me. I turn to the previously stealthed guard and trigger the first of the armor's active Skills.

Abyssal Chains

Calling upon the material connection to the shadow plane, chains from the abyss erupt, binding a target in place.

Effect: Target is bound by shadow chains. Chains deal 10 points of damage per second. To break free, target must win a contested Strength test. Abyssal Chains have a Strength of 120.

Uses: 2/3

Recharge rate: 1 per hour

The chains erupt from the shadows in the ground, wrapping around the surprised, triple-armed sentient. Spiked portions of the chains dig into flesh, twisting and squeezing as they bind the surprised guard in place. Even as he begins to struggle to free himself, I move. I jump into the sky and use my hoverboots to cover the short distance between the pair of us, evading the sudden explosion of ice that attempts to contain me and the trailing fire from the remaining Hakarta guards. As I land beside the captured guard, I stare into his angry and defiant eyes.

I turn and cut, my conjured soulbound sword and the trailing blades formed by A Thousand Blades tearing into him, breaking my own binding as they impact. It doesn't matter. The weapon tears into his body and the other blades follow, widening wounds and creating new ones. Those eyes, cat-like green and purple, widen in pain and disbelief at how quickly he falls. His armor defenses, his contingency shields, and his enchantments fail one after the other, my Penetration Skill allowing me to burn through his defenses like a blowtorch through wet paper. It's one thing to know your opponent has a Skill, another to experience it.

Outside, I can sense how the other guards are attempting to break through my Sanctum Skill. They try everything, from direct physical and magical attacks to Skills that burrow through the integrity of the Sanctum. The best they can do is shorten the duration of the Skill—but two minutes is an eternity in a fight. I see a pair of the guards break away from Mikito's dot, charging toward us even as the Samurai enacts her own little surprise.

By the time my opponent falls, Slimwese's bodyguards have him on the farthest side of the cylindrical cone I've created. It's nowhere near far enough. Even as I dart forward, the Hakarta are releasing binding traps—glue, ice, and Mana absorbing grenades—in the hopes of delaying the inevitable. I dodge and crash through them when necessary, letting my Soul Shield and my other defenses take the hits. Even as I run, I take in the details.

Hakarta Close Security Mercenary Bodyguard (Level 42)
HP: 2460/2460
MP: 479/842
Conditions: Terrified, Shared Health, Berserk, Inspired Employee

There's more information of course. But over time, I've realized that all that detail is unnecessary. Not for generic fighters like these. In short order, they'll be dead and I'll be moving on. I'm grateful they're mercenaries—it means we're less likely to have issues with revenge. Those who take these kinds of jobs know the score all too well.

Then I'm up against them. My first cut is blocked, the rifle in the lead Hakarta's hand splitting apart and transforming into a pair of punch daggers with curved extensions at either end to help block attacks. The weapon has barely reset its appearance when my sword slams into it and the Hakarta's legs buckle. Even as my other blades arc toward his left side, the Hakarta has twisted and thrown a punch. A flash in the corner of my helmet shows that I'm not the only one with a shield-breaking Skill. Another third of my Soul Shield dropped with that single strike.

It's not enough. Nowhere near. I step and cut, switching hands as I conjure the original blade in one hand and cut upward, separating arm from body while my other hand grabs hold of one of the conjured blades and stabs it into him. The next few moments are all reflexive, a choreography of pain, blood, and blades before we're rudely interrupted by the remaining Hakarta.

The air temperature drops like a rock, ice forming around our bodies as it's conjured from the air and another plane. I throw myself sideways and up, trying to get out of the area of effect, but this time, going up is the wrong choice. He's inverted the stubby cone of his spell, making it so that I end up trapped by the time the spell is fully formed. Trapped in elemental ice, my Soul Shield keeps taking damage. I feel the Shield shatter, and rather than renew it, I trigger my other Skills.

First comes Vanguard of the Apocalypse. The drain on Mana is huge, but the boost in my attributes is useful. In the small gap between the ice forming around my body and the shattering of my Soul Shield, I can move. I use that tiny gap to trigger Cleave and cut at the ice that traps me. It shatters beneath the enhanced strike, the elemental ice sheared apart. As I break free, I don't stop, throwing a Blade Strike to harass the mage and the bodyguard.

I could kill Slimwese directly, but the problem is that they're all Linked to him. It's a common bodyguard Skill, one that connects the principal's health pool with their guards. It means any damage I do to Slimese will be partially or wholly absorbed by the guards. Makes it so that I have to kill the guards before I kill him. The Erethrans use it too, with the Two for One Skill.

Knowing that, I have to take down the pair. Even the brief time that I was trapped has seen the bodyguard increase his health again, pushing it back up to a third. Frustrating. Kicking forward, I close the distance as I spam the Blade Strikes, chipping away at their health. Once I'm close, I extract a trio of grenades and flick them toward Slimwese and the mage. The Mogul isn't much help in the fight, but he's doing his best, firing his oversized plasma shotgun. Even when I'm right next to his bodyguard.

Even as the Mage begins another binding spell, I'm tearing through his friend's health. Just before the ice shackles fully materialize, Ali steps in and jerks the Mage's hand. The spell shatters as the Mana he's used dispels, the little Spirit then growing to full size to land an empowered uppercut on the Mage. While the mage is busy, the Bodyguard falls. Through the Hakarta's shattered mask, I watch as he breathes his last, bloody, bubbling breath.

My hand rises then cuts down, triggering a series of Blade Strikes on the Mogul. With the Mage stuck fighting Ali, attacking Slimwese is as good as attacking the Mage. Each cut, each Strike, tears into Slimwese's expensive Master Class armor. Even when he triggers the Shield protection on the armor, it barely slows me. I don't stop moving, spinning round and round, layering my blades around him physically so that each swing, each cut pushes him around the circle and into another blade. There's no escape, no matter what he does.

"If you kill me, my insurance will double—no, triple—your bounty!" Slimwese cries.

I ignore his threats that turn into curses, the fear and panic in his voice increasing as his Shield fails. Surprisingly, he's managing the pain quite well, his ranting never ending.

"You cretin. You over-boiled goblin. Your mother was born from leeches, seduced by fauns, and lay with a clan of them to give birth to you."

Slimwese's ranting speeds up just before I stab him in the throat. He gurgles, dying as my blade twists and detaches his head from his body. The Mage falls too, the pair of them collapsing in unison. I stand beside Slimwese's body, safe under the Sanctum, and dismiss the XP notification as Ali floats back to me.

"Fifteen seconds before the Sanctum falls."

I crouch low, throwing smoke and obscuring grenades around the Sanctum's enclosed clearing to provide cover. When the Sanctum falls, plasma beams and magic spells fly, but I'm already moving, darting away in the smoke. Missiles and spells follow, chasing after my shrouded, ghostly form. Mikito pulls back at the same time, leaving a graveyard full of corpses and damaged men.

A minute later, Slimwese's corpse stirs. Flesh ripples, muscles twitch then split apart, innards, fluids, and flesh parting. From within the corpulent, headless creature, a thinner, smaller sentient emerges. The bodyguards are standing around the corpse, a pair of bodyguards with their hands outstretched to begin the process of layering their Skills on the emerging new creature.

In that gap of time, I strike. I've been waiting. Under the shade of my Sanctum, I triggered the second active ability of my armor, as well as cast invisibility on myself.

Mirror Shade

Mirror Shade creates a semi-solid doppelganger using hard light technology and Mana.

Effect: Mirror Shade creates a semi-solid doppelganger of the user for a period of ten minutes. Maximum range of doppelganger from user is fifty meters. Doppelganger has 18% physical fidelity.

Use: 0/1

Recharge Rate: 1 per 4 hours

Hidden inside the clouds of obfuscating smoke, I'd moved to hide behind the nearest tree and watch the little play go on. Once Slimwese's Second Life Skill kicks in, I call down a Beacon of the Angels. The obfuscating smoke from the grenades keeps the runes and sky-high lightshow hidden until the beacon hits.

The newly emerged Slimwese stands no chance, his body tearing apart, along with the rest of his people. I get a slew of XP notifications, including a second one for Slimwese as he "dies" again. This time around, his Second Life Skill is out of charges, his ability to raise himself—significantly reduced in Level—on cooldown. There's no third life, no chance to come back.

It ends in fire and flame for him. But I don't bother watching as I make my way back to the ship. It's enough.

***

The *Nothing's Heartbreak* takes off with a roar of overstraining engines, as both of us managed to arrive before the twenty-minute mark. Mikito's looking worse for the wear, the group bodyguards and tour guide personnel having done quite a number on the Samurai. If not for her higher Level and skill, she'd probably have died. Though if you looked at the quiet, calm face, you would never guess. Admittedly, after so many close calls, anyone would get a little blasé.

We roar into the sky as I make my way to the cockpit to find Dornalor and Harry staring at the readouts. I take the copilot's seat, eyeing my Mana as I strap in and the pressure from our acceleration increases, overloading the inertial dampers. Green skies and white clouds part, leaving us a clear run to the edges of the atmosphere.

My gaze darts around the cockpit, taking in the readings as I get ready to do my other job. Before I'm settled, the ship rocks as explosions encompass us. Yellow and red flame mixed with grey and black smoke swirl about in the thin atmosphere, even as beams of yellow and red lasers cut through the sky. The attacks throw us around a little, but we never stop accelerating as the *Heartbreak* attempts to achieve escape velocity. I feel the ripple of Mana that emanates from within the ship as Mikito triggers her ride Skills—Juggernaut Charge, Mount Armor, and Double Step. While not optimized for ships, they still work on the vehicle itself because Mikito is in the ship itself, using it as a conveyance.

I trigger Thousand Steps first, giving the ship a further boost in speed just like Double Step does. Unlike most Skills, Double Step and Thousand Steps are built to work with other speed Skills, allowing us to overlay them. Both Skills only add a few percent to the speed, but considering Dornalor has an active speed Skill on the *Heartbreak*, even that few percent throws off the next slew of attacks. On the other hand, Juggernaut Charge works to steady our path, allowing the *Heartbreak* to ignore damage and impacts that might divert its course.

The neural link connected to my spine finishes the ship's authentication procedures, allowing me to tap into the *Heartbreak*. My mind expands as sensor information from all around the ship floods into my mind. I trigger the next

Skill in my arsenal—Disengage Safeties—and help out the automated point defense. The tempo of firing picks up, the drain on the ambient Mana and the ship's batteries showing on the monitors even as the missiles aimed for us get blasted apart.

"Are you using that damn Skill again?" Dornalor snarls.

"Yup," I say absently, most of my concentration focused on the incoming missiles, doing the calculations as they attempt to avoid our point defense fire even while we corkscrew around beam attacks. I get data about where we're going microseconds before we move, and I'm forced to adjust the angle and trajectory of our lasers in that period. It'd be literally impossible for a normal human to do this—but all those points dedicated to Intelligence are coming in useful.

"Rock-loving monkey! I told you to stop using that on my ship," Dornalor says.

"Busy."

"Oh, and I'm not? I'm dodging two-thirds of the attacks by myself, and the rest of those missiles you're letting through. Even with that landfill-creating, wire-melting, fuse-blowing Skill of yours," Dornalor says. "You're paying for the damages and downtime."

"Fine."

"Just so you lovebirds know, they've scrambled a dozen fighters from the space station. ETA of about six minutes. I'm scrambling their communications and throwing up phantom readings on the System, but I doubt it's doing more than giving their AIs a workout," Ali says, rubbing his forehead as he floats alongside me. It doesn't matter how we jerk, the Spirit follows the motions of the craft without fail. After all, I'm his attachment to this portion of reality.

The background hum and groan of straining metal disappears, the noise gone as we breakthrough the atmosphere and enter space proper. The sudden lack of resistance sees us accelerating even more and I cut off Thousand Steps to conserve Mana. Missiles that were following us drop away, unable to keep up in the lack of atmosphere, so I cut the last of my Skills. I look over the damage reports, noting the decreased durability of the point defense system.

Disengage Safeties (Level 2)

All technological weapons have safeties built in. Users of this Skill recklessly disregard the mandatory safeties, deciding that they know better than the crafters, engineers, and government personnel who built and regulate the production of these technological pieces.
Effects: Increase power output from 2.5-25% depending on the weapon and its level of sophistication. Increase durability losses from use by 25-250%.
Cost: 200 Mana + 25 Mana per minute

"I told you to turn off your solar-flared Skill. The point defense is already twenty percent down," Dornalor says. "Hold on. We're going to afterburn."

I grunt, pulling the straps tight. Dornalor's eyes turn silver, his body radiating with Mana as he stretches his Skills to encompass the ship. The cockpit turns dark as armor plates fall over the screens, protecting us within. And then his Overdrive Skill kicks in, along with the afterburners. The entire ship burns brighter than the sky, durability dropping like a rock, along with our fuel.

In minutes, we're well away from the planet, pulling away from all the closest ships, stations, and planets. The ship flies forward, faster and faster, crossing the hundreds of kilometers in a second. Ships from the station and hovering destroyers chase us, but even with their Skills, none of them can keep up. Dornalor bought, rebuilt, and customized the ship with speed and stealth in mind. Also, short-term durability for when his Skills kick in like this.

Offering me a wolfish grin, Dornalor's eyes narrow as we attempt to escape the gravitational pull of the nearby planetoids. At first, I think we'll have no problem escaping—until a pair of destroyers drop from hyperspace, right in our flight path. Dornalor hisses in exasperation, his eyes darting side to side as he runs the math.

"Shields at seventy-three percent and climbing…" Ali says. "We'd need to be at at least ninety percent to survive a single shot from their primaries."

"They'd have to hit us first," Dornalor replies. The ship continues to corkscrew and twist, dodging incoming fire beam fire. Most of it is fired without any real hope of actually hitting us, but it does force us to dodge. "Diverting to exit point B still leaves us in range of the first destroyer and lets at least four of the ships behind us catch up. Point C puts us away from the fire entirely, but we'll definitely get caught by Sigma and Epsilon squadrons. No guarantee they don't have galactic mines to deploy."

"I could check," Harry offers.

"Probably too late," Dornalor says, a hand coming off the stick that he doesn't actually use to control the ship to wave away some other notifications. "We just passed breakaway for point C. And we have twenty seconds before our chance to go to route B is gone. Think you can figure that out in time?"

"Twenty…" Harry clamps his mouth shut, shaking his head before he realizes that Dornalor's probably too focused to see him. "No."

"Figured," Dornalor says.

"You know, if I knew you were going to do something like that, I'd have bought another Shielding Skill for the ship," I say.

"Yeah, no. Stop helping," Dornalor says. "I do not need your help. I've got this."

"Oh, come on, it wasn't that bad."

"You burnt out half our point defenses two runs ago. I still haven't gotten the main particle beam cannon fully fixed. At this stage, we're likely going to have to replace it and all its conduit entirely." Dornalor sounds exasperated. "Do you know how much that is going to cost?"

"Two hundred forty-three thousand Credits from the last quote you received," Ali says. "With the *Heartbreak* in docks for two weeks and one day."

"Exactly!"

Before I can point out that we still have to survive, and another Skill, even a low-level one, might offer us a little more of a survival opportunity, we reach the first interception zone. The destroyers open up with even more beam weaponry, the initial slew of high intensity fire supplemented by the next series of wider beam attacks that have a bigger radius. We're right at the edges of their effective range—any farther and even if we didn't dodge, the dispersed attack would do nothing to our shield.

We jerk and spin, bouncing at angles and speeds that are literally impossible in atmosphere. But without any major source of gravity or air resistance, we can twist and turn, corkscrew and draw zig-zags through the empty void, attacks invisible to the naked eye missing us by inches. Of course, using the sensors and AI overlays, it does look like a bad eighties' sci-fi movie.

"Fighters. Four squadrons. Liskas IV.2 and Ares Creed 2.1s," I report the moment the data updates. Not that Dornalor hasn't seen this information, but not everyone is tapped into the datastreams like me.

"I see them," Dornalor says.

"How are we going to get through?" Harry says.

"The same way we always do. By flying like a pirate," Dornalor says.

Dornalor falls silent, concentrating on the flow of attacks and sliding us between each attack. He can't dodge everything, and our Shields power levels drop and rise constantly as the engine does it best to recharge the shield. The closer we get, the greater the drain as we are struck with greater frequency. And all I can do is watch.

"Entering final zone in three," Ali says.

The tension in the cockpit rachets up. Harry can't use any of his Skills, at least not actively. His passive Skills and his high Luck stat are working for us, twisting things in our favor a little. Mikito's already doing her best with the few Skills she bought, and I only have a pair to use. I've got Thousand Steps running along with my aura, increasing regeneration rates for everyone. The problem with Skills is that many of them aren't stackable, and those that are stackable aren't that powerful.

In a well-run ship, each individual has their own area of responsibility with only the Captain having a couple of Skills that stack on top of each other. But a Pirate Captain can't afford to do that. He's got to be able to do everything himself, so his Skills are slightly different. Even if we can buy Skills from the Shop, many of the best Skills are specific, highly expensive, and require a corresponding skill knowledge to make best use of. The best we can do is offer minor help with non-specific Skills.

"Three. Two. One," Ali counts down for us all.

The moment we cross that invisible line, additional beam weaponry opens up. Missiles that have been accelerating for ages arrive next, exploding into miniature suns as nukes go off around us. Lasers briefly engage from within many of those missiles, pumping out lethal x-rays, while other solid projectiles attempt to connect and finish us.

"Here we go," Dornalor says.

His words end with the activation of his trump Skill—Pirate Fleet. Much like the doppelganger skill in my armor, multiple copies of the ship appear. We don't disappear, just become one of the twenty copies that dash outward. Unlike my Skill, the Pirate Fleet is a powerful third-tier Advanced Skill that replicates the ship in its entirety, from weapons to shields. It's not something he can hold for very long, but in the short period that it's active, it makes us an army. Unfortunately, the Skill has quite a few limitations—including the fact that it's only workable in a spaceship.

The fighters that have been closing in on us start disappearing, the doppelgangers combining their attacks to wipe one after another of them off the map. Not that we don't suffer losses too, but our ships are much more powerful than the fighters.

Perhaps it's because we are taking less damage, because our shields are receiving less of a beating as our combined Skills do something that the doppelgangers can't. Perhaps some Scanner Technician on the other side uses a Skill and realizes we're the real ship. But it only takes half a minute before the fire that was initially dispersed focuses again.

That's when the doppelgangers switch to the next stage, going on defense. They boost forward, the ships placing themselves between us and the attacks. The entire group moves in concert, a dancing snake that shifts and dodges attacks, each portion ahead of us slowly dying, disappearing in flashes of spectacular metal and dispersing Mana.

"Can we make it?" Harry asks, slightly breathless. In our crash seats, we're constantly thrown from side to side as the inertial dampers can't keep up with the motions. The man is pale, his ombre skin an unhealthy grey as his lower Constitution leaves him feeling the effects more than the rest of us.

"Coming up on the destroyers," Ali answers. He flicks a hand, making the sensor data appear in the middle of the cockpit. Not that any of us really need it, but on the 3D map, we slide through the center of the pair of destroyers, all of us boosting as we try to get around the attack.

"Point defense. Now!" Dornalor snaps at me.

I find my lips pulling into a rictus grin as I trigger my Skill. "Told you."

My mana and durability drain, but I'm intercepting short-range missiles that accelerate without care for their fuel reserves, attempting to intercept us. The AI helps me do the math, picking out the missiles we can't dodge, that will block our way. Charting the path we need to open, Dornalor, the AI, and I play a quintuple bluffing game with the ships, their staff, and their AIs. I blast apart missiles and drones, laying down new routes.

The ship creaks and groans. Our shields fail and a blast tears through the back quarter of the ship. It punches a hole through multiple decks, destroying wiring and armor plating. Blast doors slam shut, but even before that last successful attack finishes, another lands. Armor fails, first a few then dozens of holes appearing all across the ship.

"Come on, baby. Don't break my heart again. You can do this," Dornalor whispers to the ship, entreating it.

"Ali!" I snap.

The Spirit reaches out, using his greater gift of the greater elemental force, and suddenly, we're moving even faster. Beams that should hit us curve away, shifting just enough to reduce damage or send it away from vital areas. I feel him pulling upon my own Mana reserves, borrowing my connection to the System and my own talent. I lend him what aid I can, offering him as much attention as I can provide.

A portion of my mind notices that Mikito has left the dining area, doing damage control along with the droids. She's gotten quite good at in-field battle repairs, a skill picked up from the numerous run-ins we've had with both sides of the law and those who exist on the line.

"Just a little more, sweetie. Just a little… *now!*" Dornalor crows.

There's no warning as we transition from sub-light travel to hyperspace. We burn for a fraction of a second then suddenly drop out, already hundreds of thousands of kilometers away from our original position, if not more. Dornalor kicks in another Skill, masking our trail and our drop-out while shifting our position in the System records before entering hyperspace again. We'll shift positions and trajectories a half-dozen times at least, laying down a confusing trail for anyone trying to catch us. It's no guarantee, but it's unlikely the planet's defensive forces will chase us past the first three or four at most. Space is massive and getting lost in it is easy. Especially for a single ship.

Chapter 3

Half a day later, we're all gathered in the dining room, supping on the massive portions of consumables that Galactics consider an average meal. All those high attributes, all that running around killing and fighting requires energy. And while we suck down Mana to support the over-built attributes, we still need actual physical nutrients too.

"Did we lose them?" I say.

"No sign," Dornalor confirms as he chews on what looks like a purple piece of corn, twice as large and with a bitter seed within each kernel. "Even if they dropped in, we've powered down for the most part. It'd take a Tier I sensor to find us now."

"Nothing on the Shop," Harry says, confirming Dornalor's words.

None of that is that surprising after all this time. Even if our enemies are adapting to our tactics, we're adapting to theirs too. Add the fact that planetary forces have to worry and plan not just for us but for any potential attackers, and there's only so much effort they're willing to put into dealing with us. Not even a loss in reputation is that much of an issue for them since it's a given that life in the Galactic System is dangerous. Even for non-combatants.

And I have to admit, there's probably a certain degree of passive resistance. The people we're targeting are well-known asses, people who stomped on anyone beneath them. And when you're expecting the people beneath you to help out to their full efforts, well, you're probably going to find something else coming. They might not shirk their jobs entirely, but they won't be putting in overtime either. Which can often be the difference between success and failure.

At least I think so.

"One thing," Harry says.

"What?" Ali says.

"Slimwese wasn't lying about the bounty increase," Harry says.

I grunt. No surprise there, but the way Harry says it, it seems as though it isn't the usual couple hundred thousand increase or the like.

"I think we broke through a new threshold," he says.

"Out with it," I say.

"You're now part of the top hundred. Mikito's at one twenty-four," Harry says.

The top hundred most wanted individuals in this sector of the galaxy. Which still puts me in the top five hundred in the entire Galactic System mostly likely. Is it weird that I take some pride from that? "So what? It's not as if we haven't been trending for a bit."

"Kind of the difference between the best of and new on a Reddit forum, boy-o," Ali says. "You were on the radar for a few of the hunters but being in the top hundred means you're attracting all kinds of attention. Some of that will be good, but most of it will be bad."

"More importantly, it means our initial planned rest stop won't work," Dornalor says. "Cagiavis is willing to look the other way for most things, but this is the kind of heat that they can't take. We're going to have to find a new place to fix the ship. And there's going to be a lot of fixing."

I grunt. Part of our deal has been that we pay for the majority of the repairs, over and on top of our existing payments. It's an expensive deal, and one that benefits Dornalor more than us, but it isn't as if Pirate Captains are growing on trees. We were lucky to find him, especially considering the kind of work we do. And while we could learn to pilot our own ship, the issue of specialization comes into play. Never mind the fact that having someone in the actual ship, piloting it while we do our thing, is extremely helpful. There's more than one story of automated dropships being hacked, leaving their passengers stranded.

"Recommendations?" I say.

"Spaks."

"Spax?"

"It's a pirate station, boy-o." Ali's fingers dance and information blooms. "Spaks is the largest pirate haven in this quadrant of the galaxy. It's located in the middle of a particularly dense asteroid field and ringed by multiple gravitic and dimensional lock mines. Because of that and its ability to shift its location, it's yet to be rooted out."

"Not as if the Galactics want to get rid of it. Whatever they say, they need us and they know it," Dornalor says. "Now that we have no choice, we'll have to make use of it. Not that I expect a great reception for you guys."

I grunt, understanding his point. We straddle a weird line, of being bad guys and not. The real bad guys— pirates, smugglers and worse don't like us—me— while truly upstanding citizens aren't going to be happy to deal with us. It's why we generally use slightly shady ports.

"Need?" Mikito speaks up, eyes narrowing.

"The System might make it easy to contact one another, but the conversations held in there are cheaper to purchase. Even with Skills, your secrets are more easily provided. There's also something to be said about meeting people face to face. Spaks and places like it give the Galactics a place to send their dirty deeds. And, as you can tell"—Dornalor waves his hand, indicating the damaged portions of the ship. As he does so, a pop-up appears, giving me a status notification about the ship—"we need places to rest and refit. Not to say they don't try to wipe us out once in a while but doing so just raises the price on our services."

Nothing's Heartbreak (Modified Voos Fast Courier Kimi 23.4)

Core: Class 3.8 Voos Fast Courier

Speed: 9.8 Doms

Processing Unit & Software: Class B Xylik Core

Armor Rating (Space): Tier II

Stealth Rating (Space): Tier I

Hard Points: 8 (6 Used)

Soft Points: 11 (9 Used)

Crew Capacity: 5

Weaponry: 2 x Ares Beam Turrets, 4 x Missile Turrets (1 Damaged)

Defense: 1 x Imola Interplanetary Force Shield, 11 x Point Defense Lasers (5 Damaged)

Core Durability: 73% (more…)

Of course, this was just the summary. If I wanted more, I could drill down to see specific durability. Anything listed here as damaged was too damaged to actually be used. Thanks to the permissions provided to me, I could drill down a little for specific items, but there were still large sections that Dornalor had locked off. Which was perfectly fair. It was kind of like the smuggling operation he ran in his hidden storage location. It wasn't any of my business so long as it didn't impact, well, my business.

"As if you're cheap," Ali mutters.

Dornalor smirked. "Never said we were."

Ali bristled slightly, but before the Credit-grubbing Spirit could retort, I rapped my knuckles on the table. "All right, sounds like we're going to Spaks. Anything we should know?"

"Don't cause trouble," Dornalor says.

I open my hands wide and give him my biggest shit-eating grin. "When have I ever?"

***

Dornalor leaves to plot our course to the station via hyperspace jumps and some non-hyperspace travel. We could get there a lot faster if we went straight, but according to the Captain, there are protocols that must be met. Otherwise, we would receive a very hot and unwelcome greeting. Rather than continue to question the expert, I left the man to it. Instead, I focused on research about the station. Well, more like I set Harry and Ali to dig into the station via the System while I got the Cliff's Notes version later.

Mikito wandered off to complete more repairs, a never-ending task after the battle. It seemed to calm the Samurai, a form of physical meditation that did not involve swinging her naginata. It was a rather nice change, considering Mikito had once focused exclusively on training. Perhaps she was coming to accept what had happened to her and Earth. Or perhaps I was just hoping repairing things helped her, creating rather than destroying. At least one of us needs to be a fully functioning adult. Still, whatever healing or peace she has found, she still competes in the arena whenever she has a chance.

As for myself, I took the time to do what I always did when I had a few moments. I cracked open a book, stuck up my feet, and chewed on some chocolate.

"Classes, by common understanding, can be likened to the evolutions and mutations creatures and monsters undergo under the effects of the System. It is further widely accepted that Classes are the framework that mutations and evolutions are applied to sentient creatures. Among the Systemers, it is believed that without Classes, sentients would undergo rapid and unexpected mutations. The Skills, attributes, and advancements an individual is provided are then the methods that the System uses to guide a sentient's existence under the

influence of Mana. Experiments to devolve or refuse the creation of a Class have resulted in failure thus far, with those stripped of a Class via Skill or other, more arcane methods, instead receiving the 'Classless' Class. While the Class itself provides only the most basic of generic Skills, the additional attribute points on Leveling has seen the growth of a small Classless group of individuals. Continued observation of this group has seen a small, but not insignificant, increase in random mutations and Skill Choices on Class promotion.

From these experiments and others (see footnotes 85.11), it is clear that not all Classes are equal. Rare, unique, and otherwise prestigious Classes abound in all cultures, species, and civilizations known (with the exception of the I'ss and aqrabuamelu—see footnote 85.12) within the Galaxy. What, then, could the purpose be of these Classes? In all instances where such Classes have been found, it should be noted that such Classes and distinctions in status and rarity were also reflected in the species' and civilizations' existing makeup. It is possible then that the System is but creating a reflection of what is expected. The System is providing rarity and uniqueness because society as a whole expects such gradations in Classes and individuals.

Other researchers have objected to this circular reasoning. They have pointed to the fact that in many cases, the provision of such Classes occur to only select individuals, most of whom then go on to Level and gain positions of authority. Statistically, it is true that a higher majority (87.319%) of such prestige Class individuals have achieved a higher median Level and Credit worth than those with less prestigious Classes. Of course, this might be a matter of effect and cause being reversed. Those given such Classes are more likely to succeed due to the Class, rather than the Class being given to those more likely to succeed.

Examples of Classes developed with reference to previous world's known religion can be found in the...

...

...

It's clear then that a Class is not just a construct formed without regard to a civilization's beliefs and perspectives. Numerous research papers (see footnotes 123.12) on newly added societies and growing societies (footnote 123.13) has seen the development of new Classes.

40

Furthermore, new societal sub-groups have been known to create new Classes, the most well-known being the Priest of the System. Of particular interest to this work is the way Classes of lost or destroyed civilizations (footnote 123.14) continue to abide within the System. The existence of extinct Classes lends credence to the belief that the System has a need or desire for such Class data in its daily or future operations. It is clear, from our research and others (footnote 123.15), that the System does use previous Classes as a template for new Classes, creating minor variations in the final result.

However, research on the rare individuals who have achieved a prestige Class from an extinct species have been less than rigorous and…

The shift in inertia pulls me from my book, making me look up. I sigh, dismissing the book. Damn. Just when it was getting interesting.

System Quest Updated
+2840 XP Gained

I grunt, rubbing my chin. Interesting. The experience gain was somewhat higher than usual. Something there then, about Classes. The five-dimensional jigsaw puzzle of the System continues to stump me. Most days, I feel as though I stumble across a new piece of the puzzle, but I'm never given an idea of how big the puzzle is or what the final shape will be. Yet I can't help but continue asking the question.

What is the System?

***

Two days later, we find ourselves dropping out of hyperspace. There are no convenient landmarks, no planetary objects out here. In the distance, an asteroid field floats. Unlike what the movies would have you believe, even a "dense" asteroid field has rocks that are quite a distance apart. Random coincidence, overenthusiastic Master Classers, and planetary destruction might occasionally create dense fields like you see in the movies, but for the most part, these widely spaced out floating rocks are the norm. And even then, this is considered a "dense" asteroid field.

Spaks sits snugly between the asteroids, shifting its position once in a while to ensure the structure itself is not hit by too large an asteroid. On the other hand, due to its immense size, smaller rocks are ignored. Between the ever-shifting asteroids—some of which have had thrusters added to them to ensure that the entire field can't be mapped out beforehand—and the gravitic and dimensional mines, the pirate station is supposedly safe from wide-scale assaults. At least, assaults without a significant amount of planning and sacrifice.

Spaks itself is not a single space station but instead multiple waystations that are connected by flexible, metallic gateways. Station Prime sits in the center, surrounded by four overlapping fields of force that protect it from direct entry. Station Prime is the largest of the stations, with the various secondary stations growing smaller as they lead to each ring. However, each station radiates out from Prime itself, so the second ring has three stations and the third, a half-dozen. Each waystation is shaped like a disc with dock spokes radiating from the main waystation lobby, allowing spaceships to dock for repair and refuel. Each waystation connects to the others within its own zone, but between each zone, circular and hexagonal shapes are situated to block off the entrances between the fields.

"Newcomers all have to dock at the farthest station in the fifth hub. To get deeper into the station, you need to have sufficient reputation with the station. Those tubes can all be blown, keeping invaders from getting to the main station easily. The force shields are mostly there for early warning, though I wouldn't be surprised if they could be—or aren't already—reinforced by Skills," Ali says as we float up to the station under quarter power.

"How'd you know all that?" I say, cocking my head.

"I might not be a reporter, but I've got my sources too."

"You mean you asked your Spirit friends."

"I did," Ali admits.

Mikito ignores our conversation, watching the starships around us. We've all gathered in the cockpit for the trip in, camaraderie driving us to be together even if projectors could provide the same view anywhere within the ship itself. The array of ships out the viewport is interesting—both incredibly varied in design and form, yet uniform in the lack of merchant and cargo ships. On consideration, that makes sense since pirates rarely "take" ships, preferring the insurance payouts. It actually made everyone happier—the goods arrived, the pirates had liquid Credits, and the ship captains still owned their ships. It made everything more expensive, but that was a different matter entirely.

As I stare at the projections, I take in the menagerie of shapes, from the traditional triangular-forms and bulbous, spinning craft to a tentacled monstrosity. Without the need to worry about air resistance and with Skills backing up the construction, Galactic ship design has taken a turn toward whimsy. Or perhaps, considering the range of aliens, it might be a matter of taste.

"Hey, Dornalor."

"Yes?" Dornalor says, eyes darting around as he reads screens only he can see or the occasional dial on the console.

"The insurance stuff. It's normally a generic overall fee based off the value of their goods, right? What happens if a merchant ship carries something a lot more valuable than normal?"

"They pay more." Dornalor gives me a look that asks what kind of idiot I am to ask such a simple question.

"What if they don't want to? Or decided they couldn't afford it?"

"Then they're not insured." Dornalor frowns, probably trying to understand what I'm getting at.

"So a merchant could decide to pay a minimum amount to the insurance company then run more valuable cargo?" I say, scratching my head. "That seems like an easy way to cheat the system."

"Pirates run with a wide range of people, including Quartermasters, Assessors, and Merchants. Once they're on board, they'll be able to quantify what is actually being transported. Anything outside of the insurance range and..." Dornalor shrugs. "But some merchants still run the risk."

"Top hat," Mikito says, interrupting us.

"What?" I turn to Mikito, who points at a screen. I stare as a floating top hat moves to cut in line in front of a spaceship that reminds me of an eastern dragon. Unlike some of the more extreme ships, the top hat's design is mostly in the edging and side thrusters. I wave, zooming the screen in, and spot what I expected—much of the stylish additions are armor plates that look to be only minimally attached. "I guess they're not completely insane. Looks like that's basically ablative armoring."

Ali confirms my guess.

"Incoming courier the *Nothing's Heartbreak*. State the reason for your arrival," a voice cackles over the radio.

"This is John Lee of the *Nothing's Heartbreak*. We're here to restock and repair," I say.

"Acknowledged. We are transmitting the rules and regulations of Spaks station."

"Received," Dornalor say.

"Docking information transmitted. Please ensure you have the docking fee ready. If not, your vehicle will be impounded."

I frown. "What's the fee?"

"Twenty-five thousand Credits."

"What!" Mikito yelps.

I kind of agree. That's daylight robbery. Most docking fees are in the range of four to five thousand and that's enough for a week. Since space is big and building out is cheap, docking costs are generally quite low.

"Thousand hells. Are you people insane?" I say.

"Fee includes recharge, cleaning, and security. Please note that as you have arrived in Spaks's controlled space, the docking fee is already owed. Attempts to leave without payment of the docking fee will result in corrective action."

Dornalor keeps his mouth shut, but I see how he still has the ship headed for the station. After some grumbling, I acknowledge the last message and the invoice. Twenty-five thousand Credits is ridiculous, especially considering the ship uses mostly a mixture of Mana and fission materials—none of which need recharging right now.

Even so, we pull into the station after we pay the invoice. Along the way, I eye the other notifications that we receive—a wide of array of advertising messages from local businesses. Some are full three-dimensional holograms, while other advertisements are plain, text leaflets. Spaks seems to function much like a large settlement, with every kind of retail establishment, from clothing suppliers to alchemists, and a variety of established buildings including entertainment centers and an arena. About the only thing the station is missing is a dungeon.

While the advertising is amusing, especially those which are badly targeted—like, I don't want to breathe liquid carbon monoxide—I'm more interested in the security that Spaks boasts. There are numerous floating weapon turrets, individually manned or automated, as well as the enchanted, weaponized mine fields. Even from here, I can tell some of those mines are entirely too familiar.

"Chaos mines?" I say, shaking my head.

Chaos weapons are ridiculously cheap for the kind of damage they can do. Of course, they're also ridiculously useless at times. Comes with the territory of being entirely random. The trick is putting enough of them in play that the odds of a series of duds cancel themselves out. I've never used a Chaos grenade in vacuum though. I'm guessing that the already random effects get even more useless when pitted against hard physics. After all, randomly summoning a windstorm does nothing in vacuum.

Between all the time I've spent working over the security arrangements for the settlements and some light reading, I've got enough base knowledge to make a judgment of the visible defensive measures on Spaks, and what it's saying is that their threat of corrective measures is entirely real. The last thing we want to do is cross the local authorities. Even if we survived their ground game, we'd still have to escape. And that would be a bad, bad idea. Perhaps a Heroic Class with the right ship could leave, but for us poor Master Classers, we'd be blown out of the water long before we made it to the hyperspace limit.

As we slide past the defensive shields, I can't help but feel like the spider walking willingly into the snake's den.

Chapter 4

Gathered at the ship's docking port, I look over my fellow humans, noting the slight tension in Harry's body and Mikito's light smile as she props her naginata on her shoulder. Dornalor's still inside in the cockpit, dealing with the bureaucracy. He's getting quotes and negotiating repairs. And, I'm assuming, off-loading whatever smuggled goods he picked up.

"Ready?" I say.

Docking itself was the simplest thing in the world, and since we've got no cargo, we're ready within moments. Our docking location is on the outermost ring of the station. That the other ships connected here are broken down vessels and junk monstrosities tells us more than enough about our reputation. Well, that and the ever-so-helpful screen Ali shot to me.

Current Reputation:

- *Spaks station: -287*
- *Pirates (self-professed and System designated): -358*
- *Galactic Reputation: 4*

"Just so you know, those are averages. But between your previous actions and the reputation of Paladins..." Ali says as a reminder.

I get it. There's more detailed reputation information for each subgroup of course, and our Galactic Reputation is a weird mixture due to our activities. We get points for keeping our word, finishing up any adventures, and collecting bounties, then we get a bunch of points taken away because we kill our bounties and break the law. If not, our entire reputation would be higher.

"Yeah, I figured. Surprised they let us in."

"Why not? Easier to kill you if you walk right in. And they've got a reputation to maintain about being all kinds of accepting."

I watch Mikito raise an eyebrow, waiting for me to finish my mental dithering. That single movement is all that I need to know that the Samurai is getting impatient. To appease her, and because I'm fed up with myself too, I open the docking bay doors and stride out with a confidence I don't necessarily feel.

"Evening, gents," I say to the greeting party.

Perhaps a touch too arrogant, but better to play tough than weak. My eyes sweep over the half-dozen strong group, taking in the Status information of the armed and armored welcoming party. My gaze pauses a couple times, dismissing the usual boring combat Classers.

Oi Rikaama (Rebel Captain Level 29) (A)

HP: 780/780

MP: 1897/2080

Conditions: Unit Boost x 11, Linked Tech x 2, Linked Shield

The Captain is an interesting fellow, a creature that looks like a mix between a merman with frills and scales and a jellyfish. Even as I stare at the humanoid Captain, portions of its body ripple and shift, adjusting to the environment. It's a fascinating sight that's only visible because Oi's combat armor is transparent. Weapons wise, I only see a single monofilament knife and beam pistol on his hips.

I Shao (Outlaw Negotiator Level 18) (A)

HP: 780/780

MP: 1897/2080

Conditions: Truth Sense, Sense Motive, Scent of the Bottom (Line)

I Shao's round and angular, a creature of crystal and metal shaped to look—to Terran eyes—like a crystal turtle. Crystal arms end in sharp claws, though I spot colored finger paint on their tips. Unlike her friend, I Shao doesn't carry any obvious weapons.

Kros m'Kaka (Advanced Martial Artist Level 38) (A)

HP: 3890/3890

MP: 430/430

Conditions: Biochemical enhanced reflexes, Chronal distortion (Minor), Sense Weakness

"Martial artist? That's not what my Skill is saying," Mikito sends in the party chat, since I had Ali share the status information with the party. His streamlined data stream is a lot more convenient than most of the Skills.

As for Kros, he's long and angular and weirdly humanoid, like a human stretched to seven feet and given extra-long ears. That Kros is giving Mikito the same kind of considering look that she gives him almost makes me worry that they're going to challenge one another immediately.

"I figured I'd translate it. Just like I've translated the Bruiser and Techwarden's Class," Ali says.

"What is a Paladin of Erethra doing on my station?" Oi says once he's looked us over too.

"Your station?" I say.

"I'm asking the questions here."

"Could you be any more cliché?" I say, shaking my head. But still, I answer him. "We're dealing with a little fallout and need a place to settle some matters. Spaks is known for its hospitality. Now if you'll excuse us, we're going to visit the Shop."

I see the twitch, the way Oi looks at I Shao when I stretch the truth. I Shao catches it, her eyes darting toward Oi, whose eyes refocus on a readout then back to me in seconds. Interesting that the Negotiator's broader range of Skills allows it to pick up on my evasion even when I'm telling the truth. Different from Nelia's TruthSeeker ability.

"And if I told you you're not leaving this dock?" Oi says.

"Then I'd have to question Spaks's reputation." That elicits a snort from Oi, so I decide to be a little more blunt, tired of playing nice and pussyfooting. Getting stopped at the first hurdle would get us nowhere. "I'll still be coming in anyway. I need to visit the Shop, and I'm not letting some petty dictator stand in my way."

"Petty—"

"Why?" I Shao asks, a claw landing on Oi's body.

I look at the alien, but all I can see in those crystal eyes are myself. Damn, but reading body language in alien species is hard. Years and skills later, and I'm still finding it difficult when I hit a new species. It takes time to build up that catalogue of behaviors.

"Come on, you guys know the answer by now," I say. "We've drawn down enough heat that Spaks and its like are our only recourse."

"Do you have a target here?" Blunter now, focused.

"Nope. Not that I know of." I shoot a glance at Harry, who shakes his head. "Definitely not."

I Shao freezes, processing before she nods to Oi. The Rebel Captain's body ripples in violent waves as he considers, making me a little seasick just looking at him.

Eventually, Oi turns around and walks away. He's about halfway down the undulating metallic corridor before he turns around and adds, "I'll be waiting for you to mess up, Paladin."

"Well, that was nice," I say, rubbing my face.

Mikito snorts and puts Hitoshi back into her inventory. Harry chuckles dryly, moving out from where he's been hiding behind us.

"You know, I'm used to Mikito not talking much. But you do know you're allowed to talk," I say.

"Not my way to be in the story. It's pretty bad style," Harry says.

"I'm surrounded by baka. You're already part of the story. We wouldn't have made it this far without your Skills." Mikito points at Harry. "Stop trying to act as if none of this concerns you."

Harry sniffs, the long running argument between the two not likely to be resolved any time soon. Rather than wait around for them to rehash old positions, I walk away, marveling at how the walkway seems to float in the center of the undulating metal tube that makes up the corridor. Pretty damn cool tech.

"Got a bunch of options highlighted for you, boy-o. Of course, the main Shop connection is in the center of the waystation, but there are a couple of merchants in the hub itself that look interesting," Ali says.

"Good man. Do me a favor?" At Ali's nod, I continue. "Keep an ear to the ground? See if any of your people have any news about the bounty hunters. Or hell, a dungeon or some easy-to-run quests. If we're going to be here till the ship is repaired, I want us gaining experience and Credits."

"On it. While you go a-shopping, I'll go a-drinking."

Harry covers a snort of laughter with a coughing fit while Mikito, more used to Ali's antics, rolls her eyes.

***

The outer hub is quite an interesting place. Think the Mos Eisley cantina population of weird and wonderful aliens mixed with a cyberpunk sense of style, all lit by neon, silver, and copper for the metal corridors and you'd have a good idea of the aesthetic. Retail stores are inset along the walls, floating 3D hologram advertising and neon signs differentiating the various stores. Some of the stores are open wide, ready to welcome everyone; others have dark privacy screens, offering secrecy for grey market products. Like any good pirate station, there are no rules on what is or isn't for sale.

There's a grunginess in the hub that wasn't present in Prax, a certain level of destitution and blatant aggression among its residents that the more civilized station did not showcase. I admit, walking through the station and eyeballing the various stores, I'm more comfortable here than in the more "civilized" Galactic worlds. Well, except for the way we're treated.

"We don't deal with your kind here," the shopkeeper says, staring flatly at my chest.

"Humans?"

"Paladins." Eyeballs swivel on their sticks and I find an unseen force slowly pushing me out.

Down the street, Harry is rebuffed too.

Skill Used: It's My Store

It's My Store (Level 1)

A Shopkeeper's best friend, It's My Store allows the user to blackball users from their premises and sales of their merchandise.

Effect: Targeted blackball users are ejected from the premises. Sales via other formats are automatically rejected. May be resisted using a Strength or Intelligence check.

Cost: 100 Mana

I could force myself past the damn Skill, but what am I going to do? Force him to sell to me by punching him in the face? At some point, you just have to give up.

"Look, I've got good Credit," Harry's lips move as I lipread.

I don't even need to read the creature's mouth to see the results—not that I could with this angle and its lack of lips. Harry's face tells me everything that I need.

Eventually, after a period of intense frustration, we meet up at the linked Shop sphere. Not that we ever split that far apart, but we have been checking out stores individually to cover more ground.

"Any progress?" I ask softly.

"No. We're going to need to improve our reputation first," Mikito says then gestures to the sphere. "Or just use the System Shop."

"Shop it is," I say.

While we've had trouble with merchants before, this is the first time we've ever been shut out this hard. I'm debating if our new reputation is the cause or if it's just an issue with me. For a group of pirates and rebels, they're pickier about the company they keep than I expected. Then again, Erethran Paladins have had thousands of years to build up a rather uncompromising reputation. I watch as Mikito and Harry engage the Shop sphere before I touch the orb myself and feel my body twist as I'm transported away.

***

Blink and you're there, that's how fast the System's teleportation ability is. The fact that I'm in a weird semi-dimension that has significant time compression is something I still have a hard time working my mind around. Oh, I've read about Shops in my studies, but I'm still puzzled about the why and how. As best as I can tell, the dimensions and locations of the majority of merchant Shops don't actually exist. They just float around in a weird dimensional location. It's one of the reasons why it's possible to alter the flow of time. Of course, some Shops are just in-dimension locations, but they're relatively unpopular. You'd have to fall pretty far down the ladder to rely on those Shops. Among other things, pirates have a tendency to fly in and do a raid once in a while.

As for myself, well, I'm in a beautiful yellow room, one with a simple counter to greet guests, a waiting and lounge area for those wanting to take their time perusing their wares, and a couple of doors. I know, from previous experience, that those doors lead to private shopping rooms.

Old Foxy, all big toothy smiles, comes out the moment I make my appearance known. After all this time, Foxy's as much an old friend as Ali. He's not even trying to con me anymore, having decided that it makes more sense to take his cut normally. Which, I'll admit, at this point is really getting up there.

"Got a bunch of things to sell," I say after we've done the usual introductions and walked into a private room. A gesture is all I need to dump my gathered loot onto the floor. One of the advantages of having Ali around is that the Spirit often finds time to grab corpses, pieces of gear, and the System-generated loot while I concentrate on the more important part of a battle. Like staying alive.

"Another successful bounty, it looks like," Foxy says.

"Yup."

"Something is bothering you," Foxy says. Familiarity goes both ways unfortunately.

"A bit." I pause then decide to mention my worries. "We were nearly caught this time. They almost trapped us in the ship. I hate the fact that we're so reliant on Dornalor's Skills."

"You have a piloting skill already, yes?" Foxy says, and I nod. "Then do you desire an individual Skill to take over, or are you looking to aid him?"

I can fly the ship without Skills, so in many ways, there's no point in getting a boost Skill for generic piloting. In fact, if we're at the point where I'm piloting the ship myself, we're in trouble. A shot that hit the well-armored cockpit and killed Dornalor would disable the ship. Which means… "Probably something to help him. Though I'd take both if possible."

"Hmmm…" Foxy falls silent, standing there in thought as his bushy tail swings back and forth. If I'm not mistaken, the tail has gotten even larger. "I believe I have a solution. To start, here is a Pilot Skill and a hyperspace warp Skill from the Pod Racer Class."

"Pod racer?"

"Entertainers. The Class is chosen by young daredevils who race for sport, thrills, and fame. They earn a pittance of Credits entertaining the masses by running circles around interstellar circuits. They brave the occasional monsters that live in hyperspace and between the void and the occasional manufactured obstacle."

I admit, I'm frowning. I'm not entirely sure why he'd choose their skills over a more "normal" Class's.

"Please, take a look. You'll see their hyperspace skills are dependent on Mana. Useful for quick boosts on over-stressed engines. In your case, as you do not expect to use this Skill much, it suits your massive Mana pool," Foxy explains with a lolling grin.

Class Skill: Hyperspace Nitro Boost (Level 1)

When you've got to win the race, there's nothing like a hyperspace boost. This Skill links the user with his craft's hyperspace engine, providing a direct boost to its efficiency. Unlike normal speed increases for hyperspace engines, the Nitro Boost is a variable boost and runs a risk of damaging the engine.

Effect: 15% increase in hyperspace engine efficiency + variable % increase in efficiency at 1% per surplus Mana. Each additional 1% over base raises chance of catastrophic engine failure by 0.01%

Cost: 250 Mana + (surplus variable amount; minimum 200 Mana increments) per minute

Class Skill: On the Edge (Level 1)

Shuttle racers live their lives on the edge, cutting corners by feet and dodging monsters by inches. There's only one way to drive a ship with that level of precision, and no matter what those military Pilots tell you, it's with On the Edge.

Effect: +10% boost in ship handling and maneuverability. +10% passive increase in all piloting skills. +1% increase per increment of surplus Mana

Cost: 100 Mana per level + (surplus variable amount; minimum 100 Mana increments) per minute

"I'm guessing the racers just use these as boosts and rely on their real skills otherwise?" I say, cocking my head as I read the descriptions.

"Most have regular piloting, engineering, and hyperspace Skills from other Classes, but many of those are passive skills. However, due to the way the courses are set up, it's in the corners where the winners win. These Skills are then the bread and butter, at least for the Advanced Classers," Foxy says. "Also, depending on the races, sometimes non-Class Skills are barred from use. Helps keep things a little more fair, you know?"

I can't help but hear the enthusiasm in Foxy's voice. "You're a fan, I take it."

"Well, it is an exciting sport."

I mull over this new information. Still, I can't say I disagree with him. In particular, the fact that much of the boost comes from active use of my Mana rather than a passive overall boost means I won't be affecting my Mana Regeneration rates and I'll be able to throw in a ton of Mana when needed. It's very much in line with my Overload skill, which probably will make Dornalor complain, but he doesn't need to know about it.

"So how does this help?" It's not a bad single Skill, but I'm wondering if a copilot Skill or maybe even an Engineer Skill might be better.

"Well, you'll want to combine your Skills with this one," Foxy says, gesturing at the new notification he has created.

Class Skill: Temporary Forced Link (Level 1)

Most Class Skills can't be linked with another's. The instability formed between the mixing of the aura from multiple Mana sources often results in spectacular—and explosive—scenarios. For the 02m8 Symbiotes though, the need to survive within their host bodies and use their Skills has resulted in this unique Skill, allowing the Symbiote to lend their Mana and Skills. (For more persistent effects, see Mana Graft)

Effect: Skill and Skill effects are forcibly combined. Final effect results will vary depending on level of compatibility of Skills.

Cost: 250 Mana + 10 Mana per minute (plus original Skill cost)

"Symbiote?" I say, raising an eyebrow. And Mana Graft? I shudder to think about it.

"02m8 Symbiote. One of fourteen races that live in symbiotic relationships with others under the System," Foxy says. "What you're looking for is a bit of a specialty of their races. Of those, many are passive Skills—which I'm sure you'd prefer to avoid, from previous conversations—and others require portions of the anatomy that you do not have."

"Right, gotcha."

I tap on the Skill for a moment before I wave my fingers, pulling up the Credit cost of getting all three. I wince. Even after selling the items from the corpses and collecting the bounty I've earned, the entire thing will cost me a chunk of my earnings. But one of the aspects of fighting in the Galaxy is the constant need to keep updating our Skills. If we don't, if we aren't improving, then we're just asking to be countered.

"Oh, right. Can you get this sent off?" I say, pulling out the set of armor.

It's taken some damage. Not enough for it to be a major issue, but better to get it done now than have it fail on me later. While I could use the Armor's auto teleport function, I still pay for the fixes, and this way, I don't have to worry about the cooldown on its Skill. While I hand over my Master-crafted armor, I actually take a look at its stats.

Hod's Triple-Fused Armor

The product of multiple workings by the Master Blacksmith and Crafter Hodiliphious "Hod" Yalding, the Triple-Fused Armor was hand-forged from rare, System-generated material, hand-refined and reworked thrice over with multiple patented and rare alloys and materials. The final product is considered barely passable by Hod—though it would make a lesser craftsman cry.

Core: Class I Hallow Physics Mana Engine

CPU: Class B Wote Core CPU

Armor Rating: Tier I (Enhanced)

Hard Points: 9 (6 Used—Jungian Flight System, Talpidae Abyssal Horns, Luione Hard Light Projectors, Diarus Poison Stingers, Ares Type I Shield Generator, Greater Troll Cell Injectors)

Soft Points 4 (3 Used—Neural Link, Ynir HUD Imaging, Airmed Body Monitor)

Battery Capacity: 380/380

Active Skills: Abyssal Chains, Mirror Shade, Poison Grip

Attribute Bonuses: +93 Strength, +78 Agility, +51 Constitution, +44 Perception, +287 Stamina and Health Regeneration per minute

Note: Hod's Triple-Fused Armor is currently under limited warranty. Armor may be teleported to Hod's workshop for repairs once a week. All cost of repairs will be deducted from user's account.

The armor's a piece of work. Most of the attribute bonuses are side effects of the materials used, helping to concentrate and focus Mana and provide a boost to its maneuverability and Strength. The Perception and Constitution bonuses are, however, purely due to the additional equipment I had grafted onto the armor.

The HUD Imaging software is much better than anything I've ever seen, with a full array of passive and active sensors that tap directly into the System. Combined with my Eye of Insight Skill, only Master Class Skill users can sneak up on me. As for the Body Monitor and Troll Cell Generators, they boost my Constitution and thus my Stamina and Health Points.

But the real benefit of the armor comes from the Active Skills. While I'm not a huge fan of Poison Grip, the other pair of Skills have made my life much safer. Of course, after getting my ass handed to me that badly by the damn Master Classers in Irvina, I had to update both my Skill set and equipment. It took me months to slowly rework my fighting style, adding new Skills at a pace that made it possible for me to instinctively use them. If not for my upgraded Intelligence attribute, it probably would have taken even longer. Even if the hesitation before choosing your next action is in a microsecond, when you're fighting Master and Advanced Class Combat Classers, that microsecond is a ton of time. It's also one of the major differences and balancing points between Skills and spells. Skills are almost instantaneous in their activation. Spells require channeling and casting times.

Once I've handed over the armor for fixing, I buy the Skills, feeling my brain and body get a System makeover. It's nowhere near as bad as getting my Class, but it's never fun buying non-Class Skills because the System updates your mind for you. Still, it's necessary, if for no other reason than to make sure we don't end up dead.

Once I'm done, I pull up the modified Status Screen that Ali provided.

Status Screen			
Name	John Lee	Class	Erethran Paladin
Race	Human (Male)	Level	36
Titles			
Monster's Bane, Redeemer of the Dead, Duelist, Explorer, Apprentice Questor, Galactic Silver Bounty Hunter			
Health	4350	Stamina	4350
Mana	4010	Mana Regeneration	**257 (+5) / minute**
Attributes			
Strength	297	Agility	386
Constitution	435	Perception	226
Intelligence	401	Willpower	435
Charisma	164	Luck	90

Class Skills			
Mana Imbue	3*	Blade Strike*	5
Thousand Steps	1	Altered Space	2
Two are One	1	The Body's Resolve	3
Greater Detection	1	A Thousand Blades*	3
Soul Shield	4	Blink Step	2
Portal*	5	Army of One	4
Sanctum	2	Penetration	6
Aura of Chivalry	1	Eyes of Insight	1
Beacon of the Angels	2	Eye of the Storm	1
Vanguard of the Apocalypse	2	Society's Web	1
External Class Skills			
Instantaneous Inventory	1	Frenzy	1
Cleave	2	Tech Link	2
Elemental Strike	1 (Ice)	Shrunken Footsteps	1
Analyze	2	Harden	2
Quantum Lock	3	Elastic Skin	3
Disengage Safeties	2	Temporary Forced Link	1
Hyperspace Nitro Boost	1	On the Edge	1

Combat Spells	
Improved Minor Healing (IV)	Greater Regeneration (II)
Greater Healing (II)	Mana Drip (II)
Improved Mana Missile (IV)	Enhanced Lightning Strike (III)
Firestorm	Polar Zone
Freezing Blade	Improved Inferno Strike (II)
Elemental Walls (Fire, Ice, Earth, etc.)	Ice Blast
Icestorm	Improved Invisibility
Improved Mana Cage	Improved Flight
Haste	

The biggest change since we left Irvina a few years ago, beyond picking up my armor, is that I've purchased more Class Skills. Not passive Skills, but active Skills and most of them in my own Class too. Once I realized how scarce Class Skills points were, I decided to focus on upping old active Skills with Credits. It's cheaper to pick up those Skills because they're already part of my Skill set, unlike picking up something out of Class. Of course, each level costs ever more Credits, making it cheaper to reinforce a slew of low level Skills than focusing on getting a higher level overall.

On top of that, I have to admit I still prefer the flexibility of having multiple Skills to use. Since I finance our entire expedition via the sale of loot and the Credits we get from kills—and the occasional dungeon run—I don't have a lot of excess enchanted equipment. And since I have no idea when and what kind of problem might hit, more options are better.

On top of all that, the other Class Skills for the Paladin tree aren't that interesting. Oh, the third tier all have powerful Skills. Judgment of All makes Army of One look like a firecracker next to an artillery shell. Shackles of

Eternity is an evil, evil social gaeas Skill. But for the short term, increasing Penetration offers more bang for the buck. It makes our current work of killing much easier. There's also the potential of evolving the Skill, which is my current goal. Of course, at the minimum, I need eight points dedicated to it. When you only have twenty-five Skill points per Class progression, that means a minimum investment of a quarter of all my points. It's not even possible to purchase the progression, though why, I've yet to research.

Eight is also on the low end of dedicated points. From everything I've read about upgrade Skills, there's no guarantee when a Skill evolves. Two individuals putting points into the same Skill will trigger a Skill evolution at different point levels and with differing effects. The only guarantee is that the more points you put in, the more powerful the evolved Skill. But if I've got to dedicate half my points to a Skill Evolution, I'm not sure it's worth it. It's one of the reasons not every Master Classer or Heroic bothers. And why most Evolved Skills are at the first tier of a Class tree rather than the last tier.

Either way, it's not something I have to worry about right now. At least not till I get to at least eight points. If the Skill Evolution doesn't trigger then, I'll have to reconsider my choices.

"John?" Foxy coughs to get my attention.

"Armor ready, eh?"

I take the time to dress properly, checking for damages and feel before nodding. Now that my buying is all done, I need to make a call. One that I'm not particularly looking forward to.

***

"Katherine," I greet the bust-sized hologram of my ex-City Manager now Ambassador to Earth.

The woman looks older, more tired, which is saying something when System regeneration paves over issues like physical exhaustion. With a decent Constitution, the amount of sleep required drops significantly—though long-term sleep deprivation is still a problem. "John, I see you succeeded. And survived."

"Yup." I glance at the counter beside the hologram, an indicator of how much it's costing me for this conversation. Needing the entire conversation to be both encrypted and secret means that I'm bleeding Credits. It won't stop someone who has the budget, but the bar is high enough that few would. "Who's next?"

"Are you that eager to continue?" Katherine says, eyebrows drawing down and creasing her forehead.

"It's what I do, isn't it?" Even I can hear the bitterness in my voice. "So who?"

"No one. We're, well, we're good."

"Don't lie to me," I say, shaking my head. "I know the attacks haven't stopped. The trade embargoes and the assassinations."

"And they won't," Katherine confirms. "We're challenging a whole belief system, a way of doing business. Those who have something to lose, they aren't going to stop. But you don't have to be the tip of the spear anymore. You shouldn't."

"As if we have another—"

"We do. You weren't the only one who had a hard time. Or got better."

"The Champions? Those do-gooders?"

"There are others."

When I stare at Katherine, she shakes her head, refusing to elaborate. I get it. Information that isn't spoken here is information that can't be bought or spread.

"The Champions are needed on Earth anyway. Especially with the new defense system," she says.

"Defense?"

"Yes." Katherine waves.

A second later, a notification appears before me.

Planetary Defense Grid Mark 3.9 (Enhanced by Diamant's Aura of Long Suffering Displeasure)

Drawing upon ambient Mana density in a planet and donated Mana from governed cities, the planetary defense grid is a passive defense blocking illegal travel into the planet. Enhanced with Diamant's Aura of Long-Suffering Displeasure, it reduces attributes and Skills, and increases Mana cost of all illegal entrants. Furthermore, all illegal entrants are marked by the Mana draw upon their aura.

Range: 10,024.97 KM from planetary surface (actual range dependent upon actual Mana density)

Effect: All incoming and outgoing hypertravel, teleportation, portal, dimension shifting, etc. from and to planet is blocked unless otherwise permitted.

Individuals who break through or undertake illegal entry into affected area have all attributes and Skill effects reduced by 30% (actual effect dependent on Levels, resistances, and ambient Mana density) and all Mana costs increased by 25%.

All illegal entry individuals marked and may be tracked from central hub.

"Whoa."

The Planetary Defense Grid itself is not that surprising. I've seen variations of it, especially on many of the more secure planets. But this is the first time I've seen the aura enhancement and tracking aspect. That would make anyone trying to slip onto the planet for a job more difficult. Not impossible, but difficult.

"Why don't other planets have this?"

"Mana Density," Katherine says. "Layering an entire planet like this requires a significant amount of ambient Mana—something most non-Dungeon Worlds lack. Well, outside Forbidden Zones, and you know how those work."

"Just tracks and blocks incoming, but it doesn't stop smash-and-grabs." I recall our most recent exploit. Though the decrease in attributes would be annoying, it wouldn't stop us from doing our thing.

"No," Katherine says. "That's next on the agenda. We have some area-specific shielding options, but nothing planet wide. However, this gives us sufficient time and warning to port in help."

It's not perfect, but a planet-wide aura this powerful will increase the difficulty of any mission by significant margins. Add the reduced global payout fund and the higher difficulty as relevant targets keep going up in Levels and I can see how this new factor could tip things in our favor. But...

"Why stop the attacks?" I say. "If we take out a few more people, a few more organizations, we could end this."

"Because it doesn't end," Katherine says. "You can't kill everyone who ever wants to stop us; it's impossible. You've established yourself as a real threat, but now, it's time to put the threat away. So long as you live and don't take action, everyone who is acting against us or considering acting against us will be wary. If they can't figure out who you'll target—"

"Because I'm not targeting anyone."

"They'll be scared. And wasting Credits and resources watching you. In the meantime—"

"Your personnel will have an easier time getting into place to deal with them," I finish for Katherine.

The Ambassador flashes me a predatory smile and I shiver, recalling that for all that she looks younger now, Katherine was playing office politics for decades before she met me. And even if the mining sector isn't as homicidal as Galactic politics, it was no less cutthroat.

"The weapon not used, eh?"

"Exactly," Katherine says. "And if, and when, you do act again—"

"It'll just drive them more nuts," I say. "But that only works if your other people can continue to make them scared enough to not add to the bounty."

"We'll find out," Katherine says. "But they've been working the other end of the problem for the last little while, so we're confident."

"Other end?"

"You've been going after those who have been paying for the hits. And ignoring those who have been pulling the trigger," Katherine says. "We haven't."

It was a deliberate choice. There were—theoretically at least—fewer targets this way. Trigger-pullers are more common than those in power. Except the Sects, governments, and the corporations, who have entire bureaucracies in place to replace the latest target. Of course, even in those cases, it was no guarantee the replacement would continue to enact a bad plan. Which was the point of my attacks.

"Does it help?"

"It's increased the cost of each hit," Katherine says. "And we'll continue running retaliatory attacks. We have enough personnel now to run both."

I sigh and run a hand through my hair. It's enough information for now. More details would put their plans in danger. In the end, I'm not needed. Doing nothing right now is the best option. On top of that, the increased bounty will put a big target on our backs. We're going to have to be careful until we have a better grasp of what it means. Until then, lying low and pursuing some other goals might be a good idea.

If I could remember what my other goals are these days.

Chapter 5

The reminder that I no longer have a clue what I'm doing is distracting. I end up spending my time browsing through the Shop, window shopping in an attempt to avoid deeper thoughts. I even take a few moments to chat with Ali. Even after spending all that time, when I transition back, no one else has returned to this reality. Rather than clog up the way, I move away a short distance.

I know from previous conversations with Mikito that her Shop doesn't compress time as much—something about her Shop focusing more on having a wider variety of crafting stations. I'm not even entirely sure why that matters to the Samurai, but my recommendation that she change Shops was rebuked. And lord only knows what kind of Shop Harry has.

"Ali, where are you?"

"Having a drink."

"Got anything?"

"Maybe."

"Perfect! What is it?"

"Should be coming up to you just about now, boy-o."

"So, you're the Paladin," a voice, grating and full of malice, cuts through the hubbub.

To make the Shop sphere easier to access, it was placed in the middle of a courtyard that acts as one of the main thoroughfares in the station. Since teleportation and activation are a matter of touching the sphere, it works quite well. I turn my head to spot the group of five approaching me.

"Trouble," Ali concludes, his voice all too happy with itself.

I wince mentally as I read their Status information.

"You ignoring me, Paladin?" Cedric "Knuckles" Liviera says. Spikey hair, pig-faced, with bulging green and veiny purple muscles showing under a metal breastplate that glitters with electricity. Pig-face doesn't seem to wield anything but a pair of big claws and knuckle dusters.

Next to him, a lady I can only describe as a cyborg stands, silver metal and gears whirling away as she hefts a pair of bladed arms while a beam rifle sits on her shoulder, tracking my motion. I dub her Alita.

Next to Alita is a serpentine-humanoid hybrid, a naga, that has crisscrossed bandoliers of pistols, and a conical-head-shaped Elemental creature of wind. That's going to be a pain to fight. Lastly, there's a robed creature whose hood is down, hands stuffed into the sleeves of its robes, surrounded by a swarm of flying force shields. Mage of some sort I'd guess. Maybe healer.

In seconds, I've stereotyped and judged them all, slotting them into likely Classes and from there, the most likely combat scenarios. It might not be nice or PC, but stereotyping is mental shorthand that allows us to speed up our judgments. We do it all the time—pulling information from myriad sources and creating mental groups to allow us to navigate through our lives. Bad part of town—avoid. Big monster with fangs—dangerous! Creature with triple their Mana compared to health—spell user. There are exceptions, but if we had to build our mental picture of every person from a clean slate, we'd be exhausted long before the day was done.

Knuckles moves to shove me, a deliberately provocative action. I easily sidestep the motion, realizing that I am being somewhat rude by ignoring everything that he's said. It's just not that interesting.

"What?" I answer slightly irritably. Instinct tells me they're here to pick a fight, so I can't even be bothered to offer them civil discourse. What's the point if I'm going to be pounding their face in in the next minute?

As the confrontation continues, I note how the passersby clear out, their keen sense for danger telling them to get away.

"You Paladins think you're all kinds of great, don't you? But here you are with your noble ass, just a Pirate like the rest of us." Pig-face snorts loudly in my face.

I step back—not because of the danger of being blindsided but because of his breath. The scents of sulfur and other even worse unmentionables almost make me gag. "Look, potty mouth, I don't really know why you're here. Nor do I care. If you're looking for a reason to fight, let's just do this, will you?" I shake out one hand, loosening the muscles. "At least I won't have to deal with your bad breath."

I'm not taunting him just because I'm a complete ass. Even as we're speaking, Naga and Alita are flanking me, the cyborg coming in close while Naga keeps his distance. The longer I wait, the better their positioning.

It's all I need to say. The punch comes sweeping in. No over-shoulder looping punch but straight from the chest, pushed by hip and shoulder. I've backed off enough to block the punch and the subsequent follow-up hook into my ribs with one hand and an elbow. Pig-face is strong, each punch sending stinging pain through my arm. But blocking the attacks allows me to throw up a Soul Shield and turn on Aura of Chivalry.

None of these guys are low enough Level that my Skills stop them. It doesn't even make them hesitate. The wind-elemental starts casting. Knuckle's gets a haste buff and I can tell that the buff spells aren't ending. As for Robes, he hasn't done anything yet, which is a bit worrying. I'm tempted to pull out a few more nasty Skills, but I decide against showing off for now.

As the guns fire and Alita vanishes, I make my move. I trigger the QSM first, sliding into another dimension. I duck right through Knuckle—not a moment too soon, as a Skill kicks in and rips me back into "normal" space. But by that point, I'm heading for Robes, leaving behind a pair of tangler grenades as a present for the others. Meanwhile, my nerves are on fire from being yanked back into this dimension. That, however, is a pain I'm used to—and like a chronic pain sufferer, it just makes me mad.

You are Dimension Locked

You have been shifted back to your normal dimensional coordinates.

The explosion behind me and the subsequent coating of sticky, fast-hardening chemicals slows Knuckle and Alita. Their tactics are so damn predictable; tank attacks me from the front, damage dealer comes in from the back and does the shish-kebab thing. Predictable but effective. Even as I'm moving forward, I'm forced to dodge and weave as the Naga fills the air with hot lead. Bullets that I expect to dodge curve in the air to hit my fast-depleting Soul Shield. Each bullet has a different effect, some throwing up bright lights to blind me, others adding to my Mana drain. Still, nothing he does is enough to stop me from reaching the Mage.

I'm a step away from being in melee range when a blue beam fills the air, locking me in a column of light. I ram into the wall of light and bounce off before I cut away at the spongy material. Robes has her hands held up in front of her, channeling Mana into the column. Stuck I might be, but Naga and the Wind-Elemental Mage are filling the enclosed space with spells. Winds turned into razors cut at my body. Bullets blip through my shield. I layer on another Soul Shield as I cut against the trap, watching Robes flinch as the Mana drain increases with each attack.

Crowd—okay, me—control and coordination. Already Knuckle is moving to position himself in front of the fast-retreating Mage while Alita hangs out in my blind spot, waiting. Or at least I guess because, you know, blind spot. Just like their Statuses, their presence on my minimap is hidden too. I'm almost tempted to take out Alita first. Being the "rogue" in the group probably means the blocking is coming from her. Or the Mage. Either-or.

181 Damage done to Soul Shield

The damage notification flashes as a living cloud of acid slams into my shield, swirling around my torso as it attempts to work its way in. I hop backward and bump up against the edges of the containment spell. Snarling, I can only spin about, cutting at the shield and layering my usual complement of combat spells—Greater Regeneration, Mana Drip, Freezing Blade, and Haste. Each attack makes Robes twitch, her Mana falling like a rock. The Penetration Skill is nearly doubling the damage of each attack on the spell, making this a losing game for them.

"Not so high and mighty anymore, are you?" Knuckle taunts, misreading the situation entirely. He stalks over, one hand glowing red as he burns off the remainder of the tangler grenade.

As the Soul Shield breaks and the attacks impact my armor like a hail of stones, I eyeball Robes again. A thought brings up my armor's Shield, buying me more time. Time to take the fight to the next level.

An exertion of will, and swords appear, replicas of mine. Thousand Blades create multiple copies of my sword, each of which follow the movement of my cut. By the time the third sword cuts through the column, Robes's Mana pool bottoms out. The column disappears and I throw myself forward, snatching the fourth floating sword that blocks my way. I throw myself straight at Knuckle. This time, I focus on my feet, ignoring the damage I do to the metallic flooring, and shift the way my Strength attribute interacts with the world. That means the steel flooring buckles and tears, ripped apart by the sudden change in forces and lack of reinforcement.

Knuckle shrinks down and takes the hit, but he's not trained. His raw Strength stat might be higher than mine, but he doesn't know how to influence its usage. When we crash together, it's with the force of a pair of eighteen-wheelers going at two hundred kilometers an hour. He might be able to withstand it, but the floor can't. He doesn't reinforce it, not with his attributes, and so we tumble backward as I keep pushing.

That's the thing about our stats. Strength gives us physical power, but it's at such a level that there's no way normal—or hell, System-reinforced—metal could withstand our movements. So a portion of our "Strength" is devoted to "holding" the world together, reinforcing the bonds of things around us so that we don't inadvertently destroy our surroundings—or ourselves. The System takes a portion of our Strength to do that, but with a little practice, you can adjust those ratios.

I'll admit, part of the reason I'm as good as I am at shifting the bonds between molecules is also entirely due to my Elemental Affinity—Electromagnetic Force. In fact, I have a feeling part of the reason so many bruisers don't learn to do this is because the initial sensing part is nearly impossible for those without the affinity. Or magic.

Be that as it may, I've got more momentum than Knuckle, and even braced as he is, he can't stop the floor from tearing up behind him—not without devoting more Strength to it and letting me harm him. Which he instinctively won't. That means I smash him into the Mage, push both of them through the Wind-Elemental, and take all three of us toward Robes.

"The Wind-Elemental didn't just disperse?"

"Of course not, boy-o. They're made of structured air. If they could come apart without consequence, they'd just be air. That's why it has no health. It's basically Mana given life."

Even as we speak, the Wind-Elemental does disperse, the congealed air form breaking apart and swirling away. In the smoke from the beams and the slight opaqueness of the dense air, I spot the portion that it is keeping intact. The creature's core. On the other hand, the Elemental's Mana levels drop the longer it stays dispersed.

Knuckle finally gets his feet under him, the floor firming up just before we crash into Robes. As we do, my Shield gives way as Naga's bullets tear through it, fire erupting across my back and my health taking a plunge. I see Knuckle readying himself as my momentum comes to a rest. Rather than stay in one place, I spin and conjure my sword, sliding the weapon across his torso. Flesh tears, blood spills, and the rest of my floating swords dig into Knuckle in turn.

We're nearly up against the walls of the station, curious passersby watching the entire fight. I don't get to revel in my first substantial attack because Alita's sword-arms are in my face. She nearly cuts me in half with her first attack. Only a quickly reconjured sword helps me block her strike. There's enough momentum in her attack that she pushes the false edge of my blade into my armor. After that, we spin and cut, blocking and thrusting as I bring my extra swords to block her lines of attack. In seconds, I get the upper hand in our duel and I'm making the cyborg bleed black-and-blue blood.

You are Taunted by Re Dma Kaw!

Taunt Resisted!

I turn away for a second, acting as if I'm forced to focus on Knuckle. The hesitation is enough for the Naga's bullets to chip away at my armor and health, but in the corner of my eyes, I see Alita commit to her attack. There's a gap in the floating swords, a space that she throws herself through with sword-arms extended. I drop beneath her arms, ice-encrusted sword extending in a cut that strikes her stomach. A twist of my hips as I guide her body into another blade and blood gushes, her body coming apart under my attacks.

A beam attack throws me backward, catching me high on the shoulder and burning away armor. I land in someone's shop, metal and blood pooling around me. A larger bullet slams into a gap in my armor and explodes, flames licking and catching on fallen goods. As I roll aside and glance at my health, I layer a Soul Shield and hide behind the wall, out of sight.

John Lee (Erethran Paladin Level 28)

HP: 2431/4860

MP: 2265/4010

My health is dropping like a rock. Even with the Resistances to damage I've got, I'm getting hammered on four sides. I could reduce the damage, but again, I'd like to keep a few things under the hood. Each time I get my hands on one of the damn pirates, they pull me away and let the Healer fix them. I can't get to the Healer to take him down which is, like, the first rule of System-combat. Blink Stepping is out, since they've locked down the Dimensions. I might be able to punch through it but trying and failing could make me extremely vulnerable.

I feel seriously cornered here. Without pulling out some of my more powerful Skills, I'm in a bind. And tearing a giant hole in the station won't do my reputation any good.

"Damn, boy-o. I was hoping you'd offer a better show for the public. You want some help?"

I growl, anger flaring within me, threatening to take over. Rage floods my body and I stop thinking about the consequences of going too hard, too fast. Fine. They want to see what an Erethran Paladin can do? I'll show them.

I spin out of the corner at full speed, Haste pushing me faster than ever. Thousand Steps and Vanguard of the Apocalypse kick in too, giving me that brief burst of movement they're not expecting. That's enough for the spells and shots to miss. In the meantime, I conjure Steel Walls, a modification of my old Mud Wall spells.

I block off the Healer, Mage, and Naga, controlling the fighting area first. I doubt it'll last long. I'm sure they'll figure a way around the newly formed steel walls, but I don't need a lot of time. Next comes Knuckle, who I use Blade Strikes on. He's still slowed from the earlier cuts, the Freezing Blade attacks lowering his speed well below mine. I'm surprised they didn't dispel it, but that's not my problem.

The Blade Strikes tear into Knuckle, who does his best to dodge and block. I'm too busy to read the exact damage being done on his Status, but I can see the wounds that appear on his body, the way his flesh is flayed from his body, bones showing and blood flowing. A blow from behind catches my attention, my Soul Shield flickering as it nearly breaks under the single sneak attack. Too much…

But I'm pissed and injured and done with playing their game. I ignore the attack, throwing up a Soul Shield to replace the damaged one. I'm focused on Knuckle, Blade Strikes filling the air as I burn Mana like it's paper funeral money. Crossing the dozens of feet between us is easy. As the designated tank, Knuckle is geared to make people come to him, not keep them away.

I throw an overhand cut, intending to bisect him from right shoulder to left hip, and Knuckle activates another Skill. This time, my attack smashes into an unyielding Shield that cocoons the alien entirely. Intuition tells me it's a penultimate life-saving Skill, similar to my Sanctum. So I turn, leaving the remainder of my blades to impact against the defense while I face Alita.

Alita throws another stab, one that cuts through my Soul Shield only to be blocked by my sword. I catch her blade high, letting it slide down my guard and then, locked together, I shove. My higher Strength overpowers the cyborg, throwing her away from me. In the corner of my eyes, I see Robes skirt around the steel wall. Surprisingly, I see nothing of the Wind-Elemental or Naga.

But Knuckle is stuck in his Skill and Alita is annoying the heck out of me. As a damage dealer, her Health pool is probably on the lower end. Rather than let her recover, I snatch a second sword from the air and swing. Each clash of our blades leaves chips, deep cuts in her own blade-hands. Her health drops with each attack, and it's only Robes who keeps her alive. She's limited though, his Mana pool barely recovered even after downing who knows how many potions.

A blade cuts across my face and I lean back, narrowly dodging the attack before a floating, trailing blade stops her follow-up. With a moment's respite, I raise my hand and conjure Ice Blast, sending a cone of cold toward Robes. Her floating shields block the cone of ice, but it piles up, restricting his vision as a mini-glacier forms in front of him.

Knuckle snarls, slamming his fist into his own protective shield Skill, but I ignore him, turning to finish off Alita. Invulnerability Skills are powerful, but they often come with the side effect of putting you out of play.

Returning to my fight with Alita, I press my advantage. Freezing Blade slows her down, each block reducing her speed advantage. In the corner of my eye, I ignore the occasional notice of a Poison Resisted as her attempts at debuffing me fail. Once the downhill slide begins, it's only a matter of seconds before I pile on the damage, Cleave off her arms, and behead her.

Even a belated healing spell does nothing to fix the issue as I drop a thermal grenade on the remains. The scream of despair from Knuckle follows me as I sprint for Robes. Moments before I reach her, Knuckle is there, blinking into existence right before me. We smash together, my sword plunging into his body and tearing him up, but Knuckle envelops me in a hug. The next few seconds are a study in grappling as he throws me about, locking my limbs and tossing me around like a ragdoll. I've done a lot of fighting, but grappling is something I haven't ever really studied.

Unfortunately for Knuckle, one thing he isn't ready for is grappling with a bunch of floating blades. While I get cut too, I can dismiss the blades the moment one digs into me. Knuckle, on the other hand, can't, and I keep summoning them back into being, leaving our fight a pointy obstacle course. By the time he's got me facedown on the steel, a couple of blades are lodged deep in his body.

That's when I pull out my other spell—Enhanced Lightning Strike. Of course, using electricity in a place filled with steel is normally a bad idea. But I tap into my Elemental Affinity, adjusting the resistance levels of the swords embedded in his body and my own hands before letting loose. The lightning arcs, some of it still ending up in the floor and other parts in my body, but mostly it flows into the swords embedded in Knuckle's body. After that, it's only a matter of gritting my teeth as I become part of the circulation channel. Once again, my cheaty resistances mean that I take only a small portion of the damage that Knuckle does—especially since my Penetration Skill cuts down his own powerful resistances. Lights flicker, some going out, others managing to handle the surges with aplomb. The smell of roast pig fills my nose. Whether the sweet stench is coming from me or him, I'm unsure. When I feel Knuckle's grip relax, I toss aside his corpse and move to finish off Robes.

"Halt!"

I ignore the order, cutting at Robes's floating shield. There's no movement from Robes, the Healer looking perfectly calm even as I destroy one of her floating shield blocks. As I ready another attack, golden cords grab me and pull us apart. I tear and cut mine apart, but the voice comes again.

"Stop, Paladin. Or we'll join the fight."

I stop, staring at the golden cords that float all around me. Following them back to their point of origin, I see that Oi was speaking. The steel walls I conjured are melting back into the station while Oi walks forward, flanked by his people. Behind the shrinking walls, I spot Mikito with her blade stuck in the still-alive Naga, his body bisected by her weapon. Ali's hovering next to the Wind-Elemental, his hands cupped as he contains the creature in a globe of force and wind. The Spirit is glowing with power, and even from here, I feel my Elemental Affinity responding.

"About damn time." I dismiss Haste and my swords, dropping all but my regeneration buffs. I do replace my Soul Shield, just in case, but it looks as though our fight is over. For now.

"I asked you not to cause trouble, Paladin," Oi says, looking around the area. His face twitches as he takes in the torn and scorched metal of the concourse, the destroyed shop, and the numerous cut and bullet holes. All of those are slowly being fixed, the metal flowing together as the System enacts its usual cleaning routine. But as a former settlement owner, I know that costs Mana. And sometimes Credits. "Keeping this station functioning is hard enough without you destroying it."

"They started it."

"Only after your Spirit went around letting everyone know a Paladin was here."

Ali looks guilty for a second before he smooths out his face.

"Don't think I don't know you were goading them on," Oi says. "What was the point of this?"

"Yes. What was the point?" I say.

"We got bored," Ali says, smiling guilelessly. He flexes his hands, and the Wind-Elemental lets out a little shriek as it gets compressed further. I'm surprised that that hurts it, but what the hell do I know? Maybe Elementals have cores that don't like being compressed?

"Bored." Oi's voice is flat as his gaze travels to Knuckle's and Alita's corpses. He turns to I Shao, muttering softly to her before he flinches at her words. After a moment, he nods reluctantly and faces us all. "Come with us."

Mikito raises an eyebrow at me. I nod, so she pulls her weapon out of the Naga, being mostly gentle about it too. The poor guy lets out a little shriek, but already I see the wounds around his body have stopped bleeding and his skin is covering over the missing portions. The advantages of System-aided healing. Ali flicks his hand and the Wind-Elemental flies out, spinning around in a mini tornado that the Spirit ignores as he floats over to me.

"Seriously. What the hell?" I ask.

"Let's just say that Oi has a problem. He needs someone like you. He just didn't know it. So I had to make sure he realized it. Thus, this little demonstration."

"Damn it, Ali," I say out loud.

The Spirit chuckles as he floats back to me, taking station over my shoulder. All we had to do was lay low, get our ship fixed, and find something useful to do with our time. But while the companion link is mostly secure, it's not a hundred percent. Ever since we left Earth, we've had to be more careful. So I shelve the questions and wait to see what happens next.

As we walk, Harry appears from the crowd of bystanders, joining our little procession.

"And where were you?" I say.

"Right here."

I blink, then memory comes flashing back. He's right—the damn reporter was right there. As he was not directly involved, his Skill made him disappear from my perception. "Of course. I forgot. Useful Skill."

"It sure is."

As Mikito falls in and Oi's team flanks us, I can't help but wonder what the Captain could use help with. Certainly not something easy.

Chapter 6

Meeting rooms. Why is it always meeting rooms? Seriously, I get stuck in them more often than I'd like. Even after I've given up my position as a settlement owner, I seem fated to end up in these rooms. And while it might be a Galactic meeting room, beyond a table and chairs that morph to fit their users, it's no different from any other meeting room. In other words, stifling and boring.

"So are you going to tell me off?" I say, cocking an eyebrow and playing dumb.

"Consider yourself told off," Oi says with a world-weary tone, waving as if dismissing the topic. I'm a little surprised, at least until he continues. "Just try not to start any more fights."

"Me? Never. But I do have some trouble-making friends," I say.

"Hey!" Mikito crosses her arms and glares at me. "I don't start fights."

"Just end them," I say, recalling the poor Naga. "Thanks for the assist, by the way."

"Of course. It's my duty." A smile twitches Mikito's lips. "Also, I can't let you have all the fun."

"Why don't you just kick John off the station?" Harry asks with a frown.

"I would if I could," Oi says, "but he did nothing wrong. We might be pirates, but there are rules. If we break them to favor anyone, our reputation will go down. And in something like this, even if most people will think it's justifiable…"

"You know he's going to cause even more trouble. And he's just a Paladin," Harry says, pushing.

"That's why it's even more important," Oi says. "Everyone here is an outcast for one reason or another. Some are real Pirates. But others are those who don't want to play by the Galactic Council's rules. Or who have angered someone in power. We're all unwanted in the greater society. Spaks was built on the foundation that everyone—everyone—is accepted here until they break our rules. And you've yet to break any rule that would have you banned."

I blink, sitting back and staring at Oi and the rest of their team. It's... weird. But I can see their point. The Galactic Council, the System, it's broken. In so many ways. The society that's been created because of it, with the powers that make entire worlds nothing more than playthings, resources to be exploited, is intrinsically corrupt. Those with Credits, those born into powerful families or organizations have a leg up over everyone else. They get more chances to Level up, fight more monsters, buy more Skills. Corporations might be limited to some extent, but they find ways around it, forming Guilds and taking over empires on the backend. Debt-slavery is common, gaeas and serfdom an easy way to build one's power base. There are opportunities, but most of them involve throwing yourself into the middle of a Dungeon World and hoping to come out ahead.

No surprise that some people—outcasts and rebels—stand against it. But...

"Sounds a bit idealistic," I say.

"It's also practical. Spaks might be the largest of such stations, but we're only so because of our reputation. With Skills and the hyperspace routes, it wouldn't take much for other stations to overtake us," I Shao chimes in. Instead of sitting, the crystal being stands, apparently unable to bend in that manner. "Our reputation for fairness and accepting everyone is also our shield against the Council. Our supporters in the Council, those who still feel that it can be changed from within, will protect the station so long as we are 'idealistic' if you will."

I wave, deciding to dismiss the topic. Whatever the reason, it's good enough for me that they aren't going to toss us out immediately. The rest of it is politics, and that can be dealt with by others.

"With all that said. How do I get you off my station faster?" Oi says.

That question makes me pause. Normally we would never be in a station for long—get the ship fixed, get the details of our latest target from Katherine, do some preliminary research, then we're off. Harry would pull together more information from the Shop and his contacts, getting us the background we needed to ask the right questions. Staying still, staying in a fixed location, was dangerous. On the other hand, staying in transit, bouncing from random point to random point in hyperspace, made it hard for others to find us.

Now… well, now I had no target. No plan for the future. I'd had one before—or at least, if not a plan, a question. Then the Galactics and their damn games happened and I found myself forced into this new role. Forced to play Galactic boogeyman. Strange how life changes on you. How, for all your plans and beliefs, all your good intentions, you often ended up taking random diversions. For weeks, months, sometimes years. If you were lucky though, you ended up back on the main thoroughfare of your life, back to doing what you intended to.

"Can't say we'll be getting off Spaks," Ali says, cutting in when the silence drags on. "But we do need passage into the third ring."

"The third ring?" I Shao scoffs. "You might as well ask for the moon. We can barely go that deep on official business."

"But you can get us into the next ring," Ali says.

"We'd have to raise your reputation with a few Quests," Oi says.

"*What in the thousand hells? Why'd we want to go deeper?*"

In reply, Ali dumps a notification.

Land of the Forbidden

Headquarters of the "Forbidden Questors," the Land of the Forbidden contains the archives and meeting points for this heretical branch of Questors. While their theories and conjectures are outlandish and stress previously disproved hypotheses, their research on the System Quest has been known to allow stalled Questors to improve their completion rates. As such, their continued existence and research branch is—reluctantly—approved by most Questors.

Location: Third ring of the pirate station Spaks

"The System Quest? I thought you hated that damned thing," I send to Ali.

"I do. But I'm beginning to crave some quiet research time," Ali replies. *"You might be used to all this killing, but a few weeks of not getting banished would be nice."*

My eyebrows draw down in a frown, but I can't dispute the idea that quiet time might be nice. And the idea of a bunch of heretical Questors is intriguing.

"Looks like we're grinding rep," I say to Oi.

"I find it strange that a Paladin would want to raise his reputation with us Pirates," Oi says.

"Firstly, not your usual Paladin," I say. "Secondly, as you said, not all of you are Pirates. And frankly, it seems like you guys have worked out some way of getting along. Mostly. I'd prefer it if you didn't do the entire pirating thing, but so long as you don't try it on me or anyone I know, it ain't any skin off my back."

"Not your usual Paladin?" I Shao says. Crystalline eyebrows twitch in a way that I can only relate as a smirk. "Sounds exactly like a Paladin of Erethra to me. They never care unless it affects their people."

I tilt my head in consideration as I recall my mentor. Somehow, the image I Shao paints and the Paladin I knew don't line up. But really, what do I say? That she's wrong? That her view on things is incorrect? Just because I have first-hand experience, I'm not entirely sure it invalidates her own knowledge. Not as if I've ever really dealt with the other Paladins.

"What? You think the great and mighty Paladins are bastions of morality? They're just like the rest of us, caring only about themselves. But they get to trumpet being on the side of right," I Shao says.

"Moving on," Mikito says to Oi. "Do you have a quest for us?"

"I might have a job that needs completing. Two in fact. There's a ship leaving soon that needs another Master Class on it," Oi says.

"Needs?"

"For the insurance payout, of course."

"No."

Oi smirks, as if he knew that was the answer. "The other job pays better in reputation but is a lot more dangerous."

"Go on," I say.

Oi leans in, dropping his voice to a whisper. "We're going to assault the fourth ring."

"Pardon?" I cock my head, not sure I heard properly.

Ali smirks, arms crossing, obviously having known about this. It must be why he set up all this. Question is how he learnt of it, but the Spirit is surprisingly resourceful at times.

"There are two ways to enter a deeper ring as an administrator," Oi says, raising his fingers. "Firstly, make your own station so successful, you're making more than an inner station. Doing so means you'll automatically be promoted to the station you overtook. You'll also be able to bring a large number of your people and the captain—or captains—who helped improve your finances with you.

"Secondly, you launch an assault and take a station. Of course, if you fail…" Oi makes a gill ripping out gesture with his hands before smacking his hands together, which I'm assuming is his version of throat-slitting. "No one wants a failed rebellious captain in play."

"And those who join them?" I say.

"Well, it depends. For direct subordinates"—Oi gestures to his party—"they'll be put to death too. Those hired are generally spared, because mercenaries are mercenaries. Everyone knows not to trust them. Though…" Oi eyes us and smiles. "Well, that's not always the case."

"Like, say, a Paladin?" I snort. Joy. So he wants us to help him attempt a rebellion that may, or may not, work. I could grind reputation some other way. The gods know how long that'd take though—what with no one actually wanting to talk to us. "What do we get out of this?"

Oi smiles, leaning forward. "Well, let's talk."

Details about the fourth station they're targeting are easy enough to get. Living in such close quarters means information security is pretty much nonexistent. Everything from basic security measures to force numbers and distribution is all laid out. The biggest problem is the single Master Class on the fourth station we're targeting. I'm a little surprised there's only one, but it seems the real powers sit in the third layer and beyond. The fifth and fourth layers are left for Advanced Classers to play around in.

"I've never heard of this Class before," I say, frowning at the jumble of words that have appeared before me. It's the closest thing to a translation the System can offer, but it's a phonetic translation. With a waggle of his fingers, Ali makes it change and my jaw drops. "Dragon Lord?"

"It's the Master Class advancement for a Dragon Knight," Oi says. "Technically the kingdom has requested we call it a Dark Dragon Lord, but the Class is the same. Just that he's been ejected from the planet and their ranks."

"Why?" I ask.

"Don't know. Don't care," Oi says. "But ever since he was exiled, he's hired on as a bodyguard all across the Galaxy. Latest job is, well, here. Your job is to stall him until we finish dealing with the station master. Once his contract is over, he'll be neutralized."

"That might not be true." I can't help being slightly amused by the idea of a Dragon Lord playing bodyguard while the Erethran Paladin plays the attacker. Isn't it meant to be the other way around? "What's his Level?"

"Thirty-eight."

"Good," I say.

In fact, it's not. I was hoping for a much lower Level. Unlike many other Classes, the Dragon Knight Class is a direct combat Class, one meant to be on the frontlines. I assume the Dragon Lord Class might be less punchy, but still powerful. I'm going to be outclassed in terms of raw power.

"Ali, got any details on the Master Class?"

"A little from earlier research. The good news is the Dragon Lord is the most common Master Class upgrade, so the advantages they have are slightly lower than yours. Also, it doesn't sound like he's gone down the tamer route."

I almost choke at the idea of a dragon tamed by a Master Class but manage to keep my face neutral.

"Bad news," Ali says. "The Dragon Knight has a Penetration Skill similar to yours, though less powerful. Starts at around 25% and increases by number of points. So your defenses will take a hammering. He's got a lot of active Skills that will boost his damage output as well and, like you, a couple of regenerative abilities to his health. Flight might or might not come into play.

"Dragon Lords are meant to work with Dragon Knights, so they've got a few group buffs and the Dragon Fear Aura. Lots of direct stat bonuses too, along with active Skill increases. Dragon Armor is a passive damage reducer, so your Penetration Skill will be less useful. In fact, it's a reinforced damage reducer, so your bonus will be reduced further. There are a few big attack moves, but he doesn't have access to the Lord's big finisher—Ancestor's Wrath."

"How were you going to deal with him if I wasn't around?" I ask Oi, cocking my head.

"You just fought them," Oi says. "I have a feeling they intended to test themselves a little with you. And obviously failed."

My jaw shifts as I clench and unclench my teeth, shooting Ali a death glare even as the Spirit tries to look all too innocent. I grunt, though a part of me is appalled by the idea that they intended to use that group to fight the Dragon Lord. Using a group of Advanced Classers to neutralize a Master Class isn't a bad idea. It's a time-tested tactic. But you generally wanted to double your numbers when you dealt with a prestige Class.

In addition, that group's tactics were decent, but most prestige Classes have a larger number of attribute points compared to common Classes. In our fight, they did everything right, but they couldn't take my health and Mana down fast enough before I controlled the pace of the fight. A Dragon Lord would have the same advantages. It's only when you throw enough people at the problem that these advantages slow down or stop.

I consider everything said. What we'll need to do and the fact that we'd be reliant on Oi and his team to fulfill their side of the assault. I consider how it's quite possible this entire assault is already scuppered. If Ali, in a few hours, can figure out what's happening, it'd be really dumb for the other station master to miss this. I think about all that, and I realize that it's probably a bad idea. We don't have to rush. We can take our time.

But...

There's a Dragon Lord. And I have to admit, ever since I turned down the option of becoming one, I've always wondered. Did I make the right choice? I've had to compromise, make promises to the Erethrans, work with people to shore up weaknesses in my Skill. If I had chosen otherwise, could I have done better? Been better?

I might never have another chance to find out. The idea of pitting myself against him excites me in ways assassinating fat bankers does not. If I am on vacation, I'm allowed to indulge, right?

"All right, I'll take the deal if my team will work with me," I say, my mouth moving before my brain catches up.

***

Hours later, we're making our way back to the ship. One thing that worries me about this whole thing is Dornalor's reaction. Us joining this fight might mess with his reputation. And since he's a merc and not technically part of the crew, it might end up bad.

Dornalor is waiting for us in the mess hall, sipping on a greenish liquid that releases a little bubble of foul-smelling gas as we walk in.

"We're going to be moving into the fourth ring," I say.

"Oh?" Dornalor asks, raising an eyebrow.

"We just need to run a little task…" At his growing frown, I can't help but smile. "And stall a Master Class."

"Not the Dragon Lord, right?"

"Yes, him. And why would you guess it was him?" I say.

"Because I thought of the worst-possible scenario." Dornalor lets out a long sigh then rubs a spot just below his neck. "You people are ridiculous. You had to pick a fight with the one Master Class in the fourth ring you shouldn't anger."

"Oh, come on, he's not that bad," I say.

"He's the Scourge of the Thirty-Ninth Ward! A thrice-titled Monster Exterminator," Dornalor says exasperatedly. "The Locus of Destruction. Even among the Dragon Lords, he's infamous. And you want to stall him."

"We're no pushovers," I say, pointing at Mikito and myself.

"Hey!"

"Oh fine, Ali's sort of useful too."

"Not better."

"She's barely a Master Class. And you've skipped over an entire Class worth of attributes," Dornalor says, shaking his head. "You say stall, but can you beat him? Because if you start the fight, you sure as hell better be able to beat him."

The man is right. We're going into this with the expectation that we only need to hold the Dragon Lord for a few minutes. If we're wrong, we have to kill him. And with that thought, a thread of fear finally makes its way into my heart. I've fought Master Classers before, and no fight has ever gone the way I planned. They always have a trick or two, a contingency plan. From the very first Master Class Psychic, who nearly brought us all down, to the latest non-Combat Classers, it's only by playing smart that we've ever won.

"Thank you," I say, my face smoothing out.

"For what?"

"Reminding me. That this world isn't fair," I say softly. "And that there's always a price." I turn, heading to the exit. "Harry."

"Yes?"

"I'm going to need you."

"Me?"

"Yup. You too, Ali, so stop pouting."

I walk out, half-smiling as the pair follow me, grumbling. I can even hear Mikito following, though her, I never doubted.

***

A figure with a flat nose, horns which curve around and protect his forehead, and bulging muscles which ripple with each movement stands, breathing deeply as blood drips from numerous wounds. Each movement, each breath is shown in high detail in the holographic projection. In his hands is an anime-sized war hammer, the body of the weapon nearly as big as the nine-foot-tall figure. The man stands, dyed in dark red and green from the flames, soot and ash drifting from the devastated Galactic city. The crumbled towers, melted vehicles, and slain corpses are so real, I can almost smell the charred flesh and burnt plastic. This is the first combat assessment of our enemy, our target in action.

"The Thirty-Ninth Ward," Ali says, his voice subdued.

It's been twenty minutes since the start of the fight. Twenty minutes showcasing the devastation a single Dragon Lord has wrought. What should have started as a simple policing action in a residential ward became something more, something horrendous. An all-out fight between three Master Classers.

The minor break is over as another alchemical bomb goes off, a magi-chemical explosion centered on the Dragon Lord. But he's gone, the camera tracking Bolo's movement unerringly as he charges. The hammer swings down, crashing into a fist of green and gold, the resulting concussive explosion tearing down even more of the buildings. The pair exchange a flurry of blows, each strike making broken glass shatter and shatter again. And then, they separate as another explosion occurs in the midst of where they were standing.

Again and again, the three clash. Sometimes Bolo shifts direction, charging and attacking the Battle Alchemist, who transmutes matter to energy before he's interrupted by the other Master Classer. Other times, Bolo clashes with the Omiu Class III Warrior directly. The Master Classers use the full variety of Skills, spells, and abilities that they have on hand. In a way, it's a master class—pun intended—in combat tactics. And more importantly, I learn something else.

"He's better than me," I say softly when the battle comes to an end, Bolo standing over the corpse of the Omiu Warrior. Not that you can really call it a corpse—more like a puddle of viscera and bone.

"Me too," Mikito admits.

"Not me," Ali says. "But I'm awesome."

We both ignore the Spirit as I raise my hand and tick off on my fingers. "He's got to have Agility in the four hundreds. A constant speed boost Skill too, something like Thousand Steps but passive. It's about half as effective as Haste. Strength is easily in the four hundreds, and his Constitution is ridiculous at over five hundred. Lots of different active combat Skills like Triple Strike, Infernal Blow, Smash, Dragon Hammer, and more. Facing him head-on, he spams those attacks when he gets the upper hand."

"But his regeneration rates have got to be low—he relies on a lot of passives," Ali points out.

"Sure, and in a drawn-out fight, that might be disadvantageous. But he's specced Intelligence to give him a really deep Mana pool and a couple of Mana reserves. It won't matter for us."

Mikito nods and raises a finger. "That Dragon Fear Aura is going to be a problem. I saw at least three times when the aura made the Omiu flinch."

I nod, recalling the incidents. It's not an issue for me, but Mikito doesn't have the level of resistances that I have. Unlike me, the Dragon Lord has a high Charisma, so his Aura skills are much more effective than mine. "That Dragon's Breath Skill could be a problem, but he's not likely to use it in the station. Especially if we can keep him pointed at his employer."

Dragon's Breath isn't an actual breath attack, but a plasma projection technique that all Dragon Knights get at the fourth tier of their Skill tree. Of course, some will project it from their mouth. In the Dragon Lord's case, he projects the attack from his hammer, which I believe is a soulbound weapon like mine. Except he doesn't seem to be able to summon and unsummon the weapon like I can.

"Hey, Ali, that hammer—"

"Not a legacy weapon. Soulbound. It's a Dragon Lord Class Skill. I didn't expect him to get it actually," Ali says, frowning. "He must have chosen it rather than the more common taming ability. It has a regenerative function and a growth function. Looks like it has gained a few abilities already."

"Thank God for small mercies," Harry says, his eyes still wide and shell-shocked.

I wonder if the reporter is getting flashbacks to the first time he was involved with a Master Class battle. Getting attacked in Irvina while traveling has left its own mental scar on our friendly reporter's soul. And while we've tangled with our share of Master Classers since then, we've taken great pains to limit collateral damage. Quite often that meant choosing to take fights in more dangerous, better prepared locations. All to stop the kind of devastation we see.

"What do you mean the hammer has abilities too?" I say.

"Exactly what I said. At a guess, it'd probably be knockback, crushing, and probably a Strength dispersal ability." When we look confused, the Spirit explains. "You can think of it as a debuff if he hits you. Reduces the opponent's strength after each hit. It's short term, but that's what happened to the Omiu Warrior."

I grunt, crossing my arms. My sword is soulbound, but because it's part of my Class package as an Erethran Honor Guard, other than making the blade itself sharper and easier to recall, it doesn't have anything special. I'm not at all jealous that Bolo's hammer is better. Nope. Not at all.

"He also has that Charge ability. Combined with his other active Skills, it makes facing him head-on very difficult," Mikito says, fingers drumming on the table. "Crippling and slowing him down is the best option."

"Except he has that crowd control debuff Skill," I say, shaking my head. I noticed how any movement-restricting debuff cast on him seemed to either disappear very fast or not work at all. "And high innate poison resistance."

That was all information from the early part of the fight and our knowledge of the Dragon Knight Skill. It was one of the reasons why the Battle Alchemist shifted to blowing things up—both his restrictive spells and Skills and his poison globes did nothing to Bolo. The trade-off between spending Mana to gain an effect was really poor.

"Can you win?" Harry says.

Out of the corner of my eye, I see that Dornalor has made his way into the conference room and is leaning against the door.

Silence descends while Mikito and I share a look. After a moment, we chuckle and offer Harry a nod. In truth, this is a luxury. Researching our opponent, knowing his weaknesses. His tactics. With enough time and preparation, we can take him.

It's just a question of how.

Chapter 7

I pop a chocolate in my mouth and look around the room. Because we don't normally have access to the fourth ring, Oi has his reserve team—us and a bunch of other mercs—sitting in a room near one of the floating walkways, waiting. The disused office has a couple of chairs, a table, and nothing else. Most offices are like that, what with paper and computers being replaced by the System. Its main benefit is that it's large enough to contain all of us.

Once the attack begins, Oi's people will secure the shield and corridor controls, ensuring that we won't be blocked off from entering. Until then, the only thing we can do is wait. Our presence in the initial fight is unwanted and unnecessary.

It's sort of what we've been doing for the last four days. We've spent the time waiting in the ship, rarely venturing out. There was little point in doing so, as we had more than sufficient food. And when we're sick of cooking, takeaway was just a call away. We spent the majority of our time on research, the rest talking to Oi and his crew to get a better understanding of their plans. Having spent most of our saved Credits on other Skills, it wasn't as if we could pick up anything situational. And truthfully, we would also hit the issue of having too many Skills.

The System is weird. Like the old games we used to play, many of the "Basic" Skills aren't that useful after a certain point. So what if your Power Strike Skill adds 50 points of base damage? When your opponent has resistances at the 80% level with Tier II armor, then that additional 50 points is nothing. More than that, while Skills can be used almost immediately— barring a short interval when your Mana flows to activate it—the time taken to mentally prep and activate a Skill is still precious time in a fight. When changes in a fight take fractions of a second, you've got to be able to activate your Skills instinctively. And that's where having too many Skills becomes an issue, because you end up thinking too much. And if you're not, if you're just relying on instincts, then why waste the funds on buying Skills you'll never use?

It's why my active combat Skills continue to be few. There's no real point, not when I'm still getting used to the Skills I have. There's even a whole slew of thought and theory that the majority of a Combat Classer's Skills should be passives. It reduces one's Mana regeneration, but if you're not relying on it in the first place, who cares, right? And by limiting the number of Class Skills, you can focus on the actual fight. Of course, detractors point out that such individuals are also one-trick ponies.

Another area of theory crafting for combat Classers focuses on the specialists. There, you gamble on getting a great evolution for your Class Skill. Some have taken this to the extreme, doing it for each of their Classes, making them super specialized. In some cases, it's made frighteningly effective combatants. Often, those extremists end up dead.

I can see the points in all three options—passives, specializations and being a generalist—but liking all three points doesn't help you create an actual build. Thus far, I've spread my points all across the board with a major concentration on a few. Recently, I've concentrated on reinforcing Penetration. I've also added some non-Class Active Skills to my repertoire, as more and more of my go-to Skills are well-known. Smart Master Classes often plan for this, having hidden contingency Skills as trump cards. It's why I worry, a little, about our upcoming fight.

"Chocolate?" I say, offering Harry a piece.

The reporter shakes his head as he drags on a cigarette, nervously playing with a lighter. Mikito, on the other hand, is sitting quietly, legs crossed as she regulates her breathing. I once asked her what she thinks about while waiting for a fight to start and she said she was envisioning the forms she would be using.

Scary lady.

"No, thank you," Harry says. "Never had much of a sweet tooth."

"Your loss." I glance upward slightly, checking the time. Two minutes.

All around me, I note the mercenaries, pirates, and other riffraff that have been gathered. I was somewhat surprised Knuckle's group was still coming, after his and Alita's deaths. That's when I found out you can't kill a cyborg by tearing it apart—not unless you kill the heart and the brain. Which was also why I never got the experience for killing her. Part of our delay was due to Alita needing to heal up and get her body fixed. Knuckle, on the other hand, was dead like a doornail, which did leave a little resentment in play. It's why they're part of the vanguard now.

"You still worried that they're going to betray us?" Ali sends to me.

"Isn't that the way of things?"

"Oi said there's a System-contract on them. Just like with us," Ali points out.

I nod slightly, pulling up the request once more.

Accepted Quest - Stall Bolo the Dragon Lord

You have accepted a Contract to stall the Dragon Lord Bolo in the fourth ring of Spaks station during the upcoming assault. You will need to either stall the Dragon Lord until the station master is killed and the station control's taken or until the assault has failed.

Rewards: Reputation increase in Spaks, Access to the Fourth Ring (Conditional), 50,000 Credits

Penalties for failure: Loss in Reputation

Penalties for breach of Contract: Loss in Reputation. Loss in Experience. Enmity of Oi Rikaama and surviving members of the fifth ring.

It's an interesting Contract. Truth be told, we're getting paid a pittance for what we're being asked to do. Still, we get one station closer to getting access to the heretics, and that's our main goal. Once we get into the fourth ring, I need to figure out how to get to the third.

"Five minutes," Mikito says, bringing my attention back to the matter on hand.

We wait in tense silence, the assortment of weird and wonderful monsters and aliens completing last-minute checks on equipment and, in a few cases, throwing on buffs.

The Galactics deal with their pre-battle nerves and the imminent dance with the uncaring lady in different ways. The drakes are perfectly still, awaiting their prey, hiding in their reptilian instincts. Others are restless, their bodies shifting, twitching, and rolling as they try to burn off excess energy. The earth elemental is at the forefront of that, his entire body metamorphizing as he pushes his insides out and his outsides in, replacing portions of his body again and again. A mini-hydra-like creature hisses and growls at each of its own four heads, and in the corner, a single pair of hands knit.

"Bridge secured. Move out!"

The voice cackles over our earpieces, informing everyone at the same time. There's no mass stampede, no crazed rush. The people who are meant to go first lead the way while the rest of us finish our last-minute preps, layering buffs and defensive shields.

We're not the vanguard this time, but Mikito and I are right behind them. Our job isn't to fight, so I intend to hold off as much as possible. It's why I keep my Aura turned off, in the hope of not attracting too much attention. Not that I'm the only one with a Skill—notifications flash and disappear in quick order. Aura of the Green Splinter, the Mana Well, Aura of the Thrice-Chosen Wind. Each Aura layers on, providing a small boost, or sometimes canceling out another aura entirely.

Charging through the tunnels, we cross the expanse of space that separates the rings within minutes. Stars twinkle and flash peacefully out of the windows, discordant with the hum of beam weaponry and the screams of pain which welcome us. We exit the tunnel to a full-fledged battle, one which would make an anime designer weep in delight and failure. Aliens and monsters fight all around us. A power-armor-clad squadron faces off against a dryad and a werewolf on one end. A couple of dwarves kneecap what I can only call a salamander mount while its rider struggles against living metal chains. In another corner, floating in midair, a Psychic faces off against an elemental caster, unleashed energy crackling around their forms.

Madness and violence mix, explosions mixed with spells; blood and other body fluids litter the floor. Metal is torn up and compressed. Bullets whine and crack while multiple mini-missiles explode. Even through the noise dampeners in my helmet, I can physically feel the impact of the battle. All the while, notifications pop up, one after the other.

You have entered a restricted region. You do not have the required Reputation to be present at this location. You do not possess an exemption pass.
-10 Reputation with Spaks Station

Warning: This region is under emergency combat protocols. All dimensional shifting is Locked at this time. Dimensional shifting for any reason is prohibited and will result in loss of Reputation.

Emergency Quest Notification

An invasion of Spaks Station 4.82 has occurred. An emergency defense quest has been issued to all individuals in Station 4.82.
Rewards: Will be issued dependent on participation rate and results (see Spaks defense station standards 7.24.88.1 for details).

Do you accept: Y/N

Obviously I decline, though my lips curl up slightly in grim acknowledgement of the new doorway locked sign that shows up in my vision. Dimension locked. Again.

"Paladin!" Oi calls, and a little beacon lights up in my helmet.

We're all wired in, so I follow the bouncing ball as we rush past the fight. The disc-shaped station is made up of about seven pedestrian levels and a single maintenance level that stretches all across the outer layer. From each level, spokes for the various docking bays extend at angles that adjust as necessary to fit in the optimal number of ships. Our destination is the center of the station itself.

"Stay close, Harry," I say, reminding our reporter friend.

He grunts, running alongside us, his Class Skills in full effect.

A series of fast-moving red dots on my minimap is all the warning I get before a series of tiny rolling balls comes out of the corner, moving to intercept our party. My eyes narrow as the damn things stop rolling and pull apart, revealing a series of little homing missiles. Before I can react, Mikito lashes out, and a wave of flame and energy tears into the drones. The few that survive launch their attacks, the ripple fire effect of multiple explosives going off around us making running hard. The walls hold up surprisingly well, while I cut apart a couple of the drones as we rush past them. Before they can engage us further, more of the assault party gets involved.

Down corridors and through holes in the walls, we keep running. At each crossway, we pass more members of the advance team who are caught up in desperate battles. If there's a flaw in Oi's plan, it's that he needs to finish this fast. Because of the advantages the defending station has—the ability to send out quests, the defensive emplacements and shields—the only way to win is to hit fast and keep moving.

102

Minutes to get to the center. We run past battles, individuals locked in life or death fights, without turning our heads. Harry has his hands held out before him, recording everything he can. Mikito bounces along the edges, occasionally striking with her naginata to come to the aid of others. Rather than the brilliant glow of neon and station lightning, everything's muted. Stores closed, doors shut, and pedestrians hiding.

And then we're there, in a surprisingly silent area. Our headlong rush comes to a full stop in a large, partly illuminated, featureless security corridor. Harry's somewhere around, but because I'm in the middle of the fight and he's not part of our official combat party, his Skills are in full effect, minimizing his presence. I have to forcibly remember he's around, otherwise he fades into the background. As I run, I borrow Ali's eyesight for a second, the Spirit hovering near the ceiling to provide a better sightline over the heads of our stalled attack at the station core.

It's a man. A single, very recognizable, horned man dressed in what I would call medieval emerald scalemail that glints and glistens with his every breath. He stands at the entrance to the station core, his oversized hammer propped up in front of him, blocking the way into the administrative center. The Dragon Fear Aura he exudes is enough to freeze everyone, reaching deep within the brain to the lizard or other small scuttly creature we came from, reminding us that there are things—very big, very bad things—out there. And if we're real small and real quiet, it might just miss us.

The in-drawn breath and the thready exhalation reminds me that Mikito is working her way through the fear, pushing past it in her own way, using Skills and resistances to mental effects. I'm not sure how, I never asked, but I trust her to have my back when it counts. As for me, the Aura bounces right off my Class resistances, offering no more pressure than a deep water dive. Something I've, unfortunately, had too much experience with.

"Paladin." Oi's voice in my ear, his tone saying it all. I swear I almost hear a pleading note in it, but it might be my imagination.

Walking forward, I push past the still and silent forms of Oi's people and the Rebel Captain himself. They're all here, ready to take over and charge in, if they have a chance. Some of Oi's people have broken through the Aura, but none of them dare move. And so it's the simplest thing to walk forward and put myself before the Dragon Lord. It's the simplest thing in the Galaxy to stand before him and offer a nod.

Bolo Dumas Windward South; Scourge of the Thirty Ninth Ward, The Locus of Destruction, Monster Exterminator (Drake, Uzaks, Goblins), more… (Dragon Lord Level 38) (M)
_HP: 7190/7190_
_MP: 4730/4730_
Conditions: Dragon Fear Aura, Blessings of the Wind, Earth and Fire, Improved Constitution, Orichalum Skin, Sheathed Organs, Mana Drip, Greater Regeneration

"You're with them?" Bolo's voice is deep, posh sounding, and clipped. It buzzes down in the deep baritone range with a little more reverb than a human's. Might be the way his horns work with his voice box.

"I got paid." Unspoken are the words "same as you," but they hang in the air anyway.

"I am repaying a favor." The nine-foot-tall, flame-eyed, overly muscled, horned Dragon Lord says this as if it is sufficient explanation to everything. Including the fact that he isn't about to move. Which, I guess, it is.

"Ah. Pity," I say, cracking my neck. "Shall we?"

Bolo offers me a nod in return as he picks up his hammer. We stand there, gauging one another in silence. I feel Mikito moving up behind and to the side of me, while the rest of Oi's team collectively hold their breath. I don't know who blinks first, who makes the first move, but Bolo and I explode into action. I'm faster than him, with Haste on, but that's only until he engages that Charge ability of his. Then the son of a bitch almost teleports in front of me, hitting me with the hilt of his hammer and putting my momentum to a complete stop. Next, he helps me regain my momentum by spinning in place—and smashing aside a few unlucky bastards who've rushed up to help—and bringing the end of his hammer into my chest.

I go flying backward, my Soul Shield completely destroyed by that single attack. Those unlucky enough to not get out of the way of my flying body are bowled over. My body punches through metal wall after metal wall, refusing to stop as the momentum continues. Even as I try to slow myself down, get my feet under me, I can see the Dragon Lord charging after me, leaving his post to finish me off. He's not willing to give me the time or space to recover.

Silly old Lord.

Chest heaving with pain, I narrow my eyes as the grenades I left strewn along my pathway explode, one after the other. They do little more than annoy the Master Classer, coating him with flame, sticky webs, and monomolecular wires, shaving off tenths of his health. In reply, Bolo swings his giant hammer overhead. It's so large, it tears up the ceiling and opens massive rents in the floor as it comes crashing down. This time, I'm ready. I dodge sideways but find myself with an unforeseen problem.

The goddamn weapon is so big that any attempt at dodging it puts me out of position to attack the Dragon Lord. I can't hit him with a normal melee attack, not without risking getting hammered. To buy some time, I jump backward and toss a couple more grenades, only to watch shrapnel and flames lick at the Dragon Lord's impassive defenses. Anything less than a direct attack is nothing more than an annoyance, as we figured. A useful and distractingly large explosive annoyance, but an annoyance.

13 Damage Done

"I know, Ali."

Giving up on that attack for now, I keep retreating and slashing with my sword, leaving conjured blades moving in the air behind me. It slows the Dragon Lord as he navigates around the weapons or bats them aside, allowing me to call Blade Strikes to harry him further. The damage results from those attacks are marginally better than my grenades—in the hundreds when they do hit. Unfortunately, our battlefield regeneration rates are so high that if I can't put out at least five hundred points of damage a minute, it's useless.

"Stop running!" the Dragon Lord snarls, frustration on his face.

I've dropped Haste, but with the obstacles in place and his big weapon, dodging his attacks and keeping just ahead of him is mostly viable. When he does catch up and swings, I don't bother setting my feet, instead blocking with my sword and letting the momentum of the attack punch me through the ground at an angle. The strain on my arms and shoulders is not inconsequential. As Ali helpfully showcases.

-179 HP

When I pop back up to my feet and set myself, I notice that the Dragon Lord hasn't bothered to chase me. The next second, he spins about to return to his post. Damn. So he's not dumb enough to be pulled away from his post for too long. Didn't think he would be, but you never know.

"They're still trying to get through the doors. It's reinforced with a Skill," Ali sends.

My feet bunch as I throw myself upward, crossing the distance to return to where I started. I take off after Bolo, his dot and another familiar one stalled in a corridor ahead. By the time I turn the corner, the entire corridor is wrecked and the pair are down two floors. Beneath my feet, in the giant hole in the flooring, Mikito and the Dragon Lord duel. The Samurai is focused mostly on defense and—literally—cutting down his hammer, but a slight limp and distortion in her ghostly armor shows the damage that Bolo has managed to cause.

I let gravity take me to the fight as I throw out Blade Strikes. Two-thirds of them hit before the Dragon Lord notices and dodges. Each Blade Strike digs into his armor and skin, leaving lines of blood. Spinning away from the attacks, Bolo raises his weapon and hammers me into the ceiling. My reapplied Soul Shield shatters as I reach out to the surroundings to stabilize the walls, using both my Elemental Affinity and the System's attributes.

His attack costs him though, as Mikito manages to take off another chunk of the hammer. The clashes between the weapons send shockwaves through the surroundings. Even as I drop to the floor, I can see the hammer regrowing its broken portions. I take the time to reapply my Soul Shield and cast Freezing Blade before I run forward, joining the battle between the pair.

Caught between the two of us, the Dragon Lord is pinned in place. It's only a few seconds, a half dozen clashes with my Freezing Blade, before he gets the rhythm of our attacks. His return attack starts with a shoulder-charge at Mikito, smashing the Samurai through corridor walls. The attack sends a wave of flame and electricity erupting from the impact points, briefly blinding us. By the time I reach Bolo, the Dragon Lord has spun around and charged up his hammer, which he brings directly down at me even as the souped-up attack melts the ceiling. I get my sword up in time, reinforcing the flat of the blade with my other hand, but it's not enough.

The impact of the attack breaks my sword at the points of leverage, blowing out my elbows and shoulders as they fail to contain the kinetic energy of the swing. It goes further as elemental energy wraps around my body, pushing the remnants of my weapon into me, crushing my helmet and my chest as my Soul Shield pops like a soap bubble. By the time my body's inertia disappears, I've got broken bones, internal bleeding, and a shattered soul blade. My only saving grace is the fact I've been blown down a couple more levels.

-789 Damage

A wave of healing energy pops my shoulders back in place as the emergency healing vials in my suit kick in, injecting me with their healing potions. Renewed health flushes through my body, allowing me to use my arms again even as I dismiss my helmet into my inventory. I briefly consider using the Abyssal Chains to slow Bolo, but I know it would be a futile gesture. He has more than enough strength to shatter the chains. At best, I'd gain a fraction of a second. Rather than choose that, I reconjure my blade and eye the corridor before hopping away from the fast-arriving Dragon Lord.

Army of One creates multiple blades which project their modified, upgraded Blade Strikes—beams of force and Mana that cut through steel and flesh with abandon. When I conjure the attack, Bolo's eyes widen and he hunkers down behind his hammer, his body glowing as the Dragon Lord activates his own defensive spells. He tanks the attack head-on, feet dug into the floor to stabilize his position. As beams of energy given form strike the hammer, it comes apart in pieces. At first, at the edges where Mikito's weapon tore it apart. Then the center glows, cracks appearing as the energy bleeds through. It shatters, shrapnel disappearing under the onslaught of the attack.

Unlike my sword, Bolo's weapon can only replace itself by regeneration. As most of it is shattered, the weapon will take a while to regrow. It's part one of our plan to deal with the son of a bitch and straight out of the playbook to deal with Dragon Lords.

I spit a mouthful of blood and a loose tooth, feeling my ribs grate as they put themselves back into position. My eyes narrow at the smoking hole in the floor, warning klaxons going off as sparks from broken electrical conduits and glowing steel shroud us. If not for the entire station having an auto-regenerating feature and being System-built and reinforced, we'd have destroyed it already. Even then, the amount of damage we've done is significant. Our fight has taken us down multiple levels; the hole I've created has dropped Bolo onto the outer walls. If not for the fact that the outer walls of the station are reinforced, even the incidental damage from Army of One would have punched through.

The Dragon Lord reappears at the edge of the hole with a hop, the shattered remnants of his hammer in hand. The damn giant grins at me. My most damaging attack, and he's barely down a third of his health. Ali was not joking when he mentioned the effectiveness of Bolo's numerous defensive Skills.

An aura of green and red rises from Bolo's body, swirling in hypnotic patterns as they cloak his form. Bolo's subsequent charge almost catches me unaware, the Dragon Lord covering the ground between us in the time it takes me to activate a Skill. As he arrives, Mikito drops down, ready to trade places, but it's too late.

Once more, he triggers his Skills. Dragon Hammer on his own body, to give him strength and increased damage. Call of Fire, to add additional elemental damage. Triple Strike combined with Infernal Blow means that the punches blur, slamming me around like a hockey puck on a too-small rink. Even with my ability to conjure additional blades, I cannot stop the onslaught. Bolo slips around each of the blades, taking a few cuts here and there to keep striking me. He's hitting me so fast I don't even have time to move before he smashes directly into the deck, punching me through the last floor to hit the outer walls of the station.

Out here, the gravity controls are less powerful, and I can feel the immediate shift. I bounce a little more than normal before I collapse against the cold, uncaring metal. Barely healed body parts are shattered, my right hip a complete mess while the left side of my body is so much mush. I'm barely holding on, even as the layered regeneration buffs stitch me together. The only reasons I'm still conscious are Class-given pain resistances and my innate stubbornness. Pushing aside the pain, I start the next Skill, knowing it takes a little time to activate, and hope it happens in time.

Surprise shows on Bolo's face as he realizes I'm still alive. The Dragon Lord jumps down, broken hammer appearing in his hand as it fills with power, a nub of the hammer already regrown. Sanctuary, my ultimate defensive Skill, activates and places a dome of power around me that blocks the attack, letting the hammer bounce off it.

Bolo strikes the Sanctuary once more, eyeballing the defense before he turns to leave. The Dragon Lord knows better than to try to break through an invulnerability Skill.

"Clear," Mikito's voice sounds in my ear.

I offer Bolo's back a bloody grin. "Don't leave yet."

Bolo hesitates and looks over his shoulder. He's wary about another attack, another trick. Caution against a Master Classer. Smart.

A mental command is all it takes for Abyssal Chains to activate, one after the other, to hold the Dragon Lord still for a brief moment. It serves more as a distraction than an actual impediment. At the same time, I've already activated my other attack.

Beacon of the Angels doesn't do as much damage to an individual as my Army of One Skill. It's an area effect Skill, meant to control the battlefield and attack multiple targets. It deals damage to everything within its scope—people, equipment, structures. As I call the attack down on myself and the Dragon Lord, it splashes uselessly against my own Sanctuary, burning the Master Classer and melting the flooring we're standing on. I draw on my Mana Bracelet, draining it as fast as I can as I reactivate the Skill, targeting the same area. Bolo is using his own defensive Skills, a hand raised upward to form a shield while facing the damage head-on, waiting for the chains to shatter. It's a bad habit of his—trusting in his health, in his Skills, and tanking damage before retaliating. An eye for an eye, a punch for a hammer blow. Once he is hurt, he forgets for a moment his objective to retaliate.

Which is why we planned this entire beatdown.

Everything burns. And then it doesn't.

As my second Beacon ends, the outer walls finally give way. The explosive decompression from the station's outer walls snatches my sphere of safety and Bolo, throwing the pair of us into space. We end up spinning around and around in the middle of nowhere, far from the station exit I created.

"Do you think this will stop me?" Bolo says.

Of course, I can't hear him, but lipreading still works. Even without protective equipment, the Knight doesn't seem to be taking damage from the hostile environment. A slight click of Bolo's heels and mini-thrusters on his boots activate.

I ignore his antics while I slap on a new helmet and fill my lungs with oxygen, then I switch out my damaged armor for a simple all-purpose EVA jumpsuit. The heaters in the suit are a welcome addition, Sanctuary falling soon after and exposing me, prepped and ready, to the cold of space. By then, Bolo is nearly at the open rent in the station.

I eyeball his momentum, then pop open a Portal right in front of him. Being out of the station and no longer Dimension Locked, the Portal's mouth widens without a hitch. Inertia in space is a bitch. Bolo has no time to stop as he is taken into the Portal and deposited far outside the entire station complex.

The giggle that resounds in my ear is unusual and all too girly for its originator. The Samurai steps into sight at the exit, her naginata propped up on her shoulder as she tosses me a line. If Bolo had managed to dodge my Portal, Mikito's job was to push him back into it.

"I'll be damned. It worked," Harry says, shaking his head.

I turn my head from side to side, curious if I can spot the reporter and not finding him. Damn Skill.

"Ye of little faith." I catch the line Mikito throws and haul myself in. "Think he's going to be pissed?"

"Probably," Mikito says.

I can't help but chuckle, thinking of Bolo and the very, very long journey he has. Even if Bolo has the equivalent of a Portal ability, he won't be able to teleport into the station itself. Once he's outside, all I need to do is open a Portal in front of every entrance he tries to use, teleporting him right back out. So long as they keep the dimensions locked, he isn't getting back in any time soon. And if they release the dimensional locks, the attackers will be able to port right into the main station room.

All in all, we've won our confrontation with Bolo. And didn't have to kill him either.

A win-win for everyone.

Chapter 8

By the time I see the fist, it's too late for me to dodge. The punch slams me into the bulkhead, which compresses behind me, pinning me in place. The next half dozen punches crack ribs, burst internal organs, and make me cough up blood. A Soul Shield, thrown up automatically, shatters in a hail of strikes but gives me enough time to kick my opponent back.

I slump to the floor, glaring at Bolo, who is panting steps away from me, his body cloaked in flames. Now that he's been pushed back, the Dragon Lord makes no move to continue his attack. Mikito and Ali surround Bolo, ready to continue the fight but are held up by my hand.

"I see you're back," I say.

"You tricked me," Bolo says.

"Yup. Sorry about that, but actually beating you would be a chore." Bolo growls at my answer, and I dismiss it by shifting topics. "By the way, how'd you do that?"

"What?"

"The bone-breaking thing," I say, eyeing my health gauge. It's still at two-thirds full, so there's no reason for my body to be as broken as it is.

"Dragon Knight secret," Bolo says, the flames across his body flickering lower.

"Fine. Bloody inhuman monster," I mutter as I push myself to my feet.

"You know, he really isn't human. Also, neither really are you. Most people would be curled up screaming with that many broken bits."

"Oh, come on, this is nothing. Not like the Dugar Worm eating and digesting me. Or the Kodiak Bear sitting on me."

"And there's my point."

"So are you going to keep hitting me or are we done?" I say, cocking my head.

All around us, the various pirates, members of Oi's gang, and the residents of station 4.82 are looking at us, ready to move aside if things grow more heated. It was somewhat surprising—even if I had been informed that it would happen—the way everyone got on with their lives, fixing the damage and getting healed once the station was taken. It seems that these kinds of takeovers are routine enough no one gets too worked up about it. Win or lose, the people who reside in Spaks move on.

"We are done," Bolo says, extinguishing the flames around his body. He straightens up, the anger disappearing and an almost beseeching look appearing on his face as he runs a hand through his hair and along his horns. "Now what am I'm supposed to do?"

For a second, an image rises up in my eyes. Bolo, with much bigger eyes, looking at me and saying, "Senpai! You must take responsibility!" I choke, the mental image utterly ridiculous. But on closer look, I can almost see it. Now that we're not fighting, Bolo looks young. Not physically, but in the way he holds himself, the sudden shift in his temperament.

"Well, since you're no longer obligated, why not chill for a bit?" I wave. "Or, you know, you could help fix some of the damage you caused."

"I caused?" Bolo's eyes narrow. "I wasn't the aggressor here."

"But that hammer of yours tore up most of the floors."

"Only because you kept running."

"That's called strategy."

"If we were on dry land—"

"I'd change tactics," I reply, sniffing.

Bolo growls, getting right into my face. "Let's find the arena and we'll try that again."

"Oooh. Let me think about that. No."

"Coward."

"Hot-head."

"Oy! You two. Stop flirting and get over here," Ali calls.

The look we send to Ali just slides off him, but I do stomp over to the Spirit.

"What is it?" I say.

The dark-skinned Spirit chuckles and jumps up, shrinking down as he points in the direction of the station core. "We're wanted, boy-o."

I grunt in acknowledgement and fall in. Harry rejoins us, moving alongside the group while training his hands to the side to record the reconstruction. Bolo comes stomping along too, a little off-side to Mikito, who continues to watch our former enemies vigilantly.

"Harry Prince. War Correspondent," Harry says, showing both hands palm up then turning them around.

After making his hammer disappear, Bolo copies the motion, his motions a lot smoother. The moment Harry gets the return motion, he begins recording again.

"Bolo Dumas of the Windward South. Dragon Lord," Bolo says. "You were watching the fight."

"I was. I'll probably get good ratings for this."

"Reporters." Bolo sniffs, but when Harry asks to interview him, I note that Bolo doesn't reject the request.

I tune out the pair as we walk, eyeing the Galactics around us. Ever since we finished the Quest, the sideways looks of hostility and the angry sneers have reduced. I even get a few nods of acknowledgement from the station residents. I can't help but wonder if it's the higher Reputation numbers or just the fact that we have Bolo with us.

"Ah, Paladin. About time," Kros, the martial artist, says as we arrive in front of the same door that Bolo once guarded, the one that leads to the station core. Kros isn't the only one here, the rest of Oi's first party and some additional security standing guard. His gaze shifts, locking on the figure being pestered by our reporter. "What is he doing here?"

"Because I want to. Do you have a problem with that?" Bolo says with a low growl.

Kros freezes, crystal seeming to thrum with increased illumination. "Paladin…"

"Don't look at me," I say.

So long as Bolo isn't causing trouble, I'm not going to bother him. Or try to dissuade the Dragon Lord from following us. Having three Master Classes wandering around together will be more than sufficient to keep even the most antagonistic…

Oh, thousand hells.

"One second," I say to Kros then turn toward Bolo. He tilts his head, and I step closer, lowering my voice. "All right, spit it out. Who did you piss off?"

"I don't know what you mean." Bolo meets my eyes confidently, instead of down and to the side as he's done before.

He overplays his hand, and I know my hunch was right. It doesn't help his case that when I view him through Society's Web, dark strings lead from his form, threads that I've seen before in disastrous circumstances. Rather than reply, I return Bolo's stare while ignoring the mutters from Kros and his people.

Eventually the Dragon Lord crumbles. "Was it a Skill that gave it away?"

"Nope. Also, don't bother, I saw you activate that Deceit Skill," I say, blinking away the notification that Ali pushed to me. "It won't work. Not very honorable for a Dragon Lord, no?"

"It's just a title," Bolo says, but he shifts his weight needlessly while he speaks.

I almost smile but manage to keep my face still.

Eventually, Bolo sighs, realizing that his delaying tactics won't work either. "I have a few enemies in the deeper rings. When I was working for the station, I was protected, but now…"

"Now you're not. And you're using us as cover," I say.

"Yes."

"Okay." I turn back to Kros.

"Okay? What do you mean okay?" Bolo's voice rises at the end.

I go over the word I used in Galactic. Yup. Used the right term. It wasn't the same of course, but the general slang and intent transferred over. "Okay means okay. It's all good."

"Why?"

I ignore Bolo, smirking as I walk into the anteroom right before the actual command room that hosts the station core. There's little sign of the desperate life-and-death battle that played out here a few hours ago. A few slow-repairing dents, a set of mismatched chairs, and the lingering smell of blood and burnt flesh are all the clues available. Inside, Oi and I Shao wait for us.

It takes me a moment to realize what's different about the pair. They're dressed up, changed from the simple combat jumpsuits that most Adventurers wear—with some degree of styling obviously—to significantly more stylish and less practical wear. What they're wearing is viable for combat in a pinch, but it's significantly more expensive. Button down coats, flared sleeves, ruffles around the hips and visible jewelry in a variety of colors are all part of the new dress code. I recall seeing similar clothing worn by civilians in Irvina and other, more peaceful cities.

For an Adventurer, for a combat Classer, there's a balance in clothing and armor. Buy too cheap and the armor is mass produced, offering little protection. Pay too much and you bankrupt yourself because most clothing—and armor—doesn't last more than a fight or two. Even micro-woven, self-repairing armor can only do so much. The Master Class created armor I wear is an obvious exception—but the level of defense could have been achieved cheaper. What I'm paying for is the ability for my armor to be fixed. Unless you're facing combat situations extremely regularly, it's more financially viable to pick up a high defense, low durability, low repairability piece of armor. So expensive, styled clothing indicates an expectation of few, if no, violent encounters in the near future.

"You called?" I ask as I grab a seat.

Bolo sprawls in a seat he conjures himself, the giant chair shaped to take in his contours. His presence gets a little side-eye but no protest.

"Yes," Oi says. "We wanted to know your intentions."

"I didn't think we were that close yet," I say, batting my eyes at Oi. The joke falls flat for everyone but Ali, garnering me a bunch of crazy stares. I get that human humor is probably lost on the Galactics, but not even a smile from Harry and Mikito? I'm hurt.

"Your intentions?" Oi repeats.

"Not much of one," I say. "There's a Questor's library in the third ring that I'm aiming to visit. Maybe pick up a few Quests if there's something less criminal. Wait for our ship to get fixed."

"Do research on your next target?" I Shao asks, her eyes fixed on me. I can tell she's got her Skill up, the way the Mana fluctuates around her body and the pointed questioning she's using.

"Maybe," I say. Not an untruth, but it might not matter with her Skill. While some Skills function on the basis of your spoken word, checking against the unvarnished "truth," others verify against your body language, your vitals. Even minute differences, like the fact that I really mean no can be picked up— or at least, the uncertainty of my own intentions. How much she learns depends on her Skill level and her ability to read the information given to her.

"You're a Questor?" Bolo says, cutting in with a derisive tone.

"Oh yeah, boy-o over here is a real big one. Probably the biggest on Earth. He's spent more Credits buying those stupid books of his than on his equipment," Ali replies for me.

"I have not. You're exaggerating."

Ali chuckles while Bolo rolls his eyes.

I ignore the pair of comedians while focusing on Oi. "I'm assuming you called me here for more than a basic checkup."

"While it might seem as though the transition has gone off without a hitch, violent takeovers are not as organized and structured as you would think," I Shao says. "In fact, there are often individuals who harbor some resentment." A glance at Bolo who offers her a toss of his head, making his horns catch the light and glimmer. "During this initial period, it would be useful if we had a little… help."

"You want us to be your bodyguards." Mikito says, speaking up for the first time.

"Is that an issue? We could have you work as on-call support," Oi says. "If we upgrade the dimensional blockers, we could create exceptions in the blocks, allowing you to Portal in. Though the very fact that you are working for us should quell any major issues."

Being a bodyguard is going to tie us down. That's not a great option when I've got a bounty on my head. I can see the way being at their beck-and-call could bite us in the ass. On the other hand, official standing in Spaks will be useful if, or when, we have to fight the bounty hunters. Not to mention that the fame and reputation points would be useful. In fact…

"How'd that affect our Reputation scores?"

"Regular increases. Longer you stay, higher it goes. Same with any on-going contract that you fulfill."

"Assuming we agree, I'd still like to increase our reputation to enter the third ring faster," I say.

Oi and I Shao exchange looks before they smile.

I Shao leans forward. "I can help with that. We have contacts in this and the previous ring who could use further help. Individuals who can increase your Reputation much quicker."

I snort. Of course they only mention it now. For the moment at least, this works.

After that, it just became a matter of bargaining. I mostly sit back, letting Ali take over the negotiation. Harry keeps quiet, occasionally updating us on what's Galactic standard via the party chat but staying out of the conversation since he's not technically included. The entire bargaining session takes over an hour before everyone seems happy and a negotiated contract floats before us.

"Then that is agreed on?" I Shao says, double-confirming with the pair of us.

"Add me too. At the same rate," Bolo says.

The Dragon Lord has been ignored by us all through the entire discussion, chewing on some weird nut that looks like an over-sized sunflower seed. Every time he cracks one open, he makes the outer covering disappear into his inventory.

"Lord Bolo—" I Shao starts then stops as Bolo meets her gaze flatly.

I Shao shivers as Bolo lets his Dragon Fear Aura extend, wrapping us in its pants-wetting embrace. The Negotiator manages to look at Oi, who nods. A moment later, I see Bolo's eyes move as he reads a notification.

"Details of our contacts will be sent to you later," Oi says. "We will need to inform them beforehand."

We take the dismissal with aplomb, especially since Oi indicates that our services are not required right this moment. They intend to get the upgrades to the Dimensional Locks immediately, then whitelist us. In the meantime, they will be well secure in the control room. As we're dismissed, I walk toward where our ship is meant to dock.

"Harry, things are going to be a bit boring for a bit. Mind taking Dornalor with you on a fact-finding mission? I want to make sure we set up a warning system for any potential bounty hunters who might be coming for us. And get an idea of who's already here," I send over the party chat as we walk.

"On it."

"What about us?" Mikito says.

"I don't know about you, but I need a drink," I reply.

There's little we can do till we get the contacts from Oi. Not to mention just an hour ago, we were in a rather nasty battle with a Dragon Lord. The status effects from having half a dozen bones shattered might be gone, but I could still use a break.

***

"Mining?" I say slowly and disbelievingly at the first of Oi's contacts. "Really?"

"You requested quests that would increase your reputation with the station as quickly as possible, yes?" the robed attendant says. Thus far, I've yet to get a glimpse of whatever is beneath the robes, the woman having her appendages crossed in front of her and the hood down. "Spaks station is in constant need of additional ore. Or did you think we came to this asteroid belt for no reason?"

"I thought it was for security."

"Bah! The asteroid field provides only a modicum of additional security. Any good navigator could act as a spy, guiding in an invading fleet. They might lose a few, from contingencies, but not enough to really matter. A foolish myth," the contact says.

I open my mouth then shut it. Well, it does make sense. And they do need ore. Even with mass teleportation and large cargo ships, mining ore in the asteroid belt is probably the easiest way to replace anything they use. With the volume of ships docking everyday—and the production of even more vessels—the demand must be intense. But… "Is there nothing else?"

"Your friend is browsing through the rest of the list," the robed speaker says, inclining her head toward Ali. "But you provided me the parameters of short term, high reputation, high return. Mining is the answer."

Ali speaks up, fingers twitching as he browses. "Lots of bounties. Mostly privateers and bounty hunters who have been taking out pirate ships."

"Pass," Mikito says.

"Figured. No joining pirate crews either, right? Though they do serve the best rum," Ali mutters. "Ooooh. Fetch and deliver requests. If we knew of these, we could have brought some loot from Earth."

"Not helpful," I say, crossing my arms.

While Ali continues to mutter to himself, I turn my attention to the mining quests. Technically, they're not all direct mining quests, but they're all related to it. Three catch my attention.

Collection Quest: Gather 1000 SGUs of Iron (Repeatable quest)
Ore must be delivered to station 4.82 for Quest to be completed.
Reward: +1 Reputation, +7,389 Credits

"SGU?"

"Standard Galactic Units."

"Oh." I shrug and notice the Credit amount flicker on the notification, adjusting its payout in real time.

After a moment, I dismiss the notification. Even if we could modify the ship to mine, I have no idea how long it'd take to mine a 1000 SGUs. If it takes too long, the rental cost would eat up any potential profits. And even if reputation is what we're grinding, I'm not looking to lose Credits either.

Escort Quest:* Bountiful Eyes *requires additional security

Due to potential difficulties in their latest expedition, the Bountiful Eyes *requires additional security. Inquire at the* Eyes *for more information.*

Reward: +20 Station Reputation, +14,500 Credits

"That's a lot of reputation for guarding something," I say with a frown. "For that matter, how can a ship offer that much?"

"It's owned by the Corellis of course." At my blank look, she continues. "The Corellis own a majority share of the businesses in the second and first ring. Because of that, any action that safeguards their interest will provide reputation bonuses. If executed properly."

"Right…" I eye the quest again then shake my head. I'll put a pin in this one, but there are no details about how long this might take or what kind of trouble to expect. Also, I don't know enough about the Corellis to choose to tie myself to them yet. Even this distantly.

***Ship Recovery:* My Second Mortgage**

The ore freighter My Second Mortgage *has suffered an unknown catastrophic failure of its primary engine. Attempts at communication with the ship have resulted in no response. Your job is to ascertain the cause of the engine failure and lack of communication and then recover the ship and all its ore.*

Reward: +12 Station Reputation, 5,000 Credits + 3% of value of recovered ship and ore

"This one sounds interesting," I say, tapping the quest.

The others crane their heads to look at it, with Mikito raising the obvious question.

"Why hasn't anyone else taken the job?" Mikito asks, looking directly at Robes.

"If you noticed, the Credits on offer are low. It's quite possible that the *Mortgage* has no ore on board, so recovering it might be a significant waste of time. In most cases, a higher recovery fee that includes the cost of the ship would be provided, but, well, it's the *Mortgage*," Robes says.

"No money, lots of reputation?" I say, guessing at what the attendant is hinting at.

At her nod, I can't help but snort. There's got to be a story there, but it's not one I'm inclined to follow. If the *Mortgage* is just floating around, we can use the *Heartbreak* to drag it back. And if it's an engine failure, Mikito and I can test out our damage control Skills.

"All right, we'll take it. Let's go visit a ghost ship."

Chapter 9

"You know, I don't mind you following us around the station, but our ship?" I say, eyeing the intrusive Dragon Lord. He's taken over the navigator's seat in the cockpit, idly eying the controls while Dornalor takes us out of the station. To say that our pilot was surprised to see Bolo in the navigator seat when he got back from running his latest errand might be underplaying it a little.

"You can't really be much of an obstacle if you aren't around," Bolo says.

"Isn't that job with Oi enough?"

"No," Bolo says. "The lungfih that Oi replaced brokered my protection as part of my deal. Oi doesn't have that level of reputation yet. My deal has no additional protection promises. I would not trust a new station master to have the contacts to enforce it anyway."

Oi was less than happy that we are leaving the station, but since he's whitelisted me to Portal in if things go badly, he reluctantly agreed to our little jaunt. I'm still wary of the Dragon Lord following us, but outside of physically tossing him out, I'm not sure I can do much but accept it. And keep an eye open for the eventual betrayal.

"I'm curious to see what this ship is about," Bolo adds.

"That makes one of us," Dornalor mutters as he eyes the navigation control. While most of the ship's controls are displayed via the System, the Neural Links, or a HUD, there's a significant amount of mundane replication too.

I let my head drop back, knocking it against the headrest of my chair. The nanoweave of the seat automatically adjusts, shifting with the added weight to make it feel as though I'm sitting on nothing at all. Quite an amazing piece of luxurious technology. Except, you know, part of the reason it's so comfortable is because it needs to be when the inertial compensators fail in the middle of a dogfight.

"You're sure we don't need to get anything else to drag the ship back?" I say.

"Drag, no. But we really should have bought some disposable drone thrusters for the operation. The stations use the drones all the time to move parts and portions of ships. You'll get a lot more of a thrust that way, rather than relying on my Skills and the ship alone."

"If we had the money, I'd do it."

"You know, I do expect to get paid my usual rate for this," Dornalor says.

I wave. "You will. My lack of funds is because I've budgeted for you."

"And your fiscal responsibility is deeply appreciated," Dornalor says. "Though I'd have preferred to have more work done on the ship before we left."

"It flies, no? All the major repairs are done?" I say.

"Yes, but that's not the point."

"And Mikito and Harry are busy fixing up more parts of the ship for free too, no?"

"Slipshod, barely acceptable work," Dornalor complains. The Pirate Captain taps a few more notifications then unbuckles. "Keep the ship on autopilot, try not to crash us. I'm going to make sure they aren't cutting into anything important."

"Oh, come on. They only did it once!"

"In the middle of a fight."

"We were getting shot at!"

"Exactly!"

I watch Dornalor stomp off, and I can't help but chuckle.

"Funny. I never expected to see a Paladin speaking so friendlily to a Pirate Captain."

"Or me, a Dragon Lord outside of Xylar," I say.

Bolo shakes his head, trying to push the conversation away from him. "A human Erethran Paladin seems a lot more interesting to me."

"You first."

Bolo shakes his head then grins. He chants, "Story. Story. Story."

"What are you? Five months old?" I say, frowning.

Bolo grins at me, mouthing the word story once more.

I groan but give in. Considering we've got a few hours until we get to the damn ghost ship, telling a little story makes sense. Of course, I have to explain how Dornalor and I met. But that means explaining what we've been doing. Which requires me to explain why we're running assassinations. And that means talking about Irvina and Earth. Eventually, I find myself telling him my story, Earth's story, in its entirety. Well, in summary in its entirety. Bolo, being who he is, stops on the most ridiculous part.

"You taunted an Ice Dragon?" Bolo says, looking me up and down. "As an Advanced Class?"

"Yeah."

"Huh." Bolo says, shaking his head. "It sounds like it was a juvenile one at most."

"No way. It was at least over a hundred levels!" I protest.

"Late juvenile. An adult would have just used a spell on you." He pauses, considering as he rubs his horns. "Unless it was pregnant."

"Huh?"

"A pregnant dragon can't use its magic. The birth of a dragon is a very Mana intensive event, requiring the full Mana flow of its parent. Interrupting that flow can result in a lesser child," Bolo explains. "It's actually a common tactic on my world."

"So you guys have a lot of dragons?" I say, cocking my head.

"We are the birthplace of those magnificent creatures," Bolo says proudly. "Our world is one of the oldest integrated planets that has not become a Forbidden Zone. And that is only because of our dragons."

I frown, leaning forward and fixing Bolo's gaze with my own.

"Your turn. Talk."

For the next hour, I get a lesson in the history—and to some extent, politics—of Xylar and Xylargh, the single unified kingdom that rules over the planet. As one of the oldest planets to have been added to the System, Xylar should have been flooded with Mana, making it a Forbidden World. But during the process of Mana over-saturation, the dragons evolved. Already a sentient race, they became something more powerful under the influence of the System. Their very presence is a Mana sink for the planet, one that has to be carefully managed.

Too many dragons and disaster strikes as a Mana vortex occurs, drawing surrounding Mana into the planet and causing rampant destruction and the breakdown of the System as it is no longer able to sustain itself from the ambient Mana. Too few dragons, and the environmental Mana levels cause uncontrolled growth of monsters, spawning dungeons and alpha monsters before the System fails once again as sentients die off, being unable to draw in and "cleanse" enough Mana. That's pretty much the story of most Forbidden Zones.

The job of the Dragon Knights is to cull and care for the population of dragons on the planet. Of course, the job is made all the harder when there are few tame dragons. Not only do the Dragon Knights need to fight the many wild dragons that make up their world, they sometimes have to do so without killing them. The fact that dragons are sentient, obstinate, and nearly as aggressive as a System-bred monster does not help. Sometimes I wonder about my own encounter with the creature on Earth. If it was sentient, why'd it chase me that far? Would I have been able to bring it to me by blowing up its hoard? Certainly, their greed and avarice for their hoard is confirmed by Bolo.

Xylar is fascinating, the world that Bolo grew up in vastly different from my own. It's a curious mixture of medieval and futuristic, with underground cities to shelter against dragon attacks and a feudal system, backed by Classes while having spaceships and modern conveniences. As we talk, I learn more of the planet and it's fascinating how the System—or their reliance on the System—has affected their entire planet. Including the way they vote.

"So Xylar voted to open another Dungeon World to teleport some dragons over?" I say, head cocked.

"Yes. And don't look at me like that. I was long exiled by then," Bolo says, and I turn down my glare a bit. "We're constantly in need of ways to control the Mana flow. Killing dragons is no easy task. And a new Dungeon World will add another location which can be flooded with Mana, reducing the increase in Mana density on our planet for at least a century. Adding a few dragons to your world will increase the length of time the Dungeon World will last, which is an overall win for us all. Losing a few dragons now, that's a small price to pay. Especially since we're overpopulated at the moment anyway."

"Huh."

"What huh?"

"Well, the Erethran Honor Guards are glorified babysitters. And you guys are glorified park rangers."

"Park rangers?" Bolo looks confused.

I chuckle to myself as I spin the chair around. Of course the man's smart enough to know I insulted him and his Class, but he's not sure how. We continue the rest of the trip to the *Second Mortgage* in frigid silence, allowing me time to review my notifications.

Quest Update: the System

You have gained another clue about the System.

+4238 XP

Another clue. I've begun to form my own theory about the System, about its purpose. It's been pretty clear for a while that the System is using all living things as giant filters for Mana. On the most basic level, our Levels are just an indication of the amount of Mana we can filter. There's also been clear research that of the amount of Mana we draw in and filter, that runs through our bodies and thus the System, and the amount of Mana that comes out via healing, spells, or is otherwise used to activate Skills is not equal. There's a loss of Mana somewhere. The amount lost is not equal all the time, though the amount is roughly one percent. Whether that loss is natural or on purpose is up for debate.

Theory—or is that hypothesis?—or not, I'm still missing a lot of information. Even if I assume that the why of the System is to be a filter, to pull unmarked ambient Mana out of the environment, there are still questions. Like how the System works, the underlying structures that make it function. Why it is built to filter Mana at all. And the who of its creator. Or creators. Those, those are the questions that still lie before me. And thus far, everything I've learnt has yet to answer any of those questions. Not to my—or the researchers'—satisfaction.

***

"John. Jooooohnnn. Baka…" Mikito's voice pulls me from my thoughts.

I blink to see her leaning over the shoulder of my chair and pointing. Before us is the ore ship the *Second Mortgage*, floating in the deep darkness of space. If not for the enhanced lighting on the screens, the wreck would be almost impossible to see as it lies dormant without a single light. Not even emergency lights illuminate the vehicle.

"Dead as dead can be," Ali says, phasing half-through me.

I growl, hating when he does that, but Ali ignores me. Harry and Dornalor have made their way back, adding themselves to the now-crowded cockpit. Dornalor's in his own seat, fingers flicking over unseen controls, making the image of the *Mortgage* shift and twist as the other spectrums of vision come online.

"What now?" I say, cocking my head.

"We explore, no? We're not allowed to tow it back without checking out the cause of the ship going dark," Bolo says, already stretching in his seat and nearly hitting Mikito. The Samurai glares at Bolo, who offers her a wide grin.

"Ah. Right." I grin. "Right. Off you go, Ali."

"What? Why me?"

Mikito laughs, clapping. "Perfect. Go!"

"You too?"

"Why not? You can phase right through the damn ship, don't need to breathe, and there's no concern about you dying," I say. "If you get banished, we'll know there's a problem."

Under our "gentle" pressure, Ali flies out of the ship to scout. Of course, I keep an eye on him in my minimap, but as we said, there's little concern. The worst thing that will happen is he gets banished. And in the meantime, we can start the work of getting the ships hooked up.

"Come on, you layabout. You're with us," I say to Bolo.

"I am sitting."

"That's not what I meant… just come," I say.

Mikito, Bolo, and I head to the ship's airlock and get into our spacesuits. Unlike human versions of the suits, these are much thinner and more flexible.

Outside of some oxygen, neither Bolo nor I require the spacesuits to survive. But having your flesh alternately freezing and healing is highly uncomfortable, to say the least.

Once we exit the ship, we make our way to the in-built hardpoints on the *Heartbreak* to attach towing cables to it. Once done, we orient ourselves and take the leap to the *Mortgage*. The actual jump, from semi-solid footing on the courier into open space, is a stomach-twisting moment. There's something terrifying about throwing yourself into the emptiness of space. It catches at your throat and constricts your breathing. Even if it's for a microsecond, the fear of falling for all eternity grabs at you, bypassing all your mental defenses to send an existential fear deep into your guts.

When I land on the ore ship, magnetic boots engaging and attaching me to the ship, I let out a breath that I never knew I was holding. Beside me, Bolo is grinning widely beneath his custom helmet. Custom work on the helmet helps to show off his horns in stark relief, making him and his armor glitter in the dark void. Mikito is inscrutable as she lands smoothly beside us, barely taking a moment to orient herself before she bounds across the ship, cable in tow and using a grappling gun as an anchor point.

"How are you so good at that?" I send over the comms.

"Bought the skills," Mikito says. "What? You never wanted to be an astronaut?"

I consider Mikito's words as I laboriously stump my way up to my designated maintenance hatch. Figuring out how to install the cables on the *Mortgage* was simple. Most of the best locations are beneath maintenance hatches with big, bright signs doing everything from warning about proper use of the hatches to their contents and how to open the hatches themselves. Galactic OSHA must be working overtime for things to be so well laid out.

"Yeah, but, you know, kid's dreams," I finally answer Mikito.

"Seriously?" Mikito says, perhaps recalling my reaction before on the ISS. Then again…

"I must agree with the Redeemer. Why settle for such a shallow dream? Any mildly competent Classer could see the stars," Bolo says.

"Not exactly the point, DL," Ali says, voice cracking. Unlike the near perfect translation of our comms, his voice is slightly distorted. Ali's method of patching into our comms as a Spirit means that there's the occasional glitch. "In other news, this place is creepy. Thus far, I've yet to see a single corpse."

"Interesting," I say, frowning at the curved hull of the ship beneath my feet. A scan of the codes on the hatch has me continuing my journey. "Any signs of a struggle?"

"I'd have said so if there was, don't you think?"

"Snippy, aren't we?" I reply. Bending, I work on the right maintenance hatch, freeing it from its mounting via the simple expedience of cutting through the locks with my sword. I flip the hatch aside, letting it fall through space, and verify that the bolt we're looking for is there. A quick hookup and I'm done. "I'm good."

"Already done."

"One second. The codes I was given aren't working. I'm attempting a hack," Bolo says.

I open my mouth to complain then shut it. No point in hurrying him. It's not as if Ali's finished his survey. Bored, I turn to eye the darkness. In the distance are a few moving asteroids, their size and distance difficult to judge without the usual landmarks to give them scale. In fact, outside of our own ship and the giant floating greenish-white tentacle creature, there's nothing else out here.

…

"Uhh… guys," I say slowly, staring at what I can only describe as the floating lovechild of a giant squid and Cthulhu.

I send a few mental commands to my helmet, and in moments, a new video image shows up for everyone. The largest tentacles seem to branch out of its body where arms should be, a layer of wiggling flesh to protect its long, snake-like body. Smaller tentacles, almost like the hairs on a spider's legs, branch out from its body, twisting and grasping at the void. There's a long silence as everyone regards the image before it's broken by exclamations of horror and disgust.

"I think we found our culprit," I say.

"Thrice-born eggs!" Bolo curses.

"Goblin shit. That's a space leviathan. A big one too," Dornalor says.

"How big?" I say.

The *Heartbreak* is just over twenty meters in length, and that thing dwarfs the ship. But I'm not entirely sure how far away it is. Dornalor, having received our notification, is already boosting away from the ore ship, having used the emergency disconnect for our cables. Dornalor's putting distance between himself and the giant monster, angling the ship around to point his weapons at it.

Adult Space Leviathan (Level 158)
HP: 128971/128971
MP: 4317/4387
Condition: Hungry, Size: Massive, Two souled, Hardened Scales.
Species Note: Space Leviathans are mutated monsters that have breached their need for a terrestrial upbringing. They live between the stars, sustaining themselves on ambient Mana and the unlucky ships they encounter on their voyages. Able to ascend to lightspeed as well as create gravity wells to pull escaping ships to themselves, they are considered one

of System space's most dangerous hazards. Space leviathans range from 89 meters in size to over a kilometer.

The adults of their kind often exhibit additional psychic abilities including enforced hypnotism, suggestion, and psychic attacks. The elders of their species have been known to exhibit the ability to fire condensed bursts of solar energy.

"Thousand Hells. Look at those hit points," I say. I could throw my Skills at it as much as I want and I'd be well out of Mana before I took down even half its health. And that's counting my blades hitting. Which, I'd have to admit, I was pretty sure would happen. Hard to miss with something that big.

"Oh God, we're going to die." Harry sounds as if he's panicking. I kind of understand that. It's not as if any of his Skills will matter if the leviathan decides to eat the ship he's in. Being collateral damage makes him just as dead.

"What is this 'size: massive' notation?" Mikito says, sounding a bit annoyed.

"Ah. Right, you haven't fought one of those," I say, realization dawning.

Before I can add anything, Bolo cuts in. "Certain creatures, due to their size, have gained the Size status. This allows them to take less damage from attacks that don't cover sufficient area. Designations like that normally start around a hundred meters or so and go from there. Hard to injure something that's the size of a building if your hammer can't reach its internals. Monsters such as this are quite common in Forbidden Zones."

Mikito swears in Japanese. After all this time, I've picked up enough to know that what she's saying is rather coarse. It's amusing how the polite, civilized Japanese woman I knew has sloughed away under the intense heat of combat and familiarity.

"It seems it'll be up to you and me, Redeemer."

"John. Just John," I say. Might as well correct him. "And no stupid 'I'm an alien' joke of calling me 'Just John'."

I eye the distance between the monster and me, considering our options, then mentally command Ali to overlay an image of my Portal options. As I do so, the leviathan drifts closer, its movement seeming to be slow but in fact covering a huge distance. It's a trick of size and perspective, one that is only revealed when it turns its body to chase after the *Nothing's Heartbreak*.

"I'll lead. You follow," I say.

No more time to chat and think. I pop open the Portal as I see Mikito and Bolo kick off in my minimap, leaving the ship and my vicinity. Obviously, the Samurai isn't going to sit and wait. Instead, her ghost steed forms beneath her legs and she rides off through the void. As I head toward the Portal, I see them heading directly for the monster rather than through my Portal. Works for me. Saves me Mana.

Myself, I appear right above its head, but distance and speed means by the time I appear, the creature has moved on from my target location. I turn on my thrusters, boosting down toward the creature who seems to be ignorant of my intentions. I put that little blessing to good use and finish layering my usual complement of buffs. As I land on the creature's back while cutting apart a couple of questing tentacles, I tense for a reaction. Even as I land lightly on the leviathan's scaley back, I see that the nubs of the tentacles I sliced off have begun to regrow.

I stomp on the scales a little, testing them out for my footing. I figure out a few things immediately. One—the scales are incredibly hard, offering no give. Two—the scales are non-metallic, as the magnetic properties of my boots fail to catch. Three—every reaction has an equal and opposite reaction.

Shoulder and hip thrusters on the suit turn back on, guiding me back onto the undulating creature's body before I float away too far. Even the short time I've been goofing around, I've lost another hundred meters. It does make me question how a giant tentacle snake can float through space by wriggling its body.

"Any time now, John!" Harry's voice is growing even more panicked.

I glance at my minimap, pulling it backward as far as possible to get an idea of what's happening. Only to realize that the leviathan is catching up on the *Heartbreak*, its tentacles close enough to reach for the ship. A mental command pulls up the rearview cameras on the *Heartbreak* and I get to see the entire scene up close, as the courier ship dips and ducks, weaving between grasping appendages.

"Right. I guess we'll start with this?" I mutter, eyeing the head as I push myself alongside the monster.

Beacon of the Angels flares to life right over the monster's head as it literally swims into the attack. The column of energy seems to manifest from nowhere, collecting the light around it before lancing downward. The attack bathes the creature's head in power, burning a large spot and blinding one of the creature's many eyes. Even as the column fades, I trigger a second then a third, targeting different areas of its head.

The fight itself is weird, the creature's thrashing a parody of atmospheric battles. There is no sound. The blood that gushes from its wounds becomes nothing more than crystals. There's a surreality to the entire thing, like being a vocal character in a silent movie. Between the filters in our audio headsets and the silence of space, when the silence is interrupted, it's all the more intense.

"Aaaarrrggh!"

The scream erupts from my mouth and from the party. Even as I gather hold of myself and push back the mental assault the leviathan leveled at us, the screams continue. A command lowers the volume, but I watch as Mikito and Bolo swerve drunkenly as they fight off the assault. Even the ship has stopped its evasive maneuvers, allowing the leviathan to catch them.

"That hurt," I bitch, mostly to myself.

If it hurt me, the others must be really feeling the effect of the psychic assault. Bolo has decent resistances, so I can see him already steadying his movements. But he's still a distance away, and the pulses of psychic power assault my mental defenses without stop. The crippling pain is much reduced, at a level I can handle. That leaves me with the task of buying my friends some time.

Around me, a dozen blades appear, spinning. I swing my hand down, now holding my own sword, and together, all the empowered Blade Strikes tear through space. I marvel at the sight as blades of force and light spin, leaving behind only a ripple that exists in my mind. They impact hard, tearing apart scales and destroying waving tentacles, digging deep into the leviathan's muscle. White and blue muscle parts while green blood disperses, crystallizing in space. The psychic assault stops then begins again, but at a lower intensity.

"Mikito! Free the ship. Bolo, get your ass over here. Harry, I know you don't like getting involved but you're going to need to start using the ship's weapons."

A mental command has me burning fuel as I attempt to keep up with the now-thrashing leviathan. I'm tempted to call forth Army of One again, but it's an expensive Skill and this fight has just started. Instead, I focus on the low energy output of Blade Strikes, pulling away from the creature to dance in the void as tentacles reach for me.

Thousand Blades comes into its own once again. Blades are grabbed and thrown, my sword swung to slice off tentacles that come too close. Big or small, when they impact my blades, they either slow down or are sliced off entirely. In either case, it gives me time by creating a razor field of sharp death. But it's still not enough.

Thus far, I've managed to avoid getting touched, but each moment, the tentacles get nearer. On closer inspection, I see that each tentacle is filled with tiny barbed hooks that surround what I can only call mouths. Getting touched by those things would be a gruesome death. In the corner of my eye, I can see how the ship's AI has taken over escape attempts, afterburners straining against the leviathan.

"I guess it's my time to shine," Ali says.

Almost directly opposite from me, the Spirit raises his hands as the ball of energy he's gathered builds up. It's not lightning per se, just pure energy contained by the Spirit's will and affinity. When Ali makes a throwing motion, the energy tears a line along the monster's hide. Scales are rent asunder, flesh and blood superheated and fried, liquid boiling away before freezing in a spray of sparkling green and pink crystals.

Once again, the leviathan roars in our minds, redoubling its psychic assault. This time around, we're ready and ride out the painful assault with aplomb. Even then, I feel warm blood dripping down my lips and chin.

Mikito and the *Heartbreak* wobble a little but recover, Dornalor taking an active role in the ship's defense. The little Samurai seems to have made it to the ship, locking herself down on the vehicle while she cuts apart tentacles. Her naginata has expanded, becoming nearly as long as the ship itself. I wonder if Hitoshi grew its new ability due to its most recent interaction with Bolo's weapon or if it was just a Skill that was never yet necessary. On top of the physical size growth, the blade of the naginata has doubled as a shell of red flame energy coats it, giving the Samurai a larger cutting area.

And cut she does. Mikito swings and chops, and with the now active weapon suite on the *Nothing's Heartbreak* and her Skills, they're slowly whittling down the fast-regenerating tentacles. Even the leviathan's ability to replace its tentacles seems to have a limit.

Using the distraction the pair has offered, I open a Portal and duck through it. I leave the Portal open long enough for the monster to send through a few of its larger tentacles. Then I slam it shut, slicing them off while I get busy using a series of Blade Strikes on its back. The damage isn't much, not once it gets discounted by the "massive" condition, but every little bit counts.

"Help! It's trying to eat me," Ali says.

"Just fade out," Harry says over the comms. "And you, eat that!"

The beam weapons on the ship fire again, burning off a pair of grasping tentacles. There's a rather vindictive glee in Harry's voice. I guess being allowed to take part in a fight can be quite therapeutic for the bystander.

"It's twin-souled. It can hurt me even if I fade out," Ali says.

"Worry not. I'm here," Bolo's voice cuts in, entirely too enthused.

"The great beyond," Dornalor curses as he catches sight of Bolo.

I kind of want to add to my own curses, but I'm busy evading the never-ending series of tentacles. I'm even forced to use one of my doppelgangers just to get out of a sticky situation. I get a glimpse of Bolo charging his attack, having made his way to the leviathan's twisted, multi-eyed head.

Bolo's hammer, once only ten feet tall, has grown to the size of the *Heartbreak*. Its handle is twice again as long as he is, and the entire thing is glowing as Infernal Blow and his other Skills empower it. The hammer blurs as Triple Strike is triggered, moving so fast that I can only see afterimages of the strikes. The leviathan buckles under the maelstrom of attacks, scales crushed and sent flying, along with sprays of blood and guts.

The Dragon Lord is pounding the monster around like a badminton player and a shuttle cock, moving so fast he's playing both sides of the court. Each attack is draining visible chunks of the monster's life, the Dragon Lord putting what damage we've done to shame.

Impressive burst damage or not, Bolo has to slow down at some point. His Mana dips heavily with each attack, and eventually the attacks stop. Even the hammer shrinks, reducing to only half its overgrown size. All our combined attacks, all our damage, and the creature still has a third of its life left.

As if the leviathan was waiting for this, the monster opens its mouth. A stream of liquid spits out, splattering Bolo. His screams are ear-rending before the audio compensators muffle him. The Dragon Lord thrashes in the void, the liquid sticky and surprisingly refusing to freeze. As Bolo struggles, tentacles wrap him up. These tentacles aren't connected to the leviathan, somehow moving on their own accord after they detach themselves in their attack against Bolo.

"Ali, we need to meet up," I send to my half-pint friend.

Mikito and the *Nothing's Heartbreak* swing away from where they've been harassing the monster, burning fission as they swoop past the creature's snout. I split off, toward the center of its body. While Bolo attempts to free himself from the tentacles as he stews in the monster's juices, Mikito and the ship take over distracting the leviathan. The Samurai spins and cuts, mostly doing her best to slice apart attacks that come their way while trusting Dornalor to dodge any lunging bites.

"Head for the X."

I curve my directions, idly slicing off more tentacles as I go. I'm skimming as close to the body as I dare, keeping a minimal distance from it to ensure that I can react when the creature ripples. Soon enough, I see the little Spirit who's shrunk himself down. Having stopped attacking, the Spirit only has to dodge the occasional tentacle that reacts to his presence rather than the concerted attacks of earlier.

"What are we doing?" Ali says.

"Fastball special."

"I should have known."

But complain as much as he can, Ali takes his place. I raise my hand and call forth the spell, the beginning portions of the enhanced lightning attack forming. But lightning—electricity—requires the movement of electrons between particles. Being in a vacuum, the spell cannot function without some modification.

There's no electric charge in a vacuum, but there is an electric field. The electric field creates the magnetic field and helps the propagation of electromagnetic waves. So instead of creating an electric current—lightning—I alter the spell and use the formed spell chamber that gathers power, then give it an outlet via my Elemental Affinity. I shift the spell itself, just enough to form what I want using my Mana Sense, then release it all.

The attack can't be seen. Not in space. Unlike my other attacks—or Ali's show-off performance—this one has no container of Mana. No wasted power escaping as light. Instead, it's pure energy directed toward the leviathan. The blast passes within inches of Ali, between his outstretched hands. As it does, the Spirit forms and enhances the spell with his own Greater Affinity. The attack condenses and multiples as Mana drains from me at triple the cost of my normal Spell. But the results are worth it.

When my beam impacts, it's like a welding torch taken to living flesh. Scales peel and part, skin crisps and burns, and muscles disintegrate. We draw a line down the monster, watching as flesh and muscle peel apart and its innards smoke and spill out. It's writhing, twisting, and turning to dodge my attack, but all it does is put more pressure on its organs, sending them spilling out of the damaged container. As it dodges, the leviathan offers even more portions of its body to my attack.

"Move it, Redeemer!"

The warning comes a little too late. The tail that I had forgotten about smacks Ali and me, sending us spinning into the darkness. Bad as that is, my Soul Shield absorbs two-thirds of the impact before it fails. My armor deals with the rest. More dangerous for me is the backlash from my modification of the spell. The cudgelled-together Mana flow bursts apart from its tenuous bindings, wracking my mind and body. I end up screaming as my cells are ripped apart, my System-gifted resistances failing.

Pain.

I float in space, my body shuddering as detached tentacles float over to wrap around my body, tightening in a deadly embrace. It crushes my armor, my flesh and bones. If I don't escape, I'll die. But I'm too busy dealing with the fallout of my spell.

Even as I scream into the void, my friends are taking advantage of the distraction and damage I've done. I spot Bolo's dot moving once more, freed from the tentacles. Mikito and the *Heartbreak* separate, the Samurai's dot darting straight toward an opening in the monster's flesh. Ready to crush the last embers of the monster's life.

In the meantime? I get crushed until Ali frees me.

Chapter 10

"What kind of slime-brained idiot alters a spell in the middle of combat?" Ali berates me.

After we'd looted the leviathan and hooked up the *Mortgage*, we adjourned to the mess hall on the *Heartbreak* for a well-deserved rest. Of course, building up the initial momentum had been interesting as we were dragging two much, much larger objects. I'd even used my newly purchased Skills to boost us. Once we were done though, Ali decided to bitch me out.

"Couldn't use the Lightning Spell as is," I point out.

"Then do something else! I could adjust the strength of your other Skills."

"The Spirit is correct. Backlash from modifying spells or Skills is significant," Bolo says. "It is impressive that you can do it, but foolish to do so in combat."

"Everyone's a critic," I say, throwing up my hands dramatically. "It worked, didn't it?" I look at Mikito and Harry, searching for support.

"Don't look at me. I'm learning lots. My next segment about modifying spells and Skills is going to be a hit," Harry says, eyes gleaming as his fingers dance in midair.

"John is baka, but we knew that," Mikito says.

"Is baka. Not a baka?" Ali says with a frown.

"Maybe?" There's hesitation in Mikito's voice. Mixing Galactic grammar and Japanese seems to be throwing Mikito for a loop.

While we bullshit about the correct way to call me an idiot in Galactic, I look toward the viewscreens, where Dornalor has us on autopilot back to the station. The entire trip is taking longer than ever since we have to tow the ship and the leviathan corpse.

A glimpse at the timetable makes me wince and search for something else to distract me. My gaze falls upon a different display, one whose contents are drawn from the hacked servers of the ore ship. In the recording, the crew of the ore ship march out, one after the other, in their spacesuits. In another portion of the display screen, external cameras show the floating bodies of the crew as they reorient themselves and fly into space, headed for the leviathan's maw.

We're lucky in a way—rather than hit us with a wide-scale hypnotism Skill, the creature decided to save its Mana and chase our little ship. It's possible that the Skill had a cooldown or a high Mana cost. Or perhaps it knew better than to hypnotize a trio of Master Classers. Our resistances are all much, much higher than the Basic crew of an ore ship.

When the leviathan eats the crew, tentacles attaching to floating bodies and tossing them in like so much meaty popcorn, I dismiss the screen. I don't need to see that.

While I've been engrossed in the macabre fate of the crew, my friends have finished their discussion and moved on to their own obsessions. Mikito's disappeared—off to train, I'm assuming—while Harry sits beside me, hands moving as he edits his next segment. And scarily enough, Ali and Bolo are sitting together, watching one of Ali's many, many recordings of Earth TV. It's somewhat comforting to me that no matter what happens to Earth, at least future generations of Galactics will still learn of the awesomeness of Jackie Chan and the Three Stooges.

Rather than bother them, I pull up the notifications I've been leaving sitting in my screen, curious to see what I've been missing.

Reputation Increase!
You have killed an Adult Space Leviathan. As a threat to all space-faring Galactics, this act has increased your reputation.
+0.12 Galactic Reputation
+12 Spaks Reputation
+1254 Spaks Station Reputation

My, oh my. That was rather nice. The Reputation bump is amazing, though it amuses me that the System split it for both the region and the station. Considering the station is the major inhabitable location in the region, the additional regional reputation is useless.

Level Up!

You have reached Level 37 as an Erethran Paladin. Stat Points automatically distributed. You have 7 Free Attributes and 1 Class Skills to distribute.

I'm tempted to assign the free points, but I hesitate, realizing that for the first time in a while, I have someone outside of Ali who has a comparable Class to talk with. Perhaps Bolo might have some interesting ideas. Of course, chatting about one's exact attributes can be difficult, but I get the feeling that Bolo isn't the conniving type. Anyway, it's not as if I intend to bare my heart to the man.

Plan made, I turn to my next notification.

New Spell Learned: Enhanced Particle Ray

A powerful Tier II spell that has been enhanced and self-taught by the Redeemer of the Dead, this spell converts raw Mana into a powerful laser beam.

Effect: Enhanced Particle Ray calls forth a beam of concentrated accelerated particles. Attack does 1000 points of damage on initial strike. Additional damage may be caused as the spell is channeled at the rate of 100 base damage per second.

Cost: 100 Mana

Continuous cast cost: 10 Mana / second

Enhanced Particle Ray may be enhanced by using the Elemental Affinity of Electromagnetic Force. Damage increased by 20% per level of affinity

The new spell is amazing. It does so much more damage than my Lightning Strike, though it doesn't have the advantage of being able to jump between opponents. Even then, the sheer amount of damage puts it at one of the most dangerous attacks, especially on a per Mana ratio. The only two major issues are that I have to channel the spell to make full use of it during combat, and as a spell, there's a delay in casting it. This spell, I intuitively know, will take longer to conjure than most of my other spells. So not something I'd use on a whim.

Elemental Affinity of Electromagnetic Force Upgraded!
Your affinity with the electromagnetic force has increased. Continue to experiment and push your ability to increase your affinity. Just don't do it without thought, boy-o.

I look up to see Ali returning a knowing gaze and a smirk. Letting out a long sigh, I nod. Fine. I deserved that one. My careless use of the spell was stupid, but learning how to convert energy and Mana, how to manipulate the forces of the universe was thrilling. I admit, I'm tempted to duck into research again. Try to figure out how Mana is used, experiment and learn new spells from the manipulation of spell matrixes and the forces of nature. Which kid didn't want to throw lightning from their hands and summon elements with a snap of their fingers? It's a tempting thought, but reality hits me soon after.

First, and perhaps most importantly, time. Research—real research—takes time. High level spell research—which is generally what I need—is at the stage medical science on Earth had reached before the System debuted. All the low hanging fruit has been plucked. The equivalent of magic's penicillin was well researched. While the variety and types of spells out there are infinite, the useful variations are much smaller. Does it matter if your spell of ice sends slushy snow or big, fat snowflakes?

At the higher levels, research required significant amounts of time, resources, and expertise to get right. Galactic magic users work in teams, each focusing on specific portions of a spell in an attempt to optimize it even further. Aiden, for all his brilliance, is just rethreading the work done by hundreds of geniuses before him. Oh, he might find a few forgotten or ignored spells which, for modern spellcasters, might be considered a surprise. But only briefly. It's not to say Aiden is wrong to do what he's doing—new cultures, new people mean new research avenues. Some of which might result in new spells. More importantly, anything he finds himself, he doesn't have to pay the System for and can then make free or cheaply available to everyone else on Earth.

As for me? I can cheat with my Elemental Affinity, but only so far. I'm all guesswork and intuition. I'd spend more time failing than succeeding and time has never been my friend.

On top of that, you've got to consider my temperament. Amusingly enough, for an ex-programmer, I always enjoyed my time outdoors and moving around more than sitting behind a desk. Reflecting on it, I know that my career choice was impacted by my father and his dreams of a stable future for me rather than my personal inclinations. If he had not been so against the outdoors, I might have found some work that way. But, well. C'est la vie. And that's not to forget how tendinitis crippled me later on, making every workday a torture of painkillers, ice, and more painkillers. Holing myself up and doing repetitive tests to figure out a new spell, a new way to manipulate Mana, would drive me even more insane.

This isn't the comic books or a bad fan fiction. I'm not the genius hero who is thrown into a medieval world with twentieth-century knowledge and the ability to remember a million important and minor engineering, alchemical, and historical details. I don't have the ability to skip decades of iterative development in manufacturing research and testing, to bank on the numerous failed tests of my brethren scientists to skip decades of failures. I can't ignore the reality that the industrial revolution was predicated on the ability of us building the machinery that built the machinery that gave us our final product.

The sad fact is, I'm the caveman in the twentieth-first century. And as the caveman, my best bet is to do what we cavemen do best—hit things very hard till they start working the way we need them to.

Closing the notifications, I let out a long breath and focus on the reality around me. Like any good caveman, I've got a carcass that needs dealing with.

*****

"Impressive. An adult space leviathan. Then again, it is the two of you," Oi says when we finally get back.

We're seated at a conference room, one close to the hull of the station and near where we docked. We hadn't even asked to meet with the station master, but Oi felt the need to come down once we arrived. One of the negatives of such a huge increase in station reputation.

"Mikito helped," I helpfully point out my friend. As did Harry, but he prefers to keep his involvement quiet. I'm not a huge fan of him sending out his news reports about our trips, but the good comes with the bad with a Reporter.

My words of rebuttal are met with a scornful glare—from Mikito of all people. I open my mouth then shut it, deciding not to air party laundry.

Oi diplomatically nods before glancing at a notification then focusing on us. "As for the leviathan's corpse? What are your plans?"

It'd been expensive, but thanks to some quick work, we'd managed to hire a few bored pirate ships to watch over the corpse while we reported in. It wasn't as if we could "dock" the leviathan's body to the station. Luckily, everyone who was anyone knew who had taken down the creature. Even the allure of a quick buck was squashed by the very real knowledge that we'd come and kick in their teeth if they tried to screw with the corpse. As such, the guards were more of a visible reminder than a necessity. I might have my own code, but killing pirate scum for stealing from me would not hurt my sleep at all.

"I understand there'll be an auction soon?" I say, cocking my head. This piece of information had been helpfully supplied by Bolo as we discussed the best way to profit from the carcass.

"The quarterly auctions in the third ring, yes." Oi's eyes narrow. "But its participants are normally only those with sufficient reputation."

"Or in-demand goods," Ali says with a smirk.

"True," Oi replies. "The auction holds many of the items we've acquired from underinsured merchants. We also have a large number of Adventurers coming in from nearby systems to sell their goods. It's often more cost-efficient to do so at a large-scale auction than in the Shop."

That is so true. The transportation costs between us and Shops has to be paid somehow, so the prices of goods reflect that cost of transportation. In a large-scale auction, if an Adventurer brings his own goods in his own inventory or other form of storage, he can generate a bigger profit. Only works for high enough value goods, which makes such auctions both a prime target and shopping ground. But…

"Your reputation won't be enough to keep the carcass alone when they start arriving en-masse," Oi says. "Get it skinned and taken apart before then. Do that, and I'll make sure you get your invitations to the auction."

I know Oi's looking for a way to get rid of us, and this works quite well. Getting to the third ring was our goal after all. I grunt an affirmative then look at Bolo. I've got a lot of skills but separating a Cthulhu-monster into its various useful parts is not one of them.

The Dragon Lord looks contemplative for a second before he grins, clapping his hands and rubbing them together. "I have the perfect person!"

Are there any more frightening words than that?

***

"Compensating much?" I mutter, staring at the giant mecha that walks out of the airlock and floats over to the waiting leviathan.

We're standing at a loading dock, staring at the projection of the mecha as it draws a sword thirty feet long from its back. The entire thing glows as a monomolecular edge is given to the weapon by a carefully layered force shield.

"Did you say something?"

I look down at the tiny Gremlin that spoke, the creature barely taller than a foot. The Gremlin speaks with a twisted accent, even for a Galactic, like he's got a mouthful of rubble and one too many tongues. His spine is so twisted, he's bent over with a highly prominent hunched back. A portion of the data I've downloaded or read in passing floats to the surface, reminding me that such a posture is considered sexy among Gremlin culture. Or Greelin culture, as they are known Galactically. Seems their name was mostly translated over, though not completely. Their ability to manage and interact with technology—in both good and bad ways—from our own legends is true too.

"No. Though I'm surprised you're using a mecha at all," I say.

"Eh. You'd be surprised what societies still cling to. Might not be as powerful as a Master Class—or heck, a good Advanced Class—but a force multiplier's a force multiplier. And when your society's made up of a bunch of support Classes…" Bolo shrugs. "Not the way we do things. But your Erethrans do it too, no?"

"To some extent. Though they focus more on weapons, ships, and artillery. Not"—I gesture to the mecha that is now taking apart the leviathan corpse—"that."

"Ah, but mecha is a Greelin's dream," Um of Lof says. "Makes a Greel feel big when you're piloting one of those."

Ali chuckles, floating over and letting his body expand. In seconds, he's bigger than all of us, which is a surprise. "There's something to be said about being big, no?"

"Aye. Makes the big-ones realize that size ain't everything," Um replies.

"But it does help." Bolo sniffs, patting the head of his hammer.

"This entire talk makes no sense," I say, looking between Ali, Um, and Bolo.

Ali and Um smirk at one another, which makes me roll my eyes.

Outside, the mecha continues to take apart the leviathan. There's a delicacy to the mecha's motions that belies the scale of the action, almost like a sushi chef parting the bones from a fish corpse. A magical swish of the hands, a twist in the hips, and a flare of thrusters and off goes the scales.

Yeah, okay. That metaphor breaks down. Fast. But you get the idea.

As pieces of the body float away, drone tugs catch the pieces and drag them into a cargo vessel. Within, I know, even more members of Um's clan are waiting, knives held aloft as they dismember the body into even smaller portions. Way I understand it, even the spoilt meat will be of use as it is chunked into smaller portions and reconstituted as high-grade monster feed. The intact portions will be cut apart and sealed, ready for sale. I have to say, even for my broad palate, the idea of eating space leviathan makes me pause, but Ali assures me it's a delicacy. In some cultures.

More importantly, the expensive crafting material will be separated, sorted, and stored until the auction. As payment, we're giving up a percentage of our earnings, but Um's clan has the numbers, the expertise, and the connections to keep the valuable crafting material safe until after the auction. They also can get rid of the less expensive, everyday materials for us, giving us an immediate Credit influx. As for where they'll keep it, Bolo and Ali muttered about a Clan-powered extra-dimensional storage space.

"We good here?" I say.

"For variations of good. If you squint. And aren't too picky," Ali says before anyone else can.

Um breaks out laughing while Bolo looks puzzled. Sometimes, humor just doesn't translate.

Um finally catches his breath, clutching his sides and slapping Ali in the knee as he pulls himself together. "We are good, Redeemer. Your leviathan is insured till the auction."

"Great. Then I've got a station to visit." I eye my new station pass and look around the fourth station ring one last time. Amusing that we barely spent any time here.

A part of me knows that there are station residents who would kill for the permit in my hand. I earned it in less time than many take to get over celebrating a good haul. But bugger them. If they complain, I'll tell them to go play in a Dungeon World for a few years and earn their Master Class.

Or, you know, kick their ass.

Whistling to myself, I walk off, heading for the closest transport tube. Time to go do some reading.

Chapter 11

It takes about half a day of bouncing from transit station to transit station to enter the third ring and our final destination. The three of us leave Dornalor in the fourth ring while we journey, the Pirate Captain busy completing repairs to the ship while researching new repair options. It's not that the distance is that far, but each transit station has its own security checkpoints, its own queues. Bolo could have breezed through the security checkpoints since he had the rep, but since the rest of us are newcomers, each checkpoint needs us to register, verify our documentation, and finally, receive their bribe to pass us down the chain. Once I figured out the last was what they were really looking for, we crossed the last few checkpoints at a good clip.

"You could have told me." I glare accusingly at Bolo, who trails along, one hand filled with popcorn, his gaze fixed on the semi-opaque viewing screen he shares with Ali. Since Harry decided to stay behind to keep filming the aftereffects of the takeover, my usual social lubricant isn't around.

"I wasn't trying to get anywhere fast." Bolo waves one butter-stained hand at me. "Now, shush. Jonathan and Kate are about to meet again after ten years."

"Wha—no. Never mind. I'm not getting involved in this." Even so, my blasted Perception and Intelligence ratings mean that the sight of John Cusack and Kate Beckinsale is enough to supply the name of the movie. Details, even irrelevant details, tend to creep up on me these days. "Ali, map please."

A muttered grumble later and I've got the map of the new station we're on. The third ring is made up of fewer stations than the fourth—rather obviously, since there's less space to cover. But each station is bigger too, broader and wider than the ones in the fourth ring. System-generated cleaning bots and Mana absorption means that everything looks as clean, but the atmosphere and the people within are subtly different. No lingering fear, no desperate gazes.

Those who have made it to the third ring are more established. There are quite a few third generation and older rebels, individuals who have grown up within the station itself, never having been part of "normal" Galactic culture.

No surprise then that the entire station feels more like Irvina than ever before. Even the Classes change, from Pirate Captains, Outcasts, Buccaneers, and Rebels to more common Classes like Courier Captains, Afterburn Pilots, Privateers, and The Loyal Opposition. Even the Levels are higher, fewer Basic Classes and a lot more Advanced Classes. There's also the usual plethora of support Classers who are needed to keep anything running, most of which have a wide range of Levels. Even with the level of basic tech available, there's only so much that you want to entrust to droids when there are Classes who can take over your toys.

While the fourth and fifth rings of Spaks mainly service the riff-raff of the galaxy, the third ring station seems geared toward the everyday needs of Spak itself. The third ring hosts a large number of manufacturing centers, warehouses, and ore smelters, with the attendant docks and facilities. A perusal of the actual station plan shows that while it might be larger than previous rings' stations, the actual useable space is smaller due to the larger facilities.

When we take the sixth twisting corridor, I'm absolutely certain of the tail. Cocking my head, I note that neither Bolo or Ali look particularly worried. As for Mikito…

"Kill or subdue?" Her question is asked in a flat, matter-of-fact tone.

"Let's maybe ask our local guide first. Don't want to step on any local toes…"

"Since when?" Bolo says. "My feet are still hurting from our encounter."

"I worry about those who matter," I snark back. "Now, you going to explain who is following us?"

Bolo doesn't look away from the notification window, though he shifts his hammer on his shoulder, far enough that he can protect himself with its head or swing away as necessary. He's silent for the space of half a corridor before he speaks. "Not one of my creditors."

At the next side corridor that comes along, I turn into it. Unlike any superhero TV show might show you, there's no convenient fire escape or dumpster to hide behind. It's a station alleyway, so it's all smooth metal, cramped corridors, and numbered doorways. Occasionally, very occasionally, those doorways have System-enabled notification messages indicating what lies behind them. More commonly, when there is a notice, it's a digital notification, piped directly to our neural links or otherwise tech-adapted viewing apparatus. System messages are considered the classy and sophisticated option, since they automatically translate to any language. That includes some of the strangest ones that involve scents, echolocation, or other, weirder senses.

The alley offers no way for me to hide from view, at least not mundanely. Good thing I've got an Invisibility spell. By the time our tails arrive, half the team—the uncaring half—is down the alleyway. Our tails take a dozen steps into the cramped, tight alleyway before they realize something is wrong. Mikito's not-so-subtle rap of the hilt of her naginata on the metal floor catches their attention, and they spin about to spot us.

"Gentlemen." I start out polite. Wasn't it Churchill who said there's no reason not to be polite when you have to kill a man? "Why exactly are you following us?"

"I told you we should have been farther back," the twisted, four-legged creature I'd seen sniffing at our trail twists one head to focus on us while the other head barks at his teammate.

His teammate looks less than impressed by being told off, the stalks of its head swaying in non-existent wind. I've run into the twig warden race before, which is why I'm amused to see one of their kind on the station. Most twig wardens run around with the Biosphere Class, starting from a basic Garden

Biosphere and advancing to a full-on Continental Biosphere. At those Levels, they're kind of like Swamp Thing—nearly impossible to kill without firebombing the entire continent. Leave even a single root alive, and, well, you're going to find out what poison ivy feels like on the inside.

"The Reaper of those Who Reaps seeks an answer," Kyle the twig warden says.

No, its name is not Kyle. But I don't speak leaf. The twig's body turns, the entire sapling moving as it shifts to focus on me, ignoring Bolo and Ali, who have stopped and are watching from farther up the alleyway. Bolo's even taken things seriously enough to pull his hammer off his shoulder. Though the show continues to play.

"We are to ensure no further saplings are stricken from the forest," Kyle adds.

"I'm not an insane murder hobo, you know."

"I am not in a position to ascertain sanity of non-sapling individuals," Kyle intones, his voice like the whistling of the wind through the leaves of a shivering aspen. "But your recent actions are of concern to station owners."

"That was Oi's fault!"

"Yet your actions made it possible," Benji—four legs—growls out, twisting his heads around and flashing Bolo and me a wide, toothy grin with separate heads. Where his tongue should be is a circular, teeth-filled, flexible tube. "And we're here to stop you."

"*Ali?*"

"*Neither are Masters. But woofie's a Pack Master, so figure he's got friends on call. And bioboy runs the entire atmospheric exchange on this station. You don't want to piss off the tree that controls your oxygen.*"

I eye Kyle more warily, then shake my head. "Why the hell am I worrying about that... Look, I'm not here to kill anyone. I'm off to see the Questor branch."

"This is not the way to their location," Benji says.

"Well, I wanted to know who was tailing us. And doing a bad job of it." Frowning, I point upward at where my implant has already located the "hidden" cameras. "Why aren't you just watching us that way?"

Benji looks at Kyle, who is as inscrutable as only a tree can be. Even the Galactic downloads on body language—and four years of running around killing and talking to them—offer no help. Certain creatures are so alien, reading their body language is impossible for me.

"Example," Mikito offers as answer, looking over the pair that block our way. "Disposable dummies?"

"You know, you've gotten a lot ruder," I say, eyeing the little Japanese woman.

She flashes me a tight smile, but never takes her eyes off the pair. Benji bristles, but I'm more interested to see if Kyle will decide to speak again.

"So. What now?" I ask.

Long seconds pass, broken only by the crunch and chewing sounds that emanate from Bolo as he returns to eating caramel popcorn, having decided that a fight isn't happening.

When the silence is broken, it's by the tree. "The radiant sun informs me that you should continue your journey. Without concern about us."

Fun.

I say that out loud then turn around and stomp away, followed by my friends. Take over one station and kill a few bad guys and you get stuck with a reputation as a troublemaker. Where is the fairness there, I ask you?

***

The Questor's Branch office is situated behind what can only be called over-fortified blast doors. I watch as three blast doors separate before I'm allowed in, and that's only because I'm able to flash my Title and Quest information. Bolo gets relegated to watching his movies in a nearby café, while Mikito takes off to find the nearest hotel. And, knowing her, a training hall.

Sometimes I wonder how far she'd go without me. Unlike me and my quixotic quest, Mikito is focused on being the hardest, nastiest, and deadliest fighter there can be. The few times I've brought up the topic of her incessant training, Mikito pointed out that she doesn't have a "cheat" like me, nor does she have the years of experience that many other Master Classers have gained. Hard work is all she can use to substitute for experience, Credits, and cheat perks. That at times it is not enough is perhaps the greatest unfairness of all.

I'll admit, I feel a little guilty about how often I drag Mikito into fights. And how little help I am. But I never wanted to be a killer. Never wanted to be a fighter. Don't get me wrong, I enjoy it. I crave the clarity of a fight, the moments free of worry and self-doubt, of second-guessing and the press of responsibility. For all that, the act of killing itself, of murdering those in my way, seems wrong. Is wrong.

Once, a long time ago, I nearly killed a man for making me think he'd done something bad. That act was nearly the breaking point for me, when I tried to reconcile my own anger and disgust with the System with what I'd become. I struggled with what we'd been taught was right—the rule of law, the presumption of innocence, the separation between judge, jury, and executioner that we, as a society, had built over years of trial and error—and the needs of a System civilization. I'd struggled, and human civilization, our mores back then, won. I didn't kill Minion because it was the right thing to do.

Since then, I've been exposed to a lot more options, a wider variety of cultures and their own rules of law. Many of those societies have been warped by the System, rules and morality changed to trust and use the System as part judge, part jury, part executioner. Classes that could read the "truth," whether by reading the person or the System recorded information. Skills that gave a glimpse of the past—from reconstructed flow of molecules and energy to tapping into a System record. Even my own Paladin Class Skills allow me to guesstimate truth, providing a level of assurance when passing judgment.

Judgment. And death. Because I've dealt a lot of that too, especially in the last few years. Oh, killing monsters is one thing—it's easy. They're monsters. Semi-sentient beings at times, but still monsters. Insane aggression, lack of morality or ability to bargain. Fighting monsters is easy, without moral or ethical implications. They want to eat you; you kill them and sometimes eat them. Might makes right.

But then you fight sentients and the rules change. The balance of right and wrong changes. Some of the people we fight and kill are just guards, working people making it through the day one paycheck at a time. You can, if you want, say that they've made their decisions, chosen to work for scumbags. Easy excuses, easy explanations for why you're allowed to hurt, maim, and kill them in the pursuit of your own objectives. Easy.

If you're willing to ignore context. Of the way Galactic Society sets up entire races, entire classes of individuals so that they have little choice. Where those who are unlucky enough to be born without connections, opportunity, or Credits are ground under, turned into slaves in all but name. A choice made under duress isn't much of a choice, and most of Galactic Society is under duress of some form or another.

Yet I don't necessarily have a better option. In a universe where a Legendary Class can take on entire planets by themselves, strength is the ultimate arbiter. Entire empires and regional powers are created for the sole purpose of making themselves a credible threat to a Legendary Class.

Other groups have gone deep, Sects forming with the goal of training and focusing all their resources on a gifted few in the hopes of creating powerful Heroics and Legendary Classes. Gaining safety under the shelter of a single individual. The rise of a single high-level Heroic has seen the rise and destruction of sects and kingdoms as the new threat challenges the existing order.

Arguments abound as to which is better. Each kind of strategy is a hard counter for the other. After all, what use is having a Sect leader who's a Legendary Class when your entire Sect has been destroyed by the swarms of lower-Class soldiers of an Empire? What use is an Empire if it cannot protect its citizens?

And round and round the Galactic power games go. Dungeon Worlds become powerful sources of growth. Forbidden World expeditions are the last hope for some to become powerful or relevant. To find the justice that they cannot find through normal means.

Might makes right. It's the truth of Galactic Society, but a part of me rebels against it. Even as I indulge in the benefits it provides, I reject the truth. If might makes right, then there is no justice, no hope of salvation for those forced by society, by the System, to stand at the lowest rung.

And that's not a Galaxy I want to live in.

"Not another absent-minded scholar," a droll voice in a thick Glaswegian accent cut across my thoughts.

I frown as I stare at the speaker, the realization that he's speaking English surprising me. The starving-thin, grey, and wrinkly man flashes me a half-smile, one that sends shivers down my spine. Almost as creepy is the fact that he's in a charcoal grey suit with a thin black tie, extra long fingers steepled in front of his chest.

"Human, right?"

I ask, "How—"

"Librarian's Helper." A hand waves down the body. "It makes me look and sound like a proper aide when I greet others in the library."

I twitch, eyeing the grey man. One of the things about perception-altering Skills like this is that while they might get some aspects right—like Style, language, looks—others can be a complete miss. Higher Levels of such Skills do better, but right now, he's making #creepylibrarian a trending tag in my brain.

"What can I do for you, Questor? New books? Movies? A data download?"

"Download?" I frowned. "I thought that was anathema to the Quest completion."

"That's what headquarters says." A slight pause before the librarian's body ripples in what I realize is meant to be a shrug, but it starts from his hips and moves up. "Results of those who have purchased such downloads have been inconclusive in our view. Known barriers to improvement at the 27, 39, 46, and 51 percentile Quest completion stages. It is believed that the download of information on the System is contraindicated by the Quest itself. Current theories… well. Are numerous."

"Go on." I wave, fascinated.

"Current prevailing theories fall into two main sections. Firstly, that downloaded data is not owned knowledge. It explains why individuals who learn the same facts do not necessarily gain the same level of accomplishment. Detractors point out that such completion rates require the System to read our minds and thoughts, which is, thus far, one of the things that is commonly believed to be System-impossible. Barring, of course, the usual System-enforced connections via Skills or equipment." The librarian holds up a single, long and clawed finger. I note how the nail is black and slightly curved as he raises a second finger to join the first. "Next. The very act of downloading the data is contraindicated. As such, while completion rates can occur, especially when one is new to the Quest, those completion rates are discounted. Completing portions of the System Quest is a common use of funds by Nobles and the affluent looking for a simple experience gain. Of course, detractors point out that if the act itself was contraindicated, no one would gain any experience and completion rates.

"Thirdly." Another pale finger. "The act of acquiring the knowledge is the important aspect of the quest completion. It is required that a Questor actually gain such knowledge himself, no matter if that gain is not in the most optimal manner. Those who hold to such a belief also often hold the belief that the ultimate answer to the Quest will be an act, an exploration of the System, rather than a dry academic treatise."

"And what do you believe?" I ask.

"You stand in the Heretics Branch." The librarian's hands come apart to encompass the bare hall we stand in. "We believe that the answer to the System Quest is not found in dry treatises or within the System itself. That the answer lies outside of the System or through it, the same way a fish cannot see the pond it lies within. Only by stepping outside of the System may we understand it."

"And that's why you're the heretics?"

"In a nutshell." The librarian did that weird shrug thing again, making me wince. "It is, shall we say, a point of long contention."

"But you're not actually rejected or kicked out."

"No."

"Just living in a pirate station."

"There are certain research topics that are more easily conducted among those already considered rebels. Fewer questions, fewer concerns."

"Interesting." I drop the topic since I'm not entirely sure I want to know what kind of research they can do here that they couldn't in regular Galactic Society, considering how lax Galactic Society was—at least in certain things. "Well, I came here for a reason and I'm just burning daylight jawing right now."

"Daylight? How quaint."

A notification appears before me—a long list of research categories that are all too familiar. A second of focus brings details to the forefront.

"So. A download or more mundane information services?" he asks.

I shake my head. "Let's go mundane."

"Disappointing. And which are we purchasing today?"

My eyes track over the titles, locating a few categories that I haven't seen before. In short order, I make my selection and highlight them, sending over the details. "These."

Almost as fast as I sent the request, my shopping list is returned to me with a list of the Credit cost for each title. I wince, seeing the total amount, but this information isn't available anywhere but here and the Shop. And compared to the Shop, these prices are more than reasonable. A quick confirmation and I see a flash on my data port as the books and studies are downloaded, ready for me to read.

Title Gained: Corrupt System Questor

Not content to gain knowledge via time-tested and well-worn tracks, the title holder has delved into forbidden knowledge and societies. This title is both a gift and a warning. Be wary, for those who stand in the way of this Questor and his answers might find themselves as part of their forbidden experiments.

Effect: +20 Luck for System Quest related events

"What the hell?" My jaw nearly drops.

"Is there a problem?"

"This Title," I snarl and point at the notification window he can't see.

Ali helpfully makes it opaque, though the librarian does not even glance at it before he answers.

"Ah, that old thing. You must be new." When my glare does not diminish, the librarian shrugs. "I had expected that all Questors who found us would have acquired it already. My apologies. I did not check."

"What the hell is with the Title?"

"Just a warning, boy-o," Ali says, yawning slightly. "Give it a rest. It's the Galactic Council's way of exerting their influence. Not a major thing."

"Not a major thing!" I growl. "It's calling me corrupt."

"Corrupt. Sullied. Focused." The librarian does that weird shrug of his again. "Language is such an imperfect thing. You have decided to learn something they have forbidden. Did you expect your actions to have no consequences?"

"Well, yes." I look around the sparse location before adding, "It wasn't as if you guys haven't been emphasizing that you're still active Questors."

"But considered heretics."

I draw a deep breath and pull out some chocolate, this one from a newly functioning chocolatier in the Swiss Alps. The Chocolatier has managed to elevate the entire art form, and the chocolates he makes can even provide boosts in attributes while tasting like heaven in your mouth. I savor the bitter tartness, the way it melts on my tongue slowly, then focus on the librarian, calmer. "How do I get rid of this?"

"Can't do it, boy-o. Hide, make it less prominent, sure. But Titles can't be removed." Ali pauses, rubbing his nose. "Well, okay. It's doable, but the Classes are all very rare and in-demand. And the Shop is expensive. Especially for a Title pushed by the Council—you'd be bidding against them." I wince but Ali's not done. "Also, you'd get it again the moment you started reading."

"So what? Suck it up?"

"Got it in one." Ali flashes me a grin. "I knew you were trainable."

Turning to the librarian, I growl out my next question. "Reading room?"

"This way." The librarian seems unperturbed by the entire discussion, waving down the way.

I stomp along, intent on milking this damn branch of everything I can now that I've gotten an unwanted Title. Just what I needed. Another complication.

Chapter 12

Projected 3D holograms, 2D video recordings, text and audio files all play, creating a cacophony of sounds and a maelstrom of color and motion. They all freeze as a call from the emergency party line cuts in, bringing silence to the library's viewing room.

"What is it, Mikito?" I snarl. If she has been thrown into another prison because she got into a fight, I'll... break her out again.

Deflating slightly with that thought, I'm surprised by Harry's voice. The Reporter is very good at keeping out of trouble, especially compared to the pair of us. "It's me. Need to ask you a few questions."

"You interrupted me for that?" I shake my head, pushing aside the irritation. I was in the groove, soaking up information by the ton, watching my System Quest experience tick up. Nowhere near as fast as a good fight, but so much safer. "What is it? And what are you doing anyway?"

"A new video series. The life and times of a rebel star," Harry says.

"We're on a pirate station."

"Mine sounds better."

"And there's already a well-known series about pirate stations. In fact, there are eleven major network series, twenty-four documentaries, and eleven on-going reality shows," Ali chimes in. "Did you know that the entire crew of one of your reality TV shows was rescued from an island and transported to Goom-ax by the Marquisse of Goom himself to increase ratings of his flagging show? He's now ranked sixth and is facing a triplicate of divorces."

"I did not know that." I wonder if it's a good or bad thing he's divorcing. For that matter, who exactly is the Marquisse, what was the show about, and why did he feel the need to put himself on display? Then again, I have my own personal War Reporter, so perhaps I should store my stones.

"Ahem." Harry says the word instead of clearing his throat, an act that makes me stare at him. Now that he has my attention, the reporter continues. "I need your expertise on something. I'm seeing a lot of echoes in the social and economic structures between Irvina and Spaks and wanted your opinion on them."

"Why me?"

"You're my resident expert on the System, no?"

I can't help but grunt in reply.

Seeing that I haven't killed the feed yet, Harry hurries on. "Right. So. Five rings around Spaks, with decreasing amounts of security and economic stability as you move away from the central station. Remind you of something?"

"Irvina, as you said. And pretty much every developed settlement," I say. "It makes sense. You want to put the most important things close to the core, from the governor's residence to the main Shop access. Heck, even your first teleportation pad often goes in close. Least likely to be damaged by rampaging monsters or invading forces. Dimensional locks, even those enforced by the System, are strongest near the core. You build defenses out from the places you need to defend, making sure you have multiple fallback points. Not a surprising similarity when it's common sense."

"What do you say of common sense? That it's not common at all?" Ali says as an aside.

I glare at the Spirit, who smirks, almost missing Harry's next words.

"Just give me a few moments to set up the scenario, okay?" Harry continues without waiting for my answer. "Now, Credits are still in use here. System Shops and teleportation work, even if teleportation is heavily restricted and require passes."

"Again, like Irvina," I say.

"Then you've got the people who have grown up here. The naturalized residents of the station. Did you know that promotion between the rings is possible but very uncommon?"

"I think we just took part in one such movement, no?"

"A violent and aggressive one. And really, it only worked for the people on the top. Any of the illegal immigrants who shifted stations while the fighting was going on will be kicked back to their previous station once they're found. If they're lucky."

"And if they're unlucky?"

"Serfdom. Or merchant bait," Harry says.

I shift in my seat, eyes narrowing. "Clarify bait."

"It's expensive getting a ship that can catch up to others in hyperspace. Even more expensive getting weapons or individuals with the right kind of Skills that can take a ship out of hyper," Harry says. "So. Drop a few live sentients in an escape pod, make sure it's banged up enough that it looks right and reads right to the System. Use a few more Skills to mess with the information available via the System, and suddenly you've got live bait in a failing escape pod."

"People fall for that?" I say.

"There's a fool born every minute," Ali says. "But it's also a matter of numbers. If you drop enough of them on enough major hyperspace routes, you'll get a bite sooner or later. Once your target drops out of hyperspace, transiting back up can take a while. Especially if you pack the escape pod with the right kind of material."

"Dimensional transit disrupting material?" I vaguely recall experiencing that in one dungeon. The monster's body was so filled with the disruptive material that it made even Blink Step—a small scale dimensional hop— impossible to use.

"Explosives."

"Oh."

"It's rare to force sentients to play bait. Most are volunteers—people desperate to escape serfdom, to make themselves useful to the pirate captains," Harry says. "Leveling's not easy outside of the dungeons or Dungeon Worlds. Fewer monsters, especially in space. A lot higher chance of death due to the hazardous environment. Get caught in the wrong 'flow' of Mana and you'll end up meeting the wrong kind of monster."

That, I knew all too well. Like the oceans of Earth, space has its own current. Except the current is made up of Mana flows. In the heavier, denser currents, high Level monsters like the Leviathans swim, living off the ambient Mana most of the time. But like the whales of Earth, many break out from the heavy currents, moving into shallower currents at irregular intervals, seeking something. Unlike System-formed Leveling zones on Dungeon Worlds, the probability of running into high Level monsters in lower level currents is high, especially as the System does not subtly guide these creatures around. It's one of the dangers of deep space travel they don't really tell you about.

"Fine. So movement is hard between rings. Life is tough. Your point?" I say, changing topic again.

"My point is that the restrictions are by design."

"Spakss's?" I say, rubbing my chin. "I'm not following."

"Not Spaks, the System. Think about it. If you've got a ship to be repaired, do you go to the guy with an Advanced Class or to the Basic Class? Credits being the same, that is? If you've got a ship that needs piloting or a spell cast?" Harry shakes his head. "Space might be less restrictive, but it also means the number of deadly encounters are higher. When you've got a choice, you go with the best.

"For those with low Levels, you either find work with an existing higher-Level crew or you venture out yourself with a small ship, staying to the safest

172

regions and hoping like hell you aren't too unlucky. If you're an Artisan, you work the cheapest, dirtiest jobs possible to scrape by."

That does kind of remind me a little bit of the way Galactic society works in Irvina. Except in Spaks, there's not even a dungeon for the pirates to grind experience, so at best, they have to venture out into the great beyond, hoping to stumble across their prey. Except…

"In Irvina, the inner zones weren't physically cut off from the rest of the city. And people could go there if they were high enough Levels."

"Of course there are differences between Irvina and Spaks. That's not the point. The point is that those in the inner zones have an unfair advantage here, just like in Irvina. They have access to better Skills, better technology and equipment, networks of crews that can be trusted to help and, in some cases, specialized access to dungeons to better themselves. Just like in Irvina."

"Space dungeons?"

"They're a thing," Ali confirms. "More like the natural formed lairs that you encountered on Earth, but some stations do invest in the creation of actual space dungeons."

That's one hell of a thought. How big would a dungeon in space actually be? Are there physical constraints? Or does the System warp space itself, like it does for normal dungeons? So many questions, so few answers—at least answers that I can get right now. But I put a bookmark on that thought because going to farm experience in a space dungeon sounds all kinds of cool.

Yes. I might actually have gone pew-pew in my mind while dodging asteroids at close—and entirely unrealistic—intervals in a spaceship. Benefits or drawbacks of a high Intelligence score.

"To the point, you're saying that the System is creating the situation? It's basically making societies have different zones or rings based off Levels?"

"I'm saying I'm seeing a pattern. But I don't know the System well enough to say for sure, and you're the System expert," Harry says.

"Ah. Well…" I frown, thinking it through. While I might be the System expert, it's more knowledge for knowledge's sake. Or knowledge to answer a single question. Sure, I get a lot of use from that information, but it really doesn't tackle sociological or societal issues. Still… "I'd say yes. I've seen much of the same things. Even in the many worlds we land on, the gradations, the differences between those in power and those without are pretty strict. There are exceptions—like the X-23—where groups move together. But where individuality is prized, there's more rigidity between social classes. It's hard for those without Credits, knowledge, or access to good Classes and the Leveling resources needed to upgrade themselves.

"Of course, that's just my view. I haven't done any real study on it. I'm sure the librarian has a book or a hundred about this topic."

"Can you look? Please?" Harry says.

Since I'm now interested, I offer Harry a nod. I've been making assumptions, but perhaps I should see what others have come up with. I kill the connection and bring up a simple messenger to notify the librarian of my new needs. This should be an interesting side research project.

***

It takes me about two hours of perusal to come to a definite conclusion. And that is that I really hate anthropological research. Especially when you add in aliens. One of the major conclusions I come to is that there is no one-size-fits-all theory for how the System changes us and our societies.

While major locations like Irvina and Spaks are, in the majority, top-down, stratified societies where Levels, Classes, and one's initial starting point are the greatest signifiers of future success, this is not always true. It's more common

174

to see such situations where personal power is a requirement, where individuality and concern about your fellow alien are valued lower. If everyone looks out for themselves and their own, then society fragments with those at the top continually building on their advantages. The only change in societal structure occurs when a powerful individual—Heroic or Legendary Class—dies without an heir of equivalent strength or when major wars happen.

Other societies, other locations have found ways to deal with the stratification of society. Some have taken communist-like structures, with individuals, groups, or even AIs taking over the dispersal of resources.

Cravior, in the Eridani Nebula, have members of their society tagged and numbered on birth. They are then put through a series of regimented trials that allow them to gain the best Class possible. Once they've received their Class, each individual is then added to the queue, with members at the head of the queue receiving the undivided attention and resources of the city. Those waiting in line behind are provided fewer resources but targeted to allow them to develop and make full use of their turn. In such a way, each individual is able to achieve as much—or as little—as they desire. No matter how much or little an individual achieves during their time at the peak, they will be put through the same rotation. Variants of this format—with more or less control by AIs, sophisticated programs, or a council of Scholars, Politicians, or Statistical Analysts—exist throughout the galaxy.

UL 53, on the other hand, is a corporate planet. Owned entirely by a single corporation, society is broken into two parts—the corporate serfs and the rest. Many children sign—or have signed for them—lifelong contracts with the corporation in order to be put through training to suit the needs of the corporation. In turn, they are given the chance to promote themselves by using corporate resources to achieve higher Levels and training in corporate-sponsored training facilities. Those who are not beholden to the corporation are forced to scurry and scramble, filling in needs where the corporation has yet to choose. However, they're locked out of all but a single dungeon unless they are able to win a space in the biannual lottery.

Borysthenis as a counter example is ruled by a council. The council itself is structured to include all walks of society—from the Classless denizens to those in all tiers of their advancement and type. Artisans, Combat Classers, retired Combatants, they are all included and given voice. The members of the council rotate too, though advisors from the appropriate non-Combat Classes are always around.

And that's not even going into individual races. Some races are weird, like the X-23s. Others are pure hive-mind creatures. The twig wardens are another, almost egalitarian culture. While those with higher tier Classes are considered important, it's more of a familial respect than a societal stricture. In any world dominated by the twig wardens, they're all part of the same biosphere and thus share success and failure.

For all that, I did notice that even the most egalitarian groups had to build workarounds for the System's tiers and Classes. It was impossible to ignore them, impossible to structure a society without taking those facts into consideration. While the System might not force people to be selfish pricks, it certainly incentivized short-term selfish actions.

Once I had my fill of that depressing research, I sent a summary of the data to Harry and killed the feeds. At some point, I'd read further into it, but for now, I'd rather do research on something a little more fun.

***

Later, much later, I pause the video recordings and fish out another strip of dried mango. These are purple, a mutated form that has a sweet-tart taste, courtesy of the mild poison. Very good and filling. No matter how much Galactic food I eat, there's just something to be said about Earth-origin items.

"What do you think?" I ask Ali, letting my gaze roam over the myriad screens. All of them show video recordings, formerly scrolling text and holographic projections of the information I've purchased. All of them on the same topic.

"I think I'm bored."

"Not that, you asshole." I wave at the screens. "Of what they've given us."

"I think even with your attributes, you're picking up maybe twenty percent of what's being shown."

"So long as it's the right twenty."

My Intelligence attribute is hundreds of times higher than a normal human's. You'd think that'd make me—make anyone—a supergenius. And in some ways, I am. I can do mathematical equations that I'd never even be able to finish in my mind at the drop of a hat. My brain can calculate angles and trajectories, translate that to the micromillimeters that I need to move to dodge a barrage of weapon fire without breaking a sweat. But in other ways, I'm still very much human. For the life of me, I can't remember the name of any of my high school teachers. I can process data, but finding new solutions, new ideas does not seem to be much faster than before.

The System attributes are both a fundamental alteration of my mind and body and a crutch that doesn't work properly. Galactic explanations delve into things like Mental Resistances, psychic potential, multi-dimensional processing, and the like. And, I admit, I can see it. There are studies of those with too low a Willpower and Mental attribute entering hyperspace and going crazy. Indications that crossing between dimensions—or hanging out between them—is just not right, not "normal," and without the System aid, we'd come apart at the seams.

Add the way the System seems to help us in the way we lean into it, and I've got a brain that can process a fight and multi-dimensional travel without a problem, play with swords, and teleport across a battlefield without feeling disoriented. I can process multiple disparate pieces of information and pull out the salient point without an issue. But I don't have an eidetic memory, and all the videos are really doing is giving me a small chance to learn what I need at a faster rate. It's a risk, and I'll probably go over some of the more interesting pieces in greater detail, but for a quick overview, there's nothing to beat it.

"Forbidden Worlds, right?" Ali grows serious, flicking his gaze over the myriad paused videos. Most are grainy, broken up. Technology does not work well in Forbidden Worlds—locations so saturated with Mana that most Mana-shielded tech breaks down. Once a world is no longer able to sustain life, when the monsters destroy civilization, most such worlds are abandoned. In the later stages of a lost world, a Forbidden World, even the System no longer functions. "I'd have thought you had enough personal experience with them already."

"Har…"

Recollection of four years of my life—fighting, struggling, and surviving in a Forbidden World—comes rushing back. My Master Class Quest, forced upon me by the Erethrans, had a nasty, nasty pre-condition. One that I would never have tried to meet if I had been given a real choice.

You see, on Forbidden Worlds, most monsters gained resistances to almost all forms of attacks, making even low-level creatures a pain to kill. Along with the lower level creatures are massive, bloated monstrosities that rampage through the world, soaking in Mana at ever-expanding amounts. They keep doing so, growing and eating till they can no longer move and become prey for smaller, lighter creatures. Before they too grew, completing the insane circle of life.

"The question has always been, what's the System, right?" I raise a hand, making it flood with Mana and calling forth a simple flame. I let it burn me, face barely twitching as I watch damage counters float up from the hand as Ali reminds me how dumb I'm being. But even as fast as the damage accumulates, my body heals it. "It functions everywhere there is enough Mana—but breaks down when there's too much of it. It doesn't break down in a straight line either—certain functions give way at the edges of Forbidden Zones while others—like Skills—function even to the farthest depths. Safe Zones, zone levels, Forts, and Settlements. They are all artificial constructions of the System itself and none last in a Forbidden Zone."

"Zone levels aren't all gone," Ali rebuts. "I recall us hiding in lower Level areas. A lot."

"Yeah, but that's from the lay of the Mana lines, which the System uses in construction of the zones." I bring up an image of a familiar blue ball. "See Mana lines on Earth, showing how the zones are mostly built along their flow? Except when they aren't. Like these national parks. Or when a settlement ends up on a Mana line and they enforce the low Mana zone around the city, siphoning environmental Mana into the city while pushing it away at the same time."

"Fine. The System makes zones and cities. So what?" Ali says.

"Well, the question is if the System is making a choice when it does that. Is the System breaking down non-core functions that don't involve individuals first by choice? Or is it a design issue? We know it's a given fact that that breakdown happens all the time, so it's one of the few 'facts' we have about the way the System works."

"Well, of course it's a fact. The research is all there. No one's going to deny the facts staring you in the face."

"Remind me to tell you about flat-earthers some time." I push aside the thought, focusing on the point I'm trying to make. "So knowing that the System attempts to preserve individual abilities and Classes the longest, the question is what's next? Well, some Questors decided to see what happens when you remove Classes in a Forbidden Zone, if new research results may be found. Perhaps a new Class, perhaps an interaction with the System that is not visible otherwise. All this"—I wave my hand around, encompassing the screens—"is done for research."

"Twisted and broken research." Ali stares at one particular image of a youngster in a cage, sitting sullen and defeated. By this point of the recording, all the crying, begging, and pleading has been done. He's resigned to his fate, his death.

"Yeah."

There's an ethical question there, one that I'm not entirely sure I want to touch. I'm not torturing the kid. In fact, that actual research was completed over a century ago. Much like how a lot of medicine in the twentieth century had grown from research conducted by the Japanese and Germans, the research I'm studying now comes from entirely unethical actions. People— sentient creatures—and animals were tortured, put through tests without their consent. Frankly, I'd kill the people involved in this research. But here I am, soaking in the data. Using it to expand on my own System Quest, my own research. Trying to find an answer.

And all the while feeling dirty and unclean, but still watching. Still learning.

I'm not sure what that says about me—but whatever it is, it's not nice. That darkness, that need to know, is probably part of the reason why Lana stopped waiting. There are places I'll go, things that I'm willing to do, to get this answer. Rightly or wrongly, I need to know.

"Either way, what they've learnt is that the System isn't just an external thing—once it changes you, it changes you. The Classes, the Skills, they're not external add-ons. The overlay we see, the notifications, those can disappear. But like our experience, our Levels, the Skills still stick around," I say, letting the flame disappear. "Our control of Mana in our body just becomes more intuitive.

"It's also why some of these researchers believe that experience is actually the System's way of categorizing our understanding of Mana. Why, when we're in a combat situation, it's the people facing the greatest danger who get the most experience. Because they're learning the most, they're the most able to grasp how to manipulate Mana better. The very act of using Mana, expanding it, makes them better Mana filters."

"Except you didn't get any experience at all in the Forbidden World," Ali counters. "You only Leveled once you left the Forbidden World. Since then, your stored experience has been part of the reason for your explosive growth. If they were right, you'd have jumped in power in the Forbidden Zone itself."

"I did get more powerful though." I conjure my sword, turning it sideways, showing Ali the plain steel—well, I call it steel, even though it's unlike any metal I know of these days—edge. "Even my sword improved while we were in the Zone."

"But not to the extent you should have."

I shrug, gesturing at the screens. "It's not as though what we're discussing is a complete theory. There are gaps, but it's clear that experience is, to some extent, based off 'real' world changes. Our Levels alter based off what we learn, as do our Class Skills. If anything, the System might be both a crutch and an aid—we're forced down a specific road while we gain Levels, but at the same time, when you achieve a new Class tier, you get the download and the changes that make it possible to use a new Class."

"That's why you read up about new Classes forming?" Ali gestures to a set of still screens. "Based off the data the Manifesters were looking at?"

"Exactly." I frown. "Remind me to let Lana and the others know of them, will you? It's amazing that an entire group of Questors have managed to hide their presence across Earth."

"Not going to make any friends that way," Ali warns.

"Meh." I shrug. Not as if I care what a group of Galactic busybodies think. But the knowledge that even an intermediate Questor has at his fingertips about the System will be important for Earth. "If they want to keep watch, they'll agree to it."

Until a new world joins the System, Earth will be the hotbed for these Galactic busybodies. The Order of Benevolent Class Manifestation Watchers are all about exploring the System as it manifests a new Skill or Class. Classes are preferred, because with the right kind of Skill, you can watch as the System attempts to form or otherwise adjust to these new Classes. In fact, from what little I gather, there were literally thousands of these bastards hanging around Earth when we joined the System, hiding their presence as they watched the addition of a new world to the System. Not that they lifted a damn finger to help us. They've got a code—mostly due to a concern about imprinting us poor barbarians with their Classes and Skills.

But now that Earth is part of the System, the number of new Classes being created rather than drawn from the giant database of the System will decrease. Already the number of Manifesters on Earth has dropped considerably. It doesn't mean they won't continue to keep an eye on us, but as we Level, hiding will get more difficult. I'm sure many of these Manifesters are hiding in plain sight, but their need to watch, to understand means that a closer and more intimate relationship is optimal. Which is where Lana and Rob might have their leverage.

"I'll just add them to the list of people who want to kill us then," Ali says. I snort, but the little Spirit continues, waving his hand to make the Class notifications disappear. "Sounds like you're leaning toward the Systemers' belief that the System is beneficent and Classes are a symptom."

"Nice word choice. Not at all prejudiced, are we?" I smirk. I've yet to get Ali's backstory in any detail, just that he's somehow beholden to the System. But the way he speaks of it and those he's served, it's clear, at least to me, that he's pretty bitter. "Maybe it is, but if it's beneficial, the System isn't very good at that."

"The Umil Branch of the Systemers would agree," the librarian answers, making me jump.

I've got a sword pointed at him before I realize that he's not a threat to anything but my pants and dignity. "Don't do that."

"You were informed of my arrival," the librarian intoned.

"I was not—you son of a bitch." I glare at Ali, who's clutching his side as he snickers. "What if I Blade Striked him!"

"Then I would have banned you from the library. After giving you a proper chastisement."

I glare at the still-snickering Ali and the librarian before throwing up my hands. "Whatever. Why are you here?"

"There is a rather noisy Dragon Lord asking for your presence. If you wish, I can send him on his way."

"Did he say why?"

"No."

I grunt, shaking my head, and look back at the video recordings. There's so much more to learn… as the multiple System Quest updates have shown me. There's still a day left till the auction happens, so I can cram a little more. And a Cleanse spell will fix any odorous issues.

As I turn back toward the screens, the librarian adds one last sentence. "If I were to guess, it probably has to do with the invasion fleet."

My neck snaps around so fast, I'd give myself whiplash if not for my high Constitution.

Chapter 13

The solar system floats in the war room in the fourth ring, a holographic projection of the area around the station and the nearest planets. I watch the loosely connected station platforms, the floating spherical rings, and the larger station pieces spin in slow-moving orbit around the giant mass of the core station. All of the pieces are broken up by lightly glimmering force shields. The flares of engine thrusters are like fireflies in the night, reminding me of the numerous ships that make Spaks their station of choice, coming in for repairs and refueling. Scattered throughout the model system are specks, some larger than others, of the asteroids that surround the station.

The peaceful serenity of the image is broken by the appearance of two dozen spaceships. They drop into space, some missing asteroids by centimeters on the projection. The moment they appear, they open fire, destroying and pulverizing multiple asteroids. Only a single ship misses it's jump, exploding in a fireball as translating matter meets asteroid.

Even as automated alarms ring throughout the station and mines dart toward the invaders, another half dozen whale-like ships appear in the now-cleared zones. The ships drop into space with no warning, outside of the sphere of control of Spaks station's dimensional locks. Each ship is situated at the cardinal points of the compass in 3D with the core station as the main focal point. Six Dimensional Smoothers, so that no matter how you rotated the view, there are two overlapping spheres of control at any time.

Each whale ship is as large as a second ring station—nearly one and a half times the kilometer-long station we're situated in—and is painted in the most garish, eye-searing colors you can imagine. Bright pink, seafoam aqua, and luminescent green is the least offensive mixture. As for the battleships, they're a hodgepodge mixture of styles and types, ranging from sleek, silverfish long vessels to a swirling mass of air and plasma, gaseous smoke given form around a hidden core.

The low rumble of station control conversations that played in the background has risen to a feverish pitch as station masters, pirate captains, and flight controllers panic at the invasion. Beside me, in the corners of the holographic playback, notification windows open, dozens of conversations transcribed and scrolling faster than the unaided human eye can read. And those are just the important ones, the traffic that the AI has highlighted for review. More of what is said is left unrecorded.

The third ring reacts first, the force shield that blocks movement between each ring snapping to full force. The fifth ring takes a fraction of a second more to react, then the rest of the rings are all on alert. The semi-transparent globes are fully opaque now, with a few ships en route crashing into the fully enforced barriers. Flares of venting oxygen and other combustible gasses appear and die away, forgotten tragedies as the interlopers take action.

Even through the projection, I can feel the hum and bone-shaking thrum as the six massive ships trigger their Dimensional Locks. The wave of blue that spreads from each of the ships is a computer-generated representation, but I feel the effects of the lock as I stand here. Each of the six gargantuan ships are Dimensional Smoothers. A single ship could lock down the station, but to stop us from escaping, they sent six of them.

As the ships lock us down, the battleships are firing on the mines and blocking attacks from hidden beam turrets. There's a short and intense battle between the automated defenses and the guardian ships, one that sees the destruction of all the automated defenses and two of the battleships. The remainder of the ships trail atmosphere, most having taken some damage. But for all their vaunted defenses, Spaks fails.

Once the situation stabilizes, the holographic projection freezes, leaving me to stare at the now-overlapping spheres of dimensional stability. No matter

186

where the station boosts to, where it runs, at least two of the smoothers will be in play. Right now, all six spheres of influence overlap us, keeping the station and its residents unable to transition to a more secure location.

"Not much more to show after that," Bolo says, striding out from the corner where he has been watching the entire proceedings. As he walks, the image turns back on, speeding up multiple times, and I watch the fireflies dart away, skipping through the gaps between the ships. None of the battleships leave their Dimensional Smoother to chase down the fleeing pirates, allowing those who were caught outside the chance to escape. "The cowards have run, leaving the rest of us here."

"I'm assuming those ships are the ones placing the Dimensional Locks on us?" I say, frowning and turning my hand sideways to look at the QSM attached to my wrist. It flickers, showing on the screen that slipping sideways is a possibility still. Interesting. It must be long-range teleportation that they're blocking, which is easier to block than short-term teleportation. "Which bands are they blocking?"

"All of them," Bolo answers curtly.

"Burrowing?"

"Walls have been thickened."

"Folding?"

"Stabilized."

"Gates?" I say, reaching for half-forgotten studies.

"Disrupted."

"Divine circles?"

"Stopped, blocked, or otherwise hampered." When I open my mouth to continue, Bolo shakes his head. "Nothing works. Every single type of long-range teleportation form is blocked. Even the Shop's teleportation options are severely limited. Someone's willing to bid up the prices such that no one but the richest is getting out."

"Damn." Dimensional smoothing isn't necessarily as easy as buying a single type of Skill and locking out an area. While yes, most Skills will block most forms of teleportation, with the myriad forms of Skills out there, some types are more efficient at blocking the shift of molecules than others. As an example, divine intervention can often transport people through most dimensional locks, since the vast majority of the time, it's just a spirit being moving you really, really fast. It's not actual teleportation like Blink Step but physical movement. "How'd they manage to get so many of those ships in play? Can't be cheap."

"They aren't," Harry confirms, looking up from behind me, where he's manipulating multiple windows at a time, news feeds in each window while he reads news reports in another. "I'm doing a story on it now—mostly for the locals though. Seems like the major players have been given the inside scoop. But this is just the opening move of a much larger campaign. The name battered around is Operation Sketch Pad."

Ah, yes. In the tradition of giving operations the most random names possible, we get Operation Sketch Pad. Though I guess wiping us off the face of the galaxy is a good artistic endeavor. Or something.

Fine. I'm stretching here, as I try to figure out what the hell to do about the fact that we're trapped on a sinking ship. Or well…

"This isn't the first time it's been tried, right?" I say. I vaguely recall that conversation…

"Nope. Multiple navies and individuals have tried to destroy Spaks. This is, like, the twenty-third major rebel nexus since the start of the System," Ali says. "Spaks herself has survived nine major attempts."

"So. They can handle this?"

"If everyone pulls together, certainly," Oi says as the doors slide open. I frown at the Captain as he gestures at the screen. "That's why we asked Bolo to retrieve you. Now that you understand the situation, you should understand the wider one." At his words, the images fade away to be replaced by a fleet of ships that take up the entire room. Even my enhanced brain can't count them all at a glance, but it's well above two hundred battleships, never mind the smaller cruisers. "This is the fleet that is on its way to us."

I frown, tilting my head. "Why aren't they here already?"

"Because they're still gathering."

My jaw drops. We might have the same number of ships orbiting the station right now, but they're mostly pirate ships—equipped with a few guns and missile tubes, but not exactly war machines. They don't have the multiple redundancies or armor a real warship would have, instead sacrificing a lot of that for cargo space. Even if the entire game of insurance payouts is rigged, it doesn't mean that the pirates can send ships without space to pick up the cargo. But, if the fleet is still gathering, the sheer numbers they're sending at us is staggering.

"It's not the level of the dragon in the fight but the level of the fight in the dragon," Bolo says.

I twitch, eyes narrowing as I wonder if he's mocking me. Or if certain concepts just translate weirdly. Probably the second. "Are you saying we have more people with higher Classes?"

"A few. They're mostly worried about the Inner Crew," Oi says, pointing downward. It takes me a moment to realize he's talking about Station Prime.

"Nine high-level Master Classers, two Heroics, and one, rumored, Legendary Class." Harry flicks me the data with a swipe of his hand. In the column is a list of the names and their Classes, along with an opposition column right next to them. "Right now, we've got public announcements of a half dozen high-Level Master Classes in the fleet, a score more on the lower end of the scale. And at least one Heroic—the Grand Admiral that's running the fleet."

There's an intake of breath at that one, more than a few people wincing. Captains, Admirals, they come in two flavors for the most part. The jack-of-all trades, like Dornalor, who can do everything and whose Skills let him do it all, just not as well. Or—and I'm guessing this is the case with the Grand Admiral—the support Class. They don't do anything but stand around looking pretty and providing general Skill boosts to everyone under them. Given enough time—and a Grand Admiral has had that time—they'll increase in Levels and Skill Points until their powers can cover everyone in their fleet, boosting their performance by a significant margin. Especially since many of their Skills won't conflict with other passive boosts.

"Correct me if I'm wrong, but if they've got enough power to pull everyone together—and I'd really like to know why now—why the hell aren't they punching through our Dimensional Lock and dropping people in?" I say.

"It's been tried before. The third and eighth attempts to be exact," Oi says. "I was around for the eighth as a child. The emergency jump made me throw up for a day—even the System couldn't help with the shock. But it meant that they lost every single one of their invaders since the Inner Crew had caught wind of the attempt and sabotaged their Smoothers beforehand. Which leads me to my point. We need to take those out."

"And you're volunteering us," I say flatly. "Not exactly sure I feel the desire to kill the poor sons of a bitches doing their jobs on those ships. I really doubt there's a convenient key to pull to stop it from working."

"You understand they intend to kill us, if you refuse," Oi says.

I point at the way, even now, some of the ships are headed out. "We can run."

"Even if they intend to kill or enslave everyone on this station? Even the children?" Oi watches as I flinch at the last, the damn Galactic radiating smugness when he continues. "Everyone, including you, is considered guilty by association. The children will be let off easy—only twenty- or thirty-year sentences. Everyone else, well…"

"Not a kind and wonderful bunch, are they?" I mutter sarcastically.

"It's the Galactic System," I Shao almost spits. "Why do you think we fight the fat, corrupt, easy-Leveled Goblin eaters?"

"Yeah, yeah," I say, waving. It's not as if the pirates and rebels are that much better. And whining about the Galactic System ignores the various cultures that have managed to work around the System. Though some of them do suffer for the lack of efficiency that their ways of doing things have created. But… "It still doesn't mean I want to kill people working their jobs. Especially if they're just doing what they need to do."

"Then perhaps you should consider the makeup of the groups," Bolo says.

A projection of names flips up in front of me, some of them quite familiar. The Thirteen Moon Sect. The Kingdom of Pewsin. The Zarrie. There are more names, many that I know are the bottom-feeders of Galactic Society. Those voted most likely to exploit. But multiple years at this has shown me to not take things at face value. Especially information that is this convenient.

"Harry?"

"Data's real."

"I think someone really needs to explain why there's a fleet attacking us right when we're visiting. And why so many of those involved are people we have beef with." I turn to look at Bolo, Ali, and Oi in turn, my face losing all traces of amusement.

Truth is, the moment I saw the encirclement, I knew that we could get out if we really wanted to. Dornalor's ship has the stealth modules to get us close to the exit, then it's just a matter of running—no matter how many mines they're in the process of planting. There's more going on than just a coincidental attack, and I'd like an answer before I make a move.

"It is, as you have assumed, not entirely a coincidence that this happened." Oi holds up one hand. "Your presence here has contributed to the arrival of many of your enemies." Another hand goes up. "But rumors of an attack have been circulating for years. The timing of the attack coincides with our auction as well, offering them the highest return."

"Har! Look at that face. You owe me ten Roma crystals," Ali crows, floating over to Bolo while holding out a hand. "Told you he'd look like that."

"How can a man, even a Master Class, be that conceited?" Bolo mutters, not at all softly, while pulling the Roma crystals from his storage.

"I am not!"

"You really are," Harry says, looking up. "Though in this case, the fact that you annoyed the Thirteen Moon Sect was particularly important. They had the sixth Dimensional Smoother that was needed. This entire operation has been boiling for years, but they've never managed to get more than five Smoothers committed at any one time."

"Then we came along. And they decided to take a swing at us."

"Well, there's also the population of the station and the influx of materials," Ali drawls. "But hey, it's more John's head that's important. The big, swelled head of his."

"As much as this is amusing," I Shao speaks up, cutting through our bickering, "we are in need of an answer. Soon."

"Fine. I get the Thirteen Moons." Never liked that group, and if they are coming for me, I figure it's time to remind them why they should back off. This isn't the first time they've sent people against me, but it's mostly been small scale attacks. Nothing like this.

One thing I've learnt in my time in the Galaxy is that you can't back down, not ever. If someone takes a swing at you, you swing back and you put them down harder than ever. Otherwise, you're just asking to be targeted again. I'll admit, people like Roxley have a more subtle manner of doing things, but there's a nice simplicity to taking your sword and cutting down every single opponent. It also means that the few times you are subtle, they're more likely to be surprised.

"Obviously," Oi confirms my request.

I let out a deep breath, resigning myself to doing what I do best. Which, in this case, is blasting a bunch of idiots into space.

***

Once I agreed, the rest of the preparations proceeded at lightning speed. It seemed that while I was being briefed, the professionals were making minor adjustments to the contingency battle plans then disseminating the plans. I could whine and bitch about being relegated to playing foot soldier, what with being a Master Class and all, but really, I'm not a tactician. I'm an ex-programmer turned Galactic hitman. While I've occasionally taken part in large scale battles, it's never been on a tactical level.

I was amused when I found out that the Galactic version of "minimal amount of data" was actually the opposite—a flood of data that allowed each ship to target any of the six Dimensional Smoothers or their backup ships. Each plan, each course, each target was given a different designation and individually specified for each of our ships so that there were literally tens of thousands of plans being disseminated. Once contact is made, the strategists and tacticians will activate the appropriate plans, ensuring our fleet can act as one while keeping the other team guessing.

It's a brutal and inelegant manner of dealing with the System's ability to leak information, but considering we know there are a ton of spies involved and—as has been shown by the surprise appearance of the Dimensional Smoothers—the enemy spies are better than ours, it works. As for myself, I'm seated next to Dornalor, waiting.

"You know, I expect to get paid for this," Dornalor says.

"Talk to Io."

"She's not seated with me."

"But she commandeered your ship. Or, well, Oi did. But Io negotiates payouts." I run through the stats of the ship via my Neural Link, assessing the remaining damage and the state of our repairs. "Nicely done, by the way. I see you had the armor upgraded."

"Only where it was needed." Dornalor shrugs, but I've known him long enough to sense the satisfaction that lies beneath that shrug. "Your friends cutting up the Leviathan gave me a good deal."

"I'd hope so. We're partners now more than customers." I make sure to stress the *we* portion of the sentence, what with Dornalor having a share of the entire Leviathan.

"The auction still going on?" Dornalor asks, absently dragging a hand along the shell along his forehead.

"Eventually. It's delayed for a few days, but it'll be completed. The plan is, if things go really bad, to have a quick impromptu one so that the buyers can take part via the System. Just means that the variety of goods will be lower— or set at a higher price." I shrug. "Um figures it'll be good for us. Get us a higher price on the sale. And since they've got clansmen outside of the boundaries, it won't cost us a dime more to transport the goods."

"Nice." Dornalor rubs the arm of his chair lovingly. "There are some upgrades I've been eying for a while. If we make enough, I'll rip out the support struts around the engine and cockpit and replace them. Add in lines for two more gauss cannons."

"Gauss?" I raise an eyebrow. "Kind of old school, isn't it? Short range too."

"Everything has its place," Dornalor says. "Unless you're telling me we won't be conducting any more ship raids."

I snort before considering his words. Since I've been told not to play Galactic assassin anymore, does that mean I won't?

While I'm thinking, Dornalor continues. "We've been lacking a hard counter to those energy shields. This seems as good a time to get one as any."

I push aside my musings. Not as if Dornalor couldn't find a use for the guns after all. Like with anything in the Galaxy, there's a very big game of rock-paper-scissors with offense and defense. Force fields are mostly energy based, so those are countered—to some extent—by mass drivers. Mass drivers are beaten back by layered and hard armor, which are easily countered by high energy weaponry. Of course, Skills and ship-wide resistances add their own layers to that. Bomb-pumped nuclear missiles might be the norm, but there's no reason you couldn't power the entire thing with the heart of a fire elemental. Or pack it full of mega porcupine quills. The thing about wars, and space battles in particular, is how wasteful they are. Which is why sending a single Master Class via a stealth ship into the opponent's ship is just as viable a tactic. Kind of like now…

"Ship upgrades rather than new Skills?" I say, just to fill in the silence as we wait.

"Mana." Dornalor shrugs. "Right now, I can run everything at full bore for nine minutes. Nearly infinitely at seventy percent settings." He cocks his head, giving me a half smile. "Can't really add any other Skills without impacting my optimal run time."

I nod rather than call out his lie about his actual run time. Or utilization percentage. Or the fact that he's not mentioning he has a few backup Skills. Underplaying your hand is a common tactic, but we've been flying together long enough that I can do the math myself.

"Until I hit my next Skill threshold, better to keep my Skills as they stand," Dornalor says.

"Not going for a Skill evolution?" I query.

Dornalor is one of those who regularly consults with Class Actuaries, individuals who—for a fee—will study and assess the best "build" for an individual dependent on their Class, attributes, and situations. In his case, Dornalor visits the Actuaries, but there are a whole host of others who approximate the very same occupation.

Obviously, there are Class guides that anyone with any sense purchases. But Class Actuaries can provide more detailed reviews, taking into account specific attributes, locations, current builds, and other Skills. The very best can even give you a probability assessment of a Skill evolution.

Becoming a Class Actuary is interesting, since it's a prestige Class with a number of—mostly—hidden requirements. Most large organizations have a few on hand though, since their help can be invaluable. Those who work freelance often have waiting lists in the years.

Dornalor doesn't answer my question and I wince internally, realizing I made another faux pas. Sometimes I forget that talking about Skills and Classes isn't done. The world feels so much like a game sometimes that I forget that for the Galactics, it's no game, it's just life. And theory-crafting your build with friends is one thing, but it's another to discuss it with relative strangers—even if that stranger is your employer.

"All ships. All ships. Plan Aquarius-Twenty-Eight-Chaos-Mana. Repeat. Aquarius-Twenty-Eight-Chaos-Mana."

196

I tilt my head as the voice and screen notifications appear. I don't tense, because this is the fourth one since we radioed in our readiness. Each time, a thousand ships run through the plans, figuring out their final locations, their necessary jump details. But the next words make me tense.

"Apricot. I repeat, apricot."

Force shields around the station go down without warning. Dimensional locks disappear. Chaos and more mundane space mines, primed for sudden changes in the environment, are turned off. Ship AIs, waiting for the command, trigger already hot engines, sending their ships through the now lowered station force shields. All around us, thrusters flare and mini-suns give birth as ships dart forward. We hover, waiting for a little before we follow, our ship in the third wave of the fleet.

Nestled deep within the sensor net of my own ship, I watch my first true fleet battle. I've read details about a few of them, but never taken part. Leading the charge to each of the six Dimensional Smoothers are our siege breakers—the largest, toughest ships we have. In most cases, they're just mining ships. But considering the nature of certain types of planetary mining, the front shielding of these ore ships are as strong, if not stronger, than most heavy cruisers. Of course, they're also a lot slower and have zero offensive armaments. Unless an enemy ship captain is dumb enough to sit still long enough for the close-range borers to fire. Dumb enough, or unlucky enough, to be in a Dimensional Smoother that has to stay still—relatively speaking—to ensure full coverage of Spaks.

Knowing that, the invading armada are focusing fire on the mining ships and our two battlecruisers. I watch as nearby enemy battleships scramble to aid the Dimensional Smoothers targeted by the pair of battlecruisers. While the battlecruisers might be a little out of date, each battlecruiser still outweighs the competing battleships by four times. Sure, the battleships might be able to swarm and destroy the battlecruisers eventually—but not before the battlecruisers can close in on the Dimensional Smoothers and hammer them. Add in the presence of the various pirate ships—many of them in the destroyer-sized range—and we've got a real scrum. If we could have gotten most of the pirates to help, this entire fight would be a non-issue; but even with threats and promises of rewards, pirates and rebels are anarchists at heart. No one really wanted to risk their livelihood and lives when someone else could do it.

When Oi revealed the presence of the pair of battlecruisers, it had been quite a surprise. Most everyone knew of the first battlecruiser—it'd been a badly held secret for years, according to Bolo—but the second one had been a real surprise. Unlike the Prime Station's battlecruiser, the second battlecruiser had been commandeered by a Rebel captain in the Dorado star cluster after a failed military coup. He'd taken the battlecruiser and its crew and ran, and only recently stopped at Spaks for repairs and refueling. A series of powerful invisibility tech, spells, and Skills had kept its presence unknown to most.

"Big, beautiful, and oh so attention grabbing," Ali says, floating up through the floor as he indicates the battlecruisers. Dornalor shoots Ali a glare but relents on not bitching out the Spirit again. It might have something to do with the amount of g-forces we're experiencing, even through the inertial compensators. "Looks like the Wererats are following their babies."

I frown, not understanding the point. "What?"

"Wererats. Babies. Nom, nom, nom." When I look horrified, Ali shakes his head. "What? Your human rats do the same too. Admittedly, Wererats consider other wererat children delicacies, so they are more prone to doing it. You meat-people are all strange anyway."

"Just… ugh." I make a face.

Dornalor shakes his head before he turns his attention back to flying us through the scrum. Even if we're flying relatively far apart in absolute physical terms, we're all moving so fast that the ships are doing the equivalent of flying in close formation. Except in our case, we're playing dodge-em as the battleships ahead of us open up, filling the void with missiles, stealthed mines, particle beam fire, gravitic locuses, and other less recognizable attacks.

"Stealth modules are holding. We should be on location in five," Dornalor says as he jerks us out of the way of a newly emergent shrapnel field, one created by opening a gap into the elemental realm of diamond.

"Got it."

I leave Dornalor to the flying, focusing instead on the overall fight. In the time we've been jawing, our siege breakers have made their way a quarter of the distance, each of them lit up like a town square Christmas tree. Behind, the pirate ships that were conned into coming along are returning fire, targeting the battleships' external gun mounts and engines. Their goal is to crack the shields then defang the battleships rather than destroy them. While beam weaponry plays the biggest part in the initial clash, hundreds of missiles are on their terminal flight, headed both ways.

Electronic counter measures come into play. Within the sensor suite, I feel the sudden increase in transmissions, the way the electromagnetic spectrum explodes in volume. My affinity hums within me, asking, begging me to use it, while my Mana Sense hums with the warping of Mana as numerous Skills come into play. Mana swirls and collects around each pirate ship as their occupants struggle for survival. The enemy fleet is too far away for me to sense, but I'm sure they're doing much the same.

Countless missiles go astray, some exploding prematurely, others going so far as to target other friendly missiles. Some head away from their initial targets only to reacquire another pirate ship. As the fleets close, point-blank counter missile lasers fire under the guidance of AIs and some extremely highly attributed Intelligence and Skilled individuals. Seconds before the missiles can hit us, point defense thins out the attack further. Then they're in our midst and my senses—all of them—go insane.

High energy bombs, concentrated into beams of energy and terror, tear into metal. Gravity bombs containing miniature black holes are released from their confines, yanking stray debris and even light into their cores. X-ray lasers. Photonic beams. In a few cases, just solid masses of metal. Those are all the kinds of missiles that go off around the pirates, technological mayhem bringing death to ships by the dozens.

If only we were targeted by something so simple.

Instead, the Thirteen Moon Sect goes for the esoteric forms of missile payloads. Half of the missiles contain elementals trapped within enchanted warheads that, on explosion, spread their freed forms across a wide range of space itself. Hundreds of kilometers their bodies expand, until they touch enough metal. And then they contract, glomping together at the contact point to form elemental invaders. Acid, fire, lightning, metal. Those are the easy to recognize elementals. There's another one that's made of candy canes, another a twisting mass of melted plastic, and even a pool of poo.

To deal with the ore miner we follow, the Thirteen Moon Sect went with something much simpler and larger. An ifrit, carried on a stealthed missile, appears in front of the ore miner. It grows and grows, fifty kilometers tall, topknot of blue hair and big grin present, just before it puts its hand out and stops the ore miner dead. Except physics still has a say in this System world, and the ore miner's momentum continues forward. Immovable object meets entirely mortal structure and the ore miner crumples like a tin can, its own engines driving its demise.

In the midst of all this, Dornalor weaves us through the attacks. We're not targeted directly by any of the missiles or beam weaponry, our superior stealth modules keeping us in the clear. But incidental death is still death. More than once, I see him activate the surface deterrents, throwing up temporary force shields to block a grasping tendril from an elemental or roll the ship around a sudden explosion of focused dimensional energy.

As much damage as the enemy fleet is doing to us, our own attacks are having an effect. At least one battleship is destroyed outright, while many others have their defenses worn down. As for the Dimensional Smoothers, the target of the majority of our attacks…

"Dimensional Smoother's force shields are down. Entry plan is a go," Bolo reports from below, in the secondary command deck where he's overseeing damage control with Mikito.

We continue to fly, the first wave of the pirate fleet entirely wiped out. The second wave ahead of us has taken significant damage, especially as the battleships—now freed from firing upon the ore ship—turn their attention to them. Thankfully, the ifrit disappears after it's done with the ore ship, its service complete.

As for us…

There is no sound in space—not outside. But within the ship, the creaks and groans of the *Heartbreak*, the sudden, painful exhalations as inertial dampers either can't keep up—or worse, act against our actual acceleration. Damage notifications float up in the corner of my eye. Nothing significant, but a constant reminder that even my toughened body is taking a beating from our dodging.

We get lucky until a half minute out, when an elemental, hidden from our senses, manages to latch on. An elemental of Space itself bypasses all our mundane defenses, barely slows down on the enchantments woven into the ship, and appears within. Damage notifications appear as the newly formed Space Elemental wrecks things by changing the spatial dimensions of the *Heartbreak* itself.

"Mikito. Bolo. Damage control!" Dornalor barks. "You. Stay there."

"Wasn't going to move." I know my job. Already the guns are online, my mind tapped directly into the weaponry. We don't fire. Haven't fired. But we're closing in so fast now that there's no way to hide our—

"Void. There goes the stealth covering," Dornalor says. "Hold on!"

"Easy for you to say!" Mikito growls over the comms.

I pull up a camera and realize that Mikito's already managed to make her way to the elemental. Lucky that she's so close. The corridor itself is no longer a smooth, regular rectangle but a weird distortion of space, certain parts jutting out, others compressed to no more than four feet in size. In the center of the corridor is the space elemental, a distortion in space itself that shifts form from cube to sphere to decahedron to pyramid and more. As Mikito enters its range, her body compresses and twists, her lead leg shrinking and lengthening to her screams of pain. The Samurai doesn't hesitate, throwing Hitoshi at the elemental rather than continue to approach it. The heavy blade floats through the air and the elemental turns to regard it.

I expect to see the polearm twist, change, maybe shift course. But Legacy weaponry have their own properties, including a solidity that even my own soulbound weapon does not. Whatever weird Skills the elemental is trying to use, it fails, and the blade sinks deep into the creature. The successful attack releases Mikito's leg, the appendage springing back to its original shape, along with portions of the corridor. But both her leg and the corridor look twisted, mangled from the changes.

As the naginata falls out of the body of the elemental as it changes form once again, the elemental again exerts its influence on external space. Only to be interrupted as Bolo crashes through the bottom flooring, his hammer leading the way.

I turn away from the fight, focusing on the space battle around us. Fighters—dozens and dozens of space fighters—scramble out of the Dimensional Smoothers and some of the battleships. The fighters are as disparate as the fleet facing us. Some of the fighters are barely large enough to contain the individuals strapped within. Others are the size of an eighteen-wheeler. The range in fighters is often dependent on the Classes they carry—some just there to bring their occupants to the fight as quickly as possible. Others are more traditional, bearing external weaponry. None of it matters to me as I target the nearest fighter, letting loose on our beam weaponry to destroy their methods of locomotion.

"Protective mines are at a higher density than expected," Dornalor snarls.

In my sensor suite, more data streams in as the stealthed mines are revealed. Hundreds of them, covering space. I watch as one of the spacesuit-fighters literally bounces off a mine, his IFF ensuring it doesn't blow up. Not even when I shoot him and catch the mine in the backblast.

"Contained high-explosives." I report the results of the attack to Dornalor. Nothing too unstable. Smart. And annoying.

"Afterburners in three." Dornalor pauses then adds, "You too."

"Got it."

Afterburners and our Class Skills synchronize, increasing our forward momentum and adding to our initial velocity. That helps us dodge attacks and puts us within range of the mines and the fighters. Things get hectic after that, though I'm relieved to see that a number of damage reports decrease as the space elemental is banished. Fire and flame wrap the *Heartbreak*. Metal tears and melts, and the constant ping of damage reports and ricocheting mass-driven projectiles echo through my skull as our shields fail within seconds.

Breach in section 3, upper deck.

Intruder detected.

All around us, pirate ships duck and dive, opening fire at beam turrets and missile ports, destroying the Dimensional Smoother's offensive and defensive options. Each attack reduces incoming fire, but casualties on our side mount too. Luminescent dots in the plot disappear innocuously, belying the truth of shrieking death and explosive decompression.

Port turret 2 damaged. Send damage control

Left wing missile pod destroyed. Closing autofeed slots.
Autofeed slots closed. Dump loaded missiles?

External loaded missiles dumped. Detonation in 3.47 seconds.

Seconds that feel like hours as our brains take in and process dozens of notifications at a time. We process and make decisions that dictate the life and death of fighters and ourselves, spinning through the void before the afterburners stop and the maneuvering thrusters kick in. We spin in place, still flying backward as our forward momentum keeps us moving, then our afterburners turn on again, braking us. Even as we do so, Dornalor is speaking.

"Kill your Skill. We hit the drop point in eight seconds."

No get ready, no good luck. Not a very sentimental guy, Dornalor.

My chair retracts, dropping through the floor and being replaced by another flowing metal version of itself as I enter an escape chute below the cockpit. As I drop, the chair I'm in is enclosed by more of the liquid metal, crash foam forming from the edges to fill in empty spaces. My connection to the ship gets cut off abruptly, leaving me mentally staggering. I don't get enough time to reorient myself before the thrusters and the electromagnetic rails around my pod trigger.

I leave our spaceship in fire and flame, to bring wreck and ruin to our enemies.

Chapter 14

Outside the ship, my stomach lurches and twists as the inertial compensators in the ship lose their efficacy. I spin through the void, headed for the Dimensional Smoother's hull, passing through interlocking beams of fire by inches. A second later, my poor mortal form in the escape pod impacts the Dimensional Smoother's hull. The escape pod's outer shell breaks up under the absurd sheering forces it's subjected to, leaving me bereft of material protection. Thankfully, not Skilled protection.

Sanctuary wraps me in its protective bubble, allowing me to bounce along the hull and tear it up. Dornalor angled our forward momentum and my own exit such that when I hit the ship, I'm at an angled collision course, allowing me to skip along the hull for a few bounces before the angles become too great. That's when I turn off Sanctuary, an act that leaves me with a headache and a new notification.

Sanctuary Skill Forcibly Canceled Before Duration Expires
Mana feedback from forced cancellation affecting all Skills in Skill branch.
Effect: -16% effectiveness of Skills in Skill branch. Sanctuary Skill unable to be used for 1 hour 27 minutes and 31 seconds.

"Arse," I snarl.

Not that I have that much time to be cursing as I trigger my suit's external thrusters, doing the best I can to bleed off the momentum and put me back on a direct crash course with the Dimensional Smoother. Our initial hope was that the combined velocities and my Sanctuary Skill would allow me to burrow directly into the ship. After all, mundane metal isn't meant to handle high speed impacts against an unyielding surface. Not when the force shields are down anyway. What we didn't expect was the damn hull to be hardened to a ridiculous degree by a Skill.

My new suit is put through its paces as I dodge the occasional point defense system targeting me. The few shots I don't manage to dodge are absorbed by my Soul Shield, which takes it all like the champ it is. Beneath that, I've got the suit's own force shield, but I'd prefer to not use that till I have to. Like Sabre's old force shield, it just isn't up to spec.

On the other hand, I find a new use for the On the Edge Skill as it seems to interact with my suit's maneuvering thrusters very well. Doesn't let me escape the incoming fighters that have decided that the fat, slow—relatively speaking—suit is easy pickings. I dissuade them with a few well-placed Blade Strikes on their first pass, more from surprise than any actual threat. While they turn around, I trigger Mirror Shade to confuse the group while the Improved Invisibility spell takes me most of the way to the Smoother itself. Unfortunately, being right on top of the Dimensional Smoother has locked down even short-range teleportation like Blink Step.

Even as I glide toward the Smoother, I can see how the initial impetus from our attack is slowing down, the pirate ships forced back as the military grade vessels pound away at the vessels. We might have numbers and enthusiasm, but they've got professionalism and mass. Each battleship is about ten times the size of a destroyer and, unlike the pirate ships, is packed full of weaponry. They don't waste space on silly things like cargo spaces or personal swimming pools.

"Stop playing around," Bolo snarls, his voice ringing in my ears. He blows past me by standing on a flat, wing-shaped board, no longer bothering to use his boot thrusters. As he does so, he swings his hammer, letting the handle grow in length so that he smashes aside an unsuspecting humanoid suit that was in the way.

"What is that? And how come you didn't use it before?" I say.

"Some of us plan for the future."

"I do too!" I snap.

I lose sight of the world as a beam weapon targets me, driving away my ability to see. Realizing that my invisibility spell is no longer working, I throw Blade Strikes again. I also add a couple of nasty floating blades to the mix, leaving tiny, almost imperceptible slow-moving mines in our wake. Experience notifications let me know that my little surprises are working.

As we finally reach the Dimensional Smoother and land beside the melted slag of a point defense cannon, I trigger the suit's gravitational boots, locking me to the hull. Bolo doesn't even bother, instead inverting himself so that he's flying upside down at an angle to the hull. Why he does that is explained when he starts swinging that hammer of his, attempting to punch a hole through the hull. Each impact is aided by the boosted acceleration of the space-board, giving each swing additional velocity and keeping him in roughly the same position.

"Where's Mikito?" I ask, scanning my minimap for the woman. The sheer volume of dots on my map is distracting, so I drop everything but my party members and nearby threats, only to find nothing. Dread runs through me, though I note she's still alive in the party screen. As is Harry, but that's no surprise. He's still on the station.

"In the ship," Bolo grunts between swings. "She dropped her pod before hitting and used her weapon to punch through. Craziest thing I've seen since Sif day."

Before I can ask, a trio of guests arrive. Two from a recessed access hatch that we missed and a third from space, literally dropping from the sky and splatting onto the hull. The third looks like nothing more than a giant space booger thrown by a Galactic giant. The blob-like creature reforms its body into a multi-tentacled, multi-legged creature, discarding the trio of thrusters it had subsumed within its body, allowing the thrusters to float off into space.

"Oh, that's just disgusting." While complaining, I'm casting a fireball spell at the creature before realizing that won't work. No oxygen out here.

Cursing my ineptitude, I watch as attacks from the pair of attackers lash out at me. Annoyed, I overreact and call forth a Beacon of the Angels. I bathe Space Booger in the area effect attack while forcing the other two to wait out the attack or move around it.

"Keep them occupied. I'm nearly through!" Bolo snaps at me.

"Yeah, yeah." As if I needed an oversized muscle-bound idiot to tell me what to do. Conjuring my swords, I crouch and get ready to dance.

***

Two minutes later, the living metal that made it so hard to punch through the hull in the first place closes off the gaping hole we just tumbled through. Air rushes back in as the environmental system returns oxygen and heated air to the corridor. As I stand, shaking off the gunk clinging to me, Bolo is edging away from the flung particulates.

"Oh, stop being a baby." I debate taking the few seconds to cast a Cleanse spell, but I've burned through a ton of Mana with Sanctum, the Beacon of the Angels, and my spells. My suit has an autoclean feature on it, so the remains of SB will be taken care of. Eventually.

"That's Slokum fluid you're tossing around. They're known to carry really nasty diseases. Strong enough to overcome even our high constitutions," Bolo says. "And unlike some people, I'm not in a fully sealed suit."

"That's your fault," I say. "Who forgets to dodge a bleeding Chaos mine?"

"You were supposed to take care of things!"

"I was. It wasn't exactly easy fighting three Advanced Classers," I snap back.

"Children. Mikito's dying here. Maybe put the egos away and get moving?" Ali chastises us, forcing me to focus on the updated minimap and the ever-so-helpful blinking yellow arrow down one corridor. In the corner of my vision, I spot how Mikito's health keeps jumping up and down.

It doesn't take us long to get to her. Unlike whatever they did to reinforce the outer hull of the Dimensional Smoother, the inner bulkheads are much more fragile. When Ali's helpful directional light points downward, we tear through the bulkheads in our way. Along the way, Bolo acts like a video game character with the way he continually spins and swings his hammer, ripping holes through the surrounding walls and flooring. If we were concerned about being subtle, we'd be putting a giant, neon flashing damage report sign above our heads. But as we aren't, extra damage is a good thing. I add to the confusion by liberally tossing grenades behind us like a hyperactive kitten in a box of packing peanuts. Every bit of damage we do makes it harder for the Smoother to function.

When we do reach Mikito, we're two-thirds of the way to the secondary engine chamber. It's also here where we find the cause for the lack of opposition. Down a ten-foot-wide corridor, Mikito's being swarmed by security drones, the robots crawling along the floor, the walls, and even the ceiling in their attempts to finish the Samurai. Ali's floating beside her, just outside the range of her naginata, tossing lightning that jumps between assailants in his best attempt at backing her up. Most of the drones are two-legged, with a pair of smaller limbs near the hip that they use for either running or firing weapons while the upper two arms are just hands with sharp blades. A quick glance gives me their unimpressive stats.

Tier II Security Drones

Durability: 89/137

Abilities: Networked AI, self-repair, Link of Omniscience

In the pause while I take in the scene, three things happen. First, Mikito manages to destroy another three drones; second, four drone parts manage to pull themselves close enough to form up and weld themselves together; and lastly, Bolo rushes right past me, turning himself into a flipping hammer of doom. He hits the corridor at an angle, tearing upward and sideways so that he misses Mikito and nearly clips Ali while clearing the corpses of the drones. Each drone corpse that he hits is imbued with additional energy that explodes and showers all of us with molten metal.

"What the hell is that about?" I snarl.

A part of me wonders where the various Sect members are, but the rest of me is rushing down the corridor. The metal gunk slides right off my Soul Shield, but I'm not a fan of friendly fire. Since Bolo cleared one side, I take the other and open up a pathway with a simple Metal Wall spell, sending a tsunami of moving metal to clear the deck.

"They're golems," Bolo explains as he drops down from the upper deck where he ended up after his little display. "Mechanical golems, but golems nonetheless. So long as whoever is controlling them has Mana, they'll keep reforming."

"But not anymore." I finish his thought, eyeing the pile of drone parts I shoved aside. Even now, I can see how parts of them are moving, my actions having put some pieces closer to one another. For a moment, I consider calling forth a Beacon of the Angels, wasteful as it might be. But between having to teleport the attack all the way in, the weird interference effect the hull has on Skills, and the size of my attack, I give it a miss. Instead, I switch to the simpler

Inferno Strike spell, hosing the entire area in flames and destroying the enchanted circuitry.

"How much Mana do you have?" Bolo says after a minute of my blasting, the Dragon Lord leaning against the shaft of his hammer.

With the way I'm baking the entrance, none of the drone golems are successfully forming. Even the newcomers are coming apart before they can reach us, giving Mikito a break to recharge and regenerate.

"Not enough to keep this up forever," I mutter.

In fact, eyeing my Mana, I'm down to less than a third. As an Erethran Guard, I have a higher base Intelligence score than a Dragon Knight, but Bolo has dedicated more of his free attributes to Intelligence, giving him a much higher Mana pool. But unlike him, I've dedicated a large amount of my attributes to Willpower. That keeps my Mana regeneration high, unlike Bolo, who relies on his passives. So when casting a low Mana cost per minute spell like this, I can keep it going much longer than Bolo can. That said, whoever is controlling the golems doesn't seem to be running out either.

"They're sharing the Mana cost. Security room, Mana drain consoles, and a single Golemancer would do the trick. Powerful, but single point of failure," Ali reports back, having done some scanning of his own.

"Can we get to it?"

As if to answer my question, Bolo holds up his hammer, shrinking down the handle a little. "No more time. I'm going to punch us a way through."

Bolo releases the hammer in an underhand throw, the hammer itself enlarging as it flies down the corridor. By the time it disappears into the orange-red flame of my handheld flamethrower spell, it covers half the corridor. I kill the spell, but I'm nowhere near as fast as Mikito, who has taken off behind the hammer.

"Hey, Leeroy, slow down!"

I run after the Samurai, wondering if this is how it feels to deal with me. A lot of my tactics follow old-school SWAT tactics that I'd read about after initial breach—move and keep moving. Once you have them on the backfoot, you want to keep going.

Bolo follows, using gauntleted fists to punch through the few drones that manage to get themselves in his way. It must be quite a sight, Bolo in his medieval plate and scale armor, ornate helmeted headdress and gauntleted fist, running alongside me in my high-tech powered armor and sword while he punches out the lights of semi-sentient droids. In the lead, Mikito comes to a halt, her jaw dropping as she stares at the creature holding the T-intersection.

"I thought it was too easy," I say, skidding to a halt beside Mikito.

The creature before us looks like a giant squid, floating in midair off gravitic propulsors. Its tentacles are wrapped around the hilt and body of Bolo's hammer, slowly rotating the entire thing around to face us. Against the floor, I spot multiple crushed tentacles slowly reforming and flowing back toward the squidroid, making the entire thing look like an advanced version of the T-1000.

"Interesting. It's not a Master Work, but it's strong enough to block my attacks," Bolo says, eyes roving over the creature. "It seems unfinished."

"You call that unfinished?" I protest.

In reply, Bolo raises his hand and calls his hammer back, tearing off tentacles that attempt to stop the Skill activation. The numerous tentacles begin their slow squirm back while Bolo catches his hammer in one hand. If not for the fact that his Mana took a noticeable drop, I'd never have guessed that the simple-seeming action actually required a significant investment.

"At a guess, boy-o, it's someone's advancement Quest item," Ali says. All around the squidroid, blue outlines appear, most of them no larger than my hand. Even as I spot them, they shift and morph. "Those portions are not using the liquid-metal. If you can hit them, you'd be able to do real damage."

"Fire then?"

"Won't work," Mikito says. "The metal is resistant to heat, cold, and most other elements. Area effect attacks will be blocked by the tentacles, unless you can fill the entire corridor. And even then…"

One of Mikito's advantages is that all the time in the arena means her breadth of knowledge in fighting has grown wider than mine. It's why when she corrects me, I don't even try to argue. So unless I can cover the entire area—and that mostly means a Firestorm or Beacon of the Angels—dealing with the squid might take even more time.

"Great. Suggestions? Also, why isn't it attacking us?" I say.

"Behind us," Bolo replies, turning his head at the same time. "The golem drones are reforming and gathering. And I have view of multiple other sentients incoming."

"Delay tactics."

There are ways to clear the corridor, if I really wanted to. Army of One would destroy and clear the squidroid and at least a few walls behind it. Not the main defensive wall around the engine room though—those, for obvious reasons, are significantly plated. Worse…

"If you haven't noticed, the fight outside is getting worse. The battlecruisers weren't able to take out the other Dimensional Smoother," Bolo says. The Dragon Lord seems to be able to keep track of what is going on, unlike me.

"Thousand Hells." I swing my blade a few times, sending a couple of Blade Strikes as a warning to the drone golems that continue to try to creep up from behind.

The squidroid continues to stare at us, unmoving and patient.

"Plan needs two down," I say. We could still win this. Problem is, they haven't used any of their Advanced Classes or any other hidden tricks. If we burn all our Mana getting past the distractions, we're vulnerable to whatever traps they have within. Even if there aren't, we still need to get off this ship. "Can we do it with one down?"

"Not a chance." Bolo hefts his hammer and swings it upward.

It extends, punching through the floor above and the one after that. The Dragon Lord looks upward then lets out a roar as he swings the hammer down, tearing through a few more metal struts as he impacts our own deck. And keeps going. He punches through about four before it stops.

The hammer is already shrinking to its normal size as Bolo reaches the edge of the hole. The Dragon Lord is fast, making a decision to not continue the mission that quickly. "Coming?"

Bolo drops, not bothering to wait for my answer.

"Go, John," Mikito says, stepping forward to fend off the tentacles that have suddenly woken up and are trying to tear us apart.

"Mikito—"

"I serve."

I want to argue, but Bolo's hole is closing. Rather than waste more time, I jump down, falling through all six floors before we impact the hull. In the time I took to argue with Mikito, Bolo seems to have torn through to the hull, where he's busy attempting to dent it and make our way out.

"You going to help?"

"One second." I look up, waiting for Mikito's falling form. As the hole begins to close further, I throw a series of Blade Strikes at the opposite end of the hole from her form to ensure she's still got a way to drop.

Long seconds pass before the Samurai finally drops down toward us, closely followed by the drone-golems and a slew of metallic-silver moving tentacles. In the minimap, Ali's adding a whole bunch of other red dots for our living opponents. Seems like they're done stalling.

It'd be rude to not greet our guests, so I waste a bunch of Mana by calling down a Beacon of the Angels, letting it originate a floor above where we were and come all the way to us.

A magnificent sight, the blinding white, searing mass of energy that boils skin, melts metal, and crisps enchanted cloth. The security personnel manage to mostly dodge the blast, unlike the metal droids. The attack tears through the struts, hammering the hull on this side, and catching all of us in the blast radius as well. My Soul Shield cracks, as does my armor's shield and the contingency ring's. The armor does its bit to reduce the damage even as I cook myself. Mikito's fought with me long enough to know what was coming and is crouched low, using a last-ditch protective shell enchantment to keep the damage off her.

Under the effects of my attack, Bolo is enraged even further. He swings so hard that he punches through the damaged hull plating, blasting us and our surviving assailants into space as explosive decompression takes effect. Sadly, squidroid doesn't come with us. My last glimpse of the monster droid is it gripping the edges of the tear with its tentacles. In the midst of us shooting away from the Dimensional Smoother and into the waiting arms of Dornalor as he swoops in, I can hear Bolo's shouts.

"Dragon's tooth! You're insane, Paladin!"

What was the joke? If it's insane and it works, it's not really insanity?

***

Once we break away from the firing range of the Smoother and battleships, things get a lot less hectic. I let myself drop out of the weaponry console, rubbing the back of my neck in pain as my overheated neural link sends shards of electronic pain straight into my brain. Even my increased pain resistance is doing little to stop it from aching, which gives you an idea about how bad it is.

"That should be it," Dornalor says. "The AI should be able to handle the rest of the shots."

I grunt, shaking my head in amusement. One thing I've learnt over the past few years is that what they call AIs aren't exactly that—it's a bad translation because we don't have the right word for it. Most AIs—not counting the X-23s and others of their ilk—aren't really sentient. They have extremely sophisticated base programs and a bunch of fuzzy-logic learning programs, allowing them to tackle unique problems and yes, grow. KIM, my ex-settlement AI, is a great example of that kind of program—powerful, but limited by programming. Given enough time and resources, KIM could gain actual sentience, but the mechanics of it under the System requires her to inhabit a specific type of body to do so. No jumping from System settlement core to the next, she actually needs a specific kind of core. For all that, her ability to emulate sentience can trick most of us.

Perhaps one of the biggest differences between a non-sentient, or limited, AI and a fully enabled one is the use of Mana. The X-23s, fully powered sentient AIs, and their like have a Mana pool. Droids, no matter how powerful, are unable to access Mana. They might be System-registered, but they have no Mana pool. Once a program gains full sentience, they gain a Mana pool. Or perhaps it's vice versa—the ability to have a Mana pool allows these AIs to become fully sentient.

In either case, there's still discussion about the morality and the issue of free will among AIs. That these programs are constrained to serve, even that certain types of information or knowledge is barred to them by the System and their programming, is a cause for concern among certain Galactics. It's a discussion that has on occasion gotten violent, especially when the Systemers get involved. To the Systemers, since the AIs aren't System-registered—in the sense that they've got full status sheets—they obviously can't be sentient. And, not surprisingly for a Galactic-wide religion, there are certain fanatical groups who will enforce their beliefs. Right now, we're at the point where the cultural swing leans toward the fact that limited-AIs aren't really sentient and thus aren't really slaves. They have no soul to feel hurt by being constrained by programming or the System.

Still, I can't help but worry about it. Maybe it's one too many bad sci-fi movies, but it's why I haven't picked up a personal AI of my own. Even if, in certain areas, they're much more useful than my lazy-ass Spirit.

"Shields are recharged enough," I say in agreement, cracking my neck again in a vain attempt to make my head stop hurting. "Sorry about the rear cannons."

"I'd rather lose them than the ship," Dornalor says. "That was an appropriate time to pull out the stops."

I chuckle, recalling the swarm of fighters that arrived once we broke far enough away from the Dimensional Smoother. They were surprised when our point defenses suddenly managed to reach them, burning away their thrusters and sending many of them to the scrap heap. After that, I'd used everything I could to keep the ship in one piece as we fled. Even then, the ship's more damaged than when we first arrived.

"Now what?" I say, eyeing the glowing damage reports that crisscross the board. From an internal camera, I watch as Bolo stomps back into the ship, returning from his excursion to the top where he'd been tossing his hammer around like a living wrecking ball.

"We go back, get this fixed. Let the Politicians do their thing, drag in more people. And we do it again, except this time, we come back with most everyone," Dornalor says, shaking his head. "They should have done that the first time."

"But no one wants to get their ship shot up." I shake my head at how selfish most sentients were. Oh, there are exceptions—exceptional races even. Though most of those races never went far from their home planets. Being entirely communal and unselfish has a tendency to backfire on you, especially when the Galaxy is out to get you. "Regretting not running?"

Dornalor shakes his head. "And get banned from Spaks? No thanks. It's our station of last resort around here. We lose it, and life gets infinitely harder."

I can't help but nod. Having lived on the murky grey line between the rebels and proper Galactic society, I can see his point. At least we can still land on Galactic planets, get our stuff, and go. Those with Reputation scores or Fame in the high ten thousand negatives have it even harder—finding it nearly impossible to receive any services or work in reputable locations. There are places that will turn a blind eye, and you can always shop at a System Shop, but the System Shop is expensive. And piracy still needs to be profitable to succeed.

"We'll get them the next time." Dornalor's voice is insistent and full of confidence.

Before I can answer, shrill alarms go off all around the ship. Both our heads snap sideways, notifications flooding our views as multiple interstellar translations are picked up. At first it's a couple dozen, then the numbers keep climbing until there are hundreds. Some of the first ships that translate in do so too close to the meteors or wreckage that litters the system, exploding in balls of fire. Others are destroyed by the few remaining mines that have managed to hide their presence from the battleships. But the ships after the first few seem to adjust their translations as the explosions decrease then stop. I kill the damage details, just keeping track of the numbers, watching as more ships translate in outside the Dimensionally Smoothed geography, enveloping us in a wide array of steel.

"Well. That's a problem." And I'm not even sure if it's Dornalor or me who says it.

Chapter 15

By the time we get back to the station, it's pandemonium. No one expected the fleet to arrive so fast—the last information we had was that they were still gathering. Luckily, we manage to dock without issue, whereupon Harry rushes into the ship and seals us off, breathing hard as he wipes away congealing blood on his forehead. The team—sans Dornalor, who's still handling the piloting—is all waiting at the docking hatch, so it's a bit of a surprise to see the harried-looking reporter.

"Problem?" I say, eyeing the closed doors.

"Riots," Harry says. "Everyone's scared, now that the way out is firmly shut. Lots of accusations of incompetence." A loud thud against the docking gate interrupts whatever else Harry is about to say.

A moment later, Dornalor appears in one of the viewing screens, looking grim. "They're hauling up a door buster. Get out there before they damage my ship even more."

Bolo reacts first, walking forward with his hammer held out before him. The docking gates slide open, revealing the rebel who's been punching the doors with a still-raised fist. His eyes widen as he spots Bolo and the fast-moving hammer before he's sent careening back down the corridor, bowling over the rest of the rioters. Bolo lets the hammer drop to the floor, the thump resounding down the enclosed docking gate and silencing the crowd.

"Go. Away. I won't be as gentle next time." Bolo makes the statement entirely too calmly, as if he's talking of building a staircase instead of pummeling a sentient.

The crowd sheepishly backs away, the door cracker stored in someone's inventory to allow for an expeditious retreat. It does raise the question of why they didn't just use the door cracker when we first arrived, but then again, rioting in a space station isn't exactly the action of the rational.

Grunting in appreciation of his own awesomeness, Bolo watches as the docking bay doors slide shut before he sends Harry a glare. "Draco fangs, how did you and the Inner Crew miss the fleet arrival?"

"I don't know." Harry shakes his head. "I've tried everything I can think of to parse the information, but all my sources, from the Shop to indirect feeds and foodie reports, show that the fleet is still back in Dexaz IV. Hell, I have a live running feed of one of the captain's, a well-known foodie blogger, 'live streaming' his latest meal at Koos!"

"I'm going to assume that's meant to mean something," I say.

"Philistine. Koos is the preeminent restaurant on Dexaz IV. Their live butchering and cooking of harpy meat by Master Chef Qased is considered a highlight of any foodie's life," Ali replies. "If even Olson over there can't figure out what's going on, it's got to be a disinformation campaign."

"Like the paper tanks in England?" Mikito says, cocking her head.

"Much like that. Except on a much larger scale. I'd say there's got to be at least a few Master Class Spies or Disinformation Specialists at play. Maybe a Heroic …" Ali turns to stare at Bolo.

The Dragon Lord returns the look blankly before his eyes widen. "No. Impossible. She has no reason to do it."

"That we know of. Who can read her mind?"

"For the humans here, care to expand?" I say, stomping my foot.

"No. I really don't," Ali says. When I glare, he holds up a hand. "We don't say her name. Or her nicknames. Or anything else that might trigger her attention. I've already said enough. If it is her, you'll know soon enough. And if it isn't—"

"We don't want her attention," Bolo finishes flatly.

I stare at the pair, my jaw working for a moment in frustration before I drop the question. Bolo has never looked terrified before, but I see the fear lurking in his eyes. Even Ali, the Spirit who barely cares about the material world because it can't really affect him, looks worried. Whoever this lady is, she's not someone I want to annoy just for my curiosity.

"Anyway, it might not be her. There are a few organizations—including the Erethrans—who could pull this off. A concerted effort by one of their disinformation departments could occlude and create the false narratives," Ali finishes.

"Occlude. Big word for a small man."

"Goblin shit, John."

I grin, then let the smile fade as another loud thump echoes through the room. I tilt my head, watching the vidscreens and the growing riot outside. "How long do you think this is going to last?"

"About twenty minutes."

"That fast?" Mikito says, frowning.

From our experience, most riots last a little longer than that. In answer, Bolo points at another screen, this one showing the oxygen content on the station. Which I realize is fast dropping.

"That's one way of fixing the issue," I say. Vicious and effective. With the System's healing factor, only those at the lowest levels of Constitution would die. And only if they don't run off to whatever emergency chambers there are. Which, I'm hoping, are being controlled by Oi and his men.

With nothing better to do, we find chairs and relax, keeping an eye on the door. As I wait, I pull out a piece of chocolate and consider the enemy fleet's next play. They could come in hot. With AIs working to reorient everyone and fill in gaps from the destruction, the fleet should be mostly ready to go by now. The next few minutes will answer the question if they are coming immediately or if there's something else they're after.

Once I know what they're doing, then I'll know what my next play should be. Thus far, playing foot soldier has been less effective than I'd hoped. As the velvety chocolate goodness slides down my throat, I pull out the station information, parsing together maps and 3D diagrams of the area. Perhaps it's time to get a little more proactive.

***

It doesn't even take twenty minutes for the riots to end. Through all that, there's nary a peep from the Galactic fleet. They just sit there, waiting and watching us. I barely pay attention to the solar map, my focus on the station plans, the details that I should have learned but ignored. I soak floor plans into my bones—the multiple layers of gated tubes, the fallback positions we'll need to know. I burrow into details about the inner two stations too, pulling everything that's available to me, making Harry pass me every little scrap of information he can find.

I almost ignore the summons when it comes, so immersed am I. But I eventually relent and go to the war room. If nothing else, at least someone there might have a clue as to why the fleet isn't right on us.

The war room is more a seminar room, reminiscent of a lecture hall with arena seating going down to the stage, than a place where the few and the relevant gather. The room itself is three-quarters filled with a wide variety of interested parties. Some are known factors—security personnel and Captains of the largest ships. Others are less immediately useful—Merchants and Smugglers, Craftsman and other Artisans. Oi and I Shao stand at the bottom of the room, flanked by a series of floor-to-ceiling vidscreens.

Bolo stomps to the front of the audience and glares at the couple of Captains and their security crew. They don't even pause before beating a retreat, leaving the seats available for all of us. Harry scurries off to the side, leaving us to the front as he sets up for a better view while avoiding not-so-subtle glares.

"Making friends, are we?" I mutter as I sprawl in a seat beside Bolo.

"They're not friends. Scum and villains, all of them."

"And then you wonder why people are trying to kill you."

"I do not wonder."

"I was being sarcastic, you big idiot."

I find myself falling silent like the rest of the crowd as the screens beside Oi flicker to life. The public faces of the Inner Crew appear on each screen, glowering at us. A flicker, then Ali has their data populated for me. No surprise, but all I get is their damn names. Everything else is greyed out.

Adonael K'mini, System Pinion, Spaks Station Master, Tithed Lord, One in a Million, … (Galactic Station Master Level ???) (H)

Ifd of Clan 42.1, Credits from Dregs, Connected, Slayer of Thurma Parasites, … (System Quartermaster Level ???) (M)

Corellis Solarborn, Dread Pirate Corellis, Ten Most Wanted, Robber Baron, Slayer of Thurma, Selkies, Drimana, … (Robber Baron Level ???) (M)

"Thank you for coming." Corellis the Robber Baron takes center stage. Even through the vidscreens, I can feel the tug on my emotions, the weird interplay that high level Charisma has on the mind and the emotions. It's a nudge, a twist in my tastes so that I'm more inclined to listen to him. But it's also my mental resistances that let me note and understand the affect, while making me clinically wonder exactly how high his Charisma has to be for me to sense it even through screens. "As you know, Spaks is under attack."

"No shit," Bolo mutters, but even he keeps his voice low.

"At this time, we have received a communication from the fleet facing us. They have requested that we transmit this communication to all denizens in the station." The Baron pauses, looking as if he wants to say something else but decides against it.

His image fades away, leaving a blank surface before it flares to life with a new image. The creature that stares at us is a weird, beak-faced, antlered, biped creature. A pair of arms are held behind it, the whole body of the creature covered in a simple touch-tab jumpsuit of primary purple with pink and grey highlights.

Liftom Minora, The Last Stand, Phoenix Arisen, Slayer of Goblins, Space Phantoms, Ghosts, (more), Anointed of the Third Limit (Fleet Admiral, Level 18) (H)

_HP: ???/???_

_MP: ???/???_

Conditions: ???

"Station residents and visitors to Spaks. You are surrounded. We—the fleet before you—are charged with the destruction, capture, and restraint of the station, its occupants, and its managers. To decrease the loss of life, we are offering you a chance to surrender. If you decide to do so, you will be taken into custody and judged based on all current charges laid against you. You will not receive any further charges for the defense or the illegal escape attempt." Liftom pauses. "You will be given six hours to decide your fate and arrive before us. Those who refuse to surrender will be charged as accessories to the defense of a Pirate Station, at the very least. Additional charges will be laid depending on the vigor of your defense and the actions taken during your illegal resistance. Any resistance will be dealt with appropriately and with all reasonable force."

228

The Admiral holds that flat, no-nonsense stare for a tense silence, letting his words hang in the air before his image shudders and disappears. There's a long moment of quiet as everyone takes in what was said before everyone talks at once, some muttering about taking the offer while others are looking into space, staring at their rap sheets. It's amusing, in some ways, but rather depressing in others.

"I'm assuming us giving up is a bad, bad idea," I send to Ali, who snorts.

"Well, you did just try to destroy a multi-billion Credit ship. And have a bounty that states dead, rather than dead or alive."

I laugh grimly, looking at Mikito, who shrugs phlegmatically. When I turn toward Harry, the reporter shakes his head.

"Don't worry about me. I'm a War Reporter. Registered and all."

"Cheater." I shake my head and turn to the last of the group, only to find Bolo looking pensive. A flash of fear then anger runs through me, the anger chasing away the fear. These days, I've realized that some of my anger is misplaced, so I eye it and the fear contemplatively. Technically, Bolo isn't part of the crew, just a hanger-on. But I'll admit, I've gotten used to the big lug. "You coming?"

"Come to where?" Bolo sniffs and looks at the pirates and rebels around us, disdain in his eyes. "Unlike many, I have conducted no wrong in the wider Galactic world. My sins are mine and mine alone."

"In other words, there's nothing keeping you here," I say. "Then why join us on the earlier fight?"

Bolo shrugged. "I was paid. There was a possibility that we could succeed and escape. Now, matters have changed. Continuing to stay here seems foolish, does it not?"

"Depends," I say, gesturing to the now-blank screens.

Oi and I Shao are conversing with their own party, offering words of assurance before the group splits up to allay fears among the crowd.

"On?"

"If you can trust them to keep their word. If you want to continue using the station in the future. If you think the station itself has some use in a world like this." I cock my head, a little heat entering my voice. "If you like being pushed around by a bunch of bullies."

"I'm surprised to hear you standing up for us, Paladin," Oi says as he approaches us. "I had believed you were not a fan of us pirates."

"I'm not," I say. "You guys might not be as bad as our historical pirates, but there's still blood on your hands. But those bastards out there aren't any better than you. Worse even, in some cases. Even if they are, legally, allowed to do what they do."

"What is legal is not necessarily moral," I Shao intones, then sighs. "Still, they are smart."

"You're talking about the pronouncement." When I Shao nods, I let my eyes wander over the crowd. A few sneak out the doors even as Dornalor updates my feed from the ship, letting me know that some ships are already taking off. "Creating dissent within. I do wonder, why didn't the Inner Crew stop it? Are they that certain they can win with what they have left?"

"Hardly," Oi says. "But the Lady of Shadows is in play. And in her field, no one dares to deal with her."

"She's confirmed then?" Ali says.

Harry freezes, holding his whole body still but for his fingers. Those twitch in rapid motion as he calls up screens and data. Dark brows crease, eyes growing more intent as he reads. It's an interesting reaction, made more so when Bolo pales at I Shao's nod of confirmation.

"All right. Someone want to tell me what the hell is going on?" I say grumpily.

"The Lady of Shadows is her unofficial name. No one likes to talk of her, though she is one of the Seated members of the Galactic Council," Oi says, naming one of the nine members of the Inner Council of the Galactic System. Permanent members, the ones who enforce the final, planet-bending rules of the Galactic System and who also, with their decisions, may overrule or create new, lasting guidelines. I looked into what, exactly, they could do once, and found that even the smallest piece of substantiated information was worth the entire net worth of Earth itself.

"Legendary Class?" I ask.

"Probably," Bolo chimes in. "She's the only one who could have hidden the movement of the entire navy by herself. At least, this seamlessly. Other organizations could try, but there are often gaps. And it's why the Crew didn't bother trying to hide the Admiral's speech. If she wanted the announcement known, she would have made sure."

"So why is a Legendary Class messing with us?" I say, waving. "And why now?"

Oi can only shrug, not having any answers himself. "I'm here to invite you—both of you—to the actual war room. It's time for us to discuss what we will do when they attack."

I nod then turn to look at Bolo. The Dragon Lord looks conflicted, unsure of what to do as he stares past the bulkheads toward the waiting fleet.

He hesitates for a long time, but in the end, Bolo lets out a low huff of rueful humor and nods. "I'll come."

I almost want to ask why but decide against it. It could be as easy as an idiosyncratic need to finish what he started—something I do recall the Dragon Lord having showcased in the past. For all his talk of practicality and disdain for the pirates, the Dragon Lord seems quite comfortable here. As we follow Oi, I keep the live feed from Dornalor going, watching as numerous ships leave the outer limits of our shields and enter the waiting arms of our enemies. Weakening us all.

***

"I'm assuming we're letting them go because stopping them would end with us in a fight," I say to I Shao, who's dropped back to speak with us. The Truthteller nods, bare crystal feet ringing off the corridor as we walk. "Any estimates on how many we'd lose?"

"Not my area," I Shao says.

Harry, walking alongside, slips in next to us, eyes still flicking over cameras. I'm a little surprised he's not scrambling to the docks to film the exits. "We've already lost just over three percent of the remaining ships. I have indications of at least another four percent readying themselves, with multiple reports coming in about disturbances, fights, and the like among crews. Overall, we're likely to lose at least ten percent of our fighting strength, maybe up to twenty."

"All that without swinging a hammer," Bolo says admiringly. "The Admiral is smart."

"Might not have been his idea," I say.

We reach the inner chamber, the very same room Oi used to explain the situation to me. Except this time, it's filled with more people, including a number of the more senior Rebel Captains and other personas of note. Dominating the room as normal is the holographic projection, displaying the current situation of the battlefield.

"So what next?" I ask. "They bombard us?"

"Unlikely," one of the Rebel Captains says. "They're not that dumb." At my puzzled look, he continues speaking. "Scenario IV – B."

The projected hologram ripples then resets, and all the moving ships are gone. Now it shows a visibly smaller fleet within the shelter of the station force fields, the fronts of their ships pointed outward. Without any indication, the enemy fleet opens up, an array of railguns and other physical projectiles launched first. Next, missiles are launched after the solid projectiles have made it halfway. Lastly, just before the combined might of the missiles and projectiles hit the first force shield, beam, spell, and particle cannons fire. The hologram washes out as the sheer volume of fire overloads our eyes, just before the program corrects itself. The combined attack ripples across the shield and I watch the shield stability notification as it dips by a good quarter.

Then, something else happens. All along the attacking ships, miniature explosions appear, their own force shields glowing brighter and brighter as they're assaulted. Even as the station shield takes damage from repeated waves of attacks, the ships are assaulted by a hidden force. Before the station's force shield dips below fifty percent, the first ship goes up. Then another and another. By the time the attack lowers the force shield by a third, a quarter of their fleet are gone.

"What the hell is happening?"

"Sentient Payback," the Rebel Captain who answered me says. "We are not defenseless."

"*It's a Heroic Level Skill. Station Lord's. Damage done to the shield is returned at a certain percentage back to attackers.*" Ali helpfully fills me in, making my eyes widen in surprise. Payback Skills like that aren't unknown, but to be able to use it across the entire station is something else entirely. "*Of course, what they're missing is—*"

Another brute snarls, pounding the edge of the hologram with one of his four feet. "Too optimistic. You're forgetting the Admiral's Skill—One for All. Scenario IV – D, results only."

A ripple and the hologram disappears, refreezing as the fifth to third ring external shields disappear, the stations they protected shattered wrecks. Only the Prime Station shield and portions of the second ring stand, but the enemy fleet is in horrible shape. Eighty percent of the ships are destroyed or damaged, unable to continue their bombardment. Even someone as green as me can tell that there's no way he can punch through the remaining shield defenses with so few ships left.

"It doesn't matter. No Admiral is willing to risk losing that many," the first Rebel Captain says. I take a much closer look at him, eyeing the frills, the way he looks, and decide to name him Hornblower. His frills are sort of like horns. And being a Captain. Look, the classics have a place, you know.

"And you're all estimating this based off what we now know. You know the Inner Crew believes that there's much that has been hidden," Oi says, shaking his head. "It's why they fear the Admiral."

"Yeah. He could punch through the first shield with only eleven percent losses with his Skill," Nessos, the four-footed, maned Rebel Captain, replies. "Much lower than anything we had planned for."

"Fighting the Ironwall was never part of our plans," Oi says. "It doesn't matter what we want to happen. We just have to follow the Crew's general plan and do our part."

"Which is?" I cock my head, curious if they have any idea.

"This is the most likely scenario." Oi waves and the hologram ripples.

The entire scenario is a replay of the first scenario, except this time around, the glow around the attackers happens to all the ships at the same time. It seems the Admiral's Skill spreads the damage, meaning that everyone takes an equal portion of the damage being returned, rather than each ship taking the damage they did. Of course, the negative is that there's no way to stop the smallest and weakest ships from going up first.

They keep firing, until our first shield—the fifth ring's external shield—goes down. As expected, they lose just over ten percent of their ships, mostly the smaller ones. Each ship that gets destroyed transfers more damage to the rest of the group, meaning that the biggest and toughest will survive, with the amount of damage increasing as the fight goes on. What surprises me is that fire slackens the moment they take the shield down, the fleet turning their attention to the pirate fleet to duke it out with them. In the meantime, transports appear around the Galactic fleet and head for the fifth ring stations.

"Why are they bothering taking the fifth ring stations?"

"Rising Crescendo," Ali sends back to me. The Spirit's been reading the battle plans while I've been talking, bulking on the System data that's been transmitted and held in this room.

In place of a longer explanation, Ali sends me a notification.

Rising Crescendo (Evolved)

All stories must have appropriate buildup. Rising Crescendo ensures that the correct storytelling convention is provided to any story, forcing participants in the tale to follow the tale to its conclusion in an orderly, well-paced fashion. Poet may not designate himself as a plot point.

Effect: Poet may designate a story point that must be completed before the story may progress. Inappropriately difficult, wide-ranging, and thematically wrong plot points may be rejected or cost the Poet additional Mana.

Minimum Cost: Each designated plot point will cost Poet one eighth to one tenth of his total Mana pool per day while active. Poet may not move while using this Skill and must record the story in Poet's designated medium.

Cost: (Variable)

"Isn't that a little broken?" Even at a glance, I can tell that this looks like something anyone with half a brain could abuse. Of course, some Master Class Skills are like that, especially when they've been Evolved. It does tell me a few things though, including the fact that there's a 'Poet' in play.

"Sort of? It's an Evolved Skill, so it's a bit more wide ranging than most," Ali says. *"But while the Poet can designate the plot points, he can't do anything else. A good Assassin could take him down while he has the Skill active. Also, note that the Skill is a little vague on when it can reject a plot point."*

Still seems broken to me. The Skill notification disappears to be replaced by the specific epic that is in play—in this case, the need for the invasion force to go through each station the same way that we did. Which explains the ships that are incoming, ready to dock and drop off their people.

When the ships dock, the hologram stops and Oi walks through it, looking around at the gathered group. "We do not expect to hold the fifth ring. In fact, station masters on the fifth ring are currently readying retreat options and coordinating with those of us on the fourth ring."

"We blowing the station after they leave?" Hornblower says, appropriately.

"No. The Poet's ability forces us to leave them untouched. And don't even think about pushing through the plot blocks. I know some of you"—Oi's gaze fixes on me—"can do so. But the feedback would set us back further. We need to bleed them as they come in."

"How many rings are we going to lose?" Nessos asks, stamping his foot in impatience.

Clustered around him, just like the people around Hornblower and Oi, are other rebels who aren't powerful or confident enough to speak up. Or, perhaps, just willing to let the big mouths ask the questions we're all thinking.

"Unknown." Oi holds up a hand, stalling Nessos from speaking so that he can continue without interruption. "Best-case scenario, based off current, known forces—we beat them in the third ring."

"And worst case?"

"We lose," Bolo says with a snort. "That's the worst case, isn't it?"

"How about a survivable worst case?"

"Then, probably, we'll be fighting on Station Prime." Oi shakes his head. "Details like that are held by the Inner Crew. It is unlikely the Mistress will take any further hand in things, but with her in play, there's no guarantee that any of our plans or secrets are still hidden. We can only hope that they have underestimated our strength.

"Now, if those are all the questions, we have a lot of work to do. Even if they know what we intend to do, we still need you to know your places."

There's a lot of muted grumbling, but the rebels and pirates settle down. Over the next couple of hours, Oi goes over the myriad battle plans and contingencies, making sure everyone knows their places and what they need to do at each position. There's not a lot of subtlety here, not when the route in and out is railroaded through. Still, I have to admit, the use of the Poet's Skill means that we don't have the navy standing away and bombarding us to death, or for that matter, burning through the shields and dropping into the inner stations. Now we just need to stop them, one ring at a time.

Chapter 16

With two hours left on the Admiral's timeline, I find myself with little else to do. Dornalor has the ship in dock for repair by the remaining Mechanics and Shipwrights who haven't abandoned the station. Many have taken the navy's offer, showing how effective the little pronouncement was. Amusingly enough, some of the ship captains have even started a small side business of ferrying civilians to the navy, dumping them into the waiting hands of the Galactic fleet before turning around to pick up the next load. All for a fee, of course. Lucky for Dornalor, the majority of the Gremlin tribe we're working with has stayed, unperturbed by the idea of being caught. I have a feeling they've got their own way of hiding out if things go to hell.

Ever since our failed attack, there's been a relaxation on the restrictions for movement within the rings. In fact, the vast majority of the non-combat personnel have taken one of two routes—they've either chosen to give themselves up to the fleet or they're moving deeper into the stations. No one expects the fifth ring to hold, so most people are moving in as deep as possible. Luckily, it seems that there's enough space for the refugees to hunker down in the fourth ring, at least temporarily.

"Taking bets, taking bets. Five thousand to one, fourth ring survival. Thirty-two to one, third ring. Twelve to one, second ring." The Bookie's voice cuts through my contemplation as I wander the hallways aimlessly, unsure of what I'll do.

Ever since the emergency, they've relaxed the restrictions on Portals too, which means I can port into my position at any time, even across the shielding rings. It's where most of the others are, but I couldn't handle staying still. Which has brought me here, walking aimlessly from station to station.

"No odds on the fifth ring?" a bettor asks, and I slow down to listen, much like many others.

"No bets."

"And what about if we lose? I got five hundred Credits on that," a rough-looking humanoid with a horn that juts out from its forehead like a unicorn asks, the blue horn a jarring contrast to the creature's salmon-pink skin. There are a few hisses at his words, but Salmon Unicorn doesn't back down.

"We've got… one to eighteen on that. Payout via the System, if you win." The Bookie answers the question that comes after, assuring the winner he'll get his earnings no matter.

The reply garners more than a few hisses and catcalls, before there's a huge clamor as the crowd lays bets. It amuses me a little that the Galactics are willing to lay bets on their own destruction. On the other hand…

"*Can you place a bet?*" I send the question to Ali, not wanting to push through the group.

He's a little slow in answering, eyes glazed as he reviews data. "*No problem. What are you thinking?*"

"*No point betting on our losses. We won't be alive to take the dough. Widespread bet that we'll make it through. Third to fifth ring and overall survival.*"

"*Done. Though I'm thinking we should be considering escape plans. I'm not a big fan of going down with the ship.*"

"*Love to. Got any ideas? We need a ship, and ours is broken. Even when it does get fixed, there's no way we can break through, not right now. One problem with Rising Crescendo is it means the majority of the fleet will be around.*"

One of the negatives of the Skill is that we can't stop them from rushing through the stations. Once they land, we have to let them keep coming—otherwise, Rising Crescendo fails. It's one of the drawbacks of the Skill, but it does at least mean we don't have to worry as much about the idea of them punching through our Dimensional Locks and teleporting the entire fleet into the inner station.

It amuses me, in a way, how the interactions of Skills, technology, and Classes intersect. For every Skill, every ability in play, there's another one that checks it. Dimensional Rifts force open Dimensional Locks, which are then checkmated by Rising Crescendo. Suspect Navigation on the navy's part has made a number of very expensive portals and rifts that have been torn open through the Galactic fleet's Locks sent off-course, driving people into the waiting hands of other parties. Even the rats who ran from the sinking ship early on have reported in that they've been ambushed, smaller destroyer squadrons sent to hunt them down.

"No escape now, but not to say there won't be a chance later," Ali retorts. *"We should be ready if it crops up."*

I grunt, rubbing my temples before pushing through the crowd. *"Yeah, yeah. Think we should make a call?"*

"To who?"

"Whom. And our Erethran friends."

Ali falls silent. If there's a group that has the ability to punch through the Dimensional Locks on both sides, it'd be them. My Portal Skill isn't Evolved, something I occasionally regret. Except, of course, there's no guarantee on what kind of Evolution I would have gotten. Reading about the Erethran Guard, I learned the Honor Guard specialists in Portal Evolution have a wide range of abilities, from Extra Long Range Portals, Instantaneous Teleportation, Group Portal Shift, Semi-Permanent Portals, and of import, Lock Break. Using the Erethran General's Skill to combine Skills, they should be able to punch through. The question, of course, is whether they're willing to do so for me.

"Now?" he asks.

I consider the question and shake my head. Any contact we make now is likely to be intercepted, potentially even blocked or altered. Better to wait until things start up and this Mistress gets busy. If she's even paying attention. I admit, the introduction of a Legendary Level character to this entire thing is a bit concerning. I have no idea what she's after, but it sucks. It's been a while since I've felt like a bug in the Galactic world and I'm not liking the feeling.

"Figured. I'll set something up, just in case then. I have a few other ideas."

I raise an eyebrow and Ali flashes me a grin. There's one other possibility, before things go to hell, and it might make sense to look into it. It's not something that can be hidden, but perhaps having a few other options might make sense. Having decided on what I need to do, I shift direction, heading for the nearest Shop sphere while Ali goes to set up potential escape routes too.

***

"Your request is possible. Even in the timeframe you've requested," Foxy says, staring at the QSM he holds. "Adding a Tier I Mana Battery and adjusting the limiters is a simple fix. Tuning the QSM to work with your Portal Skill is difficult, but not impossible. But…"

"But?"

"This is a one-use option. Your Quantum State Manipulator was never built to handle being overloaded like this," Foxy says. "In addition, you should understand, the cost of the QSM has gone up significantly since our last discussion. The addition of your Earth has brought about a shift in the Galactic sphere whose ripples have only just begun to reach the edges of our domain."

"Meaning?"

"A lot of grudges are being settled."

I snort, then tap the QSM in Foxy's hands. "And people are picking up anti-personnel toys?"

"Yes. Purchases of Dimensional Locking Skills have increased, along with Skills that allow others to damage those partially shifted and the like. You humans have been quite creative with your mixture of Classes, Skills, and the way you've used your Skills. We're seeing a shift in the standard Skill purchases, especially among our clientele."

That's an interesting nugget of information. The meta build constantly shifts among the Galactics, with some Skills and abilities being more in vogue at one time compared to another. It's sort of like a giant game of *Magic the Gathering*—where all the Skills that can be the "deck winning" combination are always in play, just perhaps unknown or ignored. For a time, Dimensional Shifting was important, until Dimensional Locks were common. High Constitution, high resistance builds were powerful until poison and resistance-turning Skills came along to counter those. And so on, so forth. Add in Evolution Skills, and there's no such thing as a perfect build. It's why I like having a generic build. It means I'm not the best, but unless I'm fighting other Master Classes, I'm more than strong enough to win.

"Interesting. Have data for that?"

Foxy shakes his head. "It would be unethical to sell such information ourselves." When I smile, Foxy continues. "I would not look into purchasing our data either—we have taken precautions against that. In any case, while we are of significant import, we have always catered to a smaller clientele base than our other competitors."

"Thank you." I get the point. Instead of buying individual information, pick up the overall data trends from the System. In fact, I bet someone out there is already doing that and selling his analysis of the raw data. "But all that said, do it."

"You will not require this during the battle?"

"Nah, the next dance should be easy-peasy."

Foxy raises a single eyebrow, which, on a fox, is a weird thing to see. I chuckle at his suspicious look but ignore it.

"Anything else then, sir?"

Instead of answering him, I pop open my Status Screen. After our battle, even though we hadn't managed to complete our mission, we did get rather involved in the fight, especially toward the end when I had fun with our ship weaponry. The additional experience—mostly from the Leviathan kill earlier— has given me a new Level. Ever since I hit Level 30, my Leveling speed has slowed down significantly. Of course, compared to actual Master Classers, I'm still blazing fast, but compared to the improvements I'd seen as an Advanced Class before, this is achingly slow. Still, I have a few decisions that need making, including what to do with my new Skill points.

Thus far, I dumped the last Skill point into Penetration, and this new one was going that same way. It should put me close to my Skill evolution— theoretically. Before I decided on this, I'd actually seen a Skill Actuary. The man took in the details of my publicly available Skill use and history, pulling down my entire status screen and inputting that against the variables he and his company had created to measure against the known variations of evolutions. Theoretically, using all the information available, the Actuary can then provide a best guess estimate of what you're likely to get as a Skill evolution and how many Skill points you need. Unlike Class Actuaries, Skill Actuaries are more common since they're the Basic Class version of the same progression tree.

There are, of course, other fellows who do much the same thing—among the choices I'd seen were Witch Doctors, Rune Readers, Cosmic Data Sensors, and the like. A few hardcore groups espoused the advantages of each group over the other, but one thing I'd learned from all my reading is this—no one really knows. See, the System doesn't do time fuckery. It might provide forecasts, but those are often drawn from data sets developed by AIs,

Actuaries, or other Classes using their abilities. The System itself doesn't make estimates. In many ways, that piece of information puts quite a bit of weight behind the idea that the System isn't alive per se, but a machine. Or just really alien, like the Koo'ara who can only live in one of three states—the past, the future, and the present. Yes, they're very, very weird.

Anyway, the point is that the estimate I received was that I should see an evolution at nine Class Skill points. The most likely evolution path—at 43.87%—would be the simplest, a more powerful Penetration ability that sent a portion of the damage through, no matter the defense. The second most likely option—at 37.34%—was a corrosive Penetrative effect, one that basically did damage over time to the defense.

All this information is great and all, and if it's true, it puts me real close to seeing a more powerful Penetrative Skill. Unfortunately, between what the Rune Reader et al were up to and the fact that the Actuary had a very small dataset to pull from—and one that was particularly homogenous, unlike myself—there's a 62.183% chance that the evolution I'll actually see is nothing like what they've recommended.

When you've got a small sample size and the majority of those have decided to do quite similar builds, the unexpected nature of the evolutions is a risk. But it's still better than nothing, which is pretty much what I received from the Classes that looked toward the future. They'd just stared at me and shook their heads, muttering something about clouded futures. A little digging brought up the fact that this was happening all over the damn Galaxy as the introduction of a Dungeon World made forecasts for the future extremely turbulent. Adding a large number of fast Leveling Classes to the Galaxy has a tendency to do that. Of course, some people believe that part of the reason they have problems predicting the future is due to the conflicting information sources provided to them via Classes who don't want the future to be known and the System's own, intrinsic inability to tell the future.

All of that is to say, I might or might not get a Skill Evolution the next time I throw a point in. Which is part of the reason I've been holding off till I have a few hours of uninterrupted and safe time. Like now.

But before I do that, the biggest thing I want to do is figure out what to do about my attributes. While the new Penetration evolution could provide me a huge Skill-up, allowing me to do some real nasty damage, I've also recently received a rather clear indication that my lack of specialization is making me lag behind some of the other Master Classes. Oh, when I know what I'm in for or if I'm fighting non-prestige Classes, my attribute points are close enough that I can hold my own. But against someone like Bolo—the one-percenters— I'm coming up short. Not only have the majority of individuals with those Classes received the benefit of a lot of training through their progression, they've also gotten advice and, often, the luxury of specializing.

It's frustrating that I've not been able to specialize. Oh, it's true that I've chosen to not do so. I've spread my Skill points around a little more than I should, trying to do a little bit of everything. If I wasn't such a surly bastard, I could have worked with others, made sure I had people to back me up, protect my back. Even now, my party leans toward a hell of a lot of "punch you in the face" and not a lot of flexibility outside of that. It's not as if we have a Drone Commander, able to build and command thousands of mechanical drones, or a dedicated Elementalist, able to conjure demons from another plane. Or a Necro Lord. Never mind that one. I hate Necro Lords. Who thinks it's a good idea to hang around rotting bodies all day?

But I could have made different choices. Been better. Yet all that regret is kind of wasted effort. Humanity has this amazing ability to play "what if," as if the best option would have played out every time. Yet we don't know that. In fact, it's just as likely that something worse could have happened. I don't know how many times I've survived by the skin of my teeth in a fight because I had the Body's Resolve. Or because I had an extra point in my Soul Shield. I've saved lives with Sanctum, and I've kept my allies alive by sharing the pain with them. I've located people with Greater Detection that, these days, are high contributing members of society and others who are much better off not part of it.

That's life, really. We can go "what if" all we want, but it's worth remembering that things could have been a lot worse. Perhaps not immediately, not in the way you'd think, but down the road, fortune could easily turn. Fate is fickle and not to be trifled with.

Still, I'm human and that frustration is real. All I can do is make the best of what I can now and use what Credits I have to shore up my weaknesses, knowing that people like Bolo will always be a step ahead. That's kind of okay, since I have an advantage he'll never have—I know what it's like to really struggle, to be down to the last few health points, bleeding and wheezing, nerves on fire, and still not be willing to give up.

Foxy coughs, pulling me back from my thoughts. "Redeemer?"

"Sorry. Just thinking. Contemplating my attribute allocation."

"Ah, you have a mixed direct combat and magic build, do you not?"

"I do. I can hit most things I swing at, but I've got a relatively high Intelligence and decent regen." In fact, the majority of Galactics dump a significant portion of their free attributes into Intelligence, even when it's not part of their Class stat allocation, since a large number of Skills and spells require Mana. Can't do much if you have no Mana to feed the Skills.

It's another reason why my high attributes are a huge advantage—when you have, say, two free points and you've got to dedicate them to Intelligence to increase your Mana Pool every other Level, Prestige Classes can pull ahead with ease. Of course, that raises another question of why there's differentiation in Classes at all—why not give everyone the same Class or the same amount of Intelligence? It can't be a case of suitability, since Class selection, especially when a new world is introduced to the Galactic System, is by choice. It's not as if the System is analyzing us and going "you are more suited for X Class; you can only handle five attributes a Level." We are making the decision and living with the consequences.

Admittedly, there are records of when those decisions go wrong. Just because it can be done doesn't mean every individual should take a Prestige Class. Mana overcharge can happen. Mutations and warping of individuals due to an inability to handle the additional Mana flow is not unknown. Having too high Intelligence but not enough Willpower is a known danger. Over-balancing one particular "trait" is another. But like so much with the System, there's no guaranteed over-balanced threshold.

Even if you assume there are individual and racial limits to the kind of imbalance and even Level that an individual can attain—and the records and studies on this are highly conflicted—it still doesn't explain why the System allows people to choose Classes that are entirely unsuited for them. A bad coding error? A mistaken belief that free will is important, even if the result is suboptimal? Those are some of the questions that plague Questors like me, and thus far, there's still no clear winner.

"Not uncommon among Paladins. Though some have been more Charisma-focused solution-makers, most have gone down the route of ensuring their dictates can be backed up." I grunt at Foxy, who flashes me a needle-filled mouth. "Are you finding yourself short of Mana during battles?"

I consider Foxy's point. After a moment, I shake my head. "Not much. Might be a problem in the coming fight, but I've got decent burst damage. The Penetration Skill helps a lot—I can do a lot more damage than most with even my basic attacks."

"True," Foxy says. "And you have not used your Aura or other champion Skills much."

"Not much call for it."

"Not the way you fight, no." Foxy shrugs. "If you have trouble allocating, it is often recommended to focus on survival."

"Constitution."

"And Intelligence."

With Shield Skills, that makes sense. Throwing up another Soul Shield can often be more efficient at keeping me alive than tanking another hit—though that depends on the kind of attack, my current armor and resistances, and their penetration abilities. Still, more Mana gives me more options in a fight—I just have to have the time to use it all.

"Done. And done."

Once I split my attributes, I take a look at the changed Status Screen, letting my eyes drift to the paltry amount of Credits I have left after paying for repairs to the ship. As much as I might want to argue with Dornalor about who should be paying for what, and to whine about the increased Credit cost since the war started, having a functioning ship is the most important thing right now.

Status Screen			
Name	John Lee	Class	Erethran Paladin
Race	Human (Male)	Level	**38**
Titles			
Monster's Bane, Redeemer of the Dead, Duelist, Explorer, Apprentice Questor, Galactic Silver Bounty Hunter, Corrupt Questor			

Health	4520	Stamina	4520
Mana	4160	Mana Regeneration	357 (+5) / minute
Attributes			
Strength	304	Agility	394
Constitution	452	Perception	234
Intelligence	416	Willpower	447
Charisma	172	Luck	92
Class Skills			
Mana Imbue	3*	Blade Strike*	5
Thousand Steps	1	Altered Space	2
Two are One	1	The Body's Resolve	3
Greater Detection	1	A Thousand Blades*	3
Soul Shield	4	Blink Step	2
Portal*	5	Army of One	4
Sanctum	2	Penetration	7
Aura of Chivalry	1	Eyes of Insight	1
Beacon of the Angels	2	Eye of the Storm	1
Vanguard of the Apocalypse	2	Society's Web	1
External Class Skills			
Instantaneous Inventory	1	Frenzy	1
Cleave	2	Tech Link	2

Elemental Strike	1 (Ice)	Shrunken Footsteps	1
Analyze	2	Harden	2
Quantum Lock	3	Elastic Skin	3
Disengage Safeties	2	Temporary Forced Link	1
Hyperspace Nitro Boost	1	On the Edge	1

Combat Spells	
Improved Minor Healing (IV)	Greater Regeneration (II)
Greater Healing (II)	Mana Drip (II)
Improved Mana Missile (IV)	Enhanced Lightning Strike (III)
Firestorm	Polar Zone
Freezing Blade	Improved Inferno Strike (II)
Elemental Walls (Fire, Ice, Earth, etc.)	Ice Blast
Icestorm	Improved Invisibility
Improved Mana Cage	Improved Flight
Haste	Enhanced Particle Ray

I briefly consider buying another Thousand Blades. While getting a single extra blade isn't that useful, the additional three blades when triggering Army of One adds a decent chunk of damage. On the other hand, having an extra blade floating around me when fighting increases the complexity significantly. It's why I've held off on picking up more blades, because the training time to handle the additional blade while fighting is significant. Running into my own blade in a fight is painful, to say the least.

Other than that, there's not much I can buy without affecting my Mana Regeneration—a non-starter considering we're likely going into a long, drawn-out fight. I take a deep breath and focus. A few seconds later, the Class Skill point is allocated without an issue. I let out a breath that I barely recognize I'm holding, disappointed that nothing happened. Well, that was a waste of Credits. It also means I'm unlikely to see the Skill Evolution in this fight.

Chapter 17

Walking out of the private room in the Shop, I'm surprised to see that I have a visitor. If it was a tall, dark, and rather handsome Truinnar visitor, I'd be more than happy but, in this case, it's one I truly did not expect. Standing before me is the Librarian, still dressed in his suit and clashing heavily with the yellow décor.

"Ah, the Questor I was looking for," the Librarian says with a smile.

"What?" I cock my head, my eyes widening slightly as the creature glides forward within feet of me. I automatically step back, a hand rising to put space between us. Not that I'm worried—the Shop I'm in would not stand for violence. Any violence would result in automatic teleportation out and the initiator being banned from the premises. Or at least from being in the same location as another customer.

"Just a small thing." The Librarian's hand moves with a gentle implacability.

Automatically, I lean backward, my head turning to the side as my hand moves to intercept his. It's not rational, it's all instinct—hard-coded instinct to stop potential threats from touching me. It's all the faster because of that, but it doesn't matter. Not one bit. No matter how fast I'm moving, no matter how efficient my actions are, the hand fills my vision, refusing to be swayed. It's like the coming of old age—always guaranteed, impossible to avoid, no matter what we do.

A thumb touches the middle of my forehead, resting on my glabella, the other all-too-long fingers wrapping around to envelop the rest of my head. A part of me notes that his fingers are dry and freezing—just before a river of fire floods into my brain. My mind, already thoroughly abused by the System, is taking another beating as information, torrents of information, floods in. Everything I ever wanted to know, everything I ever intended to ask and read about, enters my brain like a shaken soda can through a pinhole.

Questions, answers, stupid inane studies, and profound dissertations on the System all arrive. I get videos of some of the grossest, most disgusting experiments that have ever been conducted to understand the nature of the System and the most basic lectures given to children. In the end, it's all data, unsorted information, none of it explained but all of it provided to me in a tidal wave of videos, text, holograms, scents, and other sensory information. It comes unpacked and in full detail, notifications flashing on and on and on even as I struggle to stay afloat in the sea of pain and data. The headache becomes a migraine which transforms into a herd of elephants doing the Viennese waltz in my head. Even through my rather ridiculous resistances, my natural stubbornness propped up by the System's Willpower adjustments, I can feel the tendrils of my shaky sanity coming apart.

When it feels like I'm done, when I can't handle any more, the data in my mind packs itself away, shrinking down from its unspooled format into compact nuggets of information. Answers that I'm desperate to find are hidden again, conclusions that I'm just beginning to reach as I see the links between information disappear. Data is compressed, the library shoved into the corners of my mind. More compressed data gets thrown onto it, the attic of my mind growing as cluttered as a ninety-year-old hoarder's living room. It helps, it helps a lot, because the data doesn't stop. It just keeps flooding in, taking an eternity in subjective time and seconds in reality.

"What is going on here?" Foxy snarls, appearing beside us.

Too late. All too late.

I find myself pressed against the closed doorway I recently exited, my eyes wide and focused on the Librarian and the ghosts of studies past. The Librarian returns my gaze, smiling with that creepy, too toothy mouth and big, wide grey eyes. Eyes that I suddenly recall seeing in all too many studies, staring down mercilessly at research subjects.

"I was but providing the Questor a gift."

As if on cue, a new Status Notification pops up.

Title Gained: Living Repository (System Research)

You are a walking repository of knowledge. Whether through choice, fate, or destiny, you are a living repository of knowledge for a specific branch of information. Your life or death may be desired by others for the information you hold. This Title may be gained multiple times for multiple forms of knowledge.

Effect: +250% Resistance to Skills and spells that invade and require access to Title holders mind. This includes Possession, Mental Invasion, Mental Links, etc.

Note: This title may be hidden.

System Quest Updated. Experience Gained

+751 XP, +238 XP, +1803 XP, +637 XP, +43 XP, …

"Some gift," I growl. At Foxy's pointed look, I wipe my face, my hand coming away stained with blood. A simple Cleanse fixes that problem and removes all traces of my blood, though I've shed enough of it that it wouldn't be hard to find if people really wanted it. "My brain feels like it's been stuffed with cotton wool soaked in lighter fluid and then lit on fire."

"I'm sorry, Librarian Feh'ral, but you have violated the rules of your entry. I must ask you to leave now." Temper cooled, Foxy is showing a hell of a lot of deference to the Librarian. Especially since he assaulted me.

"As you wish." Feh'ral bows to us both then just disappears.

Foxy turns to me, his eyes raking over my form, and points at my nose again. I blink, touching the still-bleeding nose, surprised that I've managed to keep bleeding even with the amount of health regeneration I have. Even the pain in my head has not gone away.

"What did he do?" I mutter to Foxy while holding my nose tightly and tilting my head up.

Foxy is silent, eyes unfocused as he reads a bunch of stat screens. When his eyes refocus on me, he shakes his head. "Nothing more than a data download."

"I've had those before. Never felt like this."

"That's probably because you've never had the entire Questor's library downloaded into your brain."

"Pardon?" I blink slowly, my voice still nasal from having it clamped shut.

"He downloaded all of it. The entire library." Foxy is looking at me strangely, as if I've grown another nose, three horns, and tusks. "You should not be able to handle that much information. How are you still standing?"

I consider Foxy's words. Even with my resistances and the stupid level of Intelligence I have, the Galactic is right. I should be dead. Hell, I took a couple thousand points of damage just from processing the information. Yet as I prod my brain, I realize that a lot of the data is no longer accessible. When I try to access the data, a searing pain shoots through my body that buckles my knees and makes my eyes bleed.

"Not. Doing that. Again." I wipe the blood away, retrieving some cloth to stuff my nose and clean my face.

"You learned something?"

"Yeah…" I open my mouth to explain then clamp it shut, eyes narrowing in thought. If Foxy hasn't figured out how this was done, it means that the Skill the Librarian used—and it must be a Skill—is not easily accessible. If that's the case, he's hiding that information for a reason.

"I see we Galactics have finished our corruption of you."

I laugh ruefully, but my thoughts turn back to the encounter. The way the Librarian managed to touch me, the Skill he used. And why he used it. Something fishy is going on there, and instincts borne from thousands of dangerous encounters tells me I've added to my slurry of problems.

256

***

Since I wasn't shopping, Foxy threw me out once I had mostly recovered. I still have a headache and a new status condition of Psyche Warped, which I'd missed till I left. Prodding the details, most of which had been left untranslated since Ali wasn't around, hadn't been particularly helpful. Not that it really matters beyond the countdown timer of when it'll go away. Two hours is a pain, especially when the fight is about to start.

Ali finds me when I get back to the fifth ring. *"What the hell did you do?"*

"I didn't do anything. The damn Librarian dropped the entire library into my head." I cast my gaze around, taking in the various others in the fifth ring station security room. We're all waiting, as the next part of the fight will be run by the navy. For us ground pounders, we're useless—at least till the ships dock. Quite a few screens are up, showing the surroundings and one 3D hologram of the upcoming fight.

"Duh. I knew that. I was asking what you did to him."

"Nothing. I was polite and everything the last time I saw him. You were there!"

"Uh huh." Ali frowns, staring me over then floating around me in his smaller form. He stops after making a full circuit, his face unusually concerned. *"This. This could be bad."*

"I figured. The question is, how?" As much as I've learned about the Galactic System in the last few years, my research hasn't involved the politics of Questors. Even if my new Title warns of potential trouble, I can't see how having all this information could be dangerous. After all, it's not as if the Questor's library is a hidden repository. In fact, we're generally trying to get more people involved. On the other hand, if there wasn't something

concerning in this depository, why would the Librarian do what he did? And of course, there's the title—Corrupt Questor.

"I'll look into it. But this smells fishy."

"That'd be ugly on the right."

Ali looks over involuntarily, only to catch sight of the humanoid fish-creature. As he opens his mouth to retort, a new notification appears.

New Quest Initiated: Station Defense

Defend Spaks station from the invading navy. This is a shared contribution quest.

Requirements: Stop the destruction or conquest of Spaks Station

Rewards: Variable depending on contribution percentage

Bonus Objectives: Save as many rings (0/5) as possible from destruction

As if the fleet was waiting for the quest itself, the views change as the Galactics open fire. There's no warning, no second chances. Not that most need it. Outside of a single straggling merchant transport, everyone has either docked in the safety of the inner rings, moved outside of the combat zone, or is hiding behind the fourth ring force wall, ready to launch themselves at the transports.

Just like the simulation, the Galactics open fire with the slow-moving physical projectiles first. Unlike the simplified simulation I saw, this time around, there's a much wider range of projectiles on display, from bolts of enclosed plasma and solid metal shells to even stranger things. I catch sight of feathered cannonballs with extra large eyes, their metallic bodies spinning through space as they are launched from the battleships' cannons. The feathered cannonballs are accompanied by other weird attacks including glowing green slug shells, tiny nuclear elementals barely contained in enchanted spell containers, and a weaponized concept.

Yes. Fighting in the System is weird.

Once the projectiles are on their way, with multiple ships still firing to ensure there's a continued attack on the shields, self-propelled attacks come next. Most of these are missiles, though I'm amused to see a few Advanced Classers flying along, powered by their Skills, Mana, or spacesuits. I wonder if they've been watching one too many Marvel movies, what with the flying across the thousands of kilometers to punch our shield. If I were them, I'd hang back… but it's likely they know something I don't.

Last to fire are the energy beams and line-of-sight spells and Skills. Also known as more weirdness. Projected rents in space, particle beams, matter conversion, and more flicker. The first salvo of attacks arrives at the same time, slamming into the station shield and turning it opaque under the sheer volume of damage. I turn away from the screens to watch the 3D hologram, the screen updating with damage notifications in real time as the payback Skill activates. As the fight continues, a new notification window appears.

Simulation Fidelity: 94.3% in favor of Spaks

"That's good, right?"

"As good as can be expected. We're doing more damage than we expected. Seems like there are a few Skills in play that the estimates didn't expect that are adding to the damage return and holding up the shield. On the other hand, some of those bigger Ships have better defensive Skills than expected, which is pushing up their percentage."

I grunt, flicking my eyes over the ships. Ali's right. Many of the bigger ships have their shield integrity at a higher percentage, either because they're taking less damage overall or regenerating their damage faster than expected. The gap is fast appearing, with smaller ships taking more and more damage. Some of the smallest ones even have their force shields fail.

"Why isn't the Admiral dropping them from his Skill?"

"It's an evolved Skill. Won't be that easy to adjust the parameters like that, especially mid-combat. Most likely he's restricted to who is already there and an either-or position."

"He could have chosen not to include the smaller vessels," I say. *"Or the Dimensional Smoothers."*

"You're thinking he had a choice. Something this powerful, it probably wasn't that finely controllable. Anyone who joined his fleet would be tagged with it. Could be the System even tagged a few ships we aren't seeing here with the effect." Ali shrugs. *"Intelligent Skills might be useful, but they can also be a little too smart."*

"Smart dumb, eh? I wrote a few programs like that."

The fact that the System sometimes seems like a badly programmed software program is not something I've missed. Yet in other ways, it's too organic. Too randomly acerbic with its Titles and commentary. Some of it, of course, is Ali. In a few, rather worrying cases, it's the Galactic Council or a Galactic bureaucrat somewhere, adjusting the terminology. But a lot of it is just the System. It feels like the System itself is two, maybe even three people—the System itself, pure and unadulterated, a computer program with specific notifications that it uses again and again; the Galactic Council and their random meddling and rules; and a third, controlling AI that smooths over hitches and deals with edge cases. Like the evolutions and new worlds.

"Oooh, pretty," I exclaim.

That comment is accompanied by a lot of indrawn breaths as the explosion from what I can only assume is a missile boat fills the hologram. The tiny star blooms then fades, though smaller explosions dot the hologram as the damage accumulates on the fleet's side. I spot the dispersal of escape pods from each ship. We might be destroying machinery, but the people within are mostly making it out.

The destruction is not all one-sided, as the station's shield integrity continues to drop. Even the shield's natural regeneration rate isn't enough. It lasts longer than we expected, long enough for the light show to become almost boring. Then it finally gives way with a shimmer, letting the remaining fire wing its way in.

"Brace for impact," the station master's voice comes through the loudspeakers.

In a corner, a creature with a pair of spinnerets shoots out a series of threads, anchoring itself to the walls. Most others take more mundane means of anchoring themselves. I grip the nearest railing and wait for the incidental attacks, those that were meant to destroy the shield as they miss and hit us. Once the shield goes down, the light speed attacks stop while additional dots bloom across the display as attack shuttles make their first appearance. Other larger and faster ships, with the speed and maneuverability to get in close to the exposed stations and the space to hold assault personnel, join the shuttles. In moments, the hologram is filled with hundreds of silver fireflies that dart toward us.

The booms of concussive impacts resound through the station, the backup shields failing almost immediately. The station rocks and shifts, warning lights bathing us in red and green alternating lights. Penetration rounds meant to take out the entire Spaks stations' main shields cut through the smaller branch station's defenses, tearing open metal and venting air into space. In one corner of the hologram, a station filled with water breathers is punctured, filling the immediate area with ice as it expels the station's contents.

As suddenly as the attack begins, it ends. No more incidental attacks as we enter a lull in the battle while the Galactic fleet waits for our fleet to exit the fourth ring shield and we wait for the transports to close in. Station weaponry, exposed with the shield down, open fire on the transports but do little to affect the big picture. As we wait, someone taps the hologram, shifting the view to layer Mana flows on top of the display.

"What's that for?" I could ask someone else, but I'd rather not look completely ignorant.

"They're watching for portals and other teleportation events. Mana level fluctuations can show potential exits," Ali says.

"I know that. In theory, it's possible, but the amount of changes and timeframe is so short that it's nearly impossible."

"For you. But you ain't the be all and end all, boy-o."

I frown but silently admit that with the sheer array of Skills and Classes available, it's quite possible that someone can read the telltale fluctuations. Of course, to teleport, they'd either have to create gaps in the Smoothers' locks to allow their fleet to teleport in or get close enough that they can use powerful short-range teleportations. At which point, I have to wonder, what's the point?

When the approaching shuttles hit the close-in defensive line, the clustered stealth mines and remaining defensive platforms open fire. Once they make their appearance, the Galactic fleet targets the defenses, but in the meantime, our side takes out more transports. This time around, their occupants don't all survive. Additional attacks stab from the stations, picking off the survivors. It's harsh, brutal warfare, but that's the nature of fights in the System. You can't tie up resources with damaged or injured personnel—anyone not dead is likely back in the fight in ten minutes. Potentially with more Levels. It's why some armies employ a host of Cursemongers and Poisoners, people who can make the damage they do last.

Another ship comes apart, bodies flung into space as the crystalline spaceship falls to a gravitic mine. From one torn and twisted portion, a half dozen figures emerge. Even as beam weapons target the group, a six-pointed star appears, runes of untold origin forming a magical shield. It takes the attacks, covering the fleeing members. I can see how one of them works a new spell—probably a Portal from the way the Mana flows to them—but more beams, more spells target the star shield. It flickers and tears and reforms, the

Advanced Classer putting everything she has into covering her people. I swear, I can see her eyes widen, the resignation that flashes across her quilled, alien face before her Skill fails and the beams tear into them, followed after by a teleported explosive. When the mini-nova clears, only corpses float—corpses that are picked at by the beams before they shift to the next ship.

The calculus might be simple, necessary, but I don't like it. Those who join such a fight know the risks, so they know where this ends. They have signed up for war, but lives matter, no matter the reason they are lost. It's a brutal calculus, and one that I see more than a few sentients reassessing as they consider that very soon, we're going to be on the opposite end of that equation.

"There they go." The voice is terse but liquid smooth and sweet, like someone gave maple syrup a voice and form. Kind of like that elemental that formed from our national reserves…

I tear my mind away from silly thoughts to focus on the rebel ships as they surge past the opened fourth ring shield. They zoom forward, eager to take their portion of blood. We all know that they're going to their deaths, that they're about to get blasted to pieces.

"Brave suckers," the spider-humanoid mutters, staring at the ships.

"Not that brave. They all have contingency teleport equipment," the liquid voice speaks. Surprisingly, the voice comes from a troll-rock elemental hybrid creature.

"And they work all the time. Or won't be shorted out. Right?" The spider shakes its head. "Brave."

"Look…" another voice cuts in.

But I tune them out, ignoring the argument as I know they're trying to forget the fight. We're just spectators, forced to wait for the battle that is coming to us. And so we distract ourselves with stupid arguments and old memories.

"There he is."

I follow the mental prompt from Ali, spotting Bolo's small form as he wings ahead on his surfboard. He's so small that he's nothing more than a blip to the naked, unenhanced eye. But I can see him, see how he keeps in the shadows of the ships as the Dragon Lord waits for his chance to make a difference. He's not the only individual flying out. There's someone in what I can only describe as a floating bubble, and a spinning blue circle of fire and fur, along with a few other Masters and Advanced Classers. Most though are in ships, charging into the face of danger, knowing they're going to lose. And still doing so.

The next few minutes would make any Hollywood director weep in frustration. Missiles, spells, Skills, and more are in full play as the groups close in on one another. Then the two groups make contact, dog-fighting as weapons from the fleet and stations crisscross the void, tearing into ships and bodies. The assault shuttles are, thankfully, not part of the Admiral's Skill, but the larger ships, the nimble ones, are. In such cases, these ships have an advantage, since the Admiral's Skill spreads the damage, ensuring that only a fraction of a fraction of any single attack makes its way through to any individual ship. In many cases, those ships manage to fly through without a problem. Occasionally though, one of the enemy fleet ships goes up, destroyed within the second ring or even on the outskirts as damage overloads shields. Our ships go down faster—much, much faster—as the combined weight of attacks tears them apart.

And that's when the Galactic fleet receives another nasty surprise. Packed to the gills with chaos mines and other, even more unstable items, when our ships go up, they do so with a bang. A vortex of liquid, freezing in midair and then reforming into a tear in space, yanks these ships into the gap. A quartet of ships, including one of ours, disappears into the fast-closing tear.

In another corner, a demon makes its presence known, summoned by a chaos mine. Two horns jut from its form—a form made of creepy crawlies. Its mouth widens and a stream of bugs land on a pair of ships, entangled in a boarding attack. The bugs swarm over the metal and eat into the ship. Before it can do more damage, a radiant jellyfish appears, its tentacles entangling the demon and setting off a struggle of dominance.

The battle rages in silence like all space battles, but our minds supply the screams, the cries of terror, and the shattering of metal. The smell of imagined roasted flesh and burnt plastic is so strong, I wipe at my nose, shaking it off. Sometimes, having a high Perception and Intelligence has its drawbacks.

"They're through."

Ali's soft words catch everyone's attention. There was never a way to stop them. Not really. We can only do some damage, make them bleed and hurt as they come in, force them to watch their fire as our ships and theirs tangle. Not even Bolo with his giant hammer can do more than smash the transports around before others dock. As the first good seal appears, the lights change again and a warning klaxon blares.

Now it's our turn.

Chapter 18

Nothing happens at first. We're on floor three, subsection seven, close to the inner portion of the station. Close enough that whoever manages to make their way here will be a real threat. It's an interesting plan, layering the defenses to do damage and wear people down with constant attacks rather than going for kills immediately. So long as we can pile on the damage on a continuous basis, our attackers will lose Mana and health. We're basically using fixed defenses in place of lives. In turn, watching the various screens, I see two different strategies in play on the navy side.

In one plan, we have the Juggernauts, the tanks, leading the charge. They're soaking up the damage from the traps, mines, and other defensive measures laid out in the station corridors, pushing through at speed. When their health and Mana fall too low, they switch out, letting the secondary tanks take over, allowing the guys in front to rest and recuperate. Unless they're unlucky or sloppy, they lose no one as they pass through the corridors. It's smart but requires a bunch of elites, groups of people who can take the damage and keep going.

Unlike the second group. Here, they use swarm tactics. Whether it's drones, summons, or just more warm bodies, they throw everything down the corridors without concern. Some survive. Most don't. And behind them, more people pile up. It's a wasteful, insane tactic that gives zero consideration to the people or equipment being lost. But they do it anyway—with zeal and fervor. I focus on the leaders, their eyes wide and bloodshot, foam coming from mouths and other orifices, panting in pain and excitement.

"Drugged?" I ask Ali.

"Probably. Looks like they might be Serfs or other bonded Soldiers. Sent to fight and die so that the elites behind don't have to waste their Mana."

I shudder, that furnace within me sparking, roaring aflame. I tamp it down, knowing that this is not the time. Control. I have it. My rage does not control me.

Much.

I watch as orders are barked out, a running transmission of where rebel assault groups are needed showing on one screen. On another, a small-scale map of the station shows the real-time movements of our people as the defenders are redirected to tackle and harass the elite groups. Rather than let them regenerate, we send out our people to wear them down. For the zerg swarm, support groups are sent ahead, where they use their Skills to reinforce the pre-laid defenses. Additional drones and other automated defenses are added to their corridors by the support groups, the intent shifting from wear down to slaughter. In another section of the station, I see other support Classes frantically reworking machines and weapons, altering damage types to focus on our opponents' weaknesses.

Not that the navy isn't adapting. A new breacher ship hits, its cargo of armed occupants charging out and cutting off a support team as they attempt to retreat after laying down their payload. The fight is over quickly, the support group unable to face the new invaders. And then they pile right back into the breacher ship, ready to repeat their actions.

"Smart," Spider-Rebel says. "We're going to… yes. There. We're shifting routes to deeper in the station. Keeps us safe, but we'll be forced to give up more ground."

I grunt, letting my gaze track over the 3D hologram that has taken over most of the space in the room. New orders come, and some of our people stream out. And a familiar pair of faces wander in.

"Where have you guys been?"

"My job," Harry says, pointing to the projection of the starfield.

"You were out there?"

Harry nods while Mikito offers me a small, tight smile and asks, "We miss anything?"

"Just the deaths of our hopes and dreams."

"Drama!" Ali crows, throwing a hand to his head. "But we are getting our asses kicked."

All across the station, we're being pushed back. None of our people can hold back the invaders. Worse, they're punching through the station faster than we can keep up, some groups going so far as to tear through walls and floors to shorten their route. Of course, occasionally that works against them as they release chemicals, electricity, liquid Mana, and other nasty, nasty things that keep the station running. Or the occasional booby-trapped room.

"One hundred seven percent scenario fidelity on breach conditions. One oh eight." Harry shakes his head, reading the information off the screen. "At least we're doing better in the space battle."

"But that's nearly over," Mikito says, pointing at the few ships that we have left out there.

Wrecks litter the surroundings of the station, a few occasionally bumping into the meteors that still litter the area. Not many of those left—the fight and judicious use of beam weaponry has decreased the free-floating asteroid numbers significantly. Our few remaining ships are retreating, moving to hide behind the fourth ring's defensive shield. I see a few courageous captains using tractor beams and, in one case, an open mining scoop to grab survivors before they run.

"Bolo?" I ask, frowning.

In answer, I'm directed to a close-in shot of our station. Bolo's there, swinging his hammer, batting aside nearby transports. Sometimes the hammer seems to displace its attack through time and space, the swing sending another ship hundreds of meters away flying. Due to his Skills, Bolo manages to punch through and damage what's beneath even when he attacks ships covered by the Admiral's Skill, tearing open holes in the transports with each attack. He's managing to delay the transports from coming into our station, sometimes going so far as to destroy them, but he's only one man. And one whose Mana is finite.

"Redeemer." The station master's voice blares through my ears, drawing my attention.

"Here."

"Corridor 3-21-4."

Ali flicks up a notification window even as I move, Mikito falling into step with me and Harry a few steps behind. I absently note that no one else is ordered to the same corridor, but we're both Master Classers. That makes us a tougher nut to crack than most other groups. And it's a small corridor. A small, reinforced corridor. We're going to need to that.

***

We get to the corridor first—just barely though. I've been watching our opponents on the minimap, tracking their movements, so their arrival isn't surprising. Nor are our opponents.

"Werehippos. Not again." I shake my head, spotting the group that turns the corner at a slow trot, shrugging off every attack with a nonchalance that makes me grimace.

Ali taps into their stats, trying to bypass the equipment and Skills that attempt to hide that information. I get a data readout of their estimated resistances, the amount of damage they're deflecting, guesstimates of their health.

"Not really werehippos. These guys are actually shapeshifters, where the System modified an existing species trait—" Harry shuts up when the hippos

270

let out a growl-snarl that reverberates through our chests. "I'll be right back here."

"Yeah, you do that." I shake my hand, loosening up muscles, then conjure my sword. I debate tossing down a few Shield projectors and decide against it. Those cost money.

Instead, I look at the group and decide to open big. Army of One takes a little time to charge up, but activation is almost immediate. I toss on my Aura, Eye of the Storm, and Vanguard to keep them focused on me as Mikito settles in by my side, ready to add her own attacks. I can sense beside me the fluctuations in Mana as she readies her own Advanced Class top tier Skill. Unlike mine, it focuses on taking out a single person.

When I chop down, the motion is copied by dozens of blades. Just the shockwave of the attack is enough to score the corridor, tearing out lights and wiping durable industrial paint. In retaliation, the lead hippo triggers a Skill, covering itself with a shield and glowing black and white. Still, the beams of sword energy impact the lead hippo, penetrating the shielding around his body and piercing his natural armor. Ancillary attacks are deflected off his shield into his comrades, making one stumble to a stop. The lead hippo comes apart in a welter of blood and gore, body stripped of flesh and sinew, burnt away where the blades contact but don't tear.

I note the XP notification in the corner of my mind, but I'm already stepping aside as my attack ends. Mikito steps forward and thrusts, the enlarged head of her naginata taking the least damaged hippo in the side of its body as they continue their charge. The attack looks simple, graceful even as it slips into the gap between armor plates over the heart and head. Between the momentum of Mikito's thrust and the hippo's own charge, it goes all the way in. A quick yank as the naginata shrinks and Mikito has her weapon free, the attack swinging over to take the next hippo in line as the mostly decapitated hippo slides along the floor. On my side, I throw a few Blade Strikes at the other tanks even as healing energy bathes our assailants.

Our alpha strike complete, the remaining invaders pause and return our stares. I can't help but smile a little. Perhaps they see it as taunting, because a growl rolls through the group as the secondary tanks push forward, no longer afraid. And then…

Well, then things get messy.

***

Black chains erupt from the smoking, damaged deck, rising from the shadows, drawn from the flickering light of burning fire and the occasional still working lighting strip. There are gaping holes in the deck and walls where even reinforced structures, Mana-driven repair, and Skill hardening have been unable to keep up with the damage of our fight. The chains grab the glowing, semi-solid figure that darts toward me, holding it at bay. Even then, my damage counter ticks up as the irradiated being's very presence harms me and my equipment.

Spotting the danger, Mikito steps past me and swings Hitoshi, the naginata bisecting the monster and parting the Abyssal Chains. The creature screams, two-thirds of its remaining health disappearing with that single strike. A return spin cuts the creature apart, sending its body falling. But the body continues to glow, irradiating us all. Worse, I see Mikito stagger as a trio of blasts catches her, throwing her back as they tear at her Ghostly Armor. If not for the health Hitoshi stole from the radioactive Galactic, she might have died. I feel part of the impact too, Two are One sending some of the damage to me.

"Back!" I snarl, putting myself in front of her even as I layer a Soul Shield on her while dropping Two are One.

Like Mikito, my Mana pool is down to a quarter, even after using multiple Mana injections. We've been fighting for over thirty minutes now, holding the line, but there's only so much we can do.

The shapeshifted-werehippos went down first, their tanks soaking up a ton of damage. It was only when we had finished killing them that I considered whether it would have been better for us to have kept them alive. After all, tanks generally have low damage outputs. In either case, after the shapeshifters came Elite Soldiers, a platoon of them that sat behind shields and fired at us. A simple Blink Step put me in their midst, and after I'd soaked the trap damage they'd laid for me, the ensuing carnage actually gave us ground. Mages, healers, and more melee fighters followed, wave after wave.

Over in his corner of the corridor, Ali's hovering, hands held outward as he adjusts the angles of beam attacks and spells as they fly toward us. Each change is only a small variation of the angles, but it's enough to make a portion of their attacks miss entirely. While it requires only a little of his strength, the strain of doing so for over thirty minutes with multiple attacks each second is showing on his face.

Together, we fall backward, away from the glowing rocks that were a sapient being. As we back off, the tanks and ranged fighters facing us leapfrog forward, tanks rushing upward while ranged attackers, some of them literally clinging to the ceiling as they scurry after us, lay down covering fire. As they near the glowing rock, black stone mixed with lead and other metals bubble up from the floor, covering the body.

"Damn it," I snarl.

We've been losing ground over the course of the fight—part of the reason why the entire location hasn't been entirely destroyed. We hit the end of this corridor and take the turn, my hands flicking as I add my own portion of mines to Mikito's. Not that it'll do much to slow them down, but the repeated use of these has ensured that the group don't rush headlong.

"Time to go, John," Harry says over party chat. "They're nearly at the connecting branches and the station core. If you don't leave now, they're going to block you."

"We can still hold them." I glance at the map, noting at least one more turn before we hit the station core itself. If we fall back past this corridor rather than try to hold it, we'll be able to help intercept the other group.

"Not worth it, Redeemer. The other teams are down to thirty percent effectiveness. They're waiting on you to get them out," Oi cuts in, his voice tight.

"What are you doing on here?" I frown.

This isn't Oi's station. Thus far, it's been the fifth ring station master making the calls.

"Assassin team got Yuve Yu," Oi says. "We took them out before they could take the station, but it's time to go."

The other team's inching forward down the corridor even as Mikito and I back off, Ali popping up beside us as he darts through the walls. As he comes to hover beside me, I note that Ali's form is wavering slightly, shifting in solidity, arcs of electricity dancing along the edges of his form. The Spirit's losing control of himself, his concentration shot.

"Baka. Follow the plan." Mikito says, her voice weary.

I swear but end up agreeing. The whoosh of shutting blast doors close behind us as we fall back. Even as we arrive in the station core room, the other teams are streaming in, many of them running low on Mana after having spent it on flashy and powerful top-tier attacks to give themselves space to retreat. A Space Mage standing next to the station core slaps his hands together, twisting the space further and sealing us off for a few minutes. Like my

Sanctum spell, it can lock down the area for a few minutes, so long as the Mage has the Mana.

"Redeemer. The Portal!" A four-armed cyclops hurries over, the pair of his friends in his arms barely having a sliver of health left.

Rather than answer directly, I pull the Portal into being. The cyclops offers me a quick nod as he ducks through, followed by the remaining teams. I watch, unconsciously doing a count as they keep going. When I hit sixteen and there's barely anyone left, I twitch.

"That's it?" I knew it was bad, I'd glimpsed the dots disappearing, but…

"They hit us harder than we expected," Bolo says as he appears from the corner. The Dragon Lord is smoking, steam and wisps of smoke coming off his body as blood and other viscera burn off. When he sees my raised eyebrow, Bolo shrugs. "They dropped a molten core on me."

"I… don't know what that means," I admit. As a Mana-low headache pushes against my temple, I wave him through.

"Move. They're cutting through," the Space Mage says.

"I thought that wasn't possible," Mikito says, frowning as she backs off.

Bolo heads for the Portal and steps in without hesitation, the Samurai standing right next to it.

"Anything's possible in the System. Just unlikely. The leaves turned early for us," the Mage snaps. The next second, he screams and the world snaps back into normal space. We don't move, not really, but our inner ears and that seventh sense that tells us what dimension we're in trembles, forcing all of us to stumble as space stops contorting around us.

"Time to go," I mutter, grabbing hold of the Space Mage and throwing him through the Portal.

The struggling Mage catches Mikito with one flapping hand, and rather than stop him, the Samurai steps in as well, detaching the grip the Mage has on her arm. As I get ready to step through the Portal myself, the blast doors protecting us blow apart.

I'm backing off to the Portal, only to find myself thrown aside as a blur hits me. Even as I crash into the wall, I feel more blows pummeling me as the blur keeps up the pressure. The first surprise attack shatters my newly regenerated shield from the armor. The subsequent ones strike body and armor, cracking the armor and penetrating to pile concussive attacks on my body.

I curl up slightly, trying to focus and block the attacks that are moving faster than any Haste, Blur, or speed Skill I've ever seen. I'm a giant punching bag, abused and hammered as my Mana bottoms out. The strain of holding the Portal open is making me wince, even as I hear the distant thump of approaching feet. But I can't even get my feet on the floor, the blows coming in so fast that I'm literally being pummeled into the reinforced metal of the security room.

Then, suddenly, the attacks stop as the blur slams into the wall beside me. I glimpse Ali looking intense, and my Elemental Affinity tells me he's adjusted the friction coefficient on my attacker's feet, throwing him off. But Ali's shimmering, splitting apart as he combats the System and the Skill that my attacker is using. Even now, I feel the System reasserting its influence, allowing my attacker to surge back to his feet and continue his attack.

I glimpse the Portal and Mikito's turning form as she tries to get back here. Rather than protest, I trigger my Blink Step even as I release the Portal. The world blurs and my body tears apart as the fading, unstable Portal interacts with my Blink Step as I pass through it. I fall to the ground, throwing up blood and the remainder of my breakfast.

Condition Gained: Dimensionally Challenged

Your body has been pulled into multiple dimensions at the same time. At this time, your body is suffused with the energy of multiple dimensions and is liable to take additional damage or scatter if subjected to additional dimensional strain.

Effects: -30% HP Regeneration. Unable to use or shift dimensions.

Duration: 124 Minutes

As I shudder from the Mana headache and the sudden transportation, I can only wonder. What the hell was that?

***

"Master Class speedster."

I glare at Ali as I hold a cold bottle of Apocalypse Ale to my head in the vain hope that it'll help with my headache. Not that the rest of my body isn't hurting, but the headache is the worst. The dimensional debuff added to the one I received from having all that information stuffed into my head is doing a real number on me. "Details."

"Not much. He's got a movement-oriented speed Class—specifically, a Three-Winged Messenger."

"Winged? I didn't see any—"

"It's a Class name, not a description," Ali says. "He's evolved his Winged Delivery Skill at the Advanced Level, then added more support Skills and dumped a ton of his attributes into Agility. Basically turning him into the Flash."

"Not that fast," I say.

"Depends on which version," Ali retorts.

"Kind of late for a speedster, no?"

"Didn't you hear the bit about attribute allocation?" A moment later, Ali flashes me the Status screen from my logs, something I'd been a little too busy to look at.

Devereux Alb, Champion of the Imju Global Race (219th, 220th and 221st), Monster Slayer (Trolls, Phalax,…), Thrice-Pressed Courier, … (Level 27 Three Winged Messenger)

HP: 1480/1480

MP: 1430/1430

Conditions: Blitzed, Occam's Route, Slipstream, Future Projections, Lightning Reflexes

"Low health. And Mana," I say, frowning and tapping the screen to call up information.

Occam's Route and Future Projections let him plot out the best route to move in, giving him a little bit of precognitive ability. Lightning Reflexes lets him move even faster while Slipstream reduces friction issues. As for Blitzed, it's a passive form of the Haste spell.

"Passive build." Ali shrugs. "He's all speed, all damage, but in a big area fight, he's not much use. Catch you alone though and he's got the advantage. If you hadn't closed the Portal after you, he could have followed. As it was, he might even had a chance—except then he'd be here by himself."

"Coward then."

"Not everyone has a death wish."

I do not have a death wish. If I did, I'd go pick a fight with a dragon. Yes, I know I've done that before. But, no, I really don't. I just do what has to be done. And if I'm meant to die, then, well, I was meant to have died seven, no, eight years ago.

"Whatever. If he's this low, we just need to send a bunch of area effect spells, right?"

"Skills. Spells are too slow. He'd see you cast and move," Ali points out and I grunt.

Even with my higher attributes, spells still take time to cast, unlike Skills. The higher our attributes, the easier it is for us to finish the necessary mental and Mana manipulation to make spells work. None of which is particularly useful for me since most of my area effect attacks are spells rather than Skills.

"Should I buy one?" I frown, considering the thought then glancing at the pitiful state of my wallet.

I earned a little from killing the invaders, but we only get a fraction of the Credits an individual has on them. Since neither Ali nor I had time to grab the bodies, we couldn't even loot and sell them. The rest of my funds went into fixing up the ship since, well, a way out is a good idea. Still, I could probably get a loan. The interest might be ruinous, considering the situation I'm in, and I'd probably have to put up the various properties I have on Earth as collateral, but it'd be doable.

"You could, though you could also try to slow him down. Less harm to your own, you know?"

"Tangler grenades and the like?" I nod slowly. That makes sense. Web the area, or maybe even use a Skill to alter gravity or friction or something to make him move slower. And Ali's right. If my first notice is that he's right between us, using an area effect skill without a friend-or-foe designation would mean I'd be harming my own people. Not a good idea. Then again, if he only comes when there's one of us...

"In theory. Realize he's got Skills to counter that. Or something as pedestrian as a monofilament wire laid out to tear him apart." Ali shakes his head. "He's not got this far by falling for simple tricks like that."

"Fun. Can I just let Bolo handle him?"

The big Dragon Lord's out with Mikito, having taken a twenty-minute rest to recuperate and rearm before they rejoined the fight.

A glance at the floating notification screens shows the current status of the battle in both text and image form. We've lost all the fifth ring stations, having done better in the space battle but generally worse in the station fights. There are a few notable exceptions, like stations eight and seventeen, but the navy seems to have sent some of their best against us. And thus far, a lot of the higher Level rebels have stayed out of it. Some of it, I know, is strategic — keeping the fleet guessing and holding back their own major players is important. Then there are those Classes whose Skills are just better off being used when there are larger clusters rather than the piecemeal fights we've been having. And, of course, Station Masters and their like are confined to their own stations.

Even then, our projections took a lot of that into account. And we're still losing. It's clear that our plans, the way we're distributing our forces, are leaking like a sieve to the other side. It's why they've focused their attention on areas where our best fighters aren't. Throwing just enough to slow down people like me and Bolo, sacrificing those they don't care about to our blades. Using the Messenger to try to trap me, separate me from the rest of the teams.

We're losing the information war. And with it, the rest of the war.

I struggle inwards, drawing a few glances from the tired groups. The fights have bogged down a little as our opponents attempt to enter the fourth ring. We've blown the majority of the connecting tubes between external stations, but we're forced by Rising Crescendo to keep a few connections in play. Still, that allows us to focus our forces, laying down enough covering fire and having people like Bolo and Mikito keep an eye on the tubes so the tanks can ignore the fire.

They'll push through eventually. Right now, the navy is still consolidating their gains, flying in more transports, building up their numbers and hunting down the few unlucky bastards who failed to get out in time. Eventually, they'll make the push and we won't be able to hold the tubes. Eventually, we'll be fighting in the tunnels again, trying to hold them off. Making them bleed. And hoping that something, anything changes the brutal calculus of numbers.

Chapter 19

I block the swinging tail, the spikes on its edges piercing the thinned armor on my arms as I do so. I grunt, feeling the strain on my shoulders as I push against the tail and send it backward. As I reset my stance, a four-legged cat-like creature with swinging whips connected to its forearms jumps me, proceeding to attack with its whips. I duck sideways, but the attack pierces the pink-dressed armored figure standing beside me.

"God. Damn. It!" I snarl and throw a cut at the whip-cat.

My initial attack gets blocked, but the remaining floating blades keep moving, tearing the monster apart. White light bathes the creature as a beetle-like monster from above targets it with its mouth, sending healing energy. I don't let it finish though, swinging my sword again and finishing off the cat creature by lopping off its head. As the beast dies, sending spurts of lime-green blood around, a howl erupts from the invader's back lines.

"Good job, boy-o. Piss off the Beast Trainer," Ali says. The Spirit is floating, legs crossed as he hovers above me, unseen by most. Still, the effect of his Elemental Force manipulation is clear as beams twist and jerk upward. He's pacing himself, having gotten better over the past few days at knowing which ones to adjust and which to leave alone.

I don't have time to bother with Ali as I glance at the stricken pink classer. Except she's gone, pulled back and replaced by a giant of a drake, a much larger version of Tim from Whitehorse. Unlike Tim, this one's dressed in full sci-fi combat armor. Drakey's armed with a head-to-foot glowing force shield and an anti-personnel beam turret in the other hand. Even as I look over, he catches a series of blasts on the shield and fires upon the lizard beast that's pulling back on the Beast Trainer's command. The cannon attack tears a hole in the lizard's side, but it isn't enough to finish it off.

"Less talking, more fighting." The voice that barks at us is a Drill Sergeant, an Advanced Class who's more of a support fighter than an actual damage dealer.

I'd get angry at being ordered around except that it's part of the requirement of his Class Skill—Harsh Motivation. It gives a boost to Willpower checks and, more importantly, Mana and Stamina regeneration. It's just one of the many passive Skills he's got, all of them boosting those of us on the front lines. Everything from decreased casting times to increased accuracy or decreased Mana consumption for Skills. That his passive's overlay and work with the rest of our Skills is even more important, since it's easy for such Skills to clash.

"Easy for you to say." I finish layering on my Soul Shield then throw Blade Strikes down the corridor.

A trio of bouncing balls pass the armored lizard, popping up in midair and generating force shields to catch my Blade Strikes. Two of them absorb the strikes without an issue. The third's shield shatters and the wave of force in my attack cracks it open, dropping the ball to the ground, where it sparks futilely.

***

"Redeemer! Redeemer! Redeemer!"

The cheer from behind makes me clench my teeth, but I ignore it. Ever since we lost the fourth ring, the motivation and desperation level among our group has increased significantly. It helps that even those who have been holding back have joined the fight, reinforcing our blockades. Over the last few days, we've managed to stymie their progress at the connecting tubes, especially since one of the Station Masters had the awesome idea of reducing the durability of the tubes themselves. Now the invaders have to be much more careful in their attacks, while giving us an out from Rising Crescendo.

I pause in my attacks for a moment, letting everyone else throw fire downrange as I wait for my Mana to recharge. The enemy has pulled back, hiding behind big force shields, moving armor plates taken and enchanted from monster drops or the occasional sturdy Classer. They return fire, but our mobile blockers come up to soak up the damage, creating another lull in the battle as people cycle out and Mana recharges.

"They seem to be a little less aggressive today."

"Maybe they're getting tired of banging their heads against yours. Always said you had a hard head." Ali's words might be light, but I can feel the thread of worry in his thoughts.

They've not pushed us as hard as they could. For one thing, we've not seen hide nor hair of their Master Classers since they took the fourth ring.

Rather than worry about it, I tap into the command channel. "Oi. The other connections?"

Oi's image pops up, looking worse for wear. Winning then losing your station in a span of a week must be all kinds of traumatic. "I told you you're not meant to be on this channel, Paladin! There's a dedicated channel for you Master Classers."

Unlike a regular military, since each of us Master Classers is a major power in ourselves, they have us on our specific channel. Unfortunately for Oi, I mute that channel for the most part, leaving the neural network semi-sentient AI to watch for information I need. Otherwise, I'd have to listen to the other Master Classers whine all the time.

"Bite me." I admit, I have little sympathy for his loss, considering we might all die. "Status?"

"Holding. No sign of Master Classers or a major push," I Shao cuts in.

My lips twitch as Oi flinches, the woman not meant to be on this channel either.

A change in the air, a tickling in my brain has me kill the connection and focus ahead.

"Incoming!" I warn the others even as I reach for my Skill.

When their force shields drop and the new series of attackers comes charging down the corridor, I trigger Eye of the Storm. The Skill focuses the sudden barrage of attacks on me, giving the rest of the team a chance to survive the initial onslaught. Even as I watch my Soul Shield shatter, my hands are forming the spell for an Enhanced Lightning Strike, holding it back till they're close.

When the superheated plasma and electrons jump through space, the attackers stumble and jerk to a halt. As if we're a well-rehearsed team, the remaining defenders counter charge, intent on pushing our enemies back and adding to the Galactic Fleet's losses. I drop my spell, following as I trigger Vanguard to catch up again. Whatever the fleet's up to, it's not something I can worry about right now. My job, at this moment, is to hold the line.

***

When I walk off the line, my armor's smoking and cracks show in a number of places. The thinner armor around my arms and shins, designed to allow mobility, is particularly bad, its durability down to a third of what it should be. I can't help but wince, knowing that the cost of repairs for this—especially since I'm going to need to do it through the Shop—will wipe out every Credit I've earned from the fleet personnel I've managed to end. And more.

"Are they trying to grind us down?" I ask Ali, too tired to focus my thoughts to send it at the Spirit.

"Maybe."

I'm not the only one concerned about repair costs. Around me, I can't help but overhear conversations among the returning defenders.

"Where's your axe?"

"Lost. Rusted-hoof, twice-born Galactic ran off with it in his body. Couldn't get it back before they pulled away."

"Cursed leaves. That was from that Level 70 drop, wasn't it?"

"Yeah…"

Another voice, coarser and harder. Another Sergeant or maybe just a Raider. "That is not a full loadout, soldier!"

"Sir, I was not able to buy a fourth explosive grenade, sir!"

"Oh, but you had money to clean those scales of yours real nice, didn't you?"

"Sir, yes, sir. I mean, no sir! I…"

I tune out the words as I wend through the reserve teams. We've got a five-team rotation going on. One team on the front line, one team on direct reserve and ready to step in. The team I'm moving through is secondary reserves, ready to back up the front line if things go bad. Mixed in the reserve group is mine, while the other team that was backing us up has moved to the front line. The rotation is about two and a half hours, meaning that we can cover half an Irnis day with each rotation, ensuring a five-hour full rest cycle for each group. If you're on reserve, if the team ahead does their job right, you can just chill unless things go to real hell. Such short rests periods wouldn't be viable if not for all our high Constitutions, but because of them, we can hold. For now.

I'm not the only one concerned about the slow grind in durability. I overhear more conversations as I move back to the Shop, heading for the sphere that'll send me to my very own Shop. As I step into line, I listen to the people complaining about the costs, about how the Inner Crew isn't doing enough.

Even if the station has finally gotten around to subsidising repair costs for everyone, it's only a subsidy. But while most people are complaining about how much they're losing, I'm more worried about where the station's limit is. Because there has to be a limit to the Credits the station and crew have.

"Think you can dig into their finances? Figure out how their bank account looks?" I send to Ali, hoping to assuage my worries.

"Not my area of expertise, boy-o. But I'll see if Harry can do it."

Ali's right. Harry's got the right Skills to figure something like that. Also, worst-case scenario, he could pay for it. If there's one person who's making bank, it's the reporter. Due to Harry's ability to record and provide evaluation and commentary on the entire war in real time, his records have been making bank. While none of Harry's reports include secret information, the process of repackaging it and providing professional editing and commentary makes it special.

"Thanks."

Having finally reached the end of the line, I slap my hand on the sphere and let it take me where it needs to. I leave Ali behind, no longer needing the Spirit to chaperone my purchasing. If there's one thing to be said about all this time passing, it's that I've picked up enough knowledge to not be a complete novice.

When I fade back into existence, my equipment sparkling and new, I pull the data stream to the forefront. By the time I leave the area around the Shop, I've ascertained that nothing major changed while I was gone. A few more deaths, a couple of pitched battles. Mikito had to step in once, leading a reserve regiment to shore up our defenses. They also tried accessing us via space again, cutting through the connection rings once they passed the third ring's shield and dropping people directly into space. Bolo was on that, part of the rest of the flying Classers and our remaining ships sent to pick them off.

Tactically, it makes sense that they'd try to grind us down. There are more of them than us, and as we lose Credits and people, it'll get easier and easier for them to win. We can't get reinforcements, while the fleet can. On the other hand, once we lose too many people, we'll fall back to the second ring, leaving even fewer connections and fronts for them to fight us on. It's not perfect, but it's viable for us. Unfortunately, even if we can delay the losses, according to current estimates, it's clear that we'll lose if we keep playing the defensive game.

Strategically, we still don't know the point of all this. Why attack us now? Sure, I've been given explanations that it's all because there are enough Dimensional Smoothers, that we've got an auction going on, that it's just been a matter of time. But somehow, I don't believe it. There's got to be another reason, and I'm not sure I know what it is. Call it a hunch, but I have a feeling if we figure out what they want, we might have a chance of winning. Till then, they're going to keep throwing people at us. And as they've got more people and more Credits, we're going to lose. Even if we're Leveling up with each fight, so are they. Speaking of Levels…

Next Level Completion Rate: 87%

Days of fighting Basic and Advanced Classers has pushed up my experience gain. But the biggest contributor was the flood of experience from the System Quest completion rates. When I'm not worrying about the fight, I consider the data that's still accessible in my mind, trying to make sense of it. I've taken to jotting down everything in a notepad or leaving a vocal diary, since sometimes those musings trigger a new System completion request. In fact…

System Quest Completion Rate: 69%

A huge jump, and all because the data was smashed into my brain. It's kind of amusing in that if the Librarian hadn't smashed the knowledge right into my brain, the System wouldn't have registered much of the completion rates. That it opened up a connection to the System when the Skill was being used meant that my flashes of epiphany were appropriately awarded. Now, without actively noting my thoughts, I'm not gaining experience.

"Note: System can only access thoughts when linked via a System Skill." Memories flash through my mind—research papers, recordings, data. "Supporting documents, K'mara 1938-A-3, Luzard's Maro BB4123, …" I list on and on, muttering to myself as I head for the nearest mess hall. But along the way, conflicting research comes to the forefront of my memory. "Disproving documentation, Os 7421AMOS01714, Flizard…" Conflicting research, conflicting information. It's why the System Quest hasn't been solved. Why the arguments continue to rage. Even two research programs using the same criteria can come up with different results. "Conclusion— maybe. There's another factor in play. Theory includes AI Overmind, Multiple Cognitive Recognition, First Significant Research Experience, Data Parceling…"

System Quest Updated
+14 XP

"Still at it, boy-o?" Ali says, floating down to join me as I grab a plate and ignore the stares of those who have seen me muttering to myself. Or even heard it.

"Haven't completed it yet."

"A million billion years, no one has. And you think you can." Ali sniffs.

"Exaggerating a little there," I say. "But I do have their entire library in my mind."

"And you know that isn't the only thing required," Ali retorts.

That's too true. Even with all the research done, there are still unanswered questions. Never mind the fact that others have tried the very same thing—in smaller doses at a time—and never managed to complete the quest. Even now, I wonder if I can complete the quest, if what has been done to me has destroyed my chances. Then again – the answer is the answer, right?

"Learn anything useful?"

"Well, did you know the Skills can be nerfed? Not necessarily immediately of course, but it seems that Classes and Skills themselves can see an evolution over time as a Class expands. Even those with the older versions can see their Skills altered. It happens mostly with new Classes, those that form when a new world joins, and the frequency of such changes has changed significantly," I say. "But—"

"I meant for our current predicament," Ali cuts me off.

"Ah… no."

"*You do know we're going to lose, right?*" Ali's mental voice is harsh and a touch fearful.

Surprising, considering the Spirit can't die. But he'll lose his link to this reality with my death and go back to his home dimension, waiting to be recalled. Or something like that. Spirits and companions come in a million varieties, even when they're all considered "spirits" by the System.

"*I do. But what do you think I can do about it? I'm just one Master Classer among many. And not even the strongest,*" I reply with a grunt.

I might have hunted down a bunch of bastards, but a good number weren't Combat Classers, and the rest of the time… well, I had the luxury to set the time and place for the attack. This is a completely different ballgame. This is a war.

***

After food, where most in the busy mess hall were too tired to speak with me, I make my way back to the temporary barracks. Since the third ring is the front line now, most civilians have abandoned the location, leaving more than enough space for everyone. This held especially true for the Master Classes and high-Level Advanced Classers, many of whom indulged in luxury rooms and residences throughout the stations. Even so, I found myself headed back to the main temporary barracks, an ex-warehouse location near the connecting tubes, rather than my assigned quarters. No matter how close it was, any delay would be too long if things went bad. And after living through an apocalypse and sleeping in abandoned, half-destroyed houses, it isn't that bad at all.

Inside the warehouse, I find people lying on the Galactic equivalent of military cots, hunkered around fold-out chairs, hard light benches, and in a few cases, just sitting on compressed air. Above, Galactics who prefer being high hang out. Arachne spin their webs while avians, glider humanoids, and a few eccentric humanoids lie in hammocks, floating beds, or just hang upside down. The resting defenders are all doing their own thing, resting before they're called up once more.

Some are eating, preferring the food they have stored in their Inventory to what's being served at the mess hall. I admit, it is a bit hit or miss considering they're trying to serve food for multiple races, but thanks to the System, for the most part, food is food. Barring the non-carbon-based forms, at least. Those who aren't eating are either taking some time for themselves, playing music or gambling, with games ranging from System-assisted video games to old-fashioned cards.

"Redeemer. Thank you for saving me." Pink armor appears as I walk in, revealing his neck and offering it to me in a gesture of submission. It's the weirdest sight of the day, the mohawked, flared tusk, and green skinned Galactic offering me his neck.

"I didn't really—"

"You blocked the tail. Thank you." A slight twitch of the hands opening wide before he pulls back. By now, most people know I prefer my privacy.

"Really, I didn't do anything," I mutter to his retreating back.

"Heard you took out another pair of Advanced Classers, Redeemer." The next to accost me is a known quantity, seven feet tall with a bust to match. Clad in skin-tight, scaled armor, she's striking with her red skin, spiky ears and tail, with cheekbones so sharp that they could cut you.

The woman literally oozes sex appeal, her Charisma stat powerful enough that it reaches across racial barriers and triggers my mental resistances. Just like another alien that I know. I have to admit, there are some stirrings. It's been a while. But not right now.

"Slowing down a little, are we?" she says. "If you don't keep up, I'll catch up to you yet."

"You're welcome to do so." I gesture to the front lines. "In fact, I'm sure they'd take you up right now..."

She snorts, clapping me on the shoulder and rocking me on my feet before she tromps away. A pair of desperate hangers-on offering me jealous glares before they scurry after the she-devil.

Before I've taken a dozen steps in, a pair of Galactic fox-creatures scurry up, asking for advice about their latest Level ups. They're not even really asking my advice so much as wanting an excuse to touch base.

And on and on, it continues. By the time I get to my spot near the exit doors—the signal for everyone to leave me alone—I've answered a half dozen questions, declined four challenges, and accepted the congratulations or nods of approval of a score of others. I might not be the most social of people, but after fighting with the pirates over the last few days, I'd grown to be at the very least on nodding terms with most of them.

I could learn their names, learn more about them if I wanted to. It'd just be a matter of looking up, taking in their details, spending a few minutes chatting. Being social, building the bonds that tie us together. But I don't. The harsh reality of our lives right now, much like in the first few months of the apocalypse, is that many of these people won't survive. Learning names, learning details would just increase the sense of loss I'd feel when they do fall.

But… for all that, I can't help myself. I trigger Society's Web, letting the Skill reveal the threads that bind us. I turn my head, following thread after thread, lead after lead, watching the shift as people talk, as they interact. Sometimes the intensity and colors change between others, especially when the discussion hinges upon friends. But most importantly, what is most stark are the threads that disappear, fading away as the individuals those threads belong to die.

There's a stark beauty to the web. It's a graphical overlay of the way the world works, all the petty jealousies, love, duties, and responsibilities that bind us together. Society's Web doesn't care if it's a word of thanks or a deep-set obligation of Credits and reputation. It marks them all, waiting for me to delve in.

I soak in the changes, learning more about these people in moments than I could have in hours of talking. Information, but information that lacks context. Love, hidden or expressed, burgeoning relationships and broken hearts.

Yet there's another series of threads that I focus on, threads that arise from each person and lead to the inner stations. These threads are thick, filled not with feelings but obligations, contracts. Eleven threads all lead to the Inner Crew, to the ones who control us. It's easy enough to differentiate, because almost everyone here has the same level of obligations. Of peasant to lord, of commoner to those above.

Eleven threads. And one more. This one doesn't go toward the inner rings but deeper in this very station. Leading in a very curious direction. I look down, staring at my version of the same item, at how thick my thread that goes toward the Librarian is, and I wonder—why does everyone have a thread like this? Certainly, not all here are Questors. Yet we all have a thread of obligation, of responsibility to the man. And he to us.

"*John?*" Ali interrupts my musing, forcing me to look up. "*You should rest.*"

"*Trouble?*"

"*Call it a hunch that things are about to heat up again.*"

I grunt, releasing my Skill and letting it fade away. There's something there, though it could be nothing more than a station-wide experiment. A data-gathering test for another damn research paper. The station would be a good test for a variety of ideas—from social circumstances creating variations in Skills and how the System creates and implements those Skills to a study on the experience variation in a rebel station compared to Galactic benchmarks. Compared to the threads that lead from the Inner Crew to everyone else, the thread leading to the Librarian is thin, barely there for most people.

Pushing aside the thought, I let out a breath and fix Ali with a considering look. "You sure?"

Ali can only shrug. In the end, I decide to take his hunch as gospel and lean back, resting against the cold wall. Resting till the next time I'm required to bring blood and death.

Chapter 20

Mana shackles wrap around my armor, hampering my movements even as the Gravitic Fetter targeted at my surroundings slows me down further. From the floor, small pods burst into life sending an alien-version of crawling ivy wrapping around my legs and trying to climb higher. But that's not all—I sense Mana gather behind me, in my shadow itself.

"Thousand hells! What is it with these restrictive spells?" I snarl, trying to stand straight as the spells bombard me. My Class resistances are an innate impediment to any spell directly targeting me, but these guys are using environmental restrictive spells, partially bypassing my Class's advantages.

"Stop playing, boy-o. They're already pushing your people back," Ali snaps.

Suiting words to action, the little Spirit reaches downward and jerks. The gathering Mana in my shadow suddenly disperses as the target of their action disappears under a blaze of light.

"I'm. Trying." I watch as chains, some formed from the very metal I stand upon, rise and wrap me up as the temperature drops and ice forms on my skin.

Ahead, the casters who keep targeting me with the spells have blasted through a good third of their Mana in the half minute we've been at this. But it's been worth it, at least in their estimation.

While I struggle to break out of the restrictive spells, the tanks and damage dealers have made contact. Without me stopping them, they're in the middle of punching through our front line, pushing people back with knockback skills or, in a few cases, literally over-running them. They're splintering the line, forcing us away from the chokepoint. Aura Suppression is keeping my Eye of the Storm Skill out of play. Almost as if they've done their homework and been lulling me into a sense of complacency.

"Redeemer, you need to pull more of their people to you. This is an all-hands push." Oi's voice is harsh and insistent, the gilled Captain's eyes wide and concerned. "They've got us on the backfoot here."

"Fine." I know it's petty, but it's frustrating how I'm stuck being pushed to save everyone once again.

Rather than complain, I trigger the QSM at its normal setting, watching the barriers holding me lose their grip. One issue with restrictive Skills like that is that they're affixed to one reality. I manage two steps forward before I get a new notification.

Dimension Lock instituted.

-247 HP as you are yanked back to your home dimension

Reality yawns and wraps me in its cold, uncaring embrace as my equipment and I take damage from the abrupt shift. The fact that they weren't blocking me before was probably their way of making me waste Mana or uses of the QSM. Certainly, it's currently on the fritz as it recalculates my position after the sudden change. But it's to my advantage too, as I'm free. Until the next Skill and spell hits.

I touch the edges of the Dimension Lock and find myself grinning. I feel more locks appearing, different kinds that harden the layer between worlds or add resonance to things passing between the worlds. But like me, most individuals only have Dimension Lock Skills on a purchased basis. That limits how high most people will go with such a Skill. So it only takes me shaping my Portal Skill into a pick and driving it right at the wall of their Skill to break through.

Dimension Lock breached.

-377 HP damage received

Blink Step is more powerful than the layers they have. It's just a matter of being willing to pay the price. I'm somewhat surprised they didn't find someone more powerful, but then again, this isn't a formal army like the Erethrans. They're a ragtag fleet thrown together due to concurrent interests, many of them only just beginning to get a handle on working together. Add the fact that I'm not the only individual with a movement Skill, and they might be stretched thin.

Either case, I end up in the middle of their casters. I take the fight to them, sword in hand and conjured blades following as I cut, thrust, dismember, and disarm. While most back-liners have some level of Constitution, none of them are particularly healthy. If they were, they'd be in the front. Blood splatters over my visor as I twist and kill, the Poison Stingers shooting from their hidden compartments to target those that stumble away.

My Mana Sense gives me a half-second of notice, enough time to dodge the axe that swings for my head as the wielder and a dozen of his compatriots appear, punching through the Dimension Lock like me. The next moment, the Lock tightens further, stopping any more teleport shenanigans. A part of me absently notes that this one is different, seeming to borrow strength from the Dimensional Silencers that hold the entire station in one place.

"Was this a trap?" I say as I catch a beam on my sword, splitting it apart with my own Blade Strike.

"One that you fell for. How you made it to Master Class is a mystery." A jackal-like humanoid, face seen under a clear, faceted helmet, cackles as he lowers a tri-barreled gun as big as he is.

"Really?" I grin, looking them over then eyeing the distance—a couple of hundred meters—to our front line. Surrounded by nasties. And nearly at the edge of the entrance of the floating waystation they've been staging out. "Let me show you."

Even as they swing, I get to work. First, the Luione Hard Light projector triggers. My duplicate goes for the front lines, where they put the largest and nastiest of their members—a half-ogre and a rock creature. The other is me as I bunch my legs and throw myself toward their staging area. I hit my target—an anemic, twisted creature made of metal and plastic—with my shoulder, catching it just above its center of balance. The monster folds over on impact, breath whooshing out. Strength, shifted to my feet, helps me shift his body while I tap into my Elemental Affinity to adjust the friction difference between him, myself, and the floor.

Wrapped up together, we barrel through the lines, a cannonball of human and alien, wrapped in shifting rainbow fire as a Faerie Fire spell hits, highlighting me as the real target and ignoring my doppelganger. Not that my duplicate lasts very long after, as the remainder of the fleet personnel destroy the projection. They're good—the group automatically split their attacks rather than try to guess. It doesn't matter though, since I'm now inside the waystation between floating transportation rings. The Advanced Classer I'm holding clicks and twitches, hands sharpening into points as it stabs my back. I feel his hands punch through my armor and into my body, before burning poison enters my body.

You are Poisoned!
Poison partly resisted
-4% Movement Speed and Agility

I call down Beacon of the Angels even as I hold the arms of the metal man, sprawling as much as possible while keeping him on top of me. Even if he's still injecting poison into my body, his body will be my protection. Above, my

Skill conjures in midair, bypassing the thin walls of the platform. I spread the attack as far as I can, the blinding glare of the attack hidden by the flash protector in my helmet. The platforms between stations are just rest stops, areas for enterprising entrepreneurs to sell last minute refreshments and travel supplies, areas where travellers can rest when security takes too long at their job. The entire place isn't much bigger than a football field, so Beacon of the Angels blankets the majority of the area, including me.

It hurts, the attack bypassing my armor and defenses in a way none of the others have ever done. Unfortunately, my Penetration Skill has no friend-or-foe designation; it's just damage. Bad as it might be, I know it's worse for others. So I call down the second Beacon as fast as the first. Just as fast, before the expected Skill bitchslap happens.

There's a reason why we've all been careful not to use area effect Skills like this, to not damage the ways leading in. Rising Crescendo has its own way of enforcing its strictures, and the resulting attack tears at my mind, punching through my mental defenses and imposing its will upon me. I feel a wetness on my lips as I hide beneath the burning corpse of my victim, my muscles locked in rictuses of pain.

Mental Influence Partially Resisted
Beacon of the Angels Skill Locked
Firestorm Locked
Polar Zone Locked
Improved Infernal Strike Locked
Army of One Locked
~~Duration: 18 Minutes 31 Seconds~~
Duration: 4 Minutes 1 Second

Mental Damage Taken

-1084 HP

"Hera!" A scream filled with loss and longing, one torn from the very depths of the soul resounds through the platform. It transitions into a wordless howl, going from loss to rage. The kind of anger that will follow one across the seven seas, the thirteen planets, and the hundreds of galaxies, all to sink their teeth into you.

"One. Second. I'll Be. With. You." I force myself to my feet, tossing the corpse aside as I face the fleet members.

There are holes in the floor, gaps where low quality materials or prior damage created low durability spots. Through those holes, I see writing—dense words that take the place of the flooring. From the transportation tube leading to their captured station, more fleet personnel rush in, Galactics refilling their ranks. And there's a lot to be refilled, for the majority of the support Classers here have fallen, unable to take not just one, but two applications of my Skill.

As for me, I have less than half of my own life left. My armor's smoking, damaged and patchy while it attempts to repair itself. I can't use half my Skills because of the backlash, and another portion of them are blocked. The majority of the Advanced Classers, people specifically picked out to target me, are still standing, many with full health.

"Things are not looking good for the hero, boys and girls," I mutter, palming a half dozen Chaos grenades while conjuring my sword. Yet for all my words, I can't help but grin. I trigger Harden, letting the Skill wrap around me, giving me strength. Another thought has Soul Shield layered on top, right above my armor's Force Shield.

I can't figure out why they're coming for us. What their goals are. Who the damn Librarian is or why he stuck the library in my head. Or hell, how to derail the train of my death. But this? Blood, death, and tears on the edge of failure?

This I can do.

***

Escaping my encirclement was actually easier than it seemed. Ducking into the gathering point was to help me target and find the son of a bitch who had triggered the more powerful Dimensional Lock. A quick scan, with the aid of Ali, found me the still-surviving Grushnak Naval Lieutenant. After that, it'd been a simple thing to end him and his connection to the Dimensional Smoothers that surrounded us, freeing me to Blink Step away.

Not before I dealt a little more damage with a series of quick Blade Strikes, of course. Repeated layering of Soul Shields and attacks allowed me to keep the damage up, trading Mana for health, while focusing my attacks on those already injured ensured I could finish them all off. Add in a healthy dose of Chaos Grenades, poison clouds, and Mana-eating nanites and I left the fleet personnel reeling and in pain.

Blink Stepping using Ali's line-of-sight put me back among my own people. Even the navy's attempts to stop that by erecting a wall of smoke and metal failed. Of course, I still had to punch through the rest of the Dimensional Locks, so that added to my damage, but it threw me right into battle with the front line Galactics as they clashed with my people. They never expected an enraged Master Class to pop up behind them, wielding his ever-so-dangerous sword.

After that, all we had to do was pull back under Oi's orders, heal up, and try not to get separated while we retreated. Even if we managed to pull more of their forces to us, the other teams had lost their waypoint stations. Once our resistance started crumbling, the beginning of the end was nigh. We lost the access rings and were forced to fight in the station itself, with only a short break as the fleet piled in more and more reinforcements.

We fight, making them bleed and die. We pick up bodies when we can, picking off the weak and the overextended. Defensive walls, traps, and turrets hurt the invading Galactics. Shifting walls and routes in the station allow us to hit them from the side and behind. We pop in and out, hitting them when they don't expect us, then fade away, hiding behind the cloaking spells of each station. But big as a third ring station might be, it's nowhere near big enough.

"Move, Pinkie!" I chivy the tired-looking pink-armored guard along, yanking him onto his feet and shoving him forward. "They're right on our tail."

"I thought we lost them," Monocle, the halfling with dreadlock hair and a single targeting monocle says, hauling a plasma glaive along on one shoulder.

"Go complain to them," I say. Who knows how they know, but I can see the converging red dots on my minimap.

"Oh shit. Watch the corner, boy-o."

I relay the warning to everyone before sending my thought to Ali, the Spirit scouting ahead of us. *"Trouble?"*

"Take a look for yourself."

I share his vision, surprised when I realize that I know what we're looking at. Where. This is the way to the library. After all the running around and shifting corridors, I'd gotten a little turned around. Crouched in front of the library doors is an array of fleet personnel, a full platoon and more of marines, mages, and drones. They're staring at the closed doorway, tense.

"Patching you in," Ali warns me, then, suddenly, I'm hearing a whole new conversation in Galactic.

"Do NOT enter the premises. I repeat, do not enter the premises. Subject is a Class I threat."

304

"Orders were passed on, but the Sect ignored them."

"Pull back!"

Before I can gesture for my team to back off and find a new route, especially before the team before us bumps into us, things go to hell. The security doors burst apart, a half dozen figures flying out, propelled by, all of things, data slates. The blast doors, all three of them, are no more useful than a paper screen at stopping the bodies. Well, except for the unlucky figure whose bodily integrity doesn't hold up under the pressure and comes apart. Once the thrown figures clear the doorway, the slates accelerate. Another of the Sect members body can't stand the sudden acceleration and comes apart, blood exploding as it's bisected.

"Improper Shelving. Library Ban," Ali says, eyes wide as he reads his interface. *"Goblin's Ass. How is he using those Skills at that Level?"*

I don't know. But floating out of the rubble is the Librarian. As he exits fully, the doors reform, broken pieces floating back into place as he surveys the results of his attack. The Sect members and the remaining navy personnel are all professionals, having shaken off the surprise, and are spreading out to surround the Librarian. In one ear, I hear the navy commander screaming for updates, for them to pull back, even to finish off the battle. He's panicking, his orders contradictory. I kill the tap, focusing instead on the upcoming battle.

"You are all not invited." The Librarian turns his head and fixes on a marine. "Except you. A fellow Questor is always welcome."

"You a Questor, Gehney?" one of her teammates asks, surprised.

"I am. What'd you think I was reading? The menu?"

"Quiet in the ranks!" her Sergeant barks, the pyramid-shaped figurine in his hand held up to the Librarian. "Librarian Feh'ral, you are under arrest."

The Librarian turns his head, twisting his neck while keeping the rest of its body entirely still. He focuses those grey eyes on the Sergeant and I can hear the Sergeant gulp. That's when I realize that I'm sensing a portion of the Librarian's aura, even from the distance and through my Resistances. To say it's disturbing is kind of like saying that waking up to a five-year-old standing by your bedside in the dark of the night, chanting the words "in the darkness they will come" is perfectly normal.

"No." The Librarian's answer is simple and to the point.

"Then we'll be forced to use force," the Sergeant says, voice trembling with breathless fear. But the Sergeant's talking has bought time for those thrown out of the library to steady their hearts and heal, time to spread out and focus on the Librarian.

"I would not recommend that," Feh'ral says as his hands steeple in front of his chest. That casual, non-combative motion sends a shiver of fear through my spine. And I'm not even looking to fight him.

"Stupid. You let us set up the Seven Light Eleven Heaven Formation!" One of the Sect members cackles, thrusting his hand toward the ceiling. Mana emerges from his hand and the palms of the others around.

They form a seven-sided pentacle with the Librarian in the center. Within the pentacle, eleven stars glimmer. Together, the Sect members cast a formation—basically, just a group spell—at the Librarian. Walls of Mana form, trapping Feh'ral. Within, the air itself warps and shimmers as the temperature rises again and again. On top of that, the other unharmed members of the Sect and navy open fire, their attacks passing through the walls of Mana to strike the Librarian.

Attack after attack lands. His clothes are ripped and torn, bullets and beams burning and howling. The thin, grey body is buffeted by the strikes, yet he does not part his hands or otherwise move, not even when the beam of an entire cannon blast strikes his face. Blows land for a good minute, a barrage that makes his figure disappear. Eventually, they run out of Mana or ammunition.

"Hag's tits."

"Goblin snot!"

"That's not possible."

Cries of exclamation from the attackers as they realize that all that damage, all the attacks have done nothing more than ruffle the Librarian's hair. As the shock ripples outward, the Librarian unsteeples his hands and opens them, the casual motion shattering the formation that held him still.

"*How?*" I send to Ali in pure shock.

"*He took damage. It's a Skill—Unflappable Help—that's hiding the damage.*"

"*A bluff?*"

"*Of sorts. There are ranges of damage that the Skill can hide. Most Skills start at around thirty percent of one's health. I'm surprised he sunk this many points in it… unless…*"

"*Unless?*"

Before Ali can answer me, the Librarian seems to have gotten tired of waiting. His hand twists, fingers twitching as the shards and pieces of the data slates rise. The patched doors open and more data slates appear, flying out to surround the Librarian. But that's not the end. As the fleet personnel shake off their fear and get ready to attack, the Librarian's other hand clenches. The Mana around the group freezes, stilling even when others try to rouse it.

"*Silence of the Sanctum of Learning. Skill killer.*"

What happens next is a massacre. Without Skills, without ability, the navy personnel and Sect members are forced to fight with one hand tied behind their backs. And the Librarian takes no mercy on them, using his data slates to attack them physically and his Skills to tear open their minds, making even the paltry physical defenses they raise fall apart at the appropriate moment. They fall, one after the other. Some of the fighters collapse without a single data slate touching them, as their psyches shatter.

"Boy-o. Some of those Skills I can list. Mental Impartation. Mind over Matter. Knowledge of the Masses. But there are others in there that I can't even get the System to cough up."

"Master Class Skill hidden via the System? Or Heroic?"

One of the aspects of Ali's growth is that he's still limited by my Level, and since the System technically registers him still as an Advanced Class, reaching past Master Class for his Skill delving is impossible, even if it's not blocked.

"Only a Seer knows."

As the last stubborn bastard ends up on the floor, his body carved up by the data slats and green blood dribbling from his wounds, I can't help but shake my head. They should have run. Instead, they stood and fought. And died. Brave idiots.

"You can come out now," Feh'ral calls, making me jerk. The others with me flinch, some almost looking as though they'd rather retreat.

I shake my head quickly as I make my way to greet the smiling Librarian.

"We're all friends here, yes?" I say, offering him an uncertain smile.

"Friends? Perhaps. I do require an escort." The Librarian gestures back at his library. "The attack interrupted my packing."

"Packing?" I frown, recalling the relatively empty library. When nearly everything is kept in electronic records, most of it situated in the System itself, there's not a lot of packing to do. "I…" I shake my head, recollecting the fight that just happened. You know what. If he wants to pack up the lint, I'm not going to question him on it.

"We'll be happy to escort you, sir," pink armor speaks up, bobbing a bow to the Librarian.

"Let's move. Our pursuers might have gotten delayed, but we should get going." I glance at my HUD, a little regretful that they did get delayed. After what I just saw, I have a feeling taking care of them would be a cakewalk.

Then again, the Librarian might be a Bolo. All burst damage, high Mana pool, but low Mana regen. As we head out, I can't help but glare at the question marks hovering over Feh'ral's head and wonder what secrets they hide. Wonder who, exactly, this Librarian is.

***

We've made it most of the way to the backlines, past the vanguard of the fleet attackers when I feel safe enough for us to talk. In my minimap, I can see the front line of the rebels and the lack of trouble, so I ask the question that's been burning at the tip of my tongue.

"Where are the rest of the Questors?" I say to Feh'ral, gesturing to the inner core. "I've only ever seen you and me."

"Questing," Feh'ral answers.

"No way. You're the largest non-Council library. There has got to be others visiting," I say stubbornly. "So where are they?"

"Questing." Feh'ral fixes me with his gaze by twisting his neck only, just like an owl, while the rest of his body floats forward. "Many take the opportunity to purchase information or receive a data download. But once done, few stay. They find their own opportunities in the wider Galaxy."

I frown. "Opportunities?"

"Testing," Feh'ral says. "Many of the assumptions in the papers are tested in the Forbidden Zones. Tested at places where the System and non-System reality meet. In that way, they gain greater understanding of the works and are able to produce additional studies."

"Additional…?"

A slight twitch of Feh'ral's fingers as he stares at me, then information that had been packed away in my mind blooms. I grunt as data becomes information, as dozens of studies, hundreds of papers and videos pass by me in the blink of an eye. Knowledge, given understanding.

System Quest Updated
+814 XP, +72 XP, +175 XP…

A step and then another, and the information fades, the studies going dormant. But the knowledge of spells that worked in the Zones, of races that changed and altered as the System took hold of individuals and warped them, of Classes that appeared then shattered under the pressure of too much Mana. Skills that no longer worked, or suddenly worked too well as the System gave way. Information of expedition after expedition into the heart of the Forbidden Zone. The studies might have faded, but the knowledge stays. Knowledge given, questions answered, all leaving me with ever more confusion.

I take a drink of water, clearing my suddenly dry throat. "How are you bypassing my resistances?"

"With difficulty."

I snort, but the answer does at least make me feel a little better. Even if he doesn't seem to be straining to get past my defenses. Before I can continue to question the Librarian, we find our front lines. I glance at my team, all of who've managed to regenerate back to full health.

At their nods, I sigh. "This is where we part, Librarian."

"Yes." Feh'ral continues to float forward, the front line parting to let him through. He continues to twist his neck, following me with his gaze until he is past the line, his head turned around completely. "Do not die, Questor. There are few enough true Questors left."

"True?" I call out, frustration evident in my voice.

But he's not listening. The Librarian floats into the safety of our lines, headed for the transport tubes.

"What do you mean true?" I ask.

"Redeemer?"

I sigh at Pinky. "Let's go. We got more killing to do."

"Good. I'm nearly at the next Level," Monocle says as he hefts his rifle.

I snort, mind still on the Librarian. I force my thoughts away as I turn around, heading back into the station. Time to go do what we do best then.

Chapter 21

To no one's surprise, we lose the third ring. Not even in fire and flame but in a whimper of retreating rebels and malcontents once we lose the station cores. All the defenses, all the tricks we built to turn against our enemies are returned to us, and the best we can do is make sure we're well out of the way. Most of us make it, but not everyone. Still, there are advantages to losing the ring and being forced into the larger second ring stations. Like meeting old friends again.

"Good to see you," I say to the Samurai.

This time around, space is a lot more scarce as the refugees from the first three rings are packed in with the second ring residents too. Rather stay in the already overcrowded barracks, I've chosen to use the quarters they assigned me. Which is where Mikito finds me seated on a chair and eating a snack. I let my gaze slide upward, taking in her details, and find myself smiling slightly. She's gone up in Level again.

Mikito Sato, Spear of Humanity, Blood Warden, Junior Arena Champion of Irvina, Arena Champion—Orion IV, Xumis,…; True Bound Honor (Upper Samurai Level 17) (M)
*HP: 3339/3339**
*MP: 2402/2402**
Conditions: Isoide, Jin, Rei, Meiyo, Ishiki, Ryoyo, Feudal Bond, True Bound
Galactic Reputation: 178
Galactic Fame: 147,084

A lot of her experience gain has to do with the second tier Skill True Bound. It's the next step from Feudal Bond, replacing attributes with experience. I pull up the information again, shaking my head slightly as I read over the Skill information. It's not something I'd have chosen, but ever since she gained the Skill, her experience gains have taken a step up.

True Bound (Level 1)

True Bound ties a Samurai ever closer to the fate of her Lord. In exchange for her Skill, honor, and sword, the Master exchanges a portion of his experience. This Skill is only in effect so long as the feudal status is in effect between the involved parties. If the feudal status is revoked, True Bound experience will be lost with Levels, attributes, and Class Skills locked until experience is regained. Mana Regeneration reduced by 5 permanently. Effect: User gains 10% of target Master's experience gains. This experience gain is cumulative with own experience gain.

Add Mikito doubling down on Feudal Bond and the young lady is hell on wheels in a way that doesn't show on her basic Status readout. She's got more Strength, Agility, and Perception than I do, and spending all the time in the arena means that she knows how to adjust them to her full benefit. If it weren't for the fact that we're constantly moving, she'd have a lot more championships to her name. The people at her Level just can't keep up with the prestige Classed Samurai.

"And you"—Mikito drops down to sit beside me, lowering her voice— "didn't Level?"

"I'm close," I say, shaking my head. Why am I telling her that? She should know. But I guess sometimes inane conversation is what the doctor ordered. "All those System experience results are pretty good. And the fights."

"Dragon's blood, but that's true. But what is this I hear that you haven't fought a Master Class?" Bolo says, stomping over and crossing his arms. "I've fought two. And killed one. Even your friend has dealt with one herself."

"That where the Level is from?" I ask Mikito, who nods.

I knew she was inching up, though with the sheer amount of experience a real Master Classer needs, inching is exactly the right term. Having me feed her experience helps a lot, along with her own Titles and desire to fight. Funnily enough, some Master Class kills aren't as experience heavy as others. There's a long series of tests that show that, along with an even longer list of wordy explanation. Most of it boils down to the simple fact that experience from Support Classers doesn't translate well to experience for Combat Classers who kill them. It's one reason why occasional massacres of Support Classers don't happen.

"Huh. Lucky. And why'd they send two against you?" I ask.

"Obviously, because I'm awesome." Bolo sniffs. "I still won. No matter what the Analysts say, battle is a matter of heart. Not numbers."

"But odds tell you probability," Mikito says, opening her hand sideways. "You only won because you made their underlying calculation unworkable. Aura Focus will be a problem for many and not one they expected you to have."

I raise an eyebrow in query.

Bolo almost preens. "Aura Focus lets me narrow my aura to a single individual."

I cough, thinking how Dragon Fear can knock around even the most mentally stable individual. Even I can feel it pressing against my mind when it's on. Focused, with Bolo's high Charisma, it'd be a deadly weapon. I'm almost tempted to see what it would do to my own Aura.

"Let me guess. Draco here slapped them with Aura Focus, froze one of his opponents, and went to town on them before they got a chance to recover. Spammed and killed most of his Mana, then had a long, drawn-out fight with the other Master Classer," Ali says, shaking his head. "And that's why they had to retreat, because Bolo ran out of Mana."

"I did not run out," Bolo says with a sniff. "I chose to conserve the amount I had left for a potential retaliation."

"And the rest of the Master Classers?" I say.

For obvious reasons, there aren't a lot of us who are ground pounding Master Classers. The majority of the Master Classers on our side are Captains, Quartermasters, or Navigators, individuals who run powerful ships or Support Classes. They took part in the initial battle before retreating, waiting for when the navy would be forced to commit their ships once more. Or a chance to run. As for us ground-pounding Combat Classers—outside of the Inner Crew, who have yet to take action—we have six others. Unfortunately, most of them are low Levels, just like Mikito.

"We lost Malavi." At my puzzled look, Mikito sighed. "The one that looked like a rooster."

"Oh, Birdman!" I wince as I hear myself. Sometimes, my level of insouciance with names and death can come off even harsher than I mean it to. Like now. "Sorry. How?"

"Advanced Class team. Baited him in, locked him down, then just kept hammering at his defenses. They kept pulling him deeper and deeper so that he couldn't escape," Ali says, shaking his head. "They used a bunch of nanoswarm grenades and Mana flow control spells to ensure he couldn't use most of his big Skills."

"And he was a mage."

"Rune Caster. But yes."

I sigh, rubbing my face. That means there are eight of us Master Classers left. With… "How many confirmed on their side?"

"Master Classers? Eleven that we know of."

I grunt, grateful that it's not more. Like us, a number of their Master Classers are stuck on their ships. It still doesn't make things right.

Bolo doesn't stop. "But we're certain there are a half dozen more waiting for the Inner Crew."

"Of course there are." I exhale in frustration. Then I open my eyes as I remind myself that what is, is. "Now what?"

"We consolidate and hold. The Poet has used another Skill, buying us time," Ali says, letting his gaze drift to the exit. "It won't last long—but with more of her plot points finished, she can take a little more action."

"And we're still going to force them to hit us?"

"Maybe." Bolo shrugs. "That is being decided now."

I grunt. I hate being kept out of the decision making, but it's not as if I have a better idea. Or an ability to make them listen to me. We're still caught, waiting for them to finish this. But even I know the end is near. We're getting ragged, tired from the fighting. Even if the System fixes our bodies, our minds are taking a beating.

"Chocolate?" I say, holding up the wrapped goodness.

There are a few snorts from my friends before they reach forward, taking portions of liquid gold and having a seat. For now, we can just wait.

***

Two days. That's what we've been given as the Poet uses another Skill, enforcing a break in the entire narrative of our demise. Two days to rest, relax, reequip. To build tension. Two days to buy what new Skills or spells we need to change the dynamics of the war. Except our opponents are doing the same. While I could go to the Shop to borrow their time distortion, it's not only rude but a way to get myself kicked out and banned if I abuse it. On top of that, what would a few extra days do? I can't fight anyone and poking through my brain is a marathon, not a sprint. I have to admit, I'm not the best at theory crafting a better build, not when compared to so many others out there.

The latest fight showcased my deficiencies—I still had trouble controlling a battlefield. I have no real control spells. Even if I have tangler grenades and wall spells, they could be dispersed or discarded by others. My taunt aura is now blocked by the Aura Suppression ability. And even if I do taunt, I'm beginning to hit the maximum of my survivability with my current healing and damage reduction loadouts, especially in these big fights. I could upgrade my Soul Shield again, which would increase my survival rates, but it doesn't really help with dealing with large groups of individuals.

I can see two ways of fixing that problem. The easiest is to increase my survivability, increase my ability to move on the field and then increase my damage. That's kind of the build I've been going for. It doesn't matter how many they have—if I can get to them and take them down fast, I can win. My other option, with Beacon of Angels, is pulling large groups to me and blasting them all away. That's particularly useful against Basic Classes or back line fighters, but against Advanced Class players, the wide area effect damage is often muted by their armor and resistances.

"Another Level in Beacon?" I mutter. It works, after all. And if I don't do enough damage now, I could just up it. The damage math with Penetration worked in my favor. If I did two thousand points of damage now, going up to two thousand five hundred in base damage would be a five hundred point increase in base damage. Assuming someone had a forty percent defense, then I'd be looking at a thousand two hundred points of damage initially, but a thousand five hundred after their resistances normally. However, Penetration actually deducted eighty percent of the forty percent defense, leaving it with an actual damage reduction of eight percent. In that sense, we're looking at a thousand eight hundred and forty percent base damage, or two thousand three hundred after the increase. That's four hundred and sixty points of damage increased. Of course, forty percent resistances are low these days compared to most of my opponents, but the idea holds true.

"If you want, but don't destroy any more walkways. The Poet's Skill's backlash gets worse the more times you bump up against it," Ali warns. "You don't want to see what it does if you keep testing her."

I wince and nod. That's the thing about Heroic Skills—unlike the simple description given by the System, they often have a bunch of hidden side effects. "Fine. You got any suggestions?" Ali shrugs, and I narrow my eyes. "What?"

"What what?" Ali replies.

"You always have an opinion. Now you don't?"

Ali snorts. "As if you listen. You're stubborn and pig-headed and don't even listen to the experts you pay for advice. So why should I talk?"

"Still sore about that?" I say sarcastically then shrug. "Fine. Don't worry about it. But don't ever say I never asked."

Silence lingers between us for a long time before Ali growls out, as if every word is like a tooth being pulled from his mouth, "In a war like this, you need a health stealer Skill. It'll make you last longer, especially since you're already specced for Mana Regen. Large number of idiots, high amount of health to drain.

"If you're worried about controlling the battlefield, you're going to have to either increase your Aura Skill enough that it can't be ignored—which will have the side benefit of boosting everyone on your side—or you're going to have work on environmental or individual control Skills." Ali gestures as he speaks, making little notification windows appear, showcasing a variety of Skills. A Ground Stomp that knocks people around, making it hard to move. A Bog Skill that creates mud. Shadow vines that grip and tear at individuals. A hurricane Skill that throws up gale-force winds. A fog spell that hinders vision.

And another that grips and pulls a figure to them. "Personally, I'd go for an individual control Skill. Spells take too long, especially the way you fight."

That, I can unreservedly agree with. The chant and casting time of spells doesn't work with the pace of fights that I'm involved in. If I was a real Mage, I could control distance and timing, work with golems or tanks to slow down people charging me. But I'm the tank, so that doesn't really stand up.

"You aren't going to be able to beat their control over your Aura or bump through dimensions anymore. They're going to shut you down hard now that their trap didn't work. Keep you stuck in one location and hammer at you till you fall. Unless they bring in a Master Classer."

Ali flashes me datasets of the ones I can expect. Quite a few long-range specialists, individuals who are happy to sit behind tanks and pick away at their opponents. There are a couple of front-liners that I have to worry about, with a few more Support-type Master Classers who will be sending their creations after us. Most disturbing of all, a Master Composer. Who creates creatures of musical notes.

"Fair enough. So individual crowd control, drag them close or stop them from running from me, then end it." I nod. "Up my Soul Shield or personal defense, or potentially something to drain health."

"Pretty much." Ali opens his hands wide. "If you'll take the advice."

"It's not bad."

"But you're not going to." The Spirit huffs and throws himself back to float in the air, staring into space. "I'm done."

I chuckle, having had enough fun teasing the Spirit. He's not wrong, but the Spirit has forgotten one minor point. I don't have the Credits necessary to buy all the Skills I need. Not alone. I shut my eyes, going over the data, going over the options, and find myself sighing.

Time to make a call. Time to end something that should have ended a long time ago.

∗∗∗

"John? Is something wrong?" She's as beautiful as ever. Red hair cascading down to frame her heart-shaped face. Ever-so-kissable lips and a bust that even her suit can't hide.

I let my gaze rove over Lana, drinking in the view, enjoying it before I shut away old feelings. Putting them back where them belong—in the past.

"A man can't call to say hi?" I say, cocking my head.

"A man can. You can't." Lana shakes her head, a smile dancing across her lips. "Also, Mikito hasn't called me lately. She only does that when you guys are doing something dangerous. What can I do?"

I shake my head, wondering if I'm always that easy to read. Or if it's just Lana. Then again, I never claimed to be socially adept. "My investments. The money…"

"You need Credits? I can pull a portion of the funds for a shareholder payout." Lana frowns, gesturing to call up a new notification screen. She runs her gaze over it, muttering to herself about new projects as she works out how much she could pay.

"I was thinking I could just sell it to you," I say, cutting her off before she gets too deep into the analysis.

"What? Why? I mean, I could buy you out, but on such short notice…" Lana shakes her head. "I can't get you the real value."

"That's fine. In fact, if you and KIM could see into selling all my holdings over the next few days, that'd be perfect," I say. "Faster the better, but it needs to be done in two days."

Lana calls my name again, a hand extending as if to grasp me. "What's going on?"

"Just in a bit of a fight. I need to pick up some new Skills." I tell the truth, because there's no way I'd be able to lie to her. "Up my game a little."

"Then get a Credit loan!" Lana says. "Put the shares up as collateral."

"Collateral for products in a Dungeon World?" I say, shaking my head. "You know how low they value products there. Add the fact that they're going to discount it because it's a rush, and I doubt I'd get a better deal. And you know I hate interest payments."

"Leverage is not a bad word."

"But debt is."

Lana snorts. "Don't think I haven't noticed the change of subject."

"Me?" I give her my best wide-eyed look.

That draws a laugh from the redhead. Even if I am wrong about how much I could get from the banks, getting a loan would still be a better long-term option. Especially considering how fast everything is growing. Problem is, if I die, I'd rather that everything I've earned go to someone who deserves it. To helping humanity, rather than some nameless Galactic corporation.

"Just do this favor for me. Please."

Lana nods and twitches a hand. A Credit transfer offer appears, glowing before me. I eye the amount, raising an eyebrow.

"We've done well," she says.

For a moment, I consider refusing the amount. We might have done well, but this is too much. But pride gives way to practicality, forcing me to accept the transfer.

"There'll be more, probably in the next day or two," Lana adds. "But that's what I can get to you now."

"Thank you."

"Just… take care of yourself, will you?" Lana's lips twist sideways. There's a sadness in her gaze, but also a resignation. As if she understands everything that hasn't been said.

"Of course. You too." I nod goodbye before I kill the transmission and close my eyes. One last thread, cut off. It's something that's been coming, ever since I left Earth. And now, staring at my potential death, I realize I'm never going to see that blue orb again. Never walk the green forest of home. Never get my face eaten by a crazed squirrel.

I try to find some emotion, some sense of loss or sadness. But there's nothing there. I left Earth a long time ago, and I'm only just now realizing that I never really meant to go back. Says something about how numb I am to my own feelings that it took me this long to clue in. This. This is just the last step.

A quick shake of my head discards those thoughts and meandering feelings. I've got the Credits I need. And I'll sign whatever documents Lana sends over when the time comes. For now, I've got to buy what Skills I can and start practicing. Two days isn't a lot of time to learn how to integrate Skills properly.

*****

"Come here!" I snarl, throwing out my hand.

Blue light shoots out from my hand, wrapping around Mikito's naginata that she uses to block the attack. The light attaches to the handle, gripping tight and pulling it toward me. Not willing to let Hitoshi go, Mikito is dragged forward as I activate my new Skill.

Fate's Thread (Level 2)

The Akashi'so believe that we are all but weavings in the great thread of life. Connected to one another by the great Weaver, there is not one but multiple threads between us all, woven from our interactions and histories. Fate's Thread is but a Skill expression of this belief. This Skill cannot be dodged but may be blocked. After all, all things are bound together.

Effect: Fate Thread allows the user to bind individuals together by making what is already there apparent. Thread is made physical and may be used to pull, tie, and bind.
Duration: 2 minutes
Cost: 60 Mana

Each of my floating blades cuts into her, tearing at her defenses as she jumps and twists in the air. I laugh, watching her spin to reduce the damage, then when she's all the way past my floating swords, past my defenses, I dodge her palm strike by kicking her through the blades again.

"Owww!" Mikito lands and rolls, coming back up without her weapon. Her clothing and armor are torn up, barely shreds hanging from her frame even as the Ghost Armor Skill repairs itself. If she was wearing her real armor, it wouldn't be this bad, but this is just training. No need to get equipment damaged while we train. "You're getting better at that."

"And you're getting predictable." I drop Hitoshi, flexing my hand to shake off the pins and needles. Damn weapon has an anti-theft attribute, making it impossible for anyone but Mikito to wield it. Even holding the weapon is painful.

"Really?" Mikito says as she stands.

Her word is the only warning I get before I'm yanked forward by an unseen force, her polearm jerking up to angle its blade at me as it sets itself in the ground. My first act is to dismiss my own blades rather than impale myself on them. My second is to bat at her weapon. But the tiny, nearly invisible strings she somehow looped around me while we were fighting restrain my actions enough for Hitoshi to reset itself fully and impale me.

A focused surge of strength is enough to break the threads, but by that time, the naginata has sent more poison into my System, slowing me down even through my resistance. While I look at the Samurai, I find her gone—

only to feel Mikito place her dagger on my neck. Impaled and trapped, I give up.

"My win," Mikito says, then she yanks her weapon out of my chest without a trace of delicacy.

"Just because I've got a pain resistance doesn't mean you have to abuse me," I complain, rubbing the bleeding wound and waiting for my healing to kick in.

Mikito chuckles, eyeing the damage in my chest. Already, my System-enabled healing has stopped the bleeding, leaving only a fast closing wound in my body.

"How's the new Skill?" Bolo says, coming over from where he's been watching and clapping me on the shoulder. "Good, right?"

"Owwww. And it's okay." I eyeball the Skill that Bolo recommended. The one that all Dragon Knights are recommended to take.

Peasant's Fury (Level 1)

No one knows loss more than the powerless. The Downtrodden Peasant has taken the fury of the powerless and made it his own, gifting them the strength to go on so long as they manage to make others feel the same loss that they did. -5 Mana Regeneration per Second

Effect: User receives a 0.1% regeneration effect of damage dealt for each 1% of health loss.

"Bah! With your Penetration ability and your tendency to lose health, this is perfect for you," Bolo retorts. "Great for any of us with a higher Constitution. Means we can sit at a lower health level as a percentage and still get the full benefit from this."

I have to admit, he's correct. And if I hadn't dumped so much in the other out-of-Class Skill, I probably could have upgraded this one. But I have to do the best I can. Sometimes I wish I had something a little more game changing, but those are mostly Master Class Skills in combat, and I can't access any but my own.

"Again?" Mikito says, interrupting us.

I idly note that Hitoshi's clean again, my blood having been absorbed by the damn weapon. Which is not, in any way, creepy. Not at all. "Again. Bolo, you in?"

The Dragon Lord grins, hefting his hammer and walking to a starting position a short distance away. I glare at the Dragon Lord, refusing to conjure my sword until he relents and backs off farther—far enough away that the Giantification of his weapon doesn't give him an automatic hit. Mikito lets out a little laugh as she watches us but sobers up the moment I conjure my sword.

A tense second wraps us all, then as if someone fired a starting gun, we move together, dueling in a three-way fight, to make sure we're ready for our final test a day away. Even so, there's one last thing to do, one last mystery to solve.

Chapter 22

Making my way through the crowded hallways of the second ring, I can't help but grimace. Because we expect to lose the connecting tubes in the upcoming fight, the vast majority of the civilians have been pushed even deeper into the stations. While the second ring stations are bigger than the preceding stations, they now contain the populace of all three lost station rings as well as its normal population. That's brought along quite a bit of crowding and a marked lack of personal space.

The tension in the air is as thick as congealed maple syrup. There's a scant few hours left before the Poet's Skill fails and we are forced to fight again. There's been no new word from the Inner Crew. Their one and only announcement had them refusing entry to the Prime station. They've made it clear they'll let in combat specialists if things go badly, but they've also indicated that the number they'll allow in is limited due to space. Put another way, their message is simple—win or die.

The Shop portals have seen a marked increase in traffic as even the lowest Level non-Combatant tries to find funds to purchase a combat Skill or two. When that fails, they've picked up System-registered weaponry, hoping to do a little more damage. This is one case where the Admiral's earlier pronouncement is working against him. Resisting arrest and aiding and abetting a rebellion means that even non-combatants are going to be turned into Serfs. Of course, there are the hopefuls, those willing to gamble that the Admiral is lying, but they are few enough. A public renouncement of his own intentions would hit his Reputation scores significantly and make his next battle much harder to win if he tried the same tactic.

"What's the point of buying a Class Skill? If you loan me fifteen thousand Credits, we can use it to send Yu-er out." Small, bespectacled, and green, the spiky-eared almost Goblin-like speaker entreats a Yerrick. "Please. We've been friends for decades."

"You've raised enough to teleport him already?" The Yerrick is surprised, his voice rising so much so that others turn to him. The Yerrick glares around, making the others look aside until he reaches me and my curious gaze. He holds it for a second before he turns away, realizing he's not going to intimidate me.

"Yes. Yes." Softer, Greenie continues. "Please. I don't want him to die here or be enslaved."

"Knotted fur! Fine." The Yerrick makes a gesture, sending the Credits directly via the System.

I shake my head, continuing the walk. It's amazing they've managed to raise so much that they're able to punch through the Dimensional Silencers.

"Are you idiots?" another voice, shrill and musical like a thin reed whistle, cuts in. The speaker looks like a standing beetle, its voice coming from a set of thin tubes that jut from under its mouths and curl back to where its lungs would be, small holes opening and closing to allow the creature to speak. "Didn't you hear that they are redirecting teleports?"

"I'm paying more than those idiots! They won't be able to stop me," the Gremlin cries as the Yerrick glares at him.

"Har. You can afford more than the Galactics?"

The bug's pronouncement makes more than a few people fall silent. Individual teleportation via the System was possible, but the bug's comments cast a shade of fear over the speakers. Such ability was not just possible but likely. A quick check early on had shown that certain individuals were further restricted via other Skills, making teleportation ruinously expensive. Among those, not surprisingly, were my team and me.

I shake my head and push ahead. As interesting as listening to others is, as enlightening as it might be, the fact stood that I have a goal here. When I finally arrive at the building housing the library's temporary location, the doors slide open without prompting. Within, the office is blessedly free of people—just a few roving Questors, most using the quiet of the new library to relax. I'm amused to see that above their heads, their System Completion rates are being shown. Most have barely enough to qualify. I guess these are who the Librarian meant by fake Questors. Pushing aside my amusement, I find my target standing by himself at the back, a data slate in his hand.

"Who are you?" I ask the moment I close in on Feh'ral.

The way he fought. The fact that, even now, he is able to establish a place like this, when space is at premium. Ali's inability to read his Status screen. There's a mystery here, and if I'm about to fall, I want it answered. Beside me, Ali has face-palmed at my blunt questioning.

"The Librarian," Feh'ral replies, the data slate disappearing from his hand as he fixes me with that unnerving gaze of his.

I shudder slightly, even though the damn Librarian isn't using his aura. High Charisma perhaps? An intuition of his deadliness? Or he could just be really creepy. "Funny. I've never seen a librarian take out an Advanced Class attack squad. Or even have one sent after them."

"Some people desire knowledge more than others. And some prefer to keep such knowledge to themselves."

"Thousand hells…" I exhale, fixing him with a glare, dropping my voice as I do so. "You're telling me this after you stick the entire damn library in my head."

"I am telling you this because I did." Feh'ral turns his head slightly, fixing his gaze on the others within the room.

One by one, they notice his silent regard and take the not-so-subtle hint, edging out of the library. All but a single Grimlak whose head is bent, big beard shifting with each breathy exhalation as he naps. Feh'ral regards the dwarf for a second more before the sleeping Grimlak is picked up by unseen hands and thrown out the open doors.

Once the doors slide closed, Feh'ral turns back to me. "This conversation is best done alone."

"Without the Questors you said weren't here?" I snapped.

"They are not true Questors." Feh'ral's voice is filled with disdain, confirming my guess. "Though they might have the Title, they have not the heart."

"The heart to pursue an endless Quest that no one has completed in thousands of years," Ali drawls. "Yes. They're the impractical, silly ones."

In reply, the Librarian fixes Ali with a flat gaze, making the Spirit squirm before he returns his gaze to me. "You have questions."

"One. Who are you? Really?"

"And I have informed you. I am the Librarian of the Land of the Forbidden," Feh'ral states.

"So why are they trying to kill you, Librarian?" I continue. "It can't be for the library, no matter what you say. The System already makes it available to everyone. You're just the cheaper alternative."

Feh'ral doesn't rise to the prodding, seeming unconcerned about my backhanded insult. "I do not, for obvious reasons, have a clear idea of their reasoning. But if I were to forward a hypothesis, it is most likely because I have hit a threshold in the System Quest."

"Threshold?"

"Ninety point one percent."

My jaw drops, and Ali literally drops a half-foot before he catches himself and continues floating.

The Spirit recovers before me, his voice hoarse and disbelieving. "That's not possible. No one has ever gotten over ninety percent."

"Incorrect. That information has been hidden, but…" The Librarian fixes his gaze on me and I can feel information unfold within my mind again.

I wince as studies, pictures, lists, and video recordings appear. Dozens of individuals, almost all of them Corrupt Questors, all of them reaching the same point. And the last image of the Librarian staring at an image of a familiar blue planet alongside a litany of information before a new notification appears.

System Quest Updated

+1,283,217 XP

"He's right," I croak to Ali, who is still shaking his head in denial. "So very right."

"Why? How could they hide that information?" Ali says, shaking his head. "It could change everything!"

"Precisely," Feh'ral intones.

"They hid an entire fleet," I say, mind sprinting to new conclusions. My eyes narrow, my throat growing dry. "They hid an entire fleet." I repeat the words slowly, tasting them, running through the implications. "The Council knows."

"That is what has been theorized," Feh'ral says.

"They're after you." I gesture, taking in the station and all of us caught up in this mess. "All of this. It's because of you. You put all of us in danger because you had to finish this damn Quest!"

"Yes."

I breathe in and out, anger threatening to spill over from its tightly wrapped container as I think of the people forced to suffer because he couldn't stop. Knowing that what he did could—would—draw the attention of the Council.

But another part of me, the same part that has needed an answer, cannot help but wonder—why are they hiding this news? Why…

Data flickers, shudders, as my mind unwraps. Data becomes information as I grasp the edges of the conspiracy, of information that never made sense. Of studies that were meant to be truthful, that were meant to be reliable, suddenly thrown into a different light. My eyes dart from side to side as I read information only I can see, threads of information spinning through my mind.

System Quest Updated

+21XP, +712XP, +1274XP,…

System Quest Completion Rate: 78.1%

Level Up!

You have reached Level 39 as an Erethran Paladin. Stat Points automatically distributed. You have 7 Free Attributes and 1 Class Skill Point to distribute.

"You feel it too, do you not?" And for the first time, the Librarian smiles. It's chilling rather than comforting, sending shivers down my back. "The call. It is the question of the ages. The only one worth asking, for those of us caught in the web of the System. The only thing that can give meaning to this life."

I shake my head, trying to deny his words. Trying to ignore the fascination. But it's a futile effort. A fool's errand.

"Oy. You idiot," Ali says, smacking me on the back of my head with those tiny hands of his. "They'll be coming for you next."

"In time," Feh'ral acknowledges Ali's words. "But I have taken steps to ensure it is not soon. My actions with you have been shrouded. In time, they will break through. But even for the Lady, it will take time."

"Great," I mutter sarcastically. "Thanks for that." That I am, in a weird way, actually grateful is kind of scary. But it doesn't matter, not right now. "How are you going to fix this?"

The Librarian cocks his head. "Fix this?"

"Yes. Fix. As in solve the problem of you sending all of us to our deaths. You must have a plan, or else all this"—I tap my head—"is for nothing."

"I expect that you will find a way out, Questor. You have some ability to do so. I am somewhat surprised that you have not already left."

I growl, shaking my head. "What? Teleport out and get thrown into a trap? Run away in a ship through their entire navy? Exactly how did you expect this to happen?"

The Librarian looks at me flatly. After a time, he sighs. "Perhaps I overestimated you."

"No. Shit." I prod him with a finger. "You're what, Heroic? Legendary?" Something changes, a shift so small that I don't notice it on a conscious level, but my jaw drops again. "You're a bloody Legendary?"

The slightest inclination of his head.

My jaw drops. "Gods above. You're the Legendary. The one on the Inner Crew."

"I am not part of the official management of the station," Feh'ral denies. "Though I do have ties to them."

That explains the threads, the way we all wrap around him. Why we're all affected by him, by his actions. I call Society's Web to life, letting my gaze run over his form, the threads. Understanding even more. His decisions reaching out to all of us, putting our lives at risk. I glare at him, then prod him with my finger again, an action that still elicits no reaction.

"You're going to talk to the Inner Crew and help us figure a way out of this. For all of us."

"Are you threatening me?" Feh'ral asks, a tinge of curiosity rather than anger in his voice. As if the thought a mere Master Class could threaten him is laughable.

Kind of is.

"Yes." I draw a deep breath, pulling information together, piecing data into a single packet, then putting it in a data transfer for Harry. "Because you want—you need—me to bring this library out of here. Maybe it's because you've got someone coming to pull it out of me later. Maybe because you yourself aren't sure if you're going to survive this." I cock my head as I let my eyes rove down a trio of particularly thick threads. Threads that reach toward the same spot in Irvina, that make me shudder even though they're just threads. Except... "They're coming for you, aren't they?"

The Librarian inclines his head and I suck in a breath. Of course. How do you kill a Legendary? You set other Legendaries on them. It's why he hasn't acted. The moment he exposes himself, when he's at his most vulnerable after fighting off others, then they'll find him. They're going to wear him down, drain his Mana with small fry, then hit him. At least, that's how I'd do it.

"If you are done..."

"No." I shake my head while Ali stares between us. He doesn't look happy, but the Spirit knows better than to get in my way when I'm in this mood. "No. You're still going to help us. We can't win without you. But perhaps we can provide enough of a distraction that you can get away. And if not..."

"If not?"

"Well, we all die. Which isn't much of a difference from now, no?" I say.

The Librarian seems to consider that. Staring at my head, and somehow, I feel as though he's staring into my head. At the library he's socked away, that I'm holding for him. For the future of these Corrupt Questors. Countless seconds, he regards me, the silence stretching out like plastic wrap over leftovers. And then he breaks it by floating toward me, making me step away instinctively. But he doesn't stop, just continuing to float to the door.

He's halfway there before I catch up with him, falling in line, hope blooming. Maybe.

Maybe we have a chance now.

If he's not just running.

***

My concerns about Feh'ral running fade away when we enter the first ring. The Librarian blows right past the guards, his Aura sufficient to cow them long enough for orders to let us through to get to them. Not that he actually stops, somehow bypassing the electronic security locks that keep the gates closed.

The first station—Station Prime—is twice again as large as the station we just left. Corridors are wider, the main thoroughfares so big that there are buildings hanging from them. Even with the population control, I can see how crowded it is, how well-dressed and rich people are forced to rub shoulders with one another. Not surprisingly, the entire 'population control' aspect didn't actually count if you were rich or influential enough. No, the rules were for the peons, the commoners. Tempers are short, restaurants and cafes filled to the brim. Even so, I cannot help but admire the station, the stark beauty of buildings and random, weird vegetation. If we had more time…

But we don't of course. Feh'ral floats right up to one of the bullet pods that is the station's form of mass transportation. We blast off, and in minutes, we find ourselves marching past expectant guards. Many of the guards are in the high Levels of their Advanced Class, but not a single one of them looks unhappy to see the Librarian. I kind of find myself grumpy, annoyed that somehow, the mystery I had solved was not so much of a mystery to others.

But that's kind of like life, isn't it? Problems that might be unsolvable for one person are a breeze for another. Knowledge varies between individuals and groups, creating inequalities of opportunity and liability. Expertise and solutions often never line up. Until, sometimes, they do. And then the world can change.

When Feh'ral comes to a stop, I jerk to a halt beside him, caught up in my own thoughts. The Master Class guards standing before the door have stepped aside, but the door itself stays closed. They seem surprised but still at a single look from Feh'ral. Rather than moving to open the door, the Librarian just stands before it. When I open my mouth to question him, an image shimmers, a notification window given three dimensions.

In the display is a war room, one that's decked out with more notification screens, 3D holographic projectors, and simple data screens than any I've been in. For all the quantity and quality, the details are all too familiar—a litany of our losses, a listing of the forces arrayed against us. Within, eleven individuals—each of them radiating strength and confidence—are seated in a semi-circle, while aides stand behind them in the corners of the room. And right in the center, dominating the room, is an all-too-familiar hologram of our surroundings, this one playing out another tragic scenario.

"I told you it wouldn't work." Clad in a cross-buttoned navy blue tunic, the Truinnar snaps and gestures, killing the hologram. "We don't have enough people to break out."

"*Pirate Lord Krill. Master Class,*" Ali helpfully supplies.

"If we could force them to take out the shield and then storm us…" a barrel-chested, four-armed figure with clay-skin says. A series of unknowable tools rest beside his stumpy feet.

"*Station Master Engineer Shinwah.*"

"And I've told you before. If you make me break Rising Crescendo, I will not be able to use it again. In fact, much of my Skills will be blocked." The

336

speaker this time is a seafoam green flower creature, her head a mix of petals and humanoid features. Most significantly, a pair of large eyes without pupils. "You insisted I use it, even though I recommended against the use of my Skill for this very reason. Now, here we are. Forced to choose."

"Poet, right?"

"Got it in one, boy-o. Eurynome the Poet of Spring."

"If we hadn't, they'd have rushed us already." This comes from a stereotypical-looking barbarian Hakarta with a pair of war axes resting against the armrests of his chair. At this point, I've had enough surprises that I don't even blink at the fur-covered Orc, even though the typical fantasy orc image has been replaced by sci-fi-armored orc soldiers after all this time. It's just been one of those days. "It was the best choice then. Dropping the Skill now and bleeding their ships is our best choice now. They'll still have to destroy the second ring stations, if they come for us, or have the defenses fire upon them. It should give us the best chance of doing damage."

"Warlord Mika. Master Class."

"Damage. And then what?" The Poet's leaf-hands shudder before she continues. "Even Adonael's Skills can only hold so long, as we know."

"Then we take the battle to them," Mika states.

"And fail," Adonael, Galactic Station Master, says. It's curious to me to see that the public faces of the Crew are mostly quiet in this discussion. Then again, I get the feeling that this argument has been going on for days. "But I believe a solution might have made itself known."

Adonael turns, fixing his gaze on us, as if he knows exactly where we're viewing him from. And considering it's his station, he probably does.

The Librarian dismisses the image even as the doors slide open, letting us in. I follow Feh'ral, a couple of steps behind, feeling self-conscious in a way I haven't since before the apocalypse. Every eye in the room fixes on Feh'ral as he floats in, hands tented in front of his chest as he regards people with those blank, overly large eyes.

"Yes, Station Master, we have a suggestion." The Librarian gestures at the location the hologram once held. A projection appears, similar but subtly different from the technologically created projection. The image of the station and the fleet are still, frozen while Feh'ral speaks. "But we will require a commitment. Of all forces."

"And the legend finally appears. Not going to run while we bleed, then?" Mika drawls, a large halberd appearing in his hands as he caresses the haft.

"I have evaluated my options and decided that aiding you will meet the majority of my goals," Feh'ral replies as if he does not see—or care about—the implied threat.

Before Mika can retort, Adonael speaks up. "Tell us your plan. Show us. Then we'll decide."

"You misunderstand. You will agree. Or you will die," Feh'ral informs Adonael and the rest of the Inner Crew.

As the silence from his cold pronouncement stretches, the Librarian raises his hand and waves it. And the new scenario plays.

Chapter 23

We sit within a supernova of energy in the *Heartbreak*, the attacks from the fleet facing us held back by the thinnest of membranes—a shield of force and Mana. Beams of energy impact the shield, turning it white and blue, flaring red and yellow as energy bleeds off. Spells, bomb-pumped lasers, and nuclear explosions all hammer the station shield, seeking our destruction. And, in turn, the Galactic fleet bleeds. The payback Skill makes them hurt, makes ships' shields fail and hulls lose integrity and we race to see who lasts longest.

It's a race we will lose. The numbers are clear, the estimates simple by this point in the battle. Some minor variations occur, new Skills purchased to increase survivability, increased refresh rates from Level Ups that alter the fate of the smart and prescient. But in the end, in a fight between Skills and numbers, we lose. We always knew we'd lose the moment the Poet dropped Rising Crescendo as per the plan. The moment we forced them to come at us through the shield. But this way, we do the most damage to their ships.

"We're going to die," Dornalor says as he sits behind the controls of his ship. The Pirate Captain keeps shooting glances at his new copilot, clearly uncomfortable with the creepy Librarian. Dornalor seems like the kind to talk too loudly in a library. Or it might be because of the Librarian's Legendary Class. Either-or.

"Everyone dies." Bolo claps Dornalor on the shoulder, grinning. "But what a story we will leave behind!"

"Seriously? Why are you here!" Dornalor snaps, shrugging off Bolo's hand.

"The view is better. I shall be at my station when the shield begins to fail."

"Why, exactly, do we have to use my ship?" the Captain bitches again, running a hand over the newly reconstructed console.

"You're sneaky McSneak," I point out.

Once the Inner Crew finally decided to listen, things had moved at lightning pace. I barely had time to get myself ready, to allocate that new Class Skill point and deal with the aftereffects before I had to make my way to the ship. Once there, I'd found the Librarian in my seat.

"I'm not the best—"

"Pretty damn close," I say. "And would you rather be out there?"

I wave at the ships surrounding us. We're floating in the midst of the other pirate ships, the few remaining cruisers and other modified freighters that the pirates have used for their raiding. Powerful, with a few big guns, but nothing like the dedicated ships the opposition is using. Well, except the few dedicated warships that the Inner Crew finally rolled out. Even then, we're badly outnumbered. Our only advantage is that the Galactic fleet will be damaged by the time the shield falls.

"Har. No thanks. I still don't believe you got them all to come out," Dornalor says.

"Pretty sure Mika roasting that protesting Captain alive got the point across," Ali says, making a face. "And there I was, eating."

"Yeah…" Dornalor represses the shudder that recollection brings before he gestures to the navigational plot. "I'll do my best to get us as close as I can, but with the amount of fire…"

"You'll do fine," I reassure the nervous Captain, putting as much confidence I can into my voice.

What I don't tell him, don't dare tell him, is that we'll be provided with as much help as the Poet can give. Due to the feedback from releasing Rising Crescendo, she's severely limited, but her story Skills—Plot Armor, Protagonist's Luck, Down but not Out—should help a lot. If she was up to speed, she could…

I shake my head, pushing aside the ifs. That way lies madness.

"Thirty-five percent," Ali says, having shrunk himself down to a fifth of his normal size so that the cockpit doesn't feel too crowded. "Time to get going, boy-o."

"The taste of battle…" Bolo's grin widens, then he turns, strolling out.

I look at the Dragon Lord's back, frowning as I try to figure out what the hell is going on with him. One second, he's talking of running away. And now, he's throwing himself into this battle with all the enthusiasm of a teenager on his first date.

"Redeemer?" Dornalor's voice rouses me.

I sigh, shaking my head. What the hell do I know about reading other races, other cultures? I can barely grasp humans. "I'm leaving, I'm leaving. Just get us close."

***

Once I reach the kitchen, I strap in beside Mikito, flashing my friend a half smile. The smell of twice-boiled pork stock with slices of char shui and fresh noodles floats in the air, reminding me of the lunch I missed. Too busy running around, too busy watching others kick the pirates into gear. As I drop in my seat, I pull out a Galactic ration bar, knowing it'll taste weird but fill the calorie void.

Mikito doesn't even twitch, her legs crossed, her eyes half-closed as she meditates, readying herself for this battle. I consider my friend as I chew, swallowing the peanut-pepper goo and following it with water before I clear my throat to get her attention.

"Thanks," I blurt when she fixes me with that flat gaze. "For everything."

"Why are you raising flags, you baka?" Mikito says, shooting me a mock glare.

"Flags?" Bolo looks around, shaking his head. "Are these Skill-based flags? What do they do?"

Mikito and I share a look before breaking out into laughter. We laugh even more as Ali floats over to explain the entire concept of death flags to Bolo. It's a great distraction, especially when the shield falls and we're forced to sit, strapped into our chairs, passive and silent, while Dornalor and Feh'ral fly us out under the cover of his Skills. All the while, the entire rebel fleet is under fire.

As we spin, swoop, reverse direction at the drop of a pin, and otherwise hide behind the rest of our ramshackle fleet, we laugh. Laugh, because the only other option is to scream in terror. Laugh, because once, long ago, a pair of Adventurers struggled to deal with overgrown wolves and Dire Bears. And now we fly through space, dodging laser beams, nuclear missiles, and tears in reality.

And when the laughter dies down, I mime planting a flag.

"Are you people insane?" Dornalor's voice comes crackling over the speakers, strained and filled with tension as he controls our ship. We aren't shooting back because that'd be a dead giveaway, but even with all his stealth Skills, the surroundings are so filled with fire that we get hit on occasion.

"How much farther?" I say, sobering.

"Five minutes. Give or take. But what are we supposed to do when we arrive?" Dornalor says.

"Just hang on for a few moments. We'll do the rest," I say.

My gaze drifts to the screen showing the battle, picking out the five wings of our attack. Of those, only three are actual threats—forces with sufficient numbers to be of real concern for the Galactic fleet. The other two wings are meant to pin down the Galactic fleet, keep them busy while the rest of us get to work.

The pair of battlecruisers lead one wing. One of the battlecruisers is barely more than a wreck, its parts scavenged to bring the other back to full fighting form. All that's left of the wrecked battlecruiser are some secondary shields, the engines, and most of the thrusters. On top of that, new armor was added where the gaping holes of the gun emplacements had been and all along the front of the battlecruiser, giving the damaged cruiser the ability to soak up fire. They've basically turned the entire battlecruiser into a giant missile, one so big that its sheer mass will do significant damage to its targeted Dimensional Smoother. The threat of the kamikaze battlecruiser forces the Galactic fleet to concentrate fire on it, allowing its compatriot to pick off the rest of its attackers without fear.

The other two main wings contain the majority of our Master Classers and high-level Advanced Classers. They carry the battle straight to the Dimensional Smoothers, with the full combat membership of the Inner Crew out in force in a show of the true might of the pirate station.

Mika, the Hakarta barbarian fighter, is bounding across space, somehow forming glowing footholds whenever he needs. Each time he reaches a ship, his attacks cut through the frail defenses of the ship itself, tearing apart armor without care for the Admiral's Skill. The axes are dual-wielded, glowing enchantments on each axe boosting their attack power. Once Mika manages to make his way in, it's only a matter of time before the entire thing self-destructs, leaving him floating in space and bounding off to the next ship. Not surprisingly, the Master Classer focuses his efforts on the larger vessels.

Yet for all the insanity of a single man destroying kilometer-long ships, it's nothing compared to others of his kind. The Pirate Lord sits in fighter jet, dog-fighting individuals and other space fighters, all the while commanding a swarm of other space fighters. His personal fleet move in independent synchronicity, like a swarm of psychically linked bees. It's as if every one of his pilots knows where every other pilot is at the same time. They cover each other's backs, coordinate fire, and dodge blind-sided attacks with equal impunity. Even worse, as each fighter is eventually destroyed, new ones launch from Prime Station, the physical bodies of the pilots safe in the confines of the station. Only the Pirate Lord is in danger, and he's so good that he barely gets hit.

Prime Station itself, with the aid of the Master Engineer, contributes to the fight, launching attacks through their final shield. Most are mundane particle beam or missile attacks, but on occasion, the main cannon in Prime Station fires. The main cannon shoots a beam of destruction half a kilometer wide and so powerful that all but the sturdiest ships fall to its attack, even through the Admiral's Skill. Each attack sees a significant drop in the entire fleet's shielding and armor. Only the fact that the main cannon requires a long charge time stops it from being a game-changer.

In another corner, a Master Summoner floats in space, beings magical and horrific forming around him and launching themselves at the attacking ships. Dragons and Titans, space-jellyfish, and a creature so horrific even my mind blanks of all but tendrils, suction cups, and mouths. So many mouths. They form in space and cross the distance to their prey in a flash, tearing at and being torn apart in a brutal display of violence.

The Inner Crew has come, and their very presence and their high-Level Skills make a difference. We cut through the fleet, many of the weaker ships falling as the damage apportioned to them exceeds their abilities to survive. Even the Dimensional Silencers see their shields fail, their regeneration rates insufficient under the renewed assault. That being said, the Silencers have multiple levels of armoring and some of the strongest Classers backing them up. All the while, in the screaming, twisting, stomach-lurching mass of combat, our men, our ships fall too. The Master Classers are spending Mana as if there's no tomorrow—but the fleet is huge and our initial sally is slowing down.

"Guys. They're in the stations," Harry's voice breaks my analysis of the fight. We left the reporter behind, his own Skills insufficient for what we expect to come. If anyone can survive the upcoming purge if we lose, it would be him. But only if he's on the station. Not that that stopped him from arguing with us. "They're pushing us back. Fast."

My mouth dries, and for a moment, memories of slaughter and the smell, the taste of defeat fills my mouth. The second ring stations are falling and I know why. Most of us ground pounder Master Classes are out here. Some of the larger ships are too big for us to take out individually, but there's nothing stopping a boarding party from getting onboard, bypassing shields and other defenses with Skills, and destroying everything from their engines to their guns. Hackers can take down their system, making ships nothing more than floating hunks of metal. Nannite swarms can eat away at struts on the inside. But to keep these people alive, our best ground pounders are necessary. And that leaves the second ring vulnerable.

"Stay safe," I tell him.

"You too."

"We're here," Dornalor growls even as we spin, lights flickering on and off as an EMP burst nearly shreds our electronics. "But they found us. Whatever you're going to do, get it done fast."

"Feh'ral—" I say, only to realize that the Librarian is already in the mess hall.

He spins slowly, marking us with his eyes. Then reality twists and bucks as the Librarian pits his ability against the pair of Dimensional Silencers that cover this area. My innards squeeze, bones twist, and flesh warps as two opposing forces contest within my body. Pain, all-encompassing pain, wraps its insidious, uncaring arms around me. And then, the world shifts.

And we find ourselves in the battleship's library.

***

No one's here. Who would stay in the library, a resting space, in the midst of a battle? That gives us the few seconds we need to reorient ourselves, deal with organs that are out of place and nerves that continue to fire as they insist they're somewhere else. In some cases, they're right. It takes seconds for the last of the Dimensional Smoother's effects to disappear, for our bodies to firmly adjust to this reality. In the meantime, I smell space, taste data slates, and feel the void on my skin.

"Everyone up?" I croak.

Mikito gives me a curt nod while Bolo cracks his neck. It's only Ali who looks green, his body fading in and out of this reality.

"I might need a bit, boy-o. There's interference on this ship itself…" Ali says, his voice fading in and out as he speaks. "All Knowledge is Not Lost was never meant to be used on others, especially not like this."

Too true. But one of the advantages of a Legendary Skill is that the user can adjust the parameters, shift it around to make it work within the sense of the Skill itself even if it did not follow the initial rules. So sending a trio of Master Classers to a library that he had no access to was something the Librarian could do, even if it was a stretch to his Skill.

"Ready?" I say, looking at each of the others.

A quick check shows that the doppelgangers, the Second Skin, and the Utility Bot are still doing their job, making it seem as if we're fighting out there. It's one reason we didn't send the Librarian—his presence is so great that there's no way they'd not locate him immediately. Even sending us is a bit of a gamble, but we're hoping it's a winning one. The next step in the plan is enacted by the twisting of a ring around my finger, a tap on the wrist from

Mikito, and a touch of an earring with Bolo. The form might be different, but the effects are the same.

Daghtree's Legendary Ring of Deception (Tier I)

A musician, poet, and artist, Daghtree's fame rose not from his sub-standard works of "art" but his array of seduction Skills from his Heartthrob Artist Class. Due to his increasing infamy, Daghtree commissioned this Legendary ring to change his appearance and continue Leveling. In the end, it is rumored that his indiscretions caught up with the infamous artist and he disappeared from Galactic sources in GCD 9,275.

Effect: Creates a powerful disguise that covers the wearer. The ring comes with six pre-loaded disguises and additional disguises may be added through expansion of charges

Duration: 1 day per charge

Charges: 3

Recharge via ambient Mana: 1 charge per Standard Galactic Unit per week

It'll take quite a powerful True Seeing Skill to cut through our disguises. These are the best that Spaks could come up with on short notice, and boy, did the Inner Crew bitch about giving up the enchantments. Once I confirm that everyone is ready, I scan the corridor outside and wave us forward, putting the map of the ship's interiors in front of me. Not to the front of the ship. Not even to the engineering rooms. We're heading to the center and just a little below, the safest point in this entire damn vessel.

Making our way through the ship is a strange experience. Keeping our heads up, a data slate in hand, we keep moving with purpose and blow past any soldier who looks at us. Bolo stays in the lead and we copy his movements, offering nods and salutes as we go along. Not that there's much of that going on, what with the ship being at battle stations. We follow Bolo's lead because the man has more military experience than we do, so he at least knows how to fake it.

As we leave behind another hurrying pair of sailors, I glance at Mikito and drop my voice. "Not much panic here."

The ship shudders, lights flicker, then things stabilize. The station's main gun must have fired again, taking out a few more ships but not doing enough to remove this ship's shield.

"Don't have to panic when you're winning," Mikito replies, her voice wry and cynical.

I snort but have to admit she's correct. Hell, this ship's barely seen any damage, the occasional shorted out light and blown fuse notwithstanding. And the sailors we see, they've all got that confident swagger of winners. As if winning is just expected.

I push aside the thread of worry, the gnawing snake of concern that sits in my stomach, turning it into my go-to fuel—anger. I remind myself that they started this fight. They came looking for us. Not because we're pirates, assassins, or killers. Not because we broke the rules, but because someone dared to ask a question. To answer it.

"You might want to stop snarling."

I smooth out my face but keep my head bowed, letting my eyes fix on the silver-steel floor. Eye the occasional breaks and rivets, which show where the ship was put together. As we trot past pale white lights and swaggering personnel, corridors broken up with navigation stripes of blue and yellow and the occasional green, I remind myself that it's just a matter of time. Time until we show them how wrong they are.

We make it about halfway to our destination before our cover is blown. Our first indication of a problem is the sudden increase in activity in my minimap, as red dots move at greater speed. The second is when those very same dots disappear, leaving me with a much smaller radius of active scanning.

I jerk my head up and open my mouth to voice a warning, only to see Bolo bounding ahead, hammer in hand. A second later, he's smashed a pair of unlucky sailors into the floor, turning the non-Combatants into lurid red paste.

"Cover blown?" Mikito queries, having turned around to eye the corridor we came from. I could tell her that no one else is showing up, but at this point, I'm not entirely sure I trust my map.

"Yup."

Bolo hefts his hammer, eyeing the corridor straight ahead. "Plan B?"

"Yes."

The word is barely out of my mouth before Bolo is charging down the corridor, winding up for his next attack. The hammer is thrown, head impacting the bulkhead before us and going through it and the wall beside it before coming to a rest inside the wall opposite. Bolo jumps through the wall and grabs the poor crewmember who's still staring at the remains of his arm before Bolo crushes him to the floor and bounds off to collect his hammer. I jog past the corpse, barely giving it more than a glance while Mikito takes the rear.

Plan B. Forget stealth, go hard and fast. Destroy anything in the way. Do as much damage as we can until we reach our goal. The plan is simple. But we've got a quarter of a kilometer of decking to go through, a ship filled with enemies, and one Heroic Class Admiral at the end of the line.

Just another day in the Galactic System.

***

"Marines!" Bolo's voice comes from ahead, almost drowned out by the explosions and screams of surprise.

I don't blame them. Trying to stop the Dragon Lord is kind of like trying to stop a runaway train with a papier-mâché roadblock. Still, I take the turn with care. Unfortunately, going straight has stopped being an option as the Captain of the Battleship, his Chief Engineer, and the Damage Control personnel have all thrown their Skills against us, reinforcing already tough bulkheads to a ridiculous degree. It's faster for us to go around and tear through doors rather than walls. Add in the fact that occasional support beams stand in our way and we're jinking a lot more than we'd like.

Around the corner, the quartet of surviving Marines have their attention split. Two are firing at the still charging back of Bolo, who ignores the attacks, while the other two have their weapons leveled and facing me when I come around the corner. They barely even flinch when my Aura brushes against their senses, Battle Spirits giving them a boost to their resolve. Combined fire from the pair strikes my Soul Shield, tearing at its edges as their Fire Support Skills add cumulative damage from working together. A Blade Strike tears one of them apart, their shared damage mitigation Skill diverting a portion of the damage to his teammates. Not enough to stop his demise, and my return backhand mixed with a Blade Strike finishes off another two. I leave Mikito the last as I take off after Bolo.

"Jump."

I do, soaring over the decking that gives way a moment later, the rush of hot air filling the corridor as the explosives set beneath the decking drop the floor. I land, grateful once again for the helmet filters that make the world a tasteless, sterile world as poison clouds bloom, brushing against my Soul Shield. I don't stop, borrowing Ali's sight to target the Abyssal Chains on the group of marines surging out of the hole, trying to bring their weapons to bear. I lock them down, giving Mikito enough time to wall-run past the platoon, letting her catch up without being bogged down. The compressed air explosion from behind is a telltale signal of Mikito leaving behind tangler grenades to slow their pursuit. We keep running, because the point of the vast majority of these attacks is to slow us down while they consolidate their troops. But it isn't going to work.

"Whelps. You will not stop me!" Another roar from Bolo, the sound of his hammer striking.

The Dragon Lord appears and disappears as we follow the floating direction arrow. I charge on, throwing Blade Strikes when necessary but always, always running.

When we make the final turn and reach the corridor that will see our target, Bolo's already stuck in. He's bleeding from a dozen cuts, even his armor insufficient to ward off the combined attacks of the platoon that was holding the door. But the defensive barriers are down, torn from their very mountings by an oversized hammer. In the midst of the marines and sailors, Bolo is spinning, a whirling dervish of metal and muscle.

"Left!" I call, throwing myself to the right even as I channel a Firestorm into my hand.

Three steps and I unleash the flames, letting it burn my targets who hunker below metal and force shields, sharing the burden of the attack. But my spells are not your everyday spells, and my ability to Penetrate their defenses sends them reeling. Once their shields fail, I'm amongst them, sword switching hands with each strike, trailing blades cutting and stabbing with equal disregard for lives.

Mikito follows along more slowly, allowing the pair of us to deal with the Galactics. The Samurai has her hands full, conjuring defensive berms and forming metallic walls to block off our route as more marines pour in to join the fight.

"Bolo. Door!" I snarl, bisecting a Truinnar marine then booting his bottom half into his friend, sending the woman and the still twitching, spurting corpse skidding across the floor to knock into another.

Blood splashes across my shielding, dripping off and leaving me untouched, free from the warmth. A red thread forms in my hand, shooting across the distance to strike a sailor that's creeping up on Mikito, and I yank him into my spinning blades. More gore, more body parts showering us all with his vital fluids. Violence, close-in violence, is a gory business—especially when you have superhuman strength.

The Dragon Lord plants his feet and twists, his hammer growing again as he catches a pair of marines and their guns before he completes his spin, releasing the weapon against the blast doors. Metal bends and warps, but the doors hold. Bolo jerks his hand back and the hammer returns, leaving a deep impression in the buckled entrance as the Dragon Lord readies another strike. Even as the hammer flies back, the doors are reforming, buffing out their own damage.

"No time. My turn," I say, jumping backward and yanking the marine I'm entangled with into my knee. The red dots in my minimap are no longer a smattering but a flood of red as their people rush us. Even our opponents' Skills can't hide the incoming numbers.

I drop the senseless, shattered body and raise my hand, sword aloft. Swords appear all around as I conjure them from thin air, more than ever before. I swing my hand down and Army of One blasts the door and anything in its way to bits. Through the smoking rubble of the door, I see our objective. The flag officer's command and control room of the flagship battleship *The Zulfiqar's Mercy.*

Except as the air clears, the Admiral is not there. Silence descends as we take in his absence, take in our failure. The battle pauses as the marines pull back and ready themselves, and we stand, staring at the quartet of Master Classers who regard us with gloating smiles.

"Did you think your little ruse would work? That we would not know?"

I'm not sure who speaks, the voice metallic and tinny, but it's derisive, gleeful. Contemptuous.

Chapter 24

Four Master Classers where there should have been one Heroic Admiral, standing in the ruins of the command and control room of the Admiral's ship. The room itself looks like a smaller version of our own war rooms, except there are a lot more chairs and stations for people to take over running the ship if needed. For all that, it's empty but for the Master Classers.

Our goal was simple. Kill the Admiral, and suddenly the fleet loses its ability to share damage. It becomes a slug fight, and between Prime Station's main cannon, the battleships, and the Master Classers, we should have been able to take out at least two Dimensional Smoothers. With two down, we could shift the station and escape the encirclement of the remaining smoothers. If we were lucky, we could take out three and make our lives a lot easier.

That was the plan. Instead, we find ourselves facing four Master Classers, four individuals who have likely been picked to deal with us especially.

"How?" Bolo croaks, staring at the group as he readies his hammer.

"How do you think? Scum like you will always betray one another." That same voice, laughter in it now.

I ignore the byplay, letting my eyes run over the group, hoping to gather as much information as possible. A lot of that information is from data we've pre-gathered, Ali populating information from what we know, information that he's assigning to the Master Classers, rather than real-time data. It'd be too easy if they didn't have something to block a read.

First is the Master Class speedster. He's known, an easy fix. I just have to hit him and he'll go down. Simple. Right… and I've got a few bridges over Vancouver to sell you. The ones that got dropped during the apocalypse.

Devereux Alb, Three Time Winner of the Sisa Cup, Too Fast for Tickets, Butcher of Goblins, Trolls,... (Level 27 Three Winged Messenger) (M)

HP: 1480/1480

MP: 1430/1430

Conditions: Blitzed, Occam's Route, Slipstream, Future Projections, Lightning Reflexes

Behind, the one that I'm assuming is talking is a birdman. Tin box around its neck gives that same croaky, gloating noise. Flames lick and dance across its frame, its eyes roving over all of us before it fixes on Mikito.

Phortala Lzz, Flame Master, Warrior of the Skies, Droughtbringer, Slayer of the Iyu Sea, ... (Level 14 Avatar of Snas the Flame Bringer) (M)

HP: 3110/3110

MP: 2430/2430

Conditions: Flame Warden, Fire Aspected, Haste, Mana Drip, Heat Regeneration

In the corner, in what can only vaguely be called a body, is a floating gas cloud. Except it's no gas, but a swarm of nannites, so dense it's given form. In the center, barely able to be seen, is the congealed form of a pixie, her body already subsumed within the swarm, given form only by thought and will. Even as we bicker, I can see tendrils of her swarm reaching for Bolo.

Elandoriel Feynori, Idea Stealer, Master Artisan, Synthetic Calamity, Swarmlord, Slayer of Griffins, ... (Level 42 Nanomanc Cybria)

HP: 1890/1890

MP: 6740/6740

Conditions: Mind in the Machine, Nanoswarm Body, Mana Locus

And lastly, standing just behind the group is a man in basic Adventurer's chic. He looks human but for the tiny horns on his forehead and those coming out of his cheekbones, the horns highlighting the swirling tattoos that glow with a sickly green light. In the few areas of exposed skin, I see more of those tattoos. Even the staff he carries looks wrong, glowing with that same sickly green light.

??? (Level ??? Acolyte of the Purple Order) (M)

HP: ???/ ???

MP: ????/ ????

Conditions: (Hidden)

"I got the rest, but the Acolyte?"

"Hidden by Dietic Interference. He wasn't even in the data downloads earlier."

"Really? And Purple?"

"It's a Skill. The Purple Order is an 'evil' order of its planet religion. Your equivalent of black or Satanic cults. Expect support Skills, diseases, and poisons. Maybe some health and damage swapping."

"Gloat over this—" One moment Bolo's talking and gesturing as if he's going to curse them out; the next he's unleashing his equivalent of a final attack. In his case, it's Dragon's Breath—an attack that erupts from the head of his weapon rather than his mouth but whose temperature makes my skin dry out even from a distance. And it's targeted at the Master Classers.

Phorta steps forward quickly, holding up his hands. The flames compress, twisting and forming a ball of plasma that he contains in his hands. He holds the attack away from his teammates, though I do note that their various defensive shields take some damage from being in close proximity to the heat. But most of it is contained, held back by the Flame Master.

"Real smart, you lizard lover. Using fire against a Fire Aspect!" Ali snaps.

As if to punctuate things, Phorta puts his hands together then jerks them apart as if he's opening curtains. The ball of plasma in the Flame Master's hands rips apart, uncorralled and forcing the Flame Master to use his Skills again to control it even as tendrils burrow into its flesh.

"Damn it! I'm still underpowered. Give me a second." Ali scowls in concentration.

But the Master Classers are no longer waiting for us to take action. One second Speedster is beside his friends, and the next, I'm punched in the chest and carried back, smashing apart marines who are too slow to move aside. Elandoriel's nannites wrap around Bolo, the Mana around him warping and disappearing even as his shields flicker, taking damage from hundreds of thousands of mini attacks at the same time. Meanwhile, Mikito cries out as she stumbles, the Acolyte pointing his hands at her as he lays a curse on the Samurai.

I try to grab at my Elemental Affinity, do the same thing that Ali did to the Speedster, but Devereux's smart. He doesn't stay still, instead shifting his position and mine constantly as he attacks, never letting me control the friction between him and the floor. In the meantime, my Soul Shield keeps getting struck, each impact shaving off fifty or sixty points.

Even when I shift tactics and try to hit him, he's so fast that I never complete my action successfully. A swing gets deflected, a knee strike gets choked off before I can get my knee high enough. An elbow that borrows the force of his attack is dodged, only to send me into the wall face first. My Soul Shield pops like an overinflated balloon, and before my armor's shield can activate, he hits the back of my neck three times, sending shooting pain down my body.

Forced into the wall, I try another tactic. Iron twists and buckles, flowing and growing as Iron Walls form around my body, hiding me away. Or at least, that was the plan, but the walls shatter, torn apart before I can finish. It does give me enough time to twist around and drop a quartet of grenades, only for them to be swept up and thrown aside.

The grenades' timers were set to go off a second after release. As fast as he is, as fast as Devereux can throw the grenades, there's only so far they can move before they explode. Two explode in balls of flame and shrapnel, enveloping the marines caught in their range. The third lets out a pitiful explosion barely larger than my fist as the sudden acceleration breaks something within. And the last doesn't even do that.

Devereux gets hit with the backblast, but it's not enough to do more than brush against the edges of his shielding. In the meantime, he grabs me and throws me aside, not intending to keep still. Flying through the air, I flick through my options. Mud Walls don't work. Polar Zone is blocked by Devereux's Skills, so it's not worth the Mana cost. Freezing Blade requires me to hit the bastard. And with him moving so fast, I'm worried he'll figure out Fate's Thread before I can use it. Beacon of the Angels could work, but while activating the Skill is immediate, the charge-up time is slow enough that Devereux would notice and dodge.

All of this flickers through my mind in seconds, my eyes roving over the environment as I search for an advantage. Then I act. Beacon of Angels begins its charge-up procedure, the edges of the attack right against where I'm still flying toward. Devereux spots it, sees how the attack would cover the entire corridor that he's been ping-ponging me down, and backs off. In the next instance, I fire Fate's Thread from my hand. I see Devereux's purposely slow smirk as he adjusts his position, dodging the Skill with ease.

Fate's Thread can't be dodged, just blocked, but Devereux doesn't know that. So while he wastes time moving out of the way of the thread that never shifts trajectory, it completes most of its flight and hits my actual target. It connects, gripping by the target's head, and I pull the Acolyte toward me as Beacon of the Angels activates, bathing the corridor in fire and flames, melting walls and crisping the few sailors remaining as well as burning me.

As the Acolyte reaches me and I charge up a second activation of the Beacon, Devereux acts. A monofilament enchanted blade strikes the Thread, but it bounces off, unable to cut apart the Skill. This is where Devereux's lack of Skills, his specialization, hurts him. By the time he's ready to act again, the Acolyte arrives, enveloped in the light and energy of my Skill. He burns, just like I do. Good news is, the damage done to the others racks up, transferring portions of his health and the marines' to me, healing singed flesh as my armor gives way.

Rule one of any fight. Take out the healer.

The Acolyte forms a purple, swirling oval Shield over himself, a Shield that pops within seconds of being subjected to my attack. He burns, but as fast as the damage appears on his body, it disappears as it is shunted away. His actual health doesn't seem to shift at all, no matter how much damage I do. And worse, the damage isn't even being sent to his teammates.

"*What the hell?*" I send my plaintive complaint to Ali, but the Spirit has his hands full.

Maybe it's the distraction of my thoughts. Maybe it's that he hasn't been able to resolve the dimensional conflict. Or it could just be that he isn't as good as his opponent. But with a scream, Ali dissolves, disappearing as he loses coherence.

In turn, Phortala lets out a laugh as he absorbs the last of the Dragon's Breath, flames licking across his skin. He laughs long enough to be stabbed by

Mikito as she charges him. Unfortunately, even as Mikito draws back her weapon, the wound she left on his body bursts with flame and seals itself.

The Beacons die off and Devereux, having spent a couple of seconds annoying Bolo with ineffectual punches, rushes back to us. Rather than tangle with him, I throw myself to the side and activate Mirror Shade at the same time, letting my doppelganger jump in the other direction. Together, we throw a series of Blade Strikes at the Acolyte while forming and tossing floating blades in the air as obstacles. It only saves us fractions of a second as Devereux dodges around the real and false weaponry, but fractions are enough. Enough for my attacks to impact the Acolyte and tear off an arm. Enough to watch it float back into place and stitch itself back together.

Then Devereux is on me, having dealt with my doppelganger. My armor's shield is down, my armor whining and smoking from the repeated attacks. Abyssal Chains erupt from the floor, trying to wrap around Devereux and missing as he keeps pushing me back. I've lost sight of the Acolyte as the Speedster spins me around, and I'm forced to fight for my life as I futilely swing at him once more.

Fate's Thread spins out, shooting from my chest and targeted at Devereux. He tries to dodge, fails, and gets drawn to me. But I find myself unable to hit him as he blocks and stops each of my attacks before I can get them off fully. Unfortunately for him, it's not just my hands he has to worry about. The floating blades of Thousand Blades hamper his movements, as does the thread, and he's forced to take wounds as we fight. But for all the damage that I'm doing, I'm on the backfoot here.

Thousand hells, but injuries, cuts, and bruises are piling up faster than the trinity of my regeneration, my defenses, and my new Skill can replace. My armor is shorting out, Devereux somehow managing to literally rip it apart as we fight. As a blade plunges into my shoulder, popping a shoulder joint out of place and the pauldron off, I give up.

I pull my armor into my storage, leaving me bare to his fist and dagger. Wounds accumulate even faster, and even when Fate's Thread disappears, Devereux sticks close, refusing to give me the chance to target his teammates again or to give up on his advantage. An uppercut spins my head and lines of light flicker in my view for a second. A blade bites into his thigh, drawing blood, and I feel the rush of energy that stitches a tooth back into place. Then the blade sinks into my stomach, pushing past my Elastic Skin and Hardened body.

Lines…

Society's Web opens before me, and as I block, I gauge the lines, the way they cluster and move. I pick the largest number, pick the direction where it should be. A mental command sends Ali in that direction, his body half reformed, invisible to anyone but me. As I block and dodge, gritting my teeth at each attack, I do my best to buy myself as much time as possible. Until Ali's ready and I conjure a Beacon of the Angels. Devereux backs off as he senses the change in Mana fluctuations around me, giving me a moment's rest. Only to look puzzled as no circle of power forms over me.

While Devereux stands there in confusion, my attention is drawn to Bolo. The Dragon Lord is fighting not just the fairy but the Acolyte. Each moment, his health takes a dip, as does his Mana, the nanoswarms implanting poisons, diseases, and virulent toxins in his blood while draining Mana from the surroundings and Bolo himself. Unable to regenerate his dwindling Mana pool, Bolo is forced to conserve his Mana as he swipes at the nanoswarm. While some of the nannites attack, millions of others form tendrils of metal and plastic that root him to the deck. Each moment, each attack is a struggle for the Dragon Lord, and all the time, the Acolyte continues to curse Bolo. If there's only one advantage to be had, it's that the pixie's swarm is destroyed by each flaming spin of his hammer. But still, they replicate and flood toward Bolo as the Master Classer drains her Mana to create even more nannites, only to have her Mana be topped off by the Acolyte.

In her own corner, Mikito is sort of holding her own. Her armor cracks and glows, repeatedly healing itself as it is assaulted by the radiant heat from Phortala. Each moment, the creature swipes and twists, flying on wings of flame as it pecks at the Samurai, kept at bay by the spinning Hitoshi. Neither seem to have the upper hand, at least not yet. But Mikito's ability to move and fight is being increasingly restricted as more and more marines pile in, opening fire and forcing her to pay attention to multiple angles.

As Devereux makes up his mind and rushes me again, the Beacon finally fires. My health takes a sudden jump upward as a rush like ten shots of espresso hits my body, washing over me like cold water on a hot summer day. Wounds close, blood stops flowing, and I find myself grinning.

"What did you do?" Devereux slows a bit, wary now.

Rather than answer him, I check the Web then trigger a second Beacon of Angels. I slam a syringe into my side, refilling my Mana, then draw hard on the Mana Bracelet, refilling my tanks as I do a quick tactical analysis. My health might be up, but overall, we're losing. Bolo might be able to hold on for a bit more, his prodigious health and regeneration sufficient to deal with the ongoing damage. But he'll fall eventually. He's fighting an endurance battle, one that restricts him and gives him no single opponent to smash apart. The worse kind of fight for the big Dragon Lord.

Mikito might win if she was fighting alone. She's more skilled and has better attributes than her opponent, but already, I can see little red dots creeping up to add their own fire to the battle. They might not be able to do much, not with the weapons they wield, but even a little help might be enough.

As for myself? My head snaps back as another fist connects with my helmet, shattering the visor. I fly backward as a knee takes me in the stomach, then Devereux is behind me, flipping me over his shoulder to change my direction to impact the floor. Conserved momentum means I skid along the floor even as Devereux charges me. My health might have been restored, but I'm still losing…

Another attack, another large flood of health. Lights flare, flicker, and twist as damage reports flood in. My attack hit more than some random location. Whether it cut through an area that was vital to the ship or was targeted at something important, it does enough damage to throw the ship into full damage control mode. Lights burn and twist, and I share Ali's vision for a second, taking in the disaster we caused. Secondary explosions continue, and I realize that we hit a loading bay for their weapons. Normally most of the damage would be contained, but Beacon of Angels and my own Penetration Skills managed to tear apart the structures meant to contain the explosions. And then, well.

Boom.

Devereux is thrown to the side, the sudden tilting of the ship and the loss of its gravitic controllers making him lose his concentration. I take advantage, attacking him with Blade Strikes while he's in the air even as we both float and spin toward the tilted floor. The Speedster has sufficient sense to twist and block, soaking up my attacks on his arms and shins. He screams in pain and sputters, half his life down in a single series of attacks. And then the wounds close as the Acolyte does his thing.

"Gods above. Plan E!" I call, landing on the sloping floor as the ship's gravity modules kick in again. The ship rights itself, tertiary blast doors and supports managing to contain the damage.

"Ooof. Radiation over here is off the charts. Give me a second, I think I might be able to help it along."

I grunt, ignoring Ali. I'm not sure how much he can do. Being pulled apart by the Avatar and coming back must have been difficult. But I'll take all the help I can get.

Mikito gets desperate, throwing Hitoshi at her opponent as she ducks away from another swooping attack and a pair of crisscrossing plasma blasts. The large grey-metal corridor is holed and scarred, filled with ash and radiating heat from the Avatar's presence. As Hitoshi plunges into the monster's chest, chains erupt from the weapon to wrap around Phortala and attach him to a corner of the glowing corridor. A single free hand allows Phortala to yank the weapon out of his chest before he lets out a yowl as Hitoshi bites back. A jerk of her hand makes the weapon return, even as the bindings that came from Hitoshi stay in place, holding Phortala still. Mikito dodges, absently throwing a half-dozen blades at some marines while she regroups with Bolo. The Dragon Lord broke away from Elandoriel by the simple expedience of releasing a wave of Mana-fueled flames, burning away all nearby nannites.

"John..." Mikito's voice is tinged with concern, but I don't have time for her.

"Go!"

Bolo swings his hammer, sending it straight up to tear apart the weakened walls. The pair fly upward, following the weapon. Mikito unleashes projected attacks to weaken the deck plating above. As the two retreat, their opponents recover, a swarm of nannites rising from the diminished body of the pixie and the Fire Avatar flaring his wings to chase the pair as he shatters the chains holding him down. The Acolyte, on the other hand, seems distracted, his head turned sideways as he stares into the sky. For once, not all his wounds have disappeared. Devereux doesn't give a damn about the others, having come back for me once he's healed.

Even as Devereux attempts to gut me, I ignore him. Instead, I call forth Army of One, swinging my sword in his and his compatriots' direction. The Speedster tries to block my falling hand, but this time around, my attack is powered by both Skill and my full Strength. He can't stop it, only deflect the blade itself. And that is insufficient to halt the Skill. Army of One fills the corridor with lethal crescents of force, Mana-imbued attacks of energy and Mana and power, each powerful enough to injure, maybe even kill if they took the attack head-on.

If it was so easy to kill a Master Class, none of us would have lasted this long. The Master Classes all react with years of honed instinct. The Acolyte throws up his shield again, but behind the shield come figures, ghostly forms that stack up ahead of the Acolyte. As the shield breaks, each of the figures is impacted, ripped apart in an all-too-real manner. They die and another replaces them, one after the other, most of them covered in wounds already.

Elandoriel forms a shield of nannites, her tiny drone minions tanking the attacks for her as she sacrifices them to protect her real body. She might avoid direct damage, but her nannites are destroyed, her nannite cloud looking patchier and significantly less dense than before.

Phortala covers himself in fire, the explosion of flame and energy fighting back against my attack. He uses the flames from the Dragon Breath attack in one short burst, covering himself in a sudden explosion of force that returns to me as a five-foot-wide cylinder of flame. I snarl, crossing my arms as I tank the blaze. But I can't help but laugh when the instinctive attack by the Avatar catches Devereux in the back, burning his arm and back.

For the first time in this fight, in either of our encounters, Devereux is entirely off his game. He wasn't expecting the way the flames cling to him and eat away at his health. He isn't used to the pain, having run from damage and pain all the time. He's used to hit and run, used to being in control. He can't run now, not with the flames sticking to him, with his nerves scorched and burnt raw. He isn't used to pain.

And for me? Pain is what I do. Pain is what I am. Pain and anger, the north and south stars of my existence. I take the flames and the pain, let them guide me as I chop down. Devereux manages to get one leg out of the way, but not the other one. I cut a hamstring, leaving him falling and open to my attacks. And then it's a simple thing to finish him off.

I exhale, feeling my health jump up, another portion of life returned to me. It's still dropping as the flames burn, eating away at my flesh. Thirty-one percent and falling. Mana at a third of my maximum. My Mana potion used, my storage bracelet drained.

And facing me, three pissed off Master Classers while my friends run.

Chapter 25

"We couldn't talk about this, could we?" I say, swinging my hands up and down on instinct to kill the flames. Surprisingly, it works. Whether it's because the flames have run out of time, they only eat a specific amount of health, or the trapped and transformed flames are nowhere near as bad as Bolo's ultimate attack, it doesn't matter. They're gone.

"Do you think your friends can escape?" A laugh from Phortala, still confident even when one of his has fallen. "There is nowhere to go. You never stood a chance."

"I know." I open my hands, conjuring swords into both hands. "We always knew."

The Acolyte tilts his head toward me, holding up a hand as Elandoriel forms Mana to finish this. "You still came. You think you have a way to win this."

"Ever wonder what the Librarian is doing?" I crack my neck, get annoyed by the half-broken helmet that hangs onto my head by a thread, and dump it back into my Inventory. Then I continue as if I never expected a reply. "Ever consider that we knew you guys would know what we were doing?"

"Ridiculous. If you did, why did you volunteer to come here? Are you that eager to die?" the Acolyte asks disinterestedly, almost as if the answer itself matters naught to him.

Of course, if it didn't, he wouldn't have stopped this fight. Above us, I hear the fading sounds of my friends breaking through the floors, perhaps even at the hull. The marines, the few who survive, have dispersed—sent off to deal with Bolo and Mikito perhaps. Or having realized how truly useless they are.

"We're wasting time!" Elandoriel hisses at the pair.

"We came because someone has to deal with you guys. Someone has to be the distraction. And, I admit, we weren't entirely sure you had moved the

Admiral. We were kind of hoping not, really," I say. "Even my friends didn't know they were bait. But they knew to trust me to go when I said so."

Metal warps, the Avatar's body rising in temperature. Enough so that Elandoriel hisses and shifts away from her own companion.

"And while you're all busy hitting us, your Admiral is getting his ass kicked," I say.

"No. We hid him—"

"You're not the only ones who can pull data. He's a Librarian for god's sake." I laugh, shaking my head. "We just had to buy him time."

"You're lying," Phortala squawks.

And is interrupted by Elandoriel. "He isn't. I just had an update. The Admiral and his men are under attack." She floats forward, the tendrils of her nanocloud reforming and shooting toward me as another cloud shields her body from the heat that Phortala emits. "I will not wait longer."

"Yeah, didn't think you would." I cut downward around me, tearing open the damaged deck. It gives way with a rending tear, the smell of acrid plastic, burnt flesh, and melted metal disappearing as a gust of clean air rushes upward and I fall. The moment I'm beneath the deck, I equip and trigger my hoverboots to skim along the new corridor. "Suckers!"

As taunts go, it's a lousy one. I'd use my Skills, but not only does Eye of the Storm require line of sight, if I stuck close enough for the Skill to work, I was too close. No. Better for me drag them along via words and intentions. Because it doesn't take them long to realize I'm headed for the one area no one wants a wrecking ball of a Master Class to go.

Spaceships in the Galactic System are strange. The System not only warps physics, it also warps the way we interact with physics and our ability to make things happen. Fission engines are easy to produce, given the right circumstances. But antimatter engines are another thing. They require a level of precision and care that might not be viable except in the best tech levels of civilization. Yet you get a Master Class Engineer, an Advanced Metal Elementalist, an Enchanter, and who knows what else, and theoretical become reality. It's the same with hyperspace engines, dimensional gates, and the rest. If you can get an Artisan with the right Skills, they can build it. There's some math involved, some science, but just as much, Skills take over. At the same time, all that warping of what should be has a cost—a level of instability that isn't apparent when everything works. But when they don't...

When they don't, the results can be quite explosive.

"He's going for the engines!" Phortala exclaims.

"Stop him!" Elandoriel snaps.

"You stop him. We need to stop his friends," the Acolyte says.

"I'm going to help the Admiral," Elandoriel says.

"As if you'd get there in time," Phortala snarls.

Their voices are all shifting, changing as I run, echoing down the corridor.

"I will not let him fall!" Elandoriel's voice flickers and cracks, then there's silence.

In turn, the sound of pursuit comes, overlapping the noise of marines and sailors trying to get in my way. Unlike Bolo, I don't try to cut my way through. Blade Strikes cost Mana and I need to save as much of mine as I can. So I take the corners and cut apart walls when following the signs take too long. All the time fighting the marines that pop up.

A few drones programmed to deal with threats drop from my Altered Space. Blocks of pure titanium take the space of the gaps I've created, tangler grenades added to create impromptu roadblocks. In others, Galactic versions of claymore mines and chaos mines are dropped, all to create confusion and concern and extract my pound of flesh.

"Get out of here. Now!" I order my team, hoping they've reached the transports. Believing they have. I have no time to check their location, how far they've gotten. If everything went as planned, they're already in a shuttle, boosting away.

It's not that far to the engines—not in a straight line, but I'm not moving in a straight line. And each fight, each wall I have cut through is another impediment, another speed bump. By the time I hit the security doors that lead to the engines, I'm nearly out of time. I can see the highlighted dots of the pair of Master Classers coming after me, Elandoriel having disappeared from my minimap. Before me is another impediment, one filled with marines and sailors, drones and force shields.

There's no more time. Not to cut my way through. Not without the others catching me.

No time, so I cheat. I make my decision as blasts ring out, impacting my newly reformed Soul Shield, bleeding it. I trigger my Skill, my evolved Skill, and watch it ripple, forming an unseen dome around my body. An idle cut into the floor makes the dome harden, giving life to it while I get ready.

Class Skill: Penetration (Level 9 - Evolved)

Few can face the judgment of a Paladin in direct combat, their ability to bypass even the toughest of defenses a frightening prospect. Reduces Mana Regeneration by 45 permanently.

Effect: Ignore all armor and defensive Skills and spells by 90%. Increases damage done to shields and structural supports by 175%.

Secondary Effect: Damage that is resisted by spells, armor, Skills and Resistances is transferred to an Evolved Skill shield at a ratio of 1 to 1.

Duration: 85 minutes

As I said, not all Skills evolve the way we expect them to. This one was not what I wanted or expected. I'd have preferred an evolution that did more damage, something that ignored defenses entirely, or perhaps added a damage-over-time effect. Something. Instead, I get to be a tank.

So I'll tank.

A hand rises, blade in it, and weapons form around me. Beam attacks rip my shield away. But it doesn't matter. My focus is ahead, my mind charting the angles I need, the location as per the vids we had purchased. Knowing where I need to hit. Where I must strike.

"*Stop him!*"

Voices, fire burning my back as the Master Classers catch up. Pain through my body, toxins running their course. Resistance notifications flashing up faster than ever, but I ignore it all. Accept the pain, the damage, as I sweep my hand down.

To end it all.

Army of One and a Paladin's ability to soak up damage. Anger and resolve formed into a single attack that's targeted at the security door and the antimatter unit hidden behind it. An antimatter unit powerful enough to run the flagship battleship of the fleet. Formed and guarded by enchantments and Artisan-worked metal.

My attacks tear through the shields thrown to safeguard the security doors. Then the security doors fall, the attacks barely slowing down. Next comes the antimatter housing of the engines themselves. Power given form, given strength. An attack of Mana and energy that burns and tears, that melts and disintegrates the casing, releasing the captured antimatter.

And the world goes white.

***

Enough antimatter to run a battleship. Power contained within a small space, bending the laws of physics. And then when the explosion propagates through air and void, the explosion finally reaches the missile batteries and enscrolled shells, calling forth secondary explosions. The batteries that feed the beam cannons, the delicate summoning circles that contain the portals to the elemental plane of energy are disrupted. More energy is released, more explosions and destruction. One after the other.

And near the heart of all that is me in my shell of power. Ifs, ands, and buts. If I had the time, I could have cut my way through and saved my Mana for Sanctum. If I had more Mana, I could have used Army of One and broken through and then hit Sanctum. But I didn't. Not after fighting and beating a Master Class and running away from three others. Penetration's shielding ability was what saved me now. Even then, even with the sheer amount of defense it provided after the damage my Skill had passed on, it was barely enough considering I was at the heart of the inferno.

Around me, the floating hulk of the battleship drifts. The explosion tore the ship asunder, sending the remnant portions spinning away. The Admiral's Skill worked against the navy now, the damage from within contained for too long as the force of the explosion rebounded again and again before the outer shell of the ship broke. In the meantime, the damage spread through the navy, destroying other ships, leaving them wrecks and setting the entire fleet on their heels. Caught in the blast, the wreckage, the survivors, and I are sent spinning through the cosmos, pulling apart from one another even as we stabilize our bodies and motions.

Having finished marveling at the damage I've done, I extract a suit and slap it on, watching as the material wraps around me before beeping its readiness. I extract the external thrusters from my Altered Storage, letting the thrusters and suit take care of the pairing. While my armor technically has thrusters, after the damage it's taken, I'm not sure I trust it. Especially if the Master Classers are coming after me.

Somewhere in my notification logs is probably information on their deaths. Or lack of it. But considering I just destroyed a battleship and the various people within it, that log is a cumbersome mess. And Ali isn't around to sort it out for me, so I keep an eye out for threats as I float, contemplating my next actions.

"John. Update." The voice cackles over my newly formed helmet, startling me with its intensity. A familiar voice. One that is a pleasure to hear.

"I'm still alive," I answer Mikito.

"We know that." The voice stays frosty, as cold as the void I float in. I'm assuming the Samurai is less than happy with the order to run when she felt it her place to stay. "We need a location update."

"Oh. Right." I glance at the map, at the distances involved. I debate what to do then shake my head. "Help the Librarian like we planned."

"Why—"

"If you guys manage to take the Admiral, I'll be able to Portal out of here once the Smoothers are down. If we don't take him down, it doesn't matter anyway." I shake my head. "Coming to get me is just a waste of time."

"Understood," Bolo replies.

The highlighted dot in my map continues its acceleration, headed toward the tiny courier ship that hosts the Admiral where he's been hiding and running the battle. It's not part of the fleet, having been stored away till its launch. It means that the Admiral's Skill isn't damaging it, while its stealth abilities kept it hidden. Until, of course, the Librarian started raising hell.

"Take care," Mikito says, sounding worried.

"You got i—" I pause, a new blip forming in my gaze. I turn my head to the side, hissing out a breath. "Well, okay. This might be… interesting."

"John?"

"Incoming fans." I trigger the jets, spinning around to watch the couple of floating figures moving toward me.

We'd been tossed apart by the explosion, but having arrested their motion, the Master Classers seem intent on closing in on me and finishing the fight. Around us, few ships have bothered to linger—beyond a small fleet of automated rescue boats. The battle is not over, and every working ship is required.

"Might want to speed it up," I say.

Three hundred Mana. It's going up with each second, but it's not enough. Not for an all-out fight. My Evolved Penetration Skill shield is holding on, but barely. The cold of the void is slowly draining it, a process that makes me laugh. On the other hand, there are numerous other enemy dots…

Where do we draw the line between our comfort and safety and our ethics? Before the apocalypse, we sat at home, protected by the sacrifices of others. Comfortable in the knowledge that violence was something other people did, something other people dealt with. And then the System came and violence was on our doorstep, in our hands, and we changed. We had to face the knowledge and commit violence ourselves to survive.

And now, here I am, blade in hand, staring at little red dots that are people, sapient individuals who have survived a calamity of my making. And I'm thinking of killing them not because they're in my way, not because they're a threat or an objective must be accomplished. But because I need—I *want* a little more of a safety margin. To save my own life.

And who's to say my life is not more important than theirs?

I float in the void, staring at the dots and my incoming doom. A pair of Master Classers. Likely low in Mana too, having spent whatever tricks they had to survive the explosion. Coming for my life after I had taken their friends, their companions. A pair that I could not beat, not even when I had my full Mana pool. My doom.

Who weighs our fates and comes up with the final tally of a worthy soul? I stare at my hand, at my sword that has reaped so many others, then laugh. Laugh, because the answer is so simple. So easy. Like all real answers.

Me.

I weigh and judge and determine. Right here, right now. No System, no gods, no unseen arbiter. Just me. My stomach aching from the laughter, my breath wheezing, grateful that none of it was escaping to my friends, I laugh. Then I dismiss my sword and stare at the incoming figures, no longer specks in the distance. Choosing to avoid staining my own soul, to avoid targeting any of those floating red dots of the surviving fleet members.

So be it. If this is the end of the line, then that's okay. I still have a chance, a fighting chance. As for those who float around, who once fought me? They could go on, never knowing how close they'd come to death. And that was fine—for the choice was mine. Because some things, some morals, some traces of humanity could not be traded away. Not even for your own life.

***

As I wait for them to close, I eye my surroundings. Put on the backfoot or not, the Galactic fleet still has the upper hand and the damn Dimensional Smoothers are still in play. The Admiral is still alive, either managing to hide or fight off the Librarian, and none of our other wings have managed to destroy a single Smoother. I'm slightly surprised, but a Heroic Class Admiral with his staff against a Legendary Artisan Librarian seems to be a bit more of an even fight than I had believed. Come to think of it, put that way, I can see how that might not be as much of a one-sided battle as I'd hoped.

In one corner of the system, the remaining pirate battlecruiser dukes it out with the majority of the remaining fleet ships, many of whom have been pulled away from other sections of the solar system. The Galactic fleet swarms the larger ship like a school of silver barracuda, beams of hard light tearing at the armor. Multiple redundancies are the only thing keeping the cruiser moving, its compatriot a floating wreck a distance away. For that matter, I absently note that the majority of the Inner Crew have either fallen or retreated—their Mana exhausted.

Of our targets, only the Dimensional Smoother the battlecruisers have been targeting looks the worse for wear. The others might be pitted, but none are venting as much atmosphere as that one, nor do the others have half their engines destroyed. I can only hope that the Prime Station will open up again. For that matter...

"What happened to the station cannon? It should have fired by now."

"It's down. Sabotage." Ali flashes the details of the two Master Classers coming toward me. *"Should I come? If I try, I might be able to get to you in time."*

I grunt, shaking my head. I doubt he'd be that much faster. In fact, I would be surprised if Ali could actually make it through the battlefield. But perhaps his desire to come is not entirely based off rational need. Realizing Ali can't see me, I send my answer mentally before studying the minimap. It's not nearly as useful as a larger notification window would be, but I can grasp the overall shape of the fight.

"Come on, you overgrown bookworm," I whisper.

The Galactic Master Classers, when they arrive, do not launch an attack immediately, giving me time to review their damage. The Acolyte looks the worse of the pair, his skin sizzling, his eyes dark and bloodshot, bared hands crisped. Only a light purple glow keeps the void from freezing his body. As for

Phortala, the Fire Elemental looks good, brimming with energy—literally, as flames lick from open wounds across his body. It's kind of amusing to see fire burning in the void, though I note how once they reach a couple of inches from his body, the flames die. A glance at Phortala's Status makes me wince, for while his health might have taken a beating, the Avatar of Flame's fully stocked on Mana. Any hope of winning is… remote.

I touch the QSM on my wrist, considering. I might be able to use it. The upgrades we've made basically boosted my ability to punch through a Dimensional Lock. Theoretically. But I'm in the overlapping Dimensional Locked fields from three different Smoothers. I had expected it to be one at most, having gotten this thing rebuilt when I expected to be fighting on a Smoother. Not for ambushing the Admiral—or playing bait. Three overlapping fields is a bit much.

"Your plan failed," the Acolyte says. "Do you have more tricks? More surprises? Or was this it?"

"And if I said yes, would you believe me?" I call my sword into my hand as I let my mind slide into that combat stance. "Look. You guys have lost your ride out. If you put your… flames… down, we'll call it a day. No one else has to die. What we do here isn't going to affect the real battle." A gesture toward the nearest Dimensional Smoother, floating a distance away. Close, if we had a working ship. But without Portals or Blink Steps, we're too slow to make a difference.

"And if we did, would you lay your neck down when it was your turn? You regenerate with each moment," the Acolyte hisses, offering me a grim smile. "Ending you now is the most logical option."

I grunt, unable to refute his point. I'm not going to put my sword down just because I'm on the losing team. "Guess you're not interested in letting me go?"

A laugh from the Acolyte is all the answer I need.

"Why do you insist on speaking with this one?" Phortala snarls, tilting his head toward where my team is supposed to arrive. "We but need to collect his head for our bounty. Then we can leave this cold, blighted place."

My grip tightens on my sword. I'm curious how they intend to begin this fight. A couple of Blade Strikes could potentially give me the opening to close in on them. Or a Soul Shield, to cover me while I rush them. I'm suddenly desperately aware that I should have invested in better thrusters, better upgrades for my secondary pieces of armor. Or is it tertiary pieces? If I can't reach them, if I can't hit them...

Mana fluctuates near me and I hit the burners, triggering a sudden acceleration. It pushes me away from the pair, but it lets me escape the sudden formation of a flame-filled cage that wraps around my previous location. Even as I bank and turn, altering the angle of my thrust, I conjure a blaster into my hand and open fire. The beam attacks strike the Acolyte's pulsing purple shield, burrowing into its defenses even as the Avatar conjures a series of mini-suns. Each of those suns spits out flame darts, the elemental-infused attacks burning even in the void of space. A part of me wonders if the spell itself is conjuring the flame or the oxygen needed, but the rest of me is busy dodging and firing, attempting to close in on the pair.

The Acolyte isn't holding still either, dodging my attacks as he casts a System-targeted corruption spell. A flicker in my notifications makes my lip compress.

You have been Cursed with GEM's Disdain!

Curse partially resisted!
Your Mana regeneration has decreased by 13.81%.

I shoot the Acolyte in return, watching as my shield firms up. Only to be bled away as another flame impacts me. As I dance and dodge, trying to close in on them, I have to be wary of the ever-growing number of flaming spheres, some of which use whips of flame. The math of this fight is simple. If I can close in, I stand a chance. The longer I stay out here, the more danger I'm in.

We spin and exchange fire, the Avatar filling the space with his little balls of flame. There are no wide area effect spells, no gouts of flame that are easy to dodge. No. This is worse. Each summoned sphere summons its own attacks, filling the air with darts of flame, each a pinprick and so dense that no matter where I go, I'm hit. The constant damage wears down my shield, leaving me exposed to the void.

Bastards.

As another flame dart hits my spacesuit, it eats a small hole in it. The suit does its best to patch the hole, but another attack adds another hole. I might have a couple of spares, but none of them are expensive or good. And the slower I am, the more I'll get hit. It's a spiral, a guarantee that I'll lose. It might take a little longer if I pull away, if I continue dodging and hoping that the Master Classer runs out of Mana. Except he's got a ton and I don't have that much health. The damage from the flames is terrifying, and if it was not for the entire battle being conducted in space, I might have lost already.

I throw up a Soul Shield to buy some time. The Skill will take some of the beating, but it won't last forever. I snarl, running through my options, feeling my skin dry and crack as it heals around the damage. Options, options, options… I scan through the surroundings, borrowing Ali's senses for a second to see how far they've come.

"Done. Do not die, Questor." A voice cuts through the silence, ringing in my ear.

I choke, missing a dodge and losing nearly two-thirds of the Soul Shield's remaining durability. The stutter in motion is due to the rather unorthodox method that Bolo and Mikito used to provide aid for the Librarian. Rather than jump into the fight, they'd launched their own penultimate attacks on the ship once they got close enough.

The courier ship's destruction left it wrecked, floating in parts and throwing its occupants about. In the midst of all that damage, the Admiral must have been easy pickings for the Librarian.

"We're on our way back," Mikito says over the comm.

I shake my head, ducking aside as I boost away from the pair. No need to fight now. I just need to survive. A Mana potion is slammed down my throat as I ignore the reduced effectiveness, using the sudden surge of Mana to refresh my battered Soul Shield. I've got an exit now—maybe, if the Smoothers…

"Smoothers. Now!" I command Mikito and get a growl in reply.

But Ali seems to have convinced them, because they turn toward the nearest.

Come on, come on…

Again and again I dodge, opening up space between my attackers and me. The damn spheres are flying after me, no longer purely attacking. Another Curse hammers into me, slowing down my reaction time. Luckily, the actual spell itself does nothing to my tech. Still, I'm on the losing end of this fight and it's showing. I don't, can't, use the rest of my Mana. Not if I want to run. Not with them so close.

Considering that last thought, I reach into my Altered Space. There are a few last things in there, a few toys and some junk that I can use. There are blocks of titanium—no more than distractions and physical cover. Others, like the chaos mines and floating drones, are meant to damage and distract but aren't particularly useful in the void of space. Some of the grenades trigger then putter out as the void of space laughs as the sonic, flashbang, and tech-driven attacks succumb to unrelenting physics.

Some are more useful. A Chaos Grenade creates a sudden attractor, pulling a pair of flaming spheres inside. Another sends a wave of healing energy, topping up a couple hundred points of health and making a pair of floating gerbil-creatures sprout solar wings. A deep ocean fish, wide-eyed, spiky, and glowing, pops into existence then freezes to death while mulch appears from another grenade.

I buy time while the rest of the rebel fleet fights. Prime Station glows, opening fire with secondary weapons on one of the Dimensional Smoothers, returning to the battle. The main cannon might be done, but the rest of its weapons now focus on a single Smoother. The Battlecruiser dies, its engines and shields overloaded, but it takes a score of ships with it as it explodes. Surprisingly, the other Battlecruiser goes off too, the paired explosion enough to destroy their target now that the Admiral is no longer alive.

Time drags on as I empty my inventory. I've bought enough time that I've regenerated a little more Mana, so I risk a Blade Strike. The attack cuts through my own obstacle, tearing apart the block of titanium and slamming into the Acolyte that it had blocked. Blood spurts as a leg is detached, the Acolyte releasing a scream. The creature spins, holding onto the stump of its thigh, bleeding out, and I see my health pop up a little, along with my shield. Just in time to take another alpha strike from Phortala, the flames washing over me as three spheres catch up and go nova.

My shield shatters and I burn, twisting in midair as the remnants of my suit crisps. I hit the release, jettisoning the destroyed thrusters before equipping another set. The entire thing takes seconds, before I'm burning fuel to get away from the next set of spheres. I swipe at my helmet, cleaning the soot away as I battle the sensation of burning and freezing, one after the other. Come on…

Another Dimensional Smoother goes down, this one targeted by the station. This time, it's the correct one. I feel the Lock disappear and I debate using my Portal, but I hold on. I can hold on. Even if my health is bottoming out, even as another Curse tears at my nerves and makes me see what isn't there. As flames fill my vision, as blood boils and my skin crisps, I hold on. A passing rebel ship opens fire on us, tossing a couple of runed shells that fill the area with metal-eating space leeches. Those distract the Master Classers for a few seconds as they burn the creatures away. A few seconds before the Master Classers return to attacking me.

Time. I buy time with health and pain. Another Smoother goes down, and I can hear my friends speaking to me. Saying words I don't have time to pay attention to. Orders fly, calling a general retreat even as the space station shifts, attempting to escape the overlapping boundaries. More orders fly, focusing attacks on the remaining targeted Dimensional Smoother. Then something happens.

Some of the Galactic fleet disappears, retreating from the fight. Others strike the flag, sending out SOS calls and calling it a day. The Smoother that was boarded drops its hold, freeing the Station of another overlapping boundary. Not one that I'm in though. The Galactics are fleeing, running.

All but the two still hounding me.

I'm still in the midst of one Smoother's hold, still stuck. Even if the QSM is meant to work, it's no guarantee. But my health is too low, my Mana refusing to regenerate. Given no choice, I reach out with my Skill. I find the portion of the world that is the center of the Station, the area I'm whitelisted to Portal into. I touch the boundaries between worlds, connect myself to the QSM, tear open the gap, and throw myself in. Just before another wave of heat washes over me, following me through the Portal.

I emerge into cool, almost freezing atmosphere. I roll across the ground, elemental fire following me before it is swept backward as the air in the room is sucked into the void. The Portal snaps closed with a relaxation of will, and I'm free. Safe.

"You really should look where you jump," a voice, all too familiar, if long unheard, says.

And I realize I'm not where I should be.

Epilogue

I escaped. So did my friends. Everyone made it back, though the fleet had pulled out, leaving behind one Dimensional Smoother and a lot of bodies. Once the problem had resolved itself, rebels and pirates flooded back, bolstering the weakened station and beginning the rebuild. The auction I'd been looking forward to went off without a hitch. Mikito even managed to pick up a new toy. Harry's Level shot up like crazy, his reports and a rather impressive story of heroism in the Station increasing his reputation. Dornalor's less happy, having lost his ship and nearly his life during the last battle. Once the station makes good on replacing the ship, they'll be joining me.

"Did he survive?" I ask Ali. A simple reconjuration brought him to my side.

"The Librarian's whereabouts and eventual fate is unknown. I see no indications that anyone ported in or out, especially anyone with the Mana signature of a Legendary Class."

I can hear the but in Ali's mental voice. The question about if we'd even be able to tell, what with the way they're all messing with the System information. Credits might not be everything, but it's close.

"I don't get it. Was he holding back in the fight because he was afraid of the Council? If he was that worried, why offer to try at all?" I shake my head, remembering the footage of the Librarian and the Admiral's fight that Harry sent to me. *"Or is he that weak?"* Ali's mental shrug sets me off on a rant, now that I've had more time to think about it. *"For that matter, if the Council wanted him dead, why didn't they just do it? There's four Legendaries on the Council and what, five Heroics, right? Assuming even the publicly accessible knowledge is correct. And not fudged downward. If they wanted him dead, they could just have Portaled in and stomped him."*

"Might be things are a little more complicated than you guessed."

Complicated. Yes, that'd be one word for it. But if that's the case, how much danger am I really in? Intuition tells me that the answer lies in my brain, wrapped away and hidden in a library stored for another. Another time. Another person. Another organization. If I could…

"Are you ready?" A voice, the same one that greeted me when I came through the Portal, interrupts my thoughts.

I turn away from the window, the view of the alien city. It's tall and sturdy towers, the people that flit between in power armor and on flying cars. I draw a deep breath and look down at the formal clothing I'm dressed in. A sky-blue military uniform with high collars, epaulets, knee-high boots, and green trimming. A single shining emblem of a griffin and crossed swords to mark who and what I am to these people. All of it pressed upon me for this very day. This very presentation.

"Lead on, MacDuff."

And Ayuri d'Malla, former Champion of Erethra, looks me over once more and nods in approval. We turn together and walk down the sumptuous hallway to meet the Queen of Erethra. To fulfill a promise I made a long time ago.

###

The End

John and friends will return in

Stars Asunder (Book 9 of the System Apocalypse)

https://readerlinks.com/l/1054489

Author's Note

Rebel Star took longer than I expected to write. A lot of that had to do with a long holiday I took with my family and my first writer's conference. That conference helped focus me on the business side, a part that I had neglected to some extent. Upon consideration, I've decided to keep hitting conferences through 2020 which will result in a slowdown in book releases, but hopefully better books and a more stable income stream.

At the time of writing, I'm working on the next and final book for the Hidden Wishes trilogy before shifting to A Thousand Li and then returning to the System Apocalypse. I have an outline for book 9, one which will focus on the Erethran Empire and John's place in the wider galaxy. The consequences of his actions will continue to impact him and Earth.

As many of you know, I've also released the first Short Story Anthology for the System Apocalypse. None of the stories are required reading for the main series, but my own story in that anthology will give context to our favorite Truinnar.

As always, I'm grateful for everyone who has followed me on this long, long journey. I hope you have enjoyed John's journey and the ever-expanding world. If you enjoyed reading the book, please do leave a review and rating.

In addition, please check out my other series, Adventures on Brad (a more traditional LitRPG fantasy), Hidden Wishes (an urban fantasy GameLit series), and A Thousand Li (a cultivation series inspired by Chinese wuxia and xianxia novels).

To support me directly, please go to my Patreon account:
-    https://www.patreon.com/taowong

For more great information about LitRPG series, check out the Facebook groups:

- LitRPG Society

    https://www.facebook.com/groups/LitRPGsociety/

- LitRPG Books

    https://www.facebook.com/groups/LitRPG.books/

About the Author

Tao Wong is an avid fantasy and sci-fi reader who spends his time working and writing in the North of Canada. He's spent way too many years doing martial arts of many forms, and having broken himself too often, he now spends his time writing about fantasy worlds.

For updates on the series and other books written by Tao Wong (and special one-shot stories), please visit the author's website:

http://www.mylifemytao.com

Subscribers to Tao's mailing list will receive exclusive access to short stories in the Thousand Li and System Apocalypse universes:

https://www.subscribepage.com/taowong

Or visit his Facebook Page: https://www.facebook.com/taowongauthor/

Glossary

Erethran Honor Guard Skill Tree

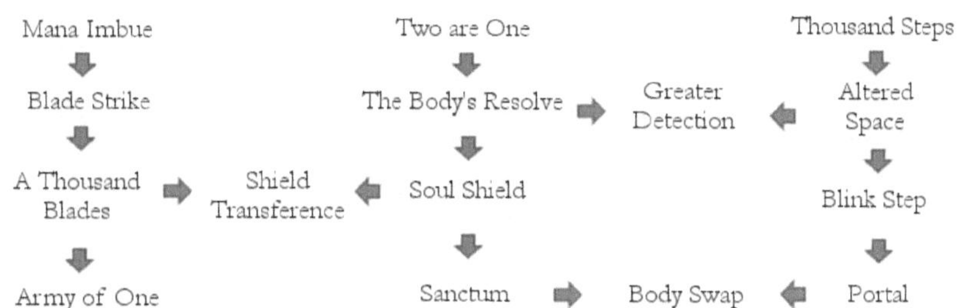

John's Erethran Honor Guard Skills

Mana Imbue (Level 3)

Soulbound weapon now permanently imbued with mana to deal more damage on each hit. +20 Base Damage (Mana). Will ignore armor and resistances. Mana regeneration reduced by 15 Mana per minute permanently.

Blade Strike (Level 5)

By projecting additional Mana and stamina into a strike, the Erethran Honor Guard's Soulbound weapon may project a strike up to 50 feet away. Cost: 50 Stamina + 50 Mana

Thousand Steps (Level 1)

Movement speed for the Honor Guard and allies are increased by 5% while skill is active. This ability is stackable with other movement-related skills. Cost: 20 Stamina + 20 Mana per minute

Altered Space (Level 2)

The Honor Guard now has access to an extra-dimensional storage location of 30 cubic meters. Items stored must be touched to be willed in and may not include living creatures or items currently affected by auras that are not the Honor Guard's. Mana regeneration reduced by 10 Mana per minute permanently.

Two are One (Level 1)

Effect: Transfer 10% of all damage from Target to Self

Cost: 5 Mana per second

The Body's Resolve (Level 3)

Effect: Increase natural health regeneration by 35%. On-going health status effects reduced by 33%. Honor Guard may now regenerate lost limbs. Mana regeneration reduced by 15 Mana per minute permanently.

Greater Detection (Level 1)

Effect: User may now detect System creatures up to 1 kilometer away. General information about strength level is provided on detection. Stealth skills, Class skills, and ambient mana density will influence the effectiveness of this skill. Mana regeneration reduced by 5 Mana per minute permanently.

A Thousand Blades (Level 3)

Creates four duplicate copies of the user's designated weapon. Duplicate copies deal base damage of copied items. May be combined with Mana Imbue and Shield Transference. Mana Cost: 3 Mana per second

Soul Shield (Level 4)

Effect: Creates a manipulable shield to cover the caster's or target's body. Shield has 1,500 Hit Points.

Cost: 250 Mana

Blink Step (Level 2)

Effect: Instantaneous teleportation via line-of-sight. May include Spirit's line of sight. Maximum range—500 meters.

Cost: 100 Mana

Portal (Level 5)

Effect: Creates a 5-meter by 5-meter portal which can connect to a previously traveled location by user. May be used by others. Maximum distance range of portals is 10,000 kilometers.

Cost: 250 Mana + 100 Mana per minute (minimum cost 350 Mana)

Army of One (Level 4)

The Honor Guard's feared penultimate combat ability, Army of One builds upon previous Skills, allowing the user to unleash an awe-inspiring attack to deal with their enemies. Attack may now be guided around minor obstacles.

Effect: Army of One allows the projection of (Number of Thousand Blades conjured weapons * 3) Blade Strike attacks up to 500 meters away from user. Each attack deals 5 * Blade Strike Level damage (inclusive of Mana Imbue and Soulbound weapon bonus)

Cost: 750 Mana

Sanctum (Level 2)

An Erethran Honor Guard's ultimate trump card in safeguarding their target, Sanctum creates a flexible shield that blocks all incoming attacks, hostile teleportations and Skills. At this Level of Skill, the user must specify dimensions of the Sanctum upon use of the Skill. The Sanctum cannot be moved while the Skill is activated.

Dimensions: Maximum 15 cubic meters.

Cost: 1,000 Mana

Duration: 2 minute and 7 seconds

Paladin of Erethra Skill Tree

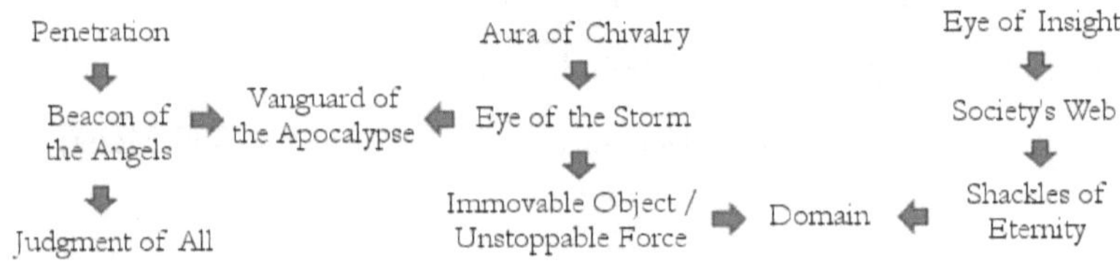

John's Paladin of Erethra Skills

Class Skill: Penetration (Level 9 - Evolved)

Few can face the judgment of a Paladin in direct combat, their ability to bypass even the toughest of defenses a frightening prospect. Reduces Mana Regeneration by 45 permanently.

Effect: Ignore all armor and defensive Skills and spells by 90%. Increases damage done to shields and structural supports by 175%.

Secondary Effect: Damage that is resisted by spells, armor, Skills and Resistances is transferred to an Evolved Skill shield at a ratio of 1 to 1.

Duration: 85 minutes

Class Skill: Aura of Chivalry (Level 1)

A Paladin's very presence can quail weak-hearted enemies and bolster the confidence of allies, whether on the battlefield or in court. The Aura of Chivalry is a double-edged sword however, focusing attention on the Paladin—potentially to their detriment. Increases success rate of Perception checks against Paladin by 10% and reduces stealth and related skills by 10% while active. Reduces Mana Regeneration by 5 Permanently.

Effect: All enemies must make a Willpower check against intimidation against user's Charisma. Failure to pass the check will cow enemies. All allies gain a 50% boost in morale for all Willpower checks and a 10% boost in confidence and probability of succeeding in relevant actions.

Note: Aura may be activated or left-off at will.

Beacon of the Angels (Level 2)

User calls down an atmospheric strike from the heavens, dealing damage over a wide area to all enemies within the beacon. The attack takes time to form, but once activated need not be concentrated upon for completion.

Effect: 1000 Mana Damage done to all enemies, structures and vehicles within the maximum 25-meter column of attack

Mana Cost: 500 Mana

Eyes of Insight (Level 1)

Under the eyes of a Paladin, all untruth and deceptions fall away. Only when the Paladin can see with clarity may he be able to judge effectively. Reduces Mana Regeneration by 5.

Effect: All Skills, Spells and abilities of a lower grade that obfuscate, hinder or deceive the Paladin are reduced in effectiveness. Level of reduction proportionate to degree of difference in grade and Skill Level.

Eye of the Storm (Level 1)

In the middle of the battlefield, the Paladin stands, seeking justice and offering judgment on all enemies. The winds of war will seek to draw both enemies and allies to you, their cruel flurries robbing enemies of their lives and bolstering the health and Mana of allies.

Effect: Eye of the Storm is an area effect buff and taunt. Psychic winds taunt enemies, forcing a Mental Resistance check to avoid attacking user. Enemies also receive 5 points of damage per second while within the influence of the Skill, with damage decreasing from the epicenter of the Skill. Allies receive a 5% increase in Mana and Health regeneration, decrease in effectiveness from Skill center. Eye of the Storm affects an area of 50 meters around the user.

Cost: 500 Mana + 20 Mana per second

Vanguard of the Apocalypse (Level 2)

Where others flee, the Paladin strides forward. Where the brave dare not advance, the Paladin charges. While the world burns, the Paladin still fights. The Paladin with this Skill is the vanguard of any fight, leading the charge against all of Erethra's enemies.

Effect: +45 to all Physical attributes, increases speed by 55% and recovery rates by 35%. This Skill is stackable on top of other attribute and speed boosting Skills or spells.

Cost: 500 Mana + 10 Stamina per second

Society's Web (Level 1)

Where the Eye of Insight provides the Paladin an understanding of the lies and mistruths told, Society's Web shows the Paladin the intricate webs that tie individuals to one another. No alliance, no betrayal, no tangled web of lies will be hidden as each interaction weaves one another closer. While the Skill provides no detailed information, a skilled Paladin can infer much from the Web.

Effect: Upon activation, the Paladin will see all threads that tie each individual to one another and automatically understand the details of each thread when focused upon.

Cost: 400 Mana + 200 Mana per minute

Other Class Skills

Frenzy (Level 1)

Effect: When activated, pain is reduced by 80%, damage increased by 30%, stamina regeneration rate increased by 20%. Mana regeneration rate decreased by 10%

Frenzy will not deactivate until all enemies have been slain. User may not retreat while Frenzy is active.

Cleave (Level 2)

Effect: Physical attacks deal 60% more base damage. Effect may be combined with other Class Skills.

Cost: 25 Mana

Elemental Strike (Level 1 - Ice)

Effect: Used to imbue a weapon with freezing damage. Adds +5 Base Damage to attacks and a 10% chance of reducing speed by 5% upon contact. Lasts for 30 seconds.

Cost: 50 Mana

Instantaneous Inventory (Maxed)

Allows user to place or remove any System-recognized item from Inventory if space allows. Includes the automatic arrangement of space in the inventory. User must be touching item.

Cost: 5 Mana per item

Shrunken Footsteps (Level 1)

Reduces System presence of user, increasing the chance of the user evading detection of System-assisted sensing Skills and equipment. Also increases cost of information purchased about user. Reduces Mana Regeneration by 5 permanently.

Tech Link (Level 2)

Effect: Tech Link allows user to increase their skill level in using a technological item, increasing input and versatility in usage of said items. Effects vary depending on item. General increase in efficiency of 10%. Mana regeneration rate decreased by 10%

Designated Technological Items: Neural Link, Hod's Triple Fused Armor

Analyze (Level 2)

Allows user to scan individuals, monsters, and System-registered objects to gather information registered with the System. Detail and level of accuracy of information is dependent on Level and any Skills or Spells in conflict with the ability. Reduces Mana regeneration by 10 permanently.

Harden (Level 2)

This Skill reinforces targeted defenses and actively weakens incoming attacks to reduce their penetrating power. A staple Skill of the Turtle Knights of Kiumma, the Harden Skill has frustrated opponents for millennia.

Effect: Reduces penetrative effects of attacks by 30% on targeted defense.

Cost: 3 Mana per second

Quantum Lock (Level 3)

A staple Skill of the M453-X Mecani-assistants, Quantum Lock blocks stealth attacks and decreases the tactical options of their enemies. While active, the Quantum Lock of the Mecani-assistants excites quantum strings in the affected area for all individuals and Skills.

Effect: All teleportation, portal, and dimensional Skills and Spells are disrupted while Quantum Lock is in effect. Forceable use of Skills and Spells while Skill is in effect will result in (Used Skill Mana Cost * 4) health in damage. Users may pay a variable amount of additional Mana when activating the Skill to decrease effect of Quantum Lock and decrease damage taken.

Requirements: 200 Willpower, 200 Intelligence

Area of Effect: 100-meter radius around user

Cost: 250 + 50 Mana per Minute

Elastic Skin (Level 3)

Elastic Skin is a permanent alteration, allowing the user to receive and absorb a small portion of damage. Damage taken reduced by 7% with 7% of damage absorbed converted to Mana. Mana Regeneration reduced by 15 permanently.

Peasant's Fury (Level 1)

No one knows loss more than the powerless. The Downtrodden Peasant has taken the fury of the powerless and made it his own, gifting them the strength to go on so long as they manage to make others feel the same loss that they did. -5 Mana Regeneration per Second

Effect: User receives a 0.1% regeneration effect of damage dealt for each 1% of health loss.

Fate's Thread (Level 2)

The Akashi'so believe that we are all but weavings in the great thread of life. Connected to one another by the great Weaver, there is not one but multiple threads between us all, woven from our interactions and histories. Fate's Thread is but a Skill expression of this belief. This Skill cannot be dodged but may be blocked. After all, all things are bound together.

Effect: Fate's Thread allows the user to bind individuals together by making what is already there apparent. Thread is made physical and may be used to pull, tie and bind.

Duration: 2 minutes

Cost: 60 Mana

Spells

Improved Minor Healing (IV)

Effect: Heals 40 Health per casting. Target must be in contact during healing. Cooldown 60 seconds.

Cost: 20 Mana

Improved Mana Missile (IV)

Effect: Creates four missiles out of pure Mana, which can be directed to damage a target. Each dart does 30 damage. Cooldown 10 seconds.

Cost: 35 Mana

Enhanced Lightning Strike

Effect: Call forth the power of the gods, casting lightning. Lightning strike may affect additional targets depending on proximity, charge and other conductive materials on-hand. Does 100 points of electrical damage.

Lightning Strike may be continuously channeled to increase damage for 10 additional damage per second.

Cost: 75 Mana.

Continuous cast cost: 5 Mana / second

Lightning Strike may be enhanced by using the Elemental Affinity of Electromagnetic Force. Damage increased by 20% per level of affinity

Greater Regeneration (II)

Effect: Increases natural health regeneration of target by 6%. Only single use of spell effective on a target at a time.

Duration: 10 minutes

Cost: 100 Mana

Firestorm

Effect: Create a firestorm with a radius of 5 meters. Deals 250 points of fire damage to those caught within. Cooldown 60 seconds.

Cost: 200 Mana

Polar Zone

Effect: Create a thirty-meter diameter blizzard that freezes all targets within one. Does 10 points of freezing damage per minute plus reduces affected individuals' speed by 5%. Cooldown 60 seconds.

Cost: 200 Mana

Greater Healing (II)

Effect: Heals 100 Health per casting. Target does not require contact during healing. Cooldown 60 seconds per target.

Cost: 75 Mana

Mana Drip (II)

Effect: Increases natural health regeneration of target by 6%. Only single use of spell effective on a target at a time.

Duration: 10 minutes

Cost: 100 Mana

Freezing Blade

Effect: Enchants weapon with a slowing effect. A 5% slowing effect is applied on a successful strike. This effect is cumulative and lasts for 1 minute. Cooldown 3 minutes.

Spell Duration: 1 minute.

Cost: 150 Mana

Improved Inferno Strike (II)

A beam of heat raised to the levels of an inferno, able to melt steel and earth on contact! The perfect spell for those looking to do a lot of damage in a short period of time.

Effect: Does 200 Points of Heat Damage

Cost: 150 Mana

Mud Walls

Unlike its more common counterpart Earthen Walls, Mud Walls focus is more on dealing slow, suffocating damage and restricting movement on the battlefield.

Effect: Does 20 Points of Suffocating Damage. -30% Movement Speed

Duration: 2 Minutes

Cost: 75 Mana

Create Water

Pulls water from the elemental plane of water. Water is pure and the highest form of water available. Conjures 1 liter of water. Cooldown: 1 minute

Cost: 50 Mana

Scry

Allows caster to view a location up to 1.7 kilometers away. Range may be extended through use of additional Mana. Caster will be stationary during this period. It is recommended caster focuses on the scry unless caster has a high level of Intelligence and Perception so as to avoid accidents. Scry may be blocked by equivalent or higher tier spells and Skills. Individuals with high perception in region of Scry may be alerted that the Skill is in use. Cooldown: 1 hour.

Cost: 25 Mana per minute.

Scrying Ward

Blocks scrying spells and their equivalent within 5 meters of caster. Higher level spells may not be blocked, but caster may be alerted about scrying attempts. Cooldown: 10 minutes

Cost: 50 Mana per minute

Improved Invisibility

Hides target's System information, aura, scent, and visual appearance. Effectiveness of spell is dependent upon Intelligence of caster and any Skills or Spells in conflict with the target.

Cost: 100 + 50 Mana per minute

Improved Mana Cage

While physically weaker than other elemental-based capture spells, Mana Cage has the advantage of being able to restrict all creatures, including semi-solid Spirits, conjured elementals, shadow beasts, and Skill users. Cooldown: 1 minute

Cost: 200 Mana + 75 Mana per minute

Improved Flight

(Fly birdie, fly! - Ali) This spell allows the user to defy gravity, using controlled bursts of Mana to combat gravity and allow the user to fly in even the most challenging of situations. The improved version of this spell allows flight even in zero gravity situations and a higher level of maneuverability. Cooldown: 1 minute

Cost: 250 Mana + 100 Mana per minute

Equipment

Hod's Triple Fused Armor

The product of multiple workings by the Master Blacksmith and Crafter Hodiliphious 'Hod' Yalding, the Triple Fused Armor was hand-forged from rare, System-generated material, hand refined and reworked trice over with multiple patented and rare alloys and materials. The final product is considered barely passable by Hod – though it would make a lesser craftsman cry.

Core: Class I Hallow Physics Mana Engine

CPU: Class B Wote Core CPU

Armor Rating: Tier I (Enhanced)

Hard Points: 9 (6 Used – Jungian Flight System, Talpidae Abyssal Horns, Luione Hard Light Projectors, Diarus Poison Stingers, Ares Type I Shield Generator, Greater Troll Cell Injectors)

Soft Points 4 (3 Used – Neural Link, Ynir HUD Imaging, Airmed Body Monitor)

Battery Capacity: 380/380

Active Skills: Abyssal Chains, Mirror Shade, Poison Grip

Attribute Bonuses: +93 Strength, +78 Agility, +51 Constitution, +44 Perception, +287 Stamina and Health Regeneration per minute

Note: Hod's Triple Fused Armor is currently under limited warranty. Armor may be teleported to Hod's workshop for repairs once a week. All cost of repairs will be deducted from user's account.

__Skills in Hod's Armor:__

Abyssal Chains

Calling upon the material connection to the shadow plane, chains from the abyss erupt, binding a target in place.

Effect: Target is bound by shadow chains. Chains deal 10 points of damage per second. To break free, target must win a contested Strength test. Abyssal Chains have a Strength of 120.

Uses: 2/3

Recharge rate: 1 per hour

Mirror Shade

Mirror Shade creates a semi-solid doppelganger using hard light technology and Mana.

Effect: Mirror Shade create a semi-solid doppelganger of the user for a period of ten minutes. Maximum range of doppelganger from user is fifty meters. Doppelganger has 18% physical fidelity.

Use: 0/1

Recharge Rate: 1 per 4 hours

Silversmith Jeupa VII Anti-Personnel Cannon (Modified & Upgraded)

This quad-barrelled anti-personnel weapon has been handcrafted by Advanced Weaponsmiths to provide the highest integration possible for an energy weapon. This particular weapon has been modified to include additional range-finding and sighting options and upgraded to increase short-term damage output at the cost of long-term durability. Barrels may be fired individually or linked.

Base Damage: 787 per barrel

Battery Capacity: 4 per barrel (16 total)

Recharge Rate: 0.25 per hour per GMU

Ares Platinum Class Tier II Armored Jumpsuit

Ares's signature Platinum Class line of armored daily wear combines the company's latest technological advancement in nanotech fiber design and the pinnacle work of an Advanced Craftsman's Skill to provide unrivalled protection for the discerning Adventurer.

Effect: +218 Defense, +14% Resistance to Kinetic and Energy Attacks. +19% Resistance against Temperature changes. Self-Cleanse, Self-Mend, Autofit Enchantments also included.

Silversmith Mark VIII Beam Pistol (Upgradeable)

Base Damage: 88

Battery Capacity: 13/13

Recharge Rate: 3 per hour per GMU

Tier IV Neural Link

Neural link may support up to 5 connections.

Current connections: Hod's Triple Fused Armor

Software Installed: Rich'lki Firewall Class IV, Omnitron III Class IV Controller

Ferlix Type I Twinned-Beam Rifle (Modified)

Base Damage: 39

Battery Capacity: 41/41

Recharge rate: 1 per hour per GMU

Tier II Sword (Soulbound Personal Weapon of an Erethran Honor Guard)

Base Damage: 397

Durability: N/A (Personal Weapon)

Special Abilities: +20 Mana Damage, Blade Strike

Kryl Ring of Regeneration

Often used as betrothal bands, Kyrl rings are highly sought after and must be ordered months in advance.

Health Regeneration: +30

Stamina Regeneration: +15

Mana Regeneration: +5

Tier III Bracer of Mana Storage

A custom work by an unknown maker, this bracer acts a storage battery for personal Mana. Useful for Mages and other Classes that rely on Mana. Mana storage ratio is 50 to 1.

Mana Capacity: 350/350

Fey-steel Dagger

Fey-steel is not actual steel but an unknown alloy. Normally reserved only for the Sidhe nobility, a small—by Galactic standards—amount of Fey-steel is released for sale each year. Fey-steel takes enchantments extremely well.

Base Damage: 28

Durability: 110/100

Special Abilities: None

Enchanted, Reinforced Toothy Throwing Knives (5)

First handcrafted from the rare drop of a Level 140 Awakened Beast by the Redeemer of the Dead, John Lee, these knives have been further processed by the Master Craftsmen I-24-988L and reinforced with orichalcum and fey-steel. The final blades have been further enchanted with Mana and piercing damage as well as a return enchantment.

Base Damage: 238

Enchantments: Return, Mana Blade (+28 Damage), Pierce (-7% defense)

Brumwell Necklace of Shadow Intent

The Brumwell necklace of shadow intent is the hallmark item of the Brumwell Clan. Enchanted by a Master Crafter, this necklace layers shadowy intents over your actions, ensuring that information about your actions are more difficult to ascertain. Ownership of such an item is both a necessity and a mark of prestige among settlement owners and other individuals of power.

Effect: Persistent effect of Shadow Intent (Level 4) results in significantly increased cost of purchasing information from the System about wearer. Effect is persistent for all actions taken while necklace is worn.

Ring of Greater Shielding

Creates a greater shield that will absorb approximately 1000 points of damage. This shield will ignore all damage that does not exceed its threshold amount of 50 points of damage while still functioning.

Max Duration: 7 Minutes

Charges: 1

Simalax Hover Boots (Tier II)

A combination of hand-crafted materials and mass-produced components, the Simalax Hover Boots are the journeyman work of Magi-Technician Lok of Irvina. Enchantments and technology mesh together in the Simalax Hover Boots, offering its wearer the ability to tread on air briefly and defy gravity and sense.

Effects: User reduces gravitational effects by 0.218 SIG. User may, on activation, hover and skate during normal and mildly turbulent atmospheric conditions. User may also use the Simalax Hover Boots to triple jump in the air, engaging the anti-gravity and hover aspects at the same time.

Duration: 1.98 SI Hours.

F'Merc Nanoswarm Mana Grenades (Tier II)

The F'Merc Nanoswarm Grenades are guaranteed to disrupt the collection of Mana in a battlefield, reducing Mana Regeneration rates for those caught in the swarm. Recommended by the I'um military, the Torra Special Forces and the No.1 Most Popular Mana Grenade as voted by the public on Boom, Boom, Boom! Magazine.

Effect: Reduces Mana Regeneration rates and spell formation in affected area by 37% ((higher effects in enclosed areas)

Radius: 10m x 10m

Daghtree's Legendary Ring of Deception (Tier I)

A musician, poet and artist, Daghtree's fame rose not from his sub-standard works of 'art' but his array of seduction Skills from his Heartthrob Artist Class. Due to his increasing infamy, Daghtree commissioned this Legendary ring to change his appearance and continue Leveling. In the end, it is rumored that his indiscretions caught up with the infamous artist and he disappeared from Galactic sources in GCD 9,275.

Effect: Creates a powerful disguise that covers the wearer. The ring comes with six pre-loaded disguises and additional disguises may be added through expansion of charges

Duration: 1 day per charge

Charges: 3

Recharge via ambient Mana: 1 charge per Galactic Standard Unit per week